I0563645

The Destined

THE DREAMLAND SERIES

Book III

E.J. Mellow

Published by Four Eyed Owl,
Village Station PO Box 204, New York, NY 10014
Editing by Dori Harrell
Cover Design by E. J. Mellow
Cover Photography by Dmitry Laudin

ISBN: 0996211497
ISBN 13: 9780996211499
ISBN ebook: 9780996211444

For Dan.
I wouldn't have gotten to the end if you weren't there from the beginning.

We grow accustom to the dark
When light is put away.

—Emily Dickinson

Chapter I

I searched for you in the stars tonight.
But I found none
that burned as bright as you.

—*Part of a letter from Dev to Molly*

THE VOICES HAVEN'T stopped all day. They are incessant, loud, and filled with terrible things. But I can't stop listening, inviting them to talk, craving them to. The news they bring is a reminder of what I need to get back for, what awaits helpless on the other side of my subconscious.

My vision blurs as I lie on my bed and watch the female anchor drone on and on, the TV's ghoulish glow filling my room in sickly flashes. Another shooting, another terrorist threat, another disgusting act carried out by the hands of humans. Does any part of them enjoy it? Or is it really all from the nightmares that infect them in their dreams? My stomach twists into an achy knot, a constant pain I've grown to live with over the weeks. Tucking my legs into my chest, I crinkle my nose as another thing I've grown accustomed to floats by.

Something is dying in my apartment.

I'm pretty sure of it. There's that sour *I should have taken the garbage out two weeks ago* stench. Something isn't right.

I should check to see if it's the trash. If my legs worked, I'd definitely check.

Too bad they don't.

They stopped working around the same time my appetite decided to skedaddle, which was around the same time my will to live flew the coop. It sounds a bit dramatic, but lately I've been on the dramatic side. When your only hope in life is torn away, you tend to act a little nutty. Anyone who says otherwise can go shove their head in my garbage.

Buzz. Buzz. Buzzzzz.

My doorbell rings, but it does little to stir me from my spot. Whoever it is, they've been relentless tonight. Ringing every few minutes. Can't they tell no one is home?

Ignoring them, I return my attention to the TV while rhythmically rubbing the concave dip of the wooden spoon I hold. It's been a weird security blanket since it was given to me, its presence bringing up happier memories. Did he hold it the same way as I do now? Did his skin brush against the same area?

Buzzzz. Buzzzzzzzzzz.

"Hush." I glare at my intercom, and to my relief the incessant ringing finally stops, the hum of the news once again the only backdrop to my thoughts. Settling into my sheets, I drape the spoon across my face and close my eyes. What I wouldn't give to be back in Terra this very moment eating with it. With him...

Bang. Bang. Bang.

I jerk up, and the utensil drops into my lap. My gaze fixes to my front door as it rattles again, the pounding of someone's fist.

"I know you're in there," booms a deep voice. "And I take no issue breaking this down if you don't let me in."

Great, someone else in my building must have buzzed him in. I purse my lips. Don't they know that's dangerous?

"Molly, you have exactly five seconds to get your butt off of whatever depressed nest you've created for yourself today and open up."

My fingers dig into my comforter, and I glance around my apartment. Nothing in here is the least bit useful for getting me out of my current predicament. Another loud *thump* makes me jump.

"One," the man bellows. *Thump.* "Two."

"For Christ's sake," I mutter and stumble out of bed.

"Three..." *Thump.* "Four."

I hurry to remove the chain.

"Five!"

I swing my door open just as Rae's fist is about to come down again. He pulls up short.

"I *do* have neighbors, you know." I scowl before turning and walking into my kitchen. He follows as I fetch a glass of water. His blond hair is pulled into a low bun tonight, and his dark skin is made darker under the dim lighting. The clothing he wears is black, always black, and I've begun to resent the color, for it forever reminds me of there...of him. I watch quietly as my Vigil protector's jaw tightens and his nose wrinkles, taking in my space. Clothes litter every inch, and from what little food I've been able to consume, take-out bags are scattered in odd corners.

"Trying to break a world record for dirtiest living conditions?" he asks as his narrowed golden eyes flicker my way. Rae's part of a race in Terra that interacts with Dreamers in their awake states as sort of guardian angels to their destinies. He also happens to be dating my best friend, Becca, even though she has no clue about this side of his or my life.

"Redecorating," I say and lean against my counter.

"Sure." He smacks my TV off, and my world suddenly drowns in silence.

"Hey, I was watching that!"

Rae ignores me as he pokes the various papers spread out on my bed, all things Dev and I are able to exchange through a small demutation box that can travel through Terra's portal. Finding the wooden spoon among the mess, Rae picks it up and cocks a brow.

I take quick steps forward and snatch it from his hand, cradling it against my chest.

"He's been giving you these to help you, not make you worse." He eyes the mess of notes entwined in my sheets before glancing to what I hold.

"It *is* helping."

"Yeah, helping you get committed," he says, bending to gather the letters.

"No!" I jump onto my bed and drape my body over them, the paper crinkling under my weight. "They're mine."

Rae sighs. "Molly, enough. I've let you wallow for a month now. You have to enter the real world."

"Why?"

"Because this amount of self-pitying is beneath you." He tries rolling me away, but I grasp the mattress more firmly. "You've been wearing the same clothes since Sunday, I'm pretty sure you haven't brushed your hair since then, and you smell." He tugs on my legs.

"So what? It's not like I have a job I need to be presentable for anymore."

It was nearly impossible to fake any semblance of normalcy after what happened with Aaron, whom I'd known as Dr. Marshall. Yes, *that* Dr. Marshall who first treated me when I got hit by lightning. He'd revealed himself as the twin brother of Aurora and the Vigil everyone thought dead after his partner, Anebel, died by the hands of the Metus. The partner he loved and who also happened to be Dev's girlfriend at the time. Soap opera–worthy conundrum, I know.

When he stabbed the Conscious blade in my gut, he severed my ability to travel to Terra while I slept. My world was now dreamless, a dark void, basically my life before the storm. So after a week of failing to show up or answer any calls or e-mails at my day job, I was canned from the marketing firm. It honestly took longer than I thought it would for Jim to drop the ax, but there's no part of me now—just like there wasn't then—that cares. My motto these days.

"Exactly." Rae grunts as he dodges one of my kicks. "So now you have even more time to train and stay in shape."

"For what?" I try fighting his grasp, but he latches on to my ankles and drags me off the bed. I hit the floor with a hard thump. "Ow!"

"I hope that hurt enough to knock some sense into you." He glares down at me. "Now don't make me do something cliché like force you into the shower with all your clothes on."

"Geez, you've been hanging around Becca too much." I rub my sore butt.

"Speaking of, I'll gladly call her over to help."

"No!" I hold up a hand. "I'll friggin take a shower."

Rae's smile is smug. "I'll get your running clothes."

"Swell," I mutter as I lift myself from the floor.

Walking to my bathroom, I slam the door and lean over my sink, staring at my reflection in the mirror. My usually lively brown eyes have dulled from the addition of dark circles that now rim them, and my skin is paler than normal, while my hair, well, let's just say stray dogs look better than I do. I pull at my stretched-out pajamas. What would Dev say if he saw me like this? The familiar ache blossoms in my stomach. How I miss the sound of his voice, his crooked grin…

Abruptly an image of his panicked blue gaze flashes before me, his fingers digging into my shoulders. *Don't go! Please make it stop!* The memory of his desperate plea before I drifted from his world, our world, haunts me, and I bite my lower lip as a throb pinches the corners of my eyes. They want to cry, but I used up all my tears a week ago. Now everything's just hollow, phantom sensations of what it once was like to feel.

Where am I supposed to go from here? What's my purpose?

Only three days after that horrible night, Rae forced me out of bed, just like now, insistent on maintaining our rigorous work-out routine. And I'm not sure if it's been for my benefit or for his—each of us searching for a way to deal with what happened and stay afloat in a quickly drowning hope. He says the Vigil are working on ways to bring me back, that no one is giving up, and neither should I. And I get this need for his conviction, I really do. My letters to Dev are filled with positivity, a carefully woven facade meant to mask my actual growing despair, because I can't escape my reality. I've been shut out, my connection to my other life severed, and I can't help feeling like I'm merely waiting on who will be my replacement. I'm not even sure if that's how it works, but the violence has only gotten worse in both Terra and Earth. A Dreamer is needed, and I don't know how much longer either world can wait to see if it will be me.

Chapter 2

I went into your room today.
Your indentation is still in the sheets,
teasing me,
as if you'll be right back.

—*Part of a letter from Dev to Molly*

BEADS OF SWEAT drip into my eyes, and I wipe them away as I lean over to catch my breath, my legs shaking from pushing them too far.

"That was one of your better times." Rae reads the stats on his watch, and I glare up at him, annoyed by his ability to never show an ounce of exhaustion after our runs. His black T-shirt barely holds any perspiration, while mine could fill a bucket if I wrung it out. We tracked a good five miles along the West Side park, a run and bike path that overlooks the Hudson River. It's our usual route that starts up by the USS *Intrepid*, passes Chelsea Piers, Battery Park, and ends with a view of the Statue of Liberty. The Lady is currently lit bright against the dark sky, a green beacon, and a lazy breeze softens the summer air. It's a perfect night for a run, and mostly all of Manhattan knows it, the path a flowing sea of bodies. Rae moves us off to the side to stretch under one of the lampposts that are evenly placed along the route, and the yellow glow highlights the sinew of muscles along his arms. I catch a few lingering stares from female admirers as they jog past.

"So you're seeing Becca tonight?" I lift my leg to the railing, massaging the tense muscle and watching the water lap rhythmically.

"Yeah, we're supposed to get dinner later. Wanna come?"

"Nope."

Rae's brows pinch in.

"I love you both," I explain, "but I'm not really in the mood to see you staring all lovey-dovey at one another other while I pretend like I'm not the third wheel."

"That was once," Rae says.

"Once too many." I switch to my other leg.

"So what will you do after this then?" Rae reties his hair into a bun. It's grown long since I've known him.

"The usual."

"Which is?"

"Just...the usual."

"Yeah, no." He shakes his head. "I'm going to tell him to stop sending you notes if they're going to turn you into a looney goon."

I raise a brow. "You mean, Looney *Tune*?"

"Is that the one with twiddle bird?"

"*Tweety*—ugh, never mind." I wave my hand dismissively. "I get your point, but please don't. They're all I have, Rae. The only things that..." I can't finish my sentence.

"I know," he says softly, placing an arm around me. "I would never actually. I just don't like seeing you like this. Either of you."

I frown. "How's he been?"

Rae seems to think over his words. "He's been...dedicated."

"What's that mean?"

"Let's just say, Dev's found a way to best exercise his need for revenge."

That doesn't sound good, and I'm about to ask for more specifics, when something in the distance catches Rae's attention, and he squints.

"Is that Jared?"

"What?" My head whips up as my stomach drops.

"It is." Rae starts waving at a man in exercise clothes looking in our direction. I quickly pull it down.

"What are you doing?!"

"I'm trying to say hi."

I duck behind him. "*Why?*"

"Molly, what's wrong with you?" He swivels so I'm in view again. "I thought you guys were on good terms."

"Yeah, but I look like a drowned porcupine. No one wants to run into their ex after a workout!"

"Well, it doesn't matter anymore, because he's gone now." Rae motions toward the path. "Wow, kind of rude of him not to come over."

"Or completely generous." I smooth back loose strands of hair that fell from my ponytail. I haven't spoken or seen Jared since the night of Becca's birthday, and running into him right now is the absolute *last* thing I can handle.

There's a beep from Rae's phone, and he pulls it from his armband, his expression growing serious as he reads some message. "Guess I'm not going to dinner with Becca after all."

"Why?"

"Because there's someone you have to meet."

"What, now?"

"Yeah."

"But I'm all sweaty." I glance to my saggy T-shirt and shorts. "Can't this wait until tomorrow?"

Rae's eyes find mine. "No, I really think you'll want to meet her now."

⇥▬◉ ◉▬⇤

My head tilts up as we pull in front of a tall office building that fills an entire block in Midtown, the dark facade of steel and glass lit by fluorescent lighting shining through a multitude of windows. This part of the city is always a cement wasteland after work hours, the sidewalks empty, the popular restaurant chains closed, as if all who inhabit it during the day willingly rushed away to forget its existence, if only for a few hours—the visual definition of a nine to five.

Paying the cab, Rae and I walk to a door that rests on the side of the main glass entrance, and I peer into the empty immaculate lobby as he removes a key card from his pocket.

"Been here before?" I ask as he slides it through a reader and a small green light flashes on.

He holds the door open for me. "A few times."

Our footsteps echo in the large space, and I turn in a circle, gazing up to the ten floors that are visible from the interior.

Rae stops at a long receptionist desk, where a security guard with thinning brown hair and a neglected paunch glances up from his magazine. The name Vita Corp hangs in flawless metal behind him.

"Hey, Carl," Rae greets the man. "Dr. Jin tell you she was expecting us?"

"Hey, Zach"—Carl smiles and shake's Rae's hand—"she sure did. You guys can head on up."

Carl merely gives me a quick nod before returning to his article.

"Zach?" I ask Rae as I follow him to the elevators.

"Zachariah Bell—one of my aliases."

"How many do you have?"

He shrugs. "A few."

"How did I not know this?"

"You never asked."

Stepping into the first open elevator, I glance at Rae. "Zach Bell...why does that sound familiar?"

A deep blush spreads across his cheeks. "I ah...might have gone through an obsessive phase with *Saved by the Bell.*"

"Oh. My. God." I slap the side of his arm while saying each word. "That is too friggin' perfect!"

Rae smiles sheepishly while I crack up, and I don't stop until a disembodied woman's voice announces we've reached the twenty-fifth floor. When the car finally opens, it reveals a scene so frighteningly familiar that goose bumps race down my arms, and I hesitate. Everything is white on top of white on top of white. Visions of the Dreamer Containment Center, the place that Dreamers train in Terra, pulse in front of me, and for a moment I question if I'm not asleep.

"You coming?" Rae asks from in front.

I blink. "Uh, yeah. Sorry, this just...reminds me a lot of Terra."

He glances through the glass partition that separates the elevator bay from the laboratory. "Yeah, I guess it sort of does." He turns back to me, his gaze searching. "Are you going to be okay?"

I slowly nod and follow him through the doors that open as we approach.

"You said this Vigil is a scientist?" I ask.

"Yeah, she's been guarding a human employee here for about ten years or so."

"*Ten years...* What does this place do?"

"A lot of different things, but their main businesses are in studying diseases and human advancements."

"Do they...do they know about Terra?"

"By the elders, no." Rae laughs.

"Then how can they help?"

"That's what we're here to find out."

We stand on a walkway that rings a two-level space and descend one of the four sets of stairs to the atrium below. Rows upon rows of clean white tables are patterned throughout the space, and I take in the variety of equipment, wires, and monitors resting on each. There are more doors off to the sides, and I wonder how many employees work here. Rae walks to the back of the room, where another glass partition sits, separating us from a stark-white lab that's visible beyond. The only things filling the chamber are a table against the far wall and a large metal contraption that rests proud in the middle, it's multitude of tubes and wires making it seem like some hi-tech and complicated engine. He knocks on the pane, and a gray-haired Asian woman pops her head up from behind the machine. Her gaze moves from Rae to linger on me before she swivels on a stool to press a button on the far wall. The glass doors unlock with a puff, and we walk inside.

"You weren't lying when you said you'd come right over," the woman says, her back to us as she scribbles something on a notepad that rests on the desk.

"You said you might have found something." Rae and I stand next to the giant machine, and I study all the protruding parts before returning my attention to the woman. She turns to face us, and I'm shocked at how young she looks, despite her silver hair, which is tied in a tight bun atop her head. She appears no older than early thirties, and with the combination of her high cheekbones, clear skin, and stormy gray eyes, she's seems not entirely of this world—which, I guess, she technically isn't.

"You must be Molly," she says and stands, taking my hand. "An honor. I'm Sonja."

"Sonja," I repeat. "It's nice to meet you."

"I wish it were under better circumstances. I was sorry to hear about what happened."

I blink at her directness. "Yes…it's been…uh."

"An adjustment," Rae finishes for me.

She nods, studying me a beat longer. "Of course. Well, I don't want to get anyone's hopes up, but we've come across a few developments that seem more promising than our past ones. So I needed you here to take some samples."

"Samples?" I ask.

"Yes, blood samples."

"Um, what?"

She looks from me to Rae. "Have you not told her about what we've been doing?"

He shifts his weight. "Not exactly. I thought it would be best if you explained, and like you said, I didn't want to get anyone's hopes up."

Sonja sighs, rubbing the sudden crease between her brows. "I wasn't planning on giving a science lesson tonight."

"Sorry, but you know this stuff makes no sense to me." Rae shrugs. "It would have ended up all backwards and upside down if I explained it."

"Okay, well, I apologize, Molly." Sonja leans against the table, her lab coat falling open slightly to reveal a gray power suit, her long legs ending in black heels. "But you'll have to accept the abridged version for now."

I nod.

"All right, so first, you know I'm a Vigil, yes? Well, my human charge is Dr. Mackenzie, who runs this lab. She also, with a bit of unknown guidance, has grown into one of the leading scientists on cell mutation and DNA transformation in your world. And while she doesn't *precisely* understand what she's trying to achieve on our end, she's been a vital part in the process. Raymond, especially, has been impressed with her capabilities."

"Raymond?" I ask, remembering the Vigil engineer I met with Elena, who gave me the Dreamer vest.

"Yes. He's been our main contact in Terra," Sonja says, placing her hands in the pockets of her lab coat. "He's been a huge asset in pushing us forward and will be portaling here soon should everything I find after today be promising."

I look between her and Rae. "And what exactly are you trying to find?"

Sonja rubs her lips together, as if organizing her next words. "Do you know what that machine is next to you?" She nods to it.

"No."

"It's an atomic-force microscope that can view individual DNA molecules."

I glance at it. "Oh, is that all?"

The Vigil woman smirks. "We've been experimenting with Crispr-Cas9. Have you heard of this?"

I raise a brow as if to say, *What do you think?*

"Well, it's a gene editing tool that works a bit like a find and replace. It can locate a gene to be edited and make the desired change. It's been put to a staggering range of uses, like creating hardier crops, making genetically modified mosquitoes that can't spread malaria, and with what we're doing here at Vita Corp, designing human cells that are resistant to certain diseases."

My jaw grows slack. "Is that even legal, the human part?"

"It's definitely highly controversial on Earth." She walks over to the microscope, checking a valve. "Because the manipulation can be done in a one-cell embryo, like sperm and egg, it can be inherited into future generations by becoming permanently sealed in the germ line of that organism."

"Which for non-science-brained people means what exactly?"

"It means"—she turns back to me—"this technology has the potential to create superhumans. You want someone immune to all disease? Check. You want them to be stronger, smarter, have red hair and blue eyes? Done."

"Jesus," I whisper.

"More like God," Sonja corrects.

There's a loud crash behind us, and I jump, turning to find Rae grimacing. "Sorry," he says and bends to pick up the broken pieces of a blue-and-green-molecule model. "I thought it was glued down."

"Maybe refrain from touching anything else?" Sonja gives him a strained smile.

"Yeah, good idea." He nods.

I look back to her. "So the government is letting you guys experiment with this?"

She snorts. "They're funding us to. This could change your world, Molly. Rid the Earth of AIDS, mental sickness—"

"Yeah, but couldn't it also be abused?"

"If placed in the wrong hands, always. But there are already laws being created to control how this technology can be used. None of that will matter to us though."

"It won't?"

"No, we won't be operating under human law if what I've found can work. We'll need to set up a secure location to complete the rest. Your world isn't ready for this yet."

The hairs on the back of my neck stand on end. "And what are you trying to do?"

"We're going to build a Molecular Chamber or, rather, finish the one that was shut down in Terra."

"Shut down?"

"Yes, this experiment was attempted—"

"Once," Ray interjects, "illegally."

A distant memory of walking with Elena in the Vigil engineers' lab and peering into an abandoned room with forgotten equipment, her words about an experiment gone too far. Was that this?

"So why are they letting you try it again, if it was going against the law there too?"

"Because you're the Dreamer," Sonja says matter of factly.

Rae comes to stand beside me. "Have you really figured it out?"

She nods. "There's still a bit more to do, of course. Tests, data gathering, et cetera, but I'm confident we can build a functional one here."

"But I still don't understand," I say with a frown. "What's this Molecular Chamber? What are you using it for?"

"It's sort of like your sleeping pod mixed with a DNA transmitter," Sonja explains. "It will scan you and do what I explained before, find and replace or insert the proper DNA."

My heart picks up pace. "The proper DNA for what?"

"To make it safe."

"Safe?"

Sonja shakes her head, a small smile appearing. "Don't you see, Molly? We might have found a way to give you the necessary elements to use our portals." She places a gentle hand on my shoulder. "You're going home. We're getting you back to Terra."

Chapter 3

My closet is organized by hues now,
my books alphabetized.
It's funny, isn't it, what we do for distractions.

—Part of a letter from Molly to Dev

DEV'S OXYGEN MASK was hot against his face, and he resisted tearing it off. He knew this discomfort was far better than exposing himself to the oppressive stench that hung thick in these tunnels. They'd been down here longer than planned, and he wasn't sure how much farther his team could hold out before he'd need to order their retreat.

"If our thermal scanner is accurate"—one of his cadet's voices spoke through his earbud—"there should be a hive down this way, sir."

Dev raised a Glower to peer down another burrowed-out shaft that connected to the one they'd been traveling through. The blue light illuminated dirt walls that glistened with a strange boiling mucus, and the air was so humid in this section that his eyes watered.

E.J. Mellow

"Yes, looks like one of their paths."

"Do you want me to set the pins this time?" Aveline came to stand next to him, her hazel gaze skimming over the sludge-crusted entrance.

By the mucus density, this hive would be larger than normal. Dev looked to his six other team members who waited in the darkened tunnel for his command. They all wore the sleek black ventilation suits, the durable material molding to every inch of their arms and legs, protecting them from the acid-riddled air that often swept through these shafts unannounced, while their hands were wrapped in skin-flexible gloves. Their mouths and noses were covered with the black breathing masks that ran under their chins to strap at the back of their necks, and though a glass shield could be activated to enclose the top portions of their faces, they were all currently down.

"No, I'll do it." Dev said and motioned for Minka.

A stocky blonde with short-cropped hair and an austere expression pushed her way through the small group. She swung a small bag from her back to her front and searched through its contents. While not a party favorite, Minka was one of the best explosive technicians Terra had, and Dev knew he was lucky to have procured her. Finding and eradicating the Metus hives that hid in the once believed, collapsed tunnels of Terra felt like a never-ending task. The paths proved to snake like an underground labyrinth across the land, and what lay waiting for them was the opposite of a prize. For some soldiers it was a permanent end. Which is why the Nocturna brought on for these missions needed to be strong, unwavering, and so far his men and women were fulfilling this role. They had yet to show fear, exhaustion, or complaint. Even when Dev gathered them for these extra runs, they followed wordlessly, with blind faith, into the devil's den.

"I'm giving you eight like last time," Minka said while taking out a rack of small titanium pins whose tops glowed cyan. "Place them as you go, and roll this"—she held up an egg-sized silver ball—"as far down the path as you can when you find the opening to their hive. We'll place emergency activation points on our way out, along with the rest of the detonators. Once we—"

"See me exit the tunnel, you'll detonate," Dev finished. "Yes, I remember from the dozens of other times we've done this."

"The procedure must be explained every time, sir. Mistakes have no room here."

"And as always, Minka, your thoroughness is appreciated." Dev took the case of explosives and strapped it into his belt. "The rest of you can make your way back out. I'll see you in a few."

While his team nodded and retraced their steps, heading to the exit that sat a mile away, Aveline didn't move.

"Remember, the Cell can be a good distance from the hive's opening and still do the job. The explosion radiance is wide." She glanced at the small ball stuck near his hip.

"Yes, I know."

"So you don't need to get as close—"

"I said I know." Dev turned from her and faced the entrance of the new tunnel.

"Do you?" she asked. "Because it seems you've been playing dumb to a lot of things lately."

He remained silent, and Aveline's sigh filtered through his earbuds. "Just…make it back, okay?"

"Always do," he said without a backward glance.

The thick mucus coating the ground suctioned to Dev's boots as he carefully traversed the tunnel, and the heat waves lapping toward him were relentless—a warning that would tell most to stay away. But Dev wasn't most, and though the thickening air became more unbearable with each step, it was merely an invitation. *Come find us*, it was saying. *I dare you.* So he kept moving, imbedding pins every few yards. The hunger to eradicate these beasts pumped through his blood like fire, his mind growing more focused and determined with each passing day, for it was another painful hour away from her, another second her features threatened to dim from his memory. Ending these nightmares was all he could do to keep him from living his own.

After turning a few corners and following the heat scanner strapped to his wrist, Dev gripped his Glower more firmly and peered around a new bend that revealed a steep slope. He stopped there to stare into an inky blackness that awaited him at the bottom—the door to their domain. The void sat unnervingly quiet, a patient threat, and Dev knew neither his light nor his night vision would be much use from here on out. The dark energy that radiated out of a Metus den had a tendency to consume any light that dared to draw near. He swallowed. Dealing with these monsters alone and even in their packs of twenty-five was manageable, but when they rested in their hives, in the pool of disease and horror that birthed them, they were terrifying. When so many were grouped together, they became one being, their orange glowing forms liquefied into a black hole of endless suffering, and even from this distance, he could sense the despair reaching toward him, ravished to have a taste of his Navitas—his life energy. If he waited much longer, the beasts would surely become aware of him and emerge. He'd seen it before, a very long time ago, when he sought retribution for another he loved that was torn from him. He'd been so close to giving up then, to letting their power manipulate him like a fly into a spider's web. Even now the phantom sensations of what they promised sent chills down his spine, the whispers of easing his pain, of taking it all away. His skin crawled at the same time it yearned for such a sweet release.

"Dev, can you hear me?" A female's voice abruptly filled his head. "We're almost out of the tunnel. How's it going?"

Dev shook away the unwanted memories before responding. "I found the entrance to their hive."

"That's good," Aveline said. "How far are you from it?"

"It's at the bottom of a slope, about seventy yards."

"Perfect. You can roll the Cell straight down from where you are."

"There's too much mucus on the ground. It'll get stuck."

A beat of silence.

"Dev…" Aveline's voice came through low and adamant. "Whatever you're thinking, I know for a fact it's not necessary. Roll the stupid thing down, and get back here."

Dev didn't respond. Instead he blinked away the beads of sweat that fell into his eyes and flipped up his face shield before making slow progress down the ascending tunnel, his feet suctioning with every step. He let Aveline rant for another second before clicking her off. He wasn't about to waste his team's time by coming all this way not to destroy the hive properly.

Dev only made it half the distance, however, before he began to taste the sickness through his mask, the heat and putrid energy now so overwhelming that it could no longer be kept out. Even if he wanted to, he could go no farther.

Implanting one last pin into the wall by his side, he reached for the Cell at his hip. Bringing it forward, he was about to activate the timer, when a strange twinge of energy caressed him, an invisible strand reaching out of the blackness below. Dev stared, his highly attuned vision trying to make out anything from the void, but it remained elusively flat yet endlessly deep. Then, like a snake striking, a fear so great leapt from the dark and wrapped around his mind, rendering him paralyzed. His heart beat violently in his chest as hopelessness filled every ounce of his being. Bile rose from his throat, and his muscles screamed in protest as whatever gripped him twisted, dove, and yanked his subconscious into something unrecognizable, mutated, and horrid. Right as he was about to scream, there was a releasing breath of fresh air, and a form appeared, a silhouette separating from the lightless backdrop.

"Molly?" he croaked out, a fissure of desperation erupting inside him. His paralysis seemed to lift, and instantly he reached for her. But she remained just beyond his grasp, forcing him to move forward, to follow her vision of dark hair and freckled cheeks that he had painfully yearned to see since the moment she vanished on the wind.

She smiled, a sweet expression, and though she said nothing, he could hear her calling to him. *I need you...come to me.*

"I will," he said. "Please, just wait for me. Stay where you are."

But she didn't seem to hear him, just kept floating farther down the path, away from him.

"No!" He quickened his pace but then came up short when her face distorted, as if something was trying to push through her skin. His stomach turned over as bits of her flesh fell away, slowly being consumed by the black tar her form stood in front of—the entrance to the Metus den. His mind became his own again, and dread washed over him as he realized the manipulation game—he had been fooled once more, and all too easily. He stepped back as a multitude of forms took shape out of the murkiness, pulsing and pushing at the thin barrier, bits of burning orange turning on behind the veil.

The Metus…were waking up.

Tendrils of nightmarish energy reached for him again, trying to regain their hold, but in a burst Dev shut his mind, threw the Cell into the mass, and turned to clamber up the slope. A howl made up of a thousand screams vibrated from behind him, and his gloved fingers dug into the mucus-laden walls as he propelled himself forward, an orange glow now growing brighter at his back. They were on him, and with a quick glance over his shoulder, he saw the creatures emerge in a condensed sludge to fill the entirety of the twelve-foot-tall tunnel. Claws and fire reached out, aware of the treat in front of them, desperate to consume it, consume him. Dev cursed as he ran, knowing he was too close to activate the Cell that he hoped was now deep within their den.

With panted breaths he crested the top of the hill and kept going, not daring to look back again. Their smell infiltrated his lungs, and it took every effort not to vomit into his mask. The concentrated number in such a small space had rendered his gear useless. The sound of their liquid cresting movements echoed in loud gushes down the tunnel, making it nearly impossible to know how close they actually were, and their high-pitched shrieks grated along every one of his nerve endings.

With a burst of determination, Dev picked up his pace.

He needed as much distance as possible to order what he would next.

"Aveline!" Dev switched on his radio.

"Dev?" Her voice came through panicked. "In all of Terra, why did you—"

"Start detonating the pins!" he instructed as he slammed into a wall at the end of his path and turned right, the blue glow from his and Minka's pins guiding the way out of the darkened tunnel.

"Dev, what's happening? We can't set them off with you still inside!"

"You have to! Start from the farthest out. I'll beat them to the exit." She made another attempt to say no, but Dev quieted her. "Aveline, I will die if you don't, and so will all of you! Detonate, NOW!"

After a second of silence, a rumble erupted from behind him. Rocks and dirt fell from above and kept falling as a patterned burst began to ignite.

The pins had been set.

With his head down, Dev raced them forward, his footing knocked unsteady every few explosions, but he righted himself and kept going, lightning in a bottle.

The sound of the monsters' pained screams filled the tunnel, the walls crushing them in their collapse. But Dev hardly registered it as his own loud breaths filled his head along with his frantic thoughts. He was still too close to trigger the Cell, but it was his only chance—their hive needed to be destroyed before most of them made it out. His only sense of relief came when he finally entered into the atrium of a large cavern. A dozen other tunnel entrances peppered the circumference of the space, all previously searched to find the hive that now chased him.

"Dev? Where are you?" Aveline's frenzied voice echoed in his ears. But he had no time to respond. Running toward the small seam of light that filtered through a hole in the ceiling, he skidded to a stop on the rocky floor and hooked himself into the waiting rope. The orange glow now grew brighter from three shafts that led to the cave—the Metus number had split up, which meant there would only be more of them.

Without stopping, he pressed a button on his harness and began zooming toward the exit above, his feet dangling in the air as he took out the Cell's detonator. If he triggered it now, he might fall back in, collapsing with everything around him, but if he waited, their hive would be empty, and some would surely get free. It was hardly a choice.

With a deceptively quiet beep, he activated the bomb.

There was a moment of nothing as Dev flew up, mere yards away from the view of the star-streaked night, but with a sudden rumble, the walls around him cracked and fissured. Large chunks of dirt and rocks fell from the cave's ceiling to crash loudly against the floor, and Dev gripped his harness more firmly as he shielded his head. This whole underground world was about to be wiped out, and he prayed to all the elders that he wouldn't be included. Like an internal gasp, waves of blue-orange lava erupted out of every tunnel—Metus mixed with the hot flame of the devouring Navitas set off from the Cell.

He covered his ears as a second explosion knocked against every atom in the space, and a burst of fire and energy kicked him from behind. Like a geyser gushing from the ground, it sent him flying the last few feet forward, through the exit of the skylight and out into the night. Dev soared as coils of smoke and flames surrounded him, a current of heat that eventually sent him smacking into the ground.

There was an audible shatter as something over his face broke apart. Acute slices of pain ripped across his cheek, and a pop sounded at his shoulder, followed by mind-numbing agony. His ears rang, his mind tumbled, and the smell of flesh burning swam around him. Pain was everywhere, everything.

And then, for the first time in Dev's life, his mind went black.

Chapter 4

*I've never been particularly jealous of the
Vigil, until now.*

—Part of a letter from Dev to Molly

THE CAFÉ IS quiet for a Friday morning, a few tables filled with New
Yorkers who have the luxury of working off site, and the tapping
of their fingers against their keyboards mixes with the soft music
playing in the background. Becca sits in front of me, her curly red
hair in a fashionable disarray across one shoulder while she shakes
a sugar packet, waiting for my response. I've been a bad companion
this morning, zoning in and out of our conversation, trying to sort
my emotions from last night's meeting with Sonja. Could I really be
close to returning to Terra? Will the transfer work? Is it even safe?
I'm hesitant to allow a full sense of relief to flood me.

I know better than that now.

But still…being even an inch closer to seeing Dev again, his
arms around me—

An impatient clearing of someone's throat brings me back to
the present, and I look up, finding Becca's green eyes pinned to me.

"Well?" she asks.

"I don't know when I'll start looking for a new job." I tear off a piece of my muffin. "I'm not really worried about it."

"Why in the world not?" She sits up straighter. "What are you going to do for money?"

"I have some saved."

This, of course, is a half-truth. The part I'm failing to mention is the Dreamer fund set up for occasions such as these. Well, Rae says it's more for health emergencies or travel expenses, but I'd easily categorize my current mental state as a health emergency.

"Since when?" Becca asks.

Something in her tone pushes away my patience. "Is this really what you want to talk about? My finances?"

"Easy, tiger." She lifts a delicate brow. "I'm just concerned. It's not like you to be so...blasé about your future, is all."

I stare out the café window, watching as an older woman walks her small dog, her jacket buttoned up to her neck to keep out the strange chill that's infiltrating our summer.

"I don't see the point in planning things anymore. Life has a way of messing it all up anyway."

Becca stays quiet for a moment, a sympathetic expression marring her brow. "I know getting fired was rough, and I can't imagine what you're going through, but I mean...you *did* just disappear, Mols. What did you expect work was going to do?"

I pop the piece of my muffin into my mouth. "I don't care about getting fired."

"Then what *do* you care about?" She slumps back into her seat. "For Christ's sake, you're like a walking corpse these days.

I hardly see you anymore, and when I do, you show up looking like this."

I frown. "What's wrong with how I look?"

Becca gives me a speaking glance. "Are you even aware that you're wearing that shirt inside out? I mean, I'm all for fashionable boldness, but not when it comes with pizza stains."

I cross my arms over my chest, hoping to cover said pizza stains. "Well, we can't *all* be as put together as you."

"True," she agrees. "But seriously, Molly. Do we need to see Dr. Marshall again? Maybe this attitude change is because of the accident. PTSD or something."

The mention of Aaron's human pseudonym stabs me right in the gut, and my arms clench around me.

"I'm fine, really," I say and attempt a smile, but I have a feeling it only makes me look like I have gas.

"I don't believe for a second you're 'fine'"—she air quotes—"but if you need me to pretend a little longer, I can do that. I swear though—if I don't see a shadow of my best friend by next week, I'm calling an intervention."

A genuine laugh escapes me.

"There she is!" Becca grins. "That gives me some hope."

Hope.

"When do you need to get back to work?" I ask, taking a sip of my coffee.

"In an hour," Becca says after she glances at her watch. "The office is always empty on summer Fridays. What are you going to do for the rest of the day?"

"Not sure. Probably call my grandpa, see how he's doing. Maybe go for a run."

"Yuck. Since when do you do that?"

"Since I heard it can be healthy for you."

"Yeah, so is yoga, and you don't come out looking like a drenched monkey. Well, unless it's hot yoga, but still. Why don't you go to my class with me tomorrow?"

I shrug. "Okay."

Becca blinks. "*Okay*?" She peers around the room. "Did Molly Spero really just agree to a work-out class?"

I roll my eyes. "All right, no need to be dramatic."

"But it's so much more fun that way." She beams a grin.

Just then the screen to my phone flashes between us, and we both look down.

"Why is Rae calling you?" Becca's brows crease.

I internally curse while declining his call. "He's probably trying to reach you or something."

"Then why didn't you answer?" She fishes into her purse for her own phone, but frowns when she finds it. "He hasn't called or texted me."

"Hunh, weird." I drop my cell into my bag.

"Yeah, weird." She watches me closely.

Crap. What possible excuse can I give to explain why my best friend's boyfriend is calling me? Besides the truth—that we've been going behind her back for months to travel to another dimension and then hang out, usually late at night or early morning, to train for combat and go on secret rendezvous to science labs. Yeah, that'll go over *really* smoothly.

"He probably wants to know what your favorite color is or something," I say. "Sometimes he calls when he's preparing some surprise for you." Becca stays silent, so I keep going. "If he ends up taking you somewhere this weekend, just act like you had no idea, okay? I'm sure he'll be upset if he found out that you knew I've been helping."

Her shoulders relax slightly. "He has been acting a little weird lately, which does happen when he's planning something."

"Yeah, like how he gave away your weekend trip to the Catskills by asking over and over if you liked the woods."

Becca smiles. "That was ridiculous."

"Exactly. That's Rae—ridiculous. If he calls again, I'll advise him to keep his cool better this time."

She nods, taking a sip of her coffee, and though she seems mollified, something in the way Becca's features stay calculating as she glances toward my bag tells me she doesn't entirely believe me.

Chapter 5

Sometimes I wake up thinking
I finally dreamt of you,
but then I realize
my heart remains still.

—Part of a letter from Molly to Dev

AVELINE'S VOICE WAS way too loud, as if she decided he wasn't in enough pain and it was her duty to rectify the situation. Dev closed his eyes and gingerly leaned his shoulder into the padded chair he sat in. *If I could only be knocked unconscious again*, he thought.

"And then you *had* to order us to detonate with you still in there. I mean, of all the moronic, suicidal—"

"You've already used those adjectives," Dev interjected, "which means you've exhausted your limited vocabulary for the day, so there's really no need for you to keep talking."

Aveline snapped her mouth shut at that but continued to fume silently beside him, her arms crossed tightly over her chest. Dev was in the recovery wing of a hospital specifically made for Nocturna soldiers. Rows of beds and chairs filled the pristine tiled space, each separated by a thin white partition allowing for some semblance of privacy. Dev was merely one among many wounded, all in various stages of healing, which, thankfully, happened a lot quicker than human standards due to the advancement of Terra's sciences. Repart Sleeves hovered around patients' arms or legs, repairing broken bones while nurses stood in front of men and women, running Stitch Scanners over open gashes and bruises. Wherever its blue light touched, minor cuts rapidly fused together, and darkened skin returned to its natural hue.

Dev had woken earlier in the ER to find a team of doctors surrounding him, the buzz of conversations and other soldiers being treated and moved into surgery filled the backdrop. They debriefed him on his injuries—a dislocated shoulder, multiple lacerations across his face, bruised ribs, and part of his back had suffered minor burns. If he ended up waking up at all, Dev had certainly thought he'd be way worse for wear. But because of the doctors' medical advancements, they fixed everything fairly rapidly, except the burns to his back, for which he had to stick around to receive a few more treatments.

He had just finished his last one and was being shown into the recovery wing when Aveline ambushed him. So while he might have survived the blast, he had yet to decide if he'd survive her fury.

"If you'd like to be helpful," Dev said, changing the subject, "you can tell me the status of the tunnels." He shifted in the chair where he sat shirtless. Strips of ointment covered his back, and he resisted the urge to scratch at the newly grown skin. It felt like a thousand ants crawling across his body.

"The status—" Aveline spluttered. "Who cares about that? You almost *died* tonight, Dev!" She threw her hands up. "I think you can take a break for one second."

"*Almost* means I didn't. I'm still as alive as you. Maybe not as animated, but still alive. So please, Aveline, the status."

With a frustrated huff, she shook her head. "All the tunnels leading to the city have been successfully collapsed. Ours was the last to be called in."

Dev nodded, his focus fixed to the tiled floor as some of the tension went out of his shoulders. "We'll need to deal with the ones on the outskirts next. See if we can recruit new teams, double our efforts. They'll certainly be a greater number of Metus out there, since they haven't been as easily maintained or monitored."

Aveline's mouth was gaped open when he glanced at her, and her left eye twitched before she snapped up his medical chart that rested beside him, flipping through his records.

"What are you doing?" He tried to grab the tablet from her, but she blocked his reach.

"Seeing if there's something in here about your brain damage, because you *have* to be suffering from something to be talking like you are. *Seriously,*" she bit out, "what's wrong with you?"

"Well, currently I'm starting to acquire a headache from this terribly annoying sound that's coming from in front of me."

A vein in Aveline's forehead strained to the surface. "*Dev,*" she hissed while throwing the tablet at him, which he easily caught. "You almost didn't make it out last night. Do you understand? You almost got buried, crushed, pulverized, taken out right alongside our enemies." She brushed a trembling hand through her hair. "I get that you need distractions. I get that you need to let out your rage for what happened to Molly, and that you miss her, but you're becoming reckless." Her eyes stayed locked to his. "This is exactly what I was afraid would happen. You're losing it. What good would your death be to her, huh? It would only make things one hundred times worse. And you know what? It's not just Molly you'd be hurting. What about me, Dev?" She stabbed a finger at her chest. "Did you ever stop to think what this is doing to me? I can't..." She swallowed her words, her voice shaking. "You can't be this selfish. I won't allow it. So until you get your head screwed on straight, you can count me out of your missions. I might have done it in the past, but I can't silently stand by you again and watch you act suicidal." And before Dev could respond, Aveline turned and stormed out of the recovery wing, her slim black form disappearing through the far door.

With a weary sigh, Dev scrubbed at his forehead as Aveline's words tumbled through him, leaving a deep ache in his chest. He knew she was right.

"She's right, you know." A familiar woman's voice spoke to him through the thin partition to his left, and Dev glanced up to see Aurora turn the corner into his cube.

She was wearing a black tank top and pants, and her strawberry-blonde hair was pulled into a messy ponytail. Her usual high cheekbones were now hollow and gaunt, and her feline-tipped green eyes, which once dazzled with the glint of a pleasurable secret, currently held only exhaustion and regret. It pained Dev more than getting the burns on his back to see his old friend in such a state, but he knew that what she suffered from was nothing he could fix, nor did he really believe he should.

Aaron, Aurora's twin brother, whom everyone had believed died, had returned to Terra. And unfortunately it had not been a cause for celebration like it should have been, for he resurrected as a crazed, bitter, heartbroken creature, seeking nothing but revenge for a love lost—Anebel, Dev's girlfriend and Aaron's Nocturna partner.

Anabel died in a tragic ambush with the Metus. And though Dev suffered her death just as badly as Aaron, Aaron ultimately believed Dev was responsible for them losing Anebel that day, making her too bold and careless. So Aaron had waited patiently in the dark, seeking retribution, which ultimately came many decades later in the form of him ripping Molly away from Terra, away from Dev, with a Conscious blade, making Dev suffer once more for loving someone. So while Dev wanted to be empathetic to Aurora's situation, he couldn't separate her from her brother. Especially when she still showed such tender sympathy and love for him, despite his recent sins and betrayal. This left Dev uncertain if he and Aurora could ever become the friends they once were.

"What are you doing here?" Dev asked.

Aurora showcased her right arm. "Seems you're not the only one that suffered a burn," she said, displaying a fresh bandage around her bicep.

"Tunnel mission or run-in?"

"A little of both." She walked over to the spare chair that sat in the corner of his alcove and slumped into it. "So you pulled the usual bullheaded Dev, huh? I heard pretty much everything through these rice-paper walls." She tapped the thin partition behind her.

"I'm not in the mood, Aurora," Dev said as he picked up the fresh T-shirt Aveline had brought him, gingerly slipping it on. His muscles ached with every small movement, and he silently grumbled. He wasn't used to such a feeling—weakness.

"Really? Because it seems you've been in a constant mood these days," came Aveline's dry reply.

"Have you been to see him today?" Dev asked, his abrupt change of topic seeming to throw Aurora off, for she visibly flinched before her lips thinned.

"I don't want to talk about him with you."

"I'm not looking for a discussion. I just want to know if you've seen him."

She studied Dev for a moment. "No, not yet."

"But you will?"

She sat up straighter, a wariness in her gaze. "Yes, I'm scheduled to visit after this."

Aaron was being held in confinement awaiting his trial, and Dev's pulse quickened at Aurora's answer. He glanced out to the sea of injured Nocturna, to the man who rested across from him, one arm draped over his face as a Repart Sleeve worked on the other. In the next alcove over, a women sat, features strained, as she clasped her half-charred leg, waiting for a nurse to attend her. This was only the first wave of the war, but such scenes continued on endlessly, the energy coming off each soldier low and dejected. Terra needed a boost, something to rally behind and raise spirits, or they would never be able to win this battle. Dev knew the one person who could do it too, who was supposed to be here giving his people hope, but she wasn't, and the thought that she possibly never would be filled him with murderous intent.

"I'll go with you." Dev stood from his chair, testing the flexibility of the bandages on his back. He didn't care if the newly healed burns left a scar. He couldn't sit here any longer.

Aurora stood with him, her eyes going wide. "I don't— No, you can't."

"You have no authority over me," Dev said curtly as he tugged on his boots. "I'm either going to go with you or go alone. Your choice."

Her face turned a shade whiter. "Fine, you can come, but let me have my time with him."

Dev nodded. "I wasn't planning on talking. I just need to see him."

She regarded him cautiously. "Why?"

Dev walked passed her. "Because sometimes you have to look the devil in the face again to remember."

⋯⊱═◉ ◉═⊰⋯

The white holding cell was bigger and cleaner than Dev would have liked. In his imaginings he pictured a tiny, damp, dark cage where random puddles of water festered in the corner while rodents skittered in for a drink. Even though rats didn't exist in Terra, Dev felt better believing they did, especially here where they could occasionally gnaw on the rag-torn clothes of their prisoner. But what he looked upon was quite the opposite, and it filled him with even more seething rage. Aaron's chamber was spacious, with a clean tiled floor, a small toilet and wash station in the corner, and a cot in the other. The only degree of satisfaction Dev got was from the absence of windows and the oppressive bright lighting of the Navitas overhead. He prayed to the elders they were kept on at all hours.

Sitting on the other side of a one-way glass, Dev watched Aurora speak with her brother. His dirty-blond hair had grown long since the weeks of his capture and currently fell messily in front of his sunken eyes, while a scraggly beard now marred his face. His white jumper sagged against his once-broad shoulders, his weight loss evident as he sat across from his sister. A table had been brought in, and his hands were bound to the center of it with thick rings of Navitas, the blue-white energy coiling together in an infinity sign. Dev viewed a profile of the arrangement, giving him access to see any movement under and atop the table. Though Dev had told Aurora he had no interest in talking with Aaron, the truth was, he wasn't allowed. After nearly killing the man with his bare hands—it took three men to haul Dev away from Aaron's unconscious and bloodied form—he was given a restraining order. The sentencing was almost laughable, for who was the real threat here? It took a bit of coaxing for the Vigil guards to allow Dev even this close, but he thought their leniency came with their shared hatred for their charge. Aaron wasn't only a traitor. Before that he was Vigil who refused his born duty. Instead he demanded to become a Nocturna guard. Dev wasn't certain, but it wouldn't come as a surprise if his people still resented him for that. Though his sister seemed untouched by such prejudice.

"Why don't you let them cut your hair?" Aurora asked, an edge of tenderness in her voice that made Dev's jaw clench. She tried reaching out to push back a long blond tendril, but Aaron turned his face away.

"Have you eaten today?" Aurora tried again.

"Would it please you if I said yes?" came Aaron's cool reply.

"It would."

"Then yes, *mia gemella*, I had a feast fit for the elders," he responded dryly, using an old endearment between the two that meant *my twin*.

Aurora didn't seem put off by his sarcasm, merely forcing a small smile while gently rubbing at her arm where the bandage was still wrapped. Aaron glanced to it.

"Have the Metus been causing more trouble?" he asked, his tone more inquisitive than concerned.

"You know I can't talk to you about that," she said, glancing to the glass where Dev and two other guards watched. A flash of annoyance passed through Aaron's features before he covered it up with blithe indifference.

"Than what can we discuss?" he asked flippantly. "The weather? I hear it will remain oddly in a constant summer night."

"Aaron, please—"

"What?" he snapped, his frustration finally shining through. "Why do you keep coming here, Aurora? Seeing me can't bring you joy. In fact, every time you come back, you look less and less presentable. Is your plan to join me in my madness?"

"You're not mad."

"Oh, I can assure you I'm quite crazed, *mia gemella*. Or haven't they told you yet?"

Aurora frowned.

"Yes, the doctors came to see me, the elders' little Vigil pets. They asked me many questions. It was so fun though, talking with them. Their reactions were the best part."

"Aaron, what are you talking about?"

"I finally answered truthfully. I told them what all of us have been thinking. You should be proud."

She shook her head. "You're not making any sense."

"Funny, that's just what they said. Well, 'not of sound mind' was the more specific wording."

Aurora blinked, seemingly lost for words.

"But it's perfect really," Aaron mused, more to himself. "A crazy person's actions are never his own, right? They can't *truly* be blamed for anything." A wicked gleam appeared in his hazel eyes. "So someone like me, well, could get away with murder."

Dev resisted charging the glass at the same moment an audible gasp escaped Aurora.

"You have to stop this, brother. Please, for my sake. Be yourself again. They might even—"

"*Myself?*" Aaron cut her off with a sneer. "And what would that be? Tell me. What is the Aaron that you so fondly remember?"

"A kind one," she snapped back. "One that would never act as you are now. Someone that was capable of love and—"

"Love." He laughed. "You would have me love again? Like *he* was able to? No, that part of me is gone."

"Even for me?" Aurora asked, a raw vulnerability present.

They regarded each other in silence, and Dev watched as Aaron's features changed from cruel disgust to sullen and sincere. "*Mia gemella*," he said softly, leaning in once more. "I'm sorry. That was not fair of me to say."

Aurora's whole body visibly relaxed at that, as if she finally got the emotional response she was craving from her brother.

"Maybe next time," he went on, "if we want these meetings to go more smoothly, you could bring me a gift, hmm? Something to help me pass my time here?"

Aurora didn't reply, only watched him warily as he shifted forward to lay his hands atop hers, his face wincing slightly when the cuffs sizzled against his skin. "Don't you want to ease my pain from being stuck in this place?"

She looked down at their connection. "Of course I do."

"Then try and bring me something sweet. Even a band will do. I just need a tiny bit of relief."

Understanding flashed through her eyes, and she pulled her hands away. "You're asking me to score you Nectus?" she asked, clearly appalled at mentioning the euphoric drug that was a Terra club favorite.

A milder dose was often mixed into the bands that adored dancers' limbs, but the more pure form, when ingested, almost instantly caused addiction. Even so, the drug wasn't illegal in Terra, only frowned upon and usually placed citizens who used it into lower brackets in their systems. The fact that Aaron seemed to crave it piqued Dev's interest greatly, and his spine straightened.

"It's been so long, *mia gemella*." He twitched slightly as he tried to scratch his arm. "My body...it hurts."

She shook her head. "Aaron, what's happened to you?"

"What I deserve," he said, his tone referencing something other than the reasons for being held in this cell.

As if suddenly realizing something, a perplexed look overtook Aurora's features. "Aaron..." She hesitated. "If you've been going through withdrawals since being put in here, that means— How have you been able to get Nectus? You said you haven't been back to Terra in decades."

Dev stepped closer to the one-sided mirror as Aurora's words hit him full force. *That Metus scum*, he thought. Aaron had been coming here right under their noses for years, getting his drug in Terra. Which meant— *By the stars*, was it possible? Who had been his contact in the city? Someone here had known he was alive, and keeping it secret. Who would do such a thing? Dev's hands clenched into fists, all of the hate boiling to the surface as he stared into the room.

As if suddenly sensing a presence on the other side of the glass, Aaron turned to peer at the wall, his sickly, dilated eyes somehow able to find Dev's, and a chill ran through him. This man represented everything Dev had loved and lost in his life, and with a bitter resolve he realized that Aaron thought the exact same thing about him. How ironic to find oneself in one's enemy.

Dev watched a now-panicked Aurora try to regain her brother's attention, knowing the danger of having Aaron suspect who might be on the other side. She called his name—nothing. She even dared to grab his chin and force his face back to her, but he didn't move. Aaron's gaze stayed trained toward Dev, a subtle understanding soaking through it.

And it took every ounce of Dev's strength to remain motionless as he held the connection. Memories of all the monsters he'd killed abruptly swam around him, the blood from their deaths forever staining his hands, the weight of it. But as Aaron's lips slowly lifted into a leering tilt and the gleam in his eyes changed into taunting pleasure, Dev thought darkly, *What's another?*

Chapter 6

I hope Rae is staying close to you.
But not too close.

—Part of a letter from Dev to Molly

HE'S CHASING ME, his gaining shadow sending my heart into overdrive as I sprint past a group of pedestrians lazily walking along the river path, and continue at a breakneck speed. My sweat turns cool against the rush of air breezing past, and my lungs burn, urging me to stop. But I can't. I only have forward now. Going back brings hesitation, uncertainty, and I have no room for that anymore. So I race the future to get here faster, for that's all I can see these days, the glimmer of hope it holds for me on the horizon. But no matter how much ground I cover, how fast I run, the end eludes me, never getting any closer—a mirage of progress.

With a growl I go faster, pushing myself the last final yards until the path I run on ends, barricaded by a railing that separates me from the water, leaving me no choice but to stop.

I bend over, panting.

"By the elders," eventually comes Rae's deep voice from behind me. "You actually beat me." His breaths are labored as he steps to my side—something I never thought I would live to hear. The week and a half following our visit to Vita Corp and learning about my possible way to get back to Terra filled me with new vigor. To say that I've become determined to regain my physical and mental strength in preparation would be putting it mildly. It's all I can think about, and now that there seems to be a game plan, a projected goal, I've found the strength to get out of bed again.

"I told you those pies would catch up with you." I wipe my face with my T-shirt and lean against the railing of the dock, the cool morning air brushing along my bare legs. We stand at our usual stopping place after running the West Side, which ends at the tip of Manhattan by the Financial District. It's still early, and a soft fog lifts off the Hudson River, the overcast sky painting the Statue of Liberty in gray rather than her usual green.

"Pies have nothing to do with it." Rae leans in. "Your improvement is outstanding."

I shrug.

"No, it really is." Rae pushes my shoulder so I face him. "I'm proud of you."

I study my hands, his words meaning more to me than I would have thought. "Thanks."

"You'll have to promise me that you'll challenge Dev to another spar the moment you get back." Rae grins. "He won't know what hit him."

Like with any mention of Dev, my chest fills with a strange mixture of excitement and sadness. "Do you really think this will work?"

He watches me closely, his golden eyes not missing a thing as wisps of his pulled-back blond hair stir softly around his dark complexion. "Yes," he says after a moment. "It'll work. With every power I have, I'll make sure it does."

I nod, the deep sincerity of his words almost knocking something loose that I've been desperate to plug forever. I hold the tears at bay.

But Rae still seems to sense my emotions, for he brings me into a hug, which I willingly embrace, man sweat and all. As his giant arms engulf me, his familiar scent of sunshine and something sweet gives me a strange sense of comfort I was unaware I needed.

"We've got this, Dreamer," he murmurs into my hair. "Your story hasn't ended just yet."

I smile at that and am about to push away and make a joke about the power of sweaty hugs, when the sound of my name being called causes Rae and me to turn, still half embracing.

Jared stands at the end of the dock, slightly out of breath from his own apparent run, staring at us. His curly, dirty-blond locks are damp from the mist in the air, and his strong biceps peek out of a gray T-shirt that clings quite flatteringly against his abs. His hazel gaze unmistakably holds a look of shock and, I'm surprised to note, anger.

Just awesome. Of course we'd run into the *one* person I wouldn't want to in a city of eight million.

"Hey, Jared," I say, stepping away from Rae and smoothing back what I'm sure is a mess of mad-scientist hair.

"Hi," he says after a moment, suspicion clearly evident in his tone.

Christ.

"I didn't know you ran down here," Rae says with a grin, and I almost smack my forehead at how bad that sounds.

"I moved," Jared says.

"You did?" I can't help asking. "But your apartment was so nice."

Jared's gaze goes back to me, and an emotion plays through it that I can't quite place. "I needed a change," he says, glancing away. "Plus, I got a promotion, so decided to buy."

"Oh, wow. That's amazing." I smile, truly happy for him.

"New York real estate is always a good investment." Rae nods. "I'm glad to hear you're doing well." He steps forward and places a friendly hand on Jared's shoulder, who visibly stiffens.

Dear Lord, is Rae really that oblivious to how we must have looked to Jared?

"Rae's been training me," I finally explain. "Getting me up at the butt crack of dawn for runs."

"You hate waking up early," Jared states matter of factly.

"Still does." Rae laughs. "Usually takes some creativity to get her out of bed."

For the love of Terra.

"What he *means*," I say, "is buzzing my door nonstop for an hour."

Jared glances between the two of us, less than convinced. "What are you training for? Are you running the New York marathon this year?"

"Oh God, no." I snort. "I just want to get in better shape."

My ex studies me, as if he's trying to take in all my differences since we broke up. I shift awkwardly, hating that I still hope he likes what he sees, despite the obvious sweat and bunched-up running shorts.

"You want to grab a bite with us?" Rae asks. "We usually go to Bean Sprout after. It's a couple blocks up from here."

"No, I should get back." Jared throws a thumb over his shoulder. "Work and all."

"Ah yeah, same here," I say, and Rae shoots me a quizzical raised brow.

"Right, well...it was...unexpected running into you guys." Jared takes a hesitant step back, looking as if he's battling with something, and I have a pretty good guess as to what that is.

"Yeah, I'm sure bumping into your ex isn't up there with great ways to start your day." *What am I even saying right now?*

Jared's responding grin is strained. "No, I can't say that it is."

We're both quiet after that, unsure where to go from here, and Rae chimes in to our awkward silence. "Well, we don't want to make you late. Maybe we could all get a drink sometime though. Catch up."

Or not.

"Yeah, maybe," Jared says while running a hand through his hair. "Enjoy your breakfast." His eyes falls to me again, and I think how strange it is to feel so distant from someone who once held me so intimately.

"Thanks," I say and then watch Jared walk up the pier, but before he gets too far, he calls back to us. "Oh, and please tell Becca I said hi."

And with one last meaningful glance my way, he turns and jogs away.

⊶⊷

The room smells strongly of bleach, and I wince as the needle pricks my vein. "How can you still not understand what just happened?" I stare at Rae from across the room. Beside me, Sonja murmurs for me to keep still as she draws a few vials of my blood.

"Because it's crazy talk. How could anyone think such a thing?"

"Um, easily. We were caught, *alone*, embracing in the early hours of the morning!"

Sonja gives us a speculative glance but remains silent as she switches one ruby-filled tube with an empty one.

The Vigil scientist's new lab is located in the back of an abandoned storefront in downtown Brooklyn. The lab is hidden behind various walls, similar to the transfer room at the Village Portal Bookstore, though at least four times bigger. A multitude of equipment fills chrome tabletops, and monitors are pushed to the far walls, displaying charts mixed with Terra's alien ancient Latin language. A half-built Molecular Chamber, from what Sonja has explained, sits at the very end of the large room, behind a clear glass partition—its white curved form seemingly innocuous in its resemblance to my sleeping pod. I have yet to inspect it more closely. A strange anxiety about everything that might go wrong while I lie in it stifles my curiosity of the thing—for now.

"There's nothing wrong with two friends hugging each other," Rae says defensively. "And I love Becca. Jared knows that."

"That doesn't stop people from cheating." Sonja enters the conversation as she pulls the needle from my arm. "Press down on this." She places a cotton ball over my vein.

"Precisely." I look back at Rae, whose posture's way too relaxed for my taste. "I think you should call her."

"And say what? It's ten in the morning. She's at work."

"I don't know—that you're madly in love with her and want to have all her babies."

"She already knows that, and even if she didn't, wouldn't that be a tad suspicious?"

I huff as I sit back in my seat.

"Your turn." Sonja swivels on her stool to face Rae, her gray ponytail swooshing behind her. She's in casual clothes today, dark jeans and a light-green sweater.

"Why are you taking his blood?" I ask as Rae shrugs out of his sweatshirt, displaying his muscular forearm, and lowers himself into the empty seat beside me.

"Because we need it," she says.

I give Sonja a derisive glare. Her habit of answering my questions without answering them really irks me. "I've gathered," I reply, "but *why* do you need it?"

"To compare, of course." Tying the rubber band around Rae's smooth dark skin, she flicks an impressively large vein that strains to the surface of his inner elbow. She swabs a disinfecting wipe.

"Compare it to mine?"

She nods as she inserts the needle, the tube filling with Rae's blood.

"What will you be looking for?"

"Differences and similarities between the two of you. While being opposite sexes makes things a little more...complicated, it shouldn't be that big of a problem."

I frown. "What are you—"

"Do you really think Jared believes we're cheating on Becca together?" Rae interjects, bringing my attention back to him, his gaze suddenly holding a fearfulness I assumed would have been there earlier.

"Unfortunately, yes."

He wipes his free palm against his running shorts. "But I would never do that to her. Why are you humans so disloyal that you could think such a thing?"

Sonja snorts as she finishes taking his blood sample and hands him a Band-Aid. "You and I both know our species can be just as bad, if not worse."

Rae frowns. "Becca wouldn't second-guess my faithfulness. I've never given her reason to."

"While you might be right," I say. "Maybe it's best we let her know we're going on runs together." Visions of her face after she saw Rae calling my phone play in my mind. "There's really no need to hide that from her, especially now that she knows I'm on a fitness kick."

"Good call." He nods.

"And it's not like she and Jared hang out," I say, feeling like I need to be the reassuring one now. "So we don't have to worry about him saying anything to her about this morning."

"Yeah, that's true." Rae gives me a relieved smile. "We're fine."

I nod. "Totally fine."

Later that night, neither Rae nor I can get ahold of Becca.

Chapter 7

The whispers of the girl who could fly
have only strengthened.
I fear the elders will finally have to tell the truth.

—Part of a letter from Dev to Molly

"AH! YOU STUPID slab of grease!" I drop the hot pan back on my stovetop, and it clatters loudly as I shake out my hand, my fingertips turning red from where they mistakenly pressed against the metal. I curse as I bring them to my mouth and struggle between walking away or throwing my potential dinner across the kitchen. The latter seems way more appealing.

After the whole no-longer-have-a-job thing, my days have become a bit freer, leading me to experiment with cooking. Which really means trying to learn the basics, like how to make pasta. Tonight's attempted dish, however, was stuffed peppers, something I watched Tim cook on occasion for Dev, Aveline, and me. He made it look so effortless, the smug Nocturna, and I frown at the indistinguishable blackened mound in front of me. I can easily hear the useless Yoda-like advice he'd be giving right about now—*The dish tell you when it's done, it will.*

Like I said, useless.

The last time I saw Tim, he was in the hospital after suffering an intensive wound from a Metus attack, one that I was thankfully able to stave off from consuming him. I know from Rae, and Dev's letters, that he's safely recovering. Even so, the memory of the gregarious, smile-wrinkled man only worsens my mood, not knowing when or if I'll ever see him again.

Grumbling, I stomp over to tug open a kitchen drawer, perusing the various pamphlets inside.

Pizza it is.

As I juggle between the difficult choices of adding extra pineapple or pepperoni, the door to my apartment rings out, making me jump. My skin prickles at whoever would be calling without warning at this time of night. I wasn't expecting Rae, but he's the only other person who visits so impromptu.

I press the intercom. "Yes?"

There's a beat of silence before I hear Becca's voice. "Let me in."

My stomach clenches into a ball of nerves. After trying to reach her all last night and earlier today, her cell eventually going straight to voicemail—something it never does—I have a very bad feeling.

I buzz her up.

Soon my door swings open, and Becca walks in followed by Rae, the blood instantly draining from my face as I take in his panicked expression. *Oh shit.*

My best friend stalks around my apartment like she's on a mission from hell. Her floral dress spins around her legs as she moves in haste, and her fiery red hair falls across her face. She shoves it out of the away in an impatient flick.

"Hey, guys," I say while stealing a glance at Rae. He's shaking his head as he stares at me, wide eyed. "Uh, to what do I owe the pleasure?"

Becca halts abruptly by the base of my bed, her green gaze on fire as it finds mine. She's been crying.

"Becca," I step forward. "What's—"

"Out with it."

"Uh? Out with wha—"

"Don't play dumb, Molly! Tell me the truth. Are you two fucking?"

The world drops from beneath me, and I feel like I've been thrown across the room.

"What? No!" Rae and I shout the last part at once.

Her face remains murderous, and a chill runs through me.

"Then how come Jared saw you two kissing?" Her words are flung like acid.

"What? When did you see Jared?"

"That doesn't matter! You two were caught making out!"

"Becca, listen to yourself. That's ridiculous."

"And why's that?"

"Because it's me!" I jab a finger into my chest. "Your *best friend* who would never do something like that. And he's Rae." I point to the man, who looks like he's about to collapse into a heap of broken dreams. "Why would Jared say something like that?"

She's silent for a moment before she says in a more dejected tone, "He said you guys were embracing."

"Embracing?" I say with raised brows. "Like perhaps in a *platonic* hug-like fashion?"

"I don't care what you want to call it!" she bursts. "He said he saw you two *alone*, early in the morning, in a suggestive position."

My teeth grind. Who knew Jared was such a gossip. "When did he tell you this?"

"He came to dinner at my sister's the other night."

Of course. I let out a frustrated groan. Her sister and Jared work together. "I knew it." I glance to Rae, who merely blinks, stunned.

"Knew what?" Becca's face is beet red, her fists balled. "What are you two hiding from me!?"

"He did *not* see us kissing"—I look her dead in the eyes—"because we weren't. Rae and I have been going on runs in the morning, and I got hit with a stupid self-pitying moment, and he was giving me a hug. That. Is. All. Please, Becca, you have to trust us."

Her nostrils flare, apparently trying to hold in her boiling rage, and her eyes narrow. "You've been running together?"

"Yes." Rae and I speak in unison again, which inflames her further.

"Then why keep it a secret? And why would Jared lie? And why is Rae calling you randomly during the day? I'm not an idiot! I see the way you two are looking at each other right now. Like you were caught. And I swear to God, you better have one hell of an explanation, because I'm about this close"—she pinches an inch of air between her pointer finger and thumb—"to setting this whole apartment on fire."

If she were anyone else, I wouldn't believe such a threat, but knowing Becca and seeing the gleam of insanity precariously ready to explode in her eyes tells me she's 100 percent capable of such an act.

I hover in a mixture of panic and desperation as my mind runs through everything I could say to explain. But we're cornered. There's no exit, and I can find no lie to remotely fix this.

"We have to tell her." I look to Rae.

"Oh God." Becca's face bleaches of color. "You *are* fucking. *How could you*!?" She bends over as a sob escapes her, and Rae and I reach for her, but he gets there first.

"No, it's not what you think!" He pulls her into his chest despite her struggles. His arm muscles bulge against his black T-shirt to keep her in place.

"Don't touch me! You sack of sh—"

"LISTEN TO ME!" he bellows as he shakes her, and she goes quiet. Neither of us have ever heard Rae raise his voice before. The effect is frightening. "I love you," he says vehemently. "I would *never* do that to you. Molly would never. Do you understand? You are my everything. I cross dimensions every day just to have a chance to be near you, to see you smile and laugh. How could you ever think I would be unfaithful?" He says the last part like the very idea makes him physically sick.

The room drowns in silence as I hold my breath. Rae slipped up, and I'm not certain if Becca even noticed. She's looking up at him, her bottom lip trembling, tears streaming down her face.

"We have been keeping something from you though," he says and then adds, "but it's not what you think. It's...more complicated."

Becca's swollen eyes dart between the two of us, her brow lifting. "What the hell could be more complicated?"

Rae presses his lips together at the same time I attempt to chew mine off. *This is it.* My two worlds about to collide like monkey fecal matter against a wall. I have a strong urge to scream and to vomit. Maybe both at the same time.

Am I about to lose my best friend?

Will she believe any of it?

But strangely mixed in with all this confused terror is the slightest, tiniest sliver of relief, because Becca will finally know, and depending on whether or not she'll ever talk to me again, at least I'll no longer have to lie.

Rae shoots me a pained glance, my own fears mirrored in his eyes before a mask of resolution covers his face. He turns back to her. "We'll tell you," he says, "but you'll need to see it to understand."

⊶⊷

There's a strange thing that can happen when driving in a car—going from one place to the next without any real recollection of getting there. The mind goes into a weird autopilot of turn left, stop, go, continue, and repeat. I barely retain the passing scenery, and whatever thoughts I have amid the journey disappear or never exist in the first place.

That's how the commute went for me as Becca, Rae, and I step out of the taxi and onto the sidewalk in front of the Village Portal Bookstore. If any words were spoken, I can't recall them. If there was a long-held awkward silence, no memory of it is present.

There's just…nothing, as if my mind went into hibernation mode in preparation for whatever's about to go down.

Peering into the darkened windows of the bookstore, my chest tightens, taking in the hanging dream catchers and various spiritual books displayed. I haven't been back since the night I was cut off, the place too painful to visit. And time still hasn't lessened the deep anguish that now mixes in with the rest of my churning, anxious emotions.

"This is what you have to show me?" Becca's skeptical voice cuts into the quiet night. Not even a random pedestrian is present in this back-alley street.

"It's inside." Rae pulls keys from his pocket and lets us in. A bell chimes against the glass as we enter, and the residual scent of incense brings up haunting memories. My heart beats in overtime as I glance to the purple drape that separates the back room, and I barely register Becca saying something, for a loud swooshing fills my ears. Flash sensations of cold, clammy hands around my neck, the prick of a blade, and liquid lightning filling my chest keeps me from being aware of anything besides forcing myself to move forward one step at a time.

"It's in here," Rae says when we enter the back room, and then he ducks inside the closet. I wait for Becca to follow, but she stops at the threshold, worry creasing her forehead.

"Um…"

"You'll see." I urge her to move just as Rae presses the button under the light switch, and the far wall begins to disappear into the floor, a beam of bright white flowing out.

Becca gasps as the three of us watch the room beyond slowly reveal itself. Everything is the same, yet completely different. The calming sensation it once gave me is now replaced with the feeling one might get visiting a disaster zone, but instead of rubble and dirt there's only stillness and white and pristine floors, no blaring sirens and flashing screens sealing my fate.

Rae and I follow Becca as she takes hesitant steps forward, her gaze bouncing around to my white coffin in the middle, then to the depowered portal in the corner—which Rae uses to travel to and from Terra—before going to the few screens that are visible in the tiled walls.

"Is this...is this some sort of fetish thing?" She turns to us with a look of horror.

"*No*," I answer, surprised to find myself resisting a grin in such a moment.

"Then what is it?"

Rae and I lock eyes before he inclines his head as if to say, *You should start.*

But where? I silently respond.

Taking a deep breath, I start at the only place that makes sense, the beginning. "Okay, remember how I told you I was having those really vivid dreams right after I got hit by lightning? To the point where I was getting confused about things and...wanted to sleep more."

She regards me cautiously but slowly nods.

"Well...it turns out that, um, the reason that was happening was because after I got hit I started transporting to another dimension while I slept." I grimace at how stupid that sounds. "And I know that sounds crazy, but it's the truth, and this place is where I go to be locked into traveling there in my subconscious for longer periods of time, and that's a portal that Rae uses to get back. And he's sort of like my guardian here on Earth, and there's this guy—"

"Okay." Rae holds up a hand, stopping my word vomit. "Let's slow down a bit." He shoots me a reproachful glare as Becca slowly backs up.

"Babe," he says softly. "I know this all seems strange and scary and—"

"Insane." One of her brows arcs.

"Improbable," he finishes. "But you'll have to keep an open mind right now. What Molly is saying, despite being somewhat inarticulate, well, is true."

Becca shakes her head, like she wants us to stop talking.

"There's another dimension," he goes on. "One that Molly travels to while she sleeps. It's called Terra Somniorum, Land of Dreams. But we call it Terra for short."

"We?" she squeaks out.

"Yes, I'm from there, from Terra." Rae begins to explain about the Vigil and the Nocturna, what each does. How our two worlds are connected and what my purpose there is. The history and importance of Dreamers and the threat of evil that manifests into human nightmares. That I, a chosen Dreamer, am called upon to bring back the balance in Terra and help stave off a war on Earth. He explains succinctly, delicately, and all the while approaching Becca until she's an arm's length away, pressed up against my sleeping pod. Rae stands there, his posture displaying that she shouldn't be afraid, his tone saying she can trust him.

I hold my breath as Becca blinks from me back up to him, a swallow bobbing her throat. "So...so you're saying you're this Vigil thing?"

Rae nods. "We aren't very different from humans. Think of it as the difference in ethnicities that you guys have here."

"But you said you're stronger than us," she says, skepticism clear in her voice. "Have the genetic makeup to be able to go through that thing in the corner without getting turned to mush."

"Yes."

"Prove it."

"What?"

"Prove it. Go through the portal and do your magic trick. *Disappear from this dimension.*" Becca says the last part in a mock spooky tone.

They stare at one another, a challenge alight in my best friend's gaze.

"I think you'll have to," I say to Rae.

"Yeah, listen to the 'Dreamer.'" She air quotes before rolling her eyes.

I glare at her. "Bec—"

"All right," Rae cuts in. "But you need to stand over there." He points to where I am, a safe distance away, and she complies, making sure not to look in my direction.

I won't lie—her ignoring me hurts, but it *is* better than her running from the room.

Walking to the portal, Rae turns on one of the panels beside it, and the ancient Latin lettering used in Terra flashes across it. He types against the screen before standing back, waiting as the portal begins to glow bright blue-white, and a high-pitched whir fills the room. My heart pumps in anticipation along with an unbearable sense of longing. Just beyond that circle is a place I've hungered to return to more than taking my next breath, and Rae can easily walk through it. Will I eventually be able to? Can I dare hope?

I glance sideways at Becca, taking in her puckered brows and lips tightly pressed together. Rae's golden eyes settle on my best friend, and it feels like he's holding her in that instant, touching her in a way that's determined, desperate, and I'm about to look away, feeling as though I'm intruding, when Rae breaks it. He squares his large shoulders, facing the portal once more, and then walks into it. Becca's breath hitches as a flash of blinding light causes us to shield our gaze, and then it's gone, and so is he.

"Rae!" Becca's eyes bulge as she steps forward. "Oh God, where did he—"

I grab her arm as she gets precariously close to the active portal. "No, we can't go through it," I say. "Just wait a second. He'll be back."

Her mouth opens and closes as she looks back and forth between me and where Rae just was. Her face is paler than normal, her red hair shocking under the fluorescent lighting.

"What's happening?" she asks in a way that reminds me of how I sounded when first learning all this.

Before I can answer, the portal flashes bright again, and Rae steps out. His blond locks are barely out of place around his dark features, his black T-shirt and jeans not even sporting a wrinkle, and I can just barely smell the sweet night air of Terra clinging to him. My heart beats longingly in my chest.

The silence is heavy as we wait for Becca's reaction. She stares at Rae like, well, like he just disappeared and reappeared through a portal.

He slowly approaches her, but she backs up, and hurt flashes in his eyes.

"I can't believe this," Becca whispers, her hand covering her mouth as she shakes her head. "I just can't. It can't be possible, right? Because that would mean... Oh God!" Her eyes grow wide as she peers at Rae. "I'm dating an alien!"

Chapter 8

I like cactuses over plants. I also like the cold over being
too hot.
Does that surprise you? Do I look leafy warm over
prickly cold?
It's funny how the details often separate knowing a
person
from not knowing them at all.

—*Part of a letter from Molly to Dev*

THE APARTMENT WAS cleaned and then cleaned again in preparation
for his arrival home. The fireplace was lit, the blue-white flames
sending shifting patterns across the living room and changing the
beige couches to a cool white hue. Dev carried an array of bever-
ages to the man who rested in the middle of one couch, a pile of
pillows propping him up.

"By the stars." Tim laughed as he saw what Dev held. "I'm
not *remotely* that thirsty."

"I didn't know what you wanted." Dev placed the tray on the
low table in front of his guardian, glancing over the cups of water,

tea, orange juice, and a drink called Traub, made from a special grape grown in Terra.

"Well, you could have easily asked." Tim smiled before pointing to the Traub. Dev handed it over, and he nestled into the couch with a sigh. Tim was still wearing the gray long-sleeve shirt and soft black pants that were given to him at the hospital, his beard extra thick, since he refused to shave until he came home. It was almost completely white now, the stress of the attack likely inducing such a change. But his hair, however, still maintained an even mix of salt and pepper.

While Tim's skin and muscles were successfully regenerated, there was still some nerve damage that the doctors said would take a few more days to repair. Dev was instructed to make sure Tim took a daily dose of nerve medication, to expedite the process.

"Do you need anything else? Are you hungry? I can go see what books you have out on your nightstand."

"My dear boy…" Tim shook his head, an amused grin marring his features as he waved Dev to sit. "I'm not an invalid. If I want to read or eat, I can certainly do all those things on my own."

Dev frowned. "They told you not to overwork yourself the first few days home."

"Yes, meaning I shouldn't go out and start fighting Metus. I'm perfectly fine to walk around here. I might even attempt to go to the bathroom." He raised his brows. "Or do you think you'll need to help with that as well?"

"Only if you promised to one day return the favor if needed," Dev said wryly.

Tim chuckled. "I'm glad to see you've still retained your humor."

Dev eyed his guardian as he settled farther into the couch. "Why wouldn't I have?"

"I'm just glad you're able to keep your spirits up. There's no use sulking, as you know."

"Yes, I know." Dev glanced toward the fire, watching as it flickered and wavered.

"Rae came to see me before I was discharged," Tim went on. "Said they were close to finding a solution."

Dev nodded, a familiar tightening settling in his stomach anytime he thought of Rae's plans.

"I'm glad to hear it. I'm sure we'll have Molly back in no time."

Before Dev could respond, the front door opened and Aveline walked in, her blonde ponytail swaying with her sure strides. Seeing who sat next to Dev, she dropped her Arcus baton into the quiver on her back and swung it off as she hurried forward.

"You're home!" She smiled and with a bounce sat beside Tim, kissing his cheek.

Though they still hadn't spoken properly since their argument at the recovery wing—Aveline doing a fine job of avoiding him—seeing her happy with the return of their guardian slid a smile onto Dev's face.

It disappeared, however, when he turned to find another person had entered their apartment. Hector closed the door behind him before slowly approaching the group, his movements languid, confident. His white hair was tied into its usual low bun at the base of his neck, underscoring his angular features, while his pale skin shone translucent under the lighting, the fireplace highlighting the wickedly carved scar across his left eye. His shrewd green gaze moved from the two people on the couch to rest on Dev.

"What are *you* doing here?" Dev asked coolly. Hector was Dev's least favorite companion of Aveline's. Though once a high-ranked Vigil protector—who they recently learned was assigned to Molly's grandfather, the chosen Dreamer before her—he'd removed himself from duty after a mysterious accident on Earth during its World War II. He was left with a vicious scar across his eye, which he refused to let Terra doctors fix, and had fallen into the less desirable crowd of underground partiers and euphoria chasers. Despite Hector's appearance of snobbish indifference and often cruel amusement, Dev easily saw it all as a carefully painted facade to hide a man running from his own ghosts. But it provoked little pity from Dev. Whatever was the cause of Hector's rather masochistic repenting behavior, it mattered little when his way of living could possibly harm Aveline. Dev didn't want his partner anywhere near such an influence.

Too bad she rarely did what Dev asked.

"I came to get you, actually," Hector said, leaning an elbow on the fireplace mantel.

"What for?"

"A summons was brought for the both of you," Aveline chimed in, picking up one of the many drinks for Tim and taking a sip.

"Well, where is it?"

Aveline gestured toward Hector, who reached into his back pocket and handed Dev a small oval chip.

He inserted it into his armband, and a message filled the screen. Dev scrunched his forehead as he read.

"Elena wants to see us?"

"So it would seem." Hector plucked an errant string from his shirt.

"Why?"

"Really, Devlin,' Hector clucked. "Must you always ask such asinine questions? We'll obviously find out when we go to her."

Dev pressed his lips together as one of his hands slowly curled into a fist.

"Hector." Aveline gave him a warning glance. "Please don't antagonize him."

"But, pet, I can hardly help it when it's so easily done." He flashed her a charming grin before turning back to Dev. "Come, General, let's not keep our dear elder waiting."

"I'm no longer a general," Dev said through clenched teeth, standing.

"Yes, well, we're both no longer a lot of things," Hector said, before opening the door for them to leave.

⋖⋗▬⊙ ⊙▬⋖⋗

They stood side by side in the spacious office, the floor-to-ceiling windows in front of them displaying a majestic view of City Hall Square. Dev's attention skimmed over the large rectangular park below, the small forms of Terra citizens maneuvering in and out of the manicured trees and pristine stone paths, a black river of movement. The buildings that surrounded the oldest part of the city were of the human neoclassical era, each adored with tall columned entryways and triangle pediments filled with intricate carved statues. For some reason, Dev found comfort in such visual history.

While most of Terra's governmental buildings were of the Greek and Roman style, none were as large and proud as City Hall, something he knew was purposefully planned. This building rested at the top of the square, the elders' chambers on the highest floor, where Hector and Dev now stood. The light from the racing stars overhead streamed into the white office and framed the current elder sitting in front of them with a soft-glowing silhouette.

Elena tapped away on various messages lighting up on her desk's surface, effectively ignoring the two men. They could easily have come back later, but Dev knew having them patiently stand before her was just another of the elder's tactics in reminding them of the difference in hierarchy. How wasteful these small games were, Dev thought, for no one needed the reminder.

Beside him, Hector stood relaxed, his arms behind his back as his constantly sly grin flirted across his lips. Dev took in a calming breath. Normally he would wear a similar air of indifference, but as of late his talent of exuding flippantness was wearing thin.

Finally, after what felt like another Earth cycle, Elena turned her messages off and leaned back in her chair.

Placing her delicate hands on either side of her armrests, she moved her cool blue gaze over them. "It's a rare sight for the two of you to stand together so amicably."

"What you command"—Hector bowed low—"we try to achieve." While the gesture was seemingly out of respect, like anything the Vigil did, it carried an edge of mockery.

"I forgot about your sting of charm, Hector." Elena stood, her white robe swaying as she walked to the front of her desk. "I've called you both here to talk about something rather precarious. Something that you both undoubtedly will resist complying with, but you will have no choice but to."

"Then why call it a discussion?" Dev asked.

Hector muffled a chuckle, while Elena merely raised a brow.

"Quite," she said. "Then let's get to the point, shall we?" She half sat on the lip of her desk. "Hector, as a Vigil you are aware of the history of the Dreamers and, with your past position, are even more acquainted with the duties of being their protector."

Dev sensed Hector stiffen.

"I am," he said.

"You are not, however, knowledgeable on our current Dreamer or the plan that is, as we speak, being set in motion to bring her back to Terra."

Both men waited for her to continue.

"Dev happens to be an expert on both."

Hector and Dev shared a glance.

"I beg your pardon, ma'am," Hector said, "but what does one have to do with the other?"

"We are in need of building a bigger team for Molly, in preparation for her return and her safety on Earth. Given what you were with her grandfather, it has been decided that you are now to be reinstated into your role as one of the chosen Dreamer's guards."

The floor seemed to drop from beneath Dev's feet, and he quickly said, "He can't be."

"It's already done."

"But there must be other Vigil in training for such a position," he countered. "Surely you can't trust *him* for this?"

Elena turned her attention to Hector, studying him. "I think you'd be surprised what I would trust Hector with. Especially now."

"Elena, this isn't a game! This is Molly, the strongest Dreamer you have admitted to ever coming in contact with. Are the elders really going to risk her safety by—"

"He is the most applicable candidate, Devlin. Besides, the few in training for the position are not yet ready, by our standards."

"But—"

"As you were so quick to point out"—Elena interrupted again—"this is not something up for discussion."

Dev snapped his jaw shut, trying not to grind his teeth to dust. *By the Metus, she was intolerable.* Hector, Molly's guard? He held back a scoff.

Turning to the Vigil, he asked, "What happened to you and Robert? What made you abandon your duty to him?"

"That is none of your concern," Hector said coolly.

"Of course it is! You've just been charged with taking care of his granddaughter and my—" Dev cut himself off. "I will *not* let you put her in harm's way."

"And I won't," Hector said, looking back to Elena, "because I cannot comply with your command."

Dev sighed in relief. "Thank Terra."

"Yes you will, Hector," Elena said.

"No." He shook his head. "I cannot relive such a thing."

"Sometimes"—the elder moved closer to him—"you must begin a story again to end it properly."

"By the stars." Dev snorted. "Must you elders always speak in tongues? Don't be tricked by their riddles, Hector. For once we agree on something. Let's see how long we can continue to."

Dev was surprised to find a pained expression creasing Hector's brow. He seemed stuck in some memory, his hand slowly lifting to touch his scarred eye. *What happened to him?* Whatever it was, Dev didn't want Molly anywhere near it. There was too much about Hector he didn't know, and the things he did…well, they were the opposite of reassuring.

"Can't you see that both of us think this is a bad idea?" Dev turned back to Elena. "Give me a meeting with the elders. I'm sure we can find another solution."

Elena didn't reply right away, merely kept her gaze trained to Hector's, a silent conversation passing between the two. Dev watched on, awkwardly shifting as he slowly witnessed the usually emotionless Vigil now experiencing an array.

"Repent for redemption," the elder eventually spoke to Hector, her voice soft, soothing. "Not damnation."

The pale-haired man took in a stuttering breath. "Yes," he said thickly. "Yes, I'll do it."

Dev blinked. "What in all of Terra just happened?"

"What always would." Elena stood back. "Now that that's settled—"

"Nothing is *settled*," Dev interjected, but Elena talked over him.

"There are still a few more things that need to be aired out"

"No, rewind please." Dev held up a hand. "What kind of mind control did you just place over Hector to get him to comply?"

"None," Hector said tightly. "My decisions are my own."

"Really? How so, when Elena just commanded we obey her?"

Hector lifted a frosty gaze to Dev. "I take this new role with honor."

"Honor? Since when did you *ever* care for such a thing?"

The Vigil's green eyes narrowed. "There's much you don't know about me, *Devlin*."

"And thank Terra for that."

"Gentlemen, please," Elena cut in. "There's only one more piece of business we need to take care of, and we must do it quickly, for your time is almost up with me."

"Then by all means"—Dev folded his arms over his chest—"continue."

She glanced at Hector. "We must discuss your involvement with Aaron."

Dev's whole body seized up. "Aaron?"

"But I already told you." Hector's shoulders hunched forward. "I didn't know who he was, what he was planning."

"Yes, no need to excite yourself," Elena reassured. "You passed the truth serum, so there is nothing to fear on our end."

The room went quiet while Hector and Elena looked to Dev, but he was too terrified to move, to breathe. For he could feel his mind being taken over by a darker force, one that would propel his hands to reach for his Arcus if what he was piecing together was true.

Slowly, and with great care, he faced the Vigil who, until this moment, he didn't believe he could hate more. "What. Did. You. Do?"

"Nothing—"

Dev seized Hector by the throat and lifted him a fraction off the ground. "What did you *do*?!"

The Vigil tried to gasp through Dev's grip, his face turning red as he frantically grabbed at his hands. Dev squeezed harder right before an invisible energy wrapped around his whole body, shocking him with an acute pain and forcing him to drop Hector.

Both men collapsed to their knees, Dev glaring up at Elena, knowing she was responsible for what just happened.

"You're insane!" Hector wheezed as he bent over coughing.

"What was your involvement with Aaron?!" Dev forced himself to his feet, moving forward.

Hector tripped as he scrambled back, but when Dev was about to lunge for him again, he was rendered paralyzed, the same energy as before holding him in place.

"Let me go," Dev bit out, his eyes pinned to Hector.

"Not until you calm yourself," Elena replied in slight boredom. "All of this is really unnecessary. Hector will tell you what you want to know. If you are to work together, this must be aired. That is, if you can spare him a moment to speak."

Dev glared at Hector, the realization of their future unity suddenly sinking in, and Hector seemed equally unhappy about it.

Tipping his chin up, Hector brushed off his clothes, seeming to revel in prolonging explaining, for it kept Dev stuck under Elena's hold. *He better run fast after this meeting. Her powers won't save him then.*

"We traded," Hector eventually said.

Dev narrowed his gaze. "In what?"

"Many things," he said. "Nectus in exchange for certain information on Robert, news about Terra for objects he could bring me from Earth. But I truly had no idea who he was. He's not the only Vigil to ever go rogue, you know."

Dev didn't know this, but that was of little concern, for as Hector continued to talk, Dev realized why Elena maintained her hold on him, forcing his feet to stay rooted to the ground, his hands stuck by his sides.

By asking Aaron to find Robert, to check in on him, Hector had led Aaron straight to Molly.

Chapter 9

My midnight,
I can't see clearly anymore.
I need you to come home.
I need the light of your star
to guide me.

—*Part of a letter from Dev to Molly*

THE SOUND OF soldering tools and metallic scents fill the lab. A contrast to the silent and less-than-pleasant aromatic taxi ride Rae and I took to the location in Brooklyn where Sonja has set up shop. Since the incident with Becca, something has definitely shifted in Rae—there's a solemn energy to him now, like his thoughts are clouded and heavy. I understand. I too feel like I'm walking under a fog these days, neither of us the best companions.

It's been almost a week since we revealed everything to Becca, which means it's also been a week since either of us has talked to her. She stayed long enough to listen to us explain further about what was going on and that while Rae was, yes, technically an alien, he was nothing like we see in the movies. *We're all aliens to someone*, I had said. While she surprisingly agreed, none of it was enough to stop her from running straight for the exit. Rae followed but was momentarily blocked by her slamming shut and locking the closet door. It only took one swift kick from Rae to open it again, but by that time I was pulling on his arm and pleading with him to let her go, to give her some space to take it all in. I mean, I'm the one who actually traveled there, and I still didn't believe it when everything was explained. I can hardly blame Becca for her reaction.

In the days that followed, Rae waited outside her apartment like a watchdog, resorting to me bringing him sandwiches, because as hard as it is to believe, I was pretty certain he wouldn't have eaten otherwise. Becca must have been staying at her sister Steph's, for she never appeared, and while he could have stalked her at work or at her sister's, I told him unless he wanted the police to get involved, he probably shouldn't. Her phone was also turned off, so neither of us knew if she saw or listened to the countless messages we left.

All we can do now is wait. And by Rae's usually lively countenance turning to an eerie sullen shadow, I know he's not handling that well. While I'm feeling the same effects of potentially losing my best friend, one of us needs to function. So it seems our roles have switched, and I'm the one nudging him to start the day and keep moving.

I watch Rae walk over to Sonja in the back of the room, his footsteps heavy, and I sigh, hoping she has some good news for us. Raymond, the Vigil scientist who helped me in Terra, is also here now. He's been coming and going for about a week, and I glance to his familiar form currently bent over one of the computers in the middle of the space. The sleeves to his white lab coat are rolled up, and his thick-rimmed glasses reflect back the blue glow from the monitor, his thinning brown hair neatly parted to one side.

"Hi, Raymond." I approach him with a grin, and his head pops up, his eyes magnified by his lenses.

"Molly, on time as usual," he says with a smile. So far Raymond's proved to be a very animated and optimistic man. Anytime I show the slightest interest in something he's doing, he falls full force into explaining what it is and its importance. If it wasn't for him, I still wouldn't know the difference between a tumor-promoting and opine-synthesis gene, and we couldn't have that now, could we?

"Sonja called to say there's been some new developments."

"Yes." His brows shoot up in excitement. "We've pretty much completed the Molecular Chamber. A few more things to test and make sure of, but it's looking good."

I try keeping my face neutral while anticipation and fear mix in my chest. I still can't believe I could actually be going back, and soon. How much will the transfer hurt? What's at risk? My Vigil companions have been rather closed lipped about the details, and my trepidation has kept me from pressing for answers.

"That's awesome," I say and look to the back of the room where the Molecular Chamber rests. Two pods, similar to the white coffin I lay in back at the Village Portal Bookstore, now sit behind the glass partition in the corner. The differences in these are the multitude of wires streaming from one to the other, a complicated spider's web, and each has a domed glass.

"Why are there two pods?" I ask.

"For each of you." Raymond clicks away on his keyboard.

I frown. "Each of us?"

But I get no answer from the Vigil who's now engrossed with a message flashing on his screen. He grumbles something about our archaic human technologies before typing away again.

Leaving Raymond to deal with whatever that is, I make my way over to Sonja and Rae, who stop their conversation as I approach. They stand by a table outside the Molecular Chamber, the chrome surface filled with various equipment and papers, none holding any real meaning to me.

"Why are there two pods in there now?" I nod to the room in front of them.

"We were just going to discuss that with you," Sonja says before furtively glancing to Rae.

"Oh?"

"Why don't we all have a seat?" She gestures to a group of chairs close by. "Raymond, can you come join us?" Sonja calls to the man, and he hurries over.

"I'm not going to like this, will I?" I say, gripping my thighs as I sit.

No answer.

"Rae? What's going on?" I turn to my friend, his hazel gaze distractedly fixated on the cement floor before it comes up to meet mine. "Did something happen in Terra? Is it Dev?"

"Dev is fine," he says, rubbing his lips together, "but Terra was dealt a pretty severe attack by the Metus earlier this week. They inflicted a great deal of damage to part of the city's wall. It wasn't breached, but things now need to move a lot quicker."

"Why didn't you mention this to me when it happened?" I ask, my heart beating faster. Dev hadn't written anything about it either.

"A lot went down that day, both Terra and here." He looks at me pointedly, and I think of Becca. "I didn't want to add any more worry onto our already stressful plate."

"But now?"

"Now we must address what needs to happen to ensure your quick return to Terra."

"Raymond said the chamber is pretty much complete, so that's good, right?"

"Yes." Rae nods, looking to Sonja. "It is."

I glance to the female Vigil. Her hair is down today, the gray locks falling right below her shoulders, but the effect does little to soften the sadness I see etched in her green gaze. I swallow. "I'm sensing there's a *but* mixed in here."

"But," Rae goes on, "we had to change the plan slightly for the chamber to be ready sooner."

"Oh my." Raymond flutters his fingers over his knee. "I thought she already knew the details."

"Not quite." Rae says.

"Oh dear," he tuts again.

"Knew what details?" I ask. "Guys, just tell me."

Rae clears his throat. "We've run out of time, Molly, and what we originally were aiming for is no longer an option."

"What were we originally aiming for?"

Sonja is the one who answers. "We were looking for a way to duplicate the unique DNA properties of the Vigil that allows us to walk freely in and out of the dimensional portal, so we could add it to your own."

"And now?"

"Now we can't duplicate per se. We can only transfer, which was the original intent of these machines."

"What does that mean, only transfer?" I ask, glancing to Rae, whose gaze is on the ground again.

"It means," she says, "what we were trying to change about the pods, we've unfortunately run out of time to explore. We can only use them as they are now, what we built from the original schematics, and what we have assurance will work."

I let out a frustration sigh. "Yes, but Sonja, what *is* that?"

She wets her lips before speaking again. "To give you the DNA required, we will need to take it from a Vigil."

A thick silence settles in the lab, everything in the universe suspended in stillness.

"What do you mean, take?" I ask slowly.

"Through the Molecular Chambers, we'll be transferring the Vigil's unique DNA to fuse with yours."

"Okay." I nod. "And what will happen to them, to the Vigil?"

"Well, luckily, replicating and inserting human DNA is what Veda Corp. does, what we have perfected, so we will be replacing what they give up with that."

As her words sink in, the periphery of my vision fish bowls out of focus. "Wait. So you're saying to make me be able to return to Terra, a Vigil has to…become human?"

Sonja's silver gaze holds mine. "Yes," she says. "That's what has to happen."

"That's crazy!" My eyes are wide, unbelieving. "Who in all of Terra would agree to such a thing? They'd be giving up everything."

No one answers me, but then again, they don't have to, for it only takes Sonja solemnly glancing to Rae to break apart my world as she silently tells me everything I don't want to know.

Chapter 10

What haunts me the most
is that I can't hold you
when you need me the most.

—*Part of a letter from Dev to Molly*

THERE'S A PHRASE people use when endless bad things happen—
when it rains, it pours. I've always hated that saying. First, it doesn't
always pour when it rains, and secondly, why are we using a mundane thing like droplets of water to describe when a person is getting broken in two by life's consistently unfair actions? It should
be rephrased to something like, *when it rains, lightning will soon strike*
you dead—I could attest to that one. Let's paint a picture that de-
scribes an iota of the pain the person is going through, because
merely being wet would be a welcome relief right about now. My
heart, lungs, blood—everything in me feels like it's being crushed
by what's just been placed in front of me.

"No." I push up out of my seat. "No, we aren't doing that."

Rae stands with me. "Molly—"

"Don't you say it!" I level a finger at him. "Don't you dare say this is what needs to be done."

"But it is."

I stare at him, incredulous, before glancing to the others. "Are you all mad?! There has to be another solution. We could...we could simulate another lightning strike, try to open that door in my brain again. Or maybe if we use whatever's in those Conscious blades, stab me with it. We can see if it reverses the effect? Two negatives make a positive, right?"

"No, Molly." The softness in Sonja's voice nearly undoes me further.

"We can wait then." I give a decided nod. "Surely we can wait a little longer to figure this out? Terra has fought wars before, where there wasn't a Dreamer present. Why can't they now?"

"This is like no other war previous," Rae says solemnly.

I tug a hand through my hair. "Does Dev know your ridiculous plan?"

"Yes."

I blink, stunned. "And he's okay with it?"

"None of us are *okay* with it," Rae says a bit sharply. "But I've thought long and hard to come to this decision, and I accept it."

I rub my forehead, a stuttered breath escaping me. "But why does it have to be *you*? Get someone else—"

"There isn't anyone else."

"There has to be. What about a Vigil prisoner or something?"

Rae shakes his head. "This is my duty—"

"Fuck your duty! I can't ask this of you! I can't kill you. I can't—"

"You're not going to kill me." He steps forward and brings me into his arms.

"Yes I will. You'll be *human*." I try pushing away, but he only holds me more tightly.

"And what's so bad about being human?"

"Stop it." I finally step out of his embrace. "You know what I'm saying. Do you even understand what you'll be giving up? Your home! Friends, Terra."

"All things you were forced to give up."

"That's different."

"Is it?"

"Yes!"

"How?"

My lips press together as I glare at him. "For one thing, if I had chosen Earth, I would have forgotten about everything I gave up. You won't. Plus, another Dreamer would have eventually come. They might still now. I'm replaceable."

"That most certainly is *not* true." Rae glowers. "You were specifically chosen for this mission, Molly, a direct descendent from the last Dreamer. There's a reason for that. And if we're going to talk about being replaceable, then what about me? There are Vigil being trained as we speak to step forward and fill my shoes."

My lips purse at that. "But none of them are *you*."

"My point exactly." His gaze softens. "None of them are you."

My shoulders droop. I'm so tired, so tired of all of this. It can never be easy, can it? I'm not asking for a completely smooth road, just one that's not filled with as many gaping potholes.

"But what will you do once you're human?"

"I'll still be your guard here. My duties on Earth won't be effected. I just won't be able to follow you into Terra. You'll have another guard to help you there. And...I'll have Becca. This might give us our chance at a proper life together."

I look into his golden eyes, the way his dark skin enhances their vibrancy and all the emotions they hold, knowing the precariousness of that statement. "You can't truly want this."

"It's not about what I want, Molly. It's about doing what's right for Terra, for you."

"But I'm not asking for you to do this for me!"

His hand rests on my shoulder. "I'm doing it so you won't have to."

My lips tremble, and I have to turn from the group as a sob escapes me. "Why?" I gasp out, covering my face with my hands, annoyed that I'm crying, since I promised myself I wouldn't do that, not anymore. Yet here I am—again. "It's too much," I say. "I'm losing too many people. I can't risk losing you too."

Rae's strong arm curls around me, bringing me back into his chest. "You're not losing me," he whispers. "This will work, and neither of us will be in any danger. I told you I'd get you back, no matter what, and I am."

"I didn't want you to sacrifice yourself to do it." I dig my fingers into his shirt.

"That's not how I see what I'm doing. I'm still going to have a life, Molly. Hopefully a happy one. It will just be a bit different than I had originally planned."

I push my face into his chest as I let the final my sobs out, knowing I still have an audience, and the last thing they need to see is the Dreamer they are counting on show weakness. So with a forced swallow, I make myself stop and brush away the tears. I can mourn separately, alone, for the first time understanding why Terra saves such a thing for behind closed doors.

Taking a deep breath, I slowly step away from Rae. There's no changing his mind, any of theirs, and deep down I understand why. But it doesn't make me feel any less horrid, selfish, and sick. There's a piece of me that's starting to hate myself. For how can my purpose on this planet be any more important than anyone else's?

Leveling a gaze on Sonja and Raymond, who both have remained silent while warily watching our exchange, I straighten my shoulders. "We should let you guys get back to work," I say. "Because before I let this man get into that machine, you better be two hundred percent certain that *nothing* will go wrong."

Chapter II

Tell me something that's made you happy recently.
I need something that will help me smile.

—*Part of a letter from Molly to Dev*

THE MEN AND women ran by in their organized rows of two as Dev placed another box of weapons onto a conveyer belt leading up to an awaiting airship. Aveline was supposed to help, but she was currently stunned motionless by his side.

"No," Aveline said with a shake of her head. "It can't be true."

"I wish it wasn't." Dev grunted as he transferred another crate. The hangar they stood in buzzed with Terra's military rushing to continue their defense along the damaged western wall of the city, where the engineers were working quickly to repair it.

"But...I thought Aaron was looking for the next Dreamer anyway and found out Molly was it when she visited him in the hospital?"

"From the sounds of it, Hector gave Aaron everything he needed to stay in the area longer when he traded information for news on Robert. He learned Robert had a granddaughter, and when she got hit by lightning…well, as crazy as he is, Aaron's not an idiot. He must have pieced together a few things. Her discussing her strange dreams with him must have solidified it. Are you going to help me with these or not?" Dev nodded to the stack of weapons.

Still in a daze, Aveline bent to pick up a crate by her feet. "Why are you so calm?"

Dev scoffed. "I certainly wasn't in Elena's office, and I hardly am now. It's taking all my strength not to hunt down your Metus turd of a boyfriend and put an end to his miserable life."

"He's not my boyfriend." Aveline scowled.

"Sure, whatever." Dev removed the crate from her still form and placed it on the belt.

"I know Hector's a lot of things," Aveline went on, "but he would never intentionally bring harm to anyone."

"Don't be so naïve." Dev shot her an annoyed glare. "People are capable of all sorts of things, and it's not like Hector surrounds himself with the most honorable of people, given his area of work."

"Still, he wouldn't willingly put anyone in danger. Especially not with what happened in his past."

Dev turned to regard Aveline carefully. "What do you know of his past?"

"Enough." Her chin tilted up.

"Tell me."

"No, I can't betray his confidence."

"*I'm* your partner, not him," Dev ground out.

"So? That's not how secrets work. You don't tell me everything about all of your friends."

Dev let out a frustrated sigh. "Just tell me this. Is what happened going to, in any way, put Molly in danger?"

Aveline looked away for a moment. "No," she said. "I think it will make her safer."

Dev's eyes narrowed. "Why would it do that?"

"Because now he has a chance at redemption."

"Well, that doesn't make me feel in the least bit better. What in all of Terra did he do, Ave?"

"You'll have to get him to tell you," she said and handed him another container.

Dev worried his bottom lip before transferring the box onto the conveyer belt, a drop of concern mixing in with his consistently palpable rage. He knew Hector abandoned his post as guardian to Molly's grandfather, Robert, during World War II. But that didn't give Dev the reason why. What could have led a Vigil to react in such a way? The ones sent out to guard Dreamers were supposed to be trained for all sorts of situations, and Dev would have thought the one assigned to watch over a chosen Dreamer would be from a hardier stock. He certainly knew Rae was. He was the bravest and most dedicated Vigil Dev knew. Which meant whatever led to Hector's abandonment must have been very bad. Would the elders really partner such a risk with Molly? Dev knew he needed to keep his faith with their choices, but lately their decisions left him more than doubtful.

"So what's going to happen to him?" Aveline asked, bringing Dev back to the loud sounds of the military hangar. A few airships took flight and zoomed up and out of the large opening in the ceiling, mixing with the shooting stars streaking by.

"Nothing," he said.

"Wha— How is that possible?"

"Everything he was doing with Aaron was legal." Dev wiped at his face with the bottom of his shirt, exposing some of his stomach and garnering a few catcalls from nearby cadets. He gave them a responding smirk before turning back to Aveline. "The Nectus and the rest of the information he shared wasn't going against any laws."

"What about the Conscious knife? Did he...was Hector responsible for that?"

Dev's knuckles turned white from how hard he was pressing them to the container he held. "Hector knew about them and admitted to mentioning something to Aaron, but only after he brought up their existence first."

"Do you believe him?"

"I don't have to. Elena said Hector passed the truth serum interrogation. But if you ask me, I think Aaron was fishing, seeing if whatever rumors he heard about the weapons were true before he went seeking them out."

There was a beat of tense silence before Aveline said, "I'm so sorry, Dev."

He looked out to the sea of action before them, a sense of weariness washing through him, and on a resigned sigh, he stepped onto the lip of the awaiting airship's cargo bay. "Come on." Dev extended a hand to Aveline. "Unfortunately, there are other monsters we have to deal with first."

Dev and Aveline strapped into their seats toward the back, Dev's team already in place as the ship's doors closed with a puff, shutting out the light from the military base. Leaning his head against his headrest, Dev pushed away his distracted thoughts to focus on what needed to be done now, instead of who was still so far away from his reach in another dimension. But even as the slick airship lifted out of the hangar and raced toward the angry glow of orange in the distance, he knew her vision would never dim, and distraction or not, he was glad for it.

Chapter 12

While cooking, I caught Tim singing with the
spatula again.
I didn't show myself until he hit the high note.
You can imagine my delight and his mortification
when I did.
Now, my midnight, you must be smiling at that.

—*Part of a letter from Dev to Molly*

THE SQUAWKING OF seagulls mixes in with the lapping of waves hitting up against the edge of the dock as the setting sun paints the Hudson River in an hombre of pink and orange, a watercolor set tipped over. Two women jog by, one laughing at something the other said, and I follow them with my eyes, watching their friendship with a sadness I hadn't previously known.

Taking in a deep breath, I turn back to stare at the water, enjoying the lightly salted air. This is the only part of the city, besides Central Park, where I can truly fill my lungs with something that doesn't smell polluted. While Manhattan is peppered with wonderful sites, people, and restaurants, the air is often fragranced with less-than-desirable surprises. I didn't realize the relief the freshness of Terra brought me until I stopped experiencing it.

Reaching for my iced coffee on the bench beside me, I take a generous sip. It's a little late in the day for caffeine, but the desire to stay up and not slip into sleep has slowly strengthened in the growing weeks. A behavior, I'm sure, wouldn't take a team of psychiatrists to figure out why.

A high-pitched squeal turns my head, and I catch a little girl grabbing for her family's dog's leash. She coos for it to keep moving like a mother to her child, evoking me to smile. My grin is short lived though, the melancholy that has circled me since leaving the lab the other day rearing forward once more. *Rae*, I think. *You're loyal to a fault.* If there were a way I could convince him not to do this, I would be smothering him with it right now. Unfortunately, I know this Vigil, and I know what's at stake. It seems like my life has been filled with a lot of decisions that are not my own lately. Funny how someone that's said to hold limitless power can feel so powerless. Slumping lower on the bench, I gaze at the shifting orange sky above. All of this only makes me more terrified for what's next. There's no room for failure now. Too many people are sacrificing things for my sake, with the belief that I'm the difference they all desperately need.

"Is this seat taken?"

I sit up with a start, finding Becca regarding me with a hesitant smile.

"Bec—" I begin to stand, but she shushes me to stay put as she joins me on the bench. "What are you doing here?"

"Rae told me where you were."

"Rae? You saw him?"

She nods.

I watch her for a moment, anxiously tapping the lid on my cup. Her red hair is pulled into a messy bun, and she wears a light-gray jacket slung over a black tank and jeans. "Are...are you guys okay?"

She takes in a deep breath and stares out at the water, her green eyes darkening to moss with the setting sun. "We will be," she says, turning back to me. "I believe you, Molly. What you guys showed me and admitted to. It took a few days to process, but...I believe you."

It's like I sprouted a thousand balloons and have begun to float, that's how light I feel after hearing her say those words. "You do?"

"Yes. I mean, if it were a lie, it would be a pretty friggin' elaborate and detailed one. What would be the point? And if I were being honest, after sitting with it, I don't really think we can be the only intelligent creatures out there." She gestures in front of us. "It's pretty narcissistic to believe, actually. I mean, we've got to get our fantasy stuff from *somewhere*, right? It can't all be make-believe."

I'm momentarily rendered speechless.

Can this really be happening?

Without thinking further, I throw my arms around her. "Oh, Bec, you don't know how happy I am to hear you say this. I thought...I thought I lost you."

She laughs lightly, returning my embrace. "Well, you kind of did for a little bit. It's not every day you learn that there are other dimensions, and your boyfriend is an alien, and your best friend is some sort of warrior badass."

"I'm not a warrior badass." I lean back.

"Um, from the sounds of it, that's exactly what you are," Becca says with raised brows. "Rae told me the things you can do there...what you *have* done. Can we say, *holy shit*?"

I hide a smile. "Yeah, I guess that's one way to describe it."

She shakes her head. "I only wish I could see it."

"I wish you could too." I squeeze her hand, the desire to share Terra, and everything else I've been forced to keep from Becca, is suddenly overwhelming. "The city, the people—everything really, it's all so...amazing," I say. "Well, when it's not getting attacked by giant smelly nightmare beasts."

She chuckles as her features soften. "I can't believe you've been dealing with this by yourself."

"Not completely by myself. I had—" I stop myself, realizing what I was about to say and not sure how Becca will react to it.

"You had Rae. It's okay. I understand. But I do think a part of my anger came from you not feeling like you could tell me about..."

"Terra," I say when it's obvious she's unsure of the name.

"Yes, that."

"I tried to tell you once, but I knew how crazy it sounded. I mean, I thought *I* was losing my mind in the beginning, before I understood what was going on."

"Yes, I remember," she says dryly. "I was there too."

"And then after...well, I'm pretty sure humans aren't allowed to know about Terra. If any do, it's very few, and I have yet to meet them."

"So you're saying I'm special."

I laugh. "I don't know if I should be concerned or grateful at how awesome you're taking this."

"Probably both," she says with a wink and settles more comfortably on the bench.

I marvel at how quickly this day has turned around. It looks like life could afford to hand me a bit of a break after all.

"Rae explained what's going to happen this weekend," Becca says after a moment.

And then there's that.

"Yes." I press my lips together. "I don't want him to do it."

"He seems to think there's no other options."

"Everyone seems to think that. And even if there are, I understand that we've run out of time to perfect them. It's not good in Terra right now. From all the violence we're seeing on Earth, I know it must be tenfold there."

She chews on the inside of her cheek while studying me. "And you're really the *only* one that can fix all this?"

I snort. "Crazy, right?"

"Not entirely." She tilts her head. "You've got an edge to you that wasn't there before. I couldn't put my finger on it until now, but you seem…mature, worldly or something."

I roll my eyes.

"I'm serious," she says. "You're still you of course, but different somehow. Your eyes…" She looks at me intently. "It's obviously they've seen things most haven't. Rae told me of your memory training."

"Geez, he really left no rock unturned."

"He better not have. I grilled him about all this until he was blue in the face."

I smile. I wouldn't have expected her to act any differently.

"It's still crazy though." She shakes her head.

"Which part?"

"That you have to somehow save two worlds from war."

I swallow, not needing the reminder. "It not just me," I say. "I have help." And then after a beat of silence, I admit, "I'm scared, Bec."

Glancing up at her, I find her watching me, compassion in her gaze. "Of course you are." She pulls both my hands into hers. "Who wouldn't be?"

"It's not just about the fighting though," I explain. "What's about to happen…if it works, it will change everything. My time in Terra won't be limited anymore. The elders, the people in charge there, I'm sure they have some sort of plan for me. I might not be able to make it back to Earth for a while. And Rae…he's giving up everything."

"Not everything," she says meaningfully.

I sigh. "No, but there are people in his life, people that he loves, that he'll never see again. And this transfer might not work. There's still risk for—"

"Let's not talk about that," Becca cuts in. "Let's not throw any bad juju around. Both of you will survive this, and it *will* work."

I can't help smiling at how much she sounds like Rae.

"And as far as giving up loved ones"—Becca drapes an arm over the back of the bench—"if what I've gathered from Rae is true, you're talking about the same someone *you* love that you were never going to see again."

I swallow, my chest tightening. "Yes."

"Chicken," Becca says gently. "I can't believe you're in love and you couldn't tell me."

"It's definitely been hard."

"Is that why you and Jared didn't work?"

"One of the reasons," I say, knowing that even if I didn't meet Dev, deep down Jared and I wouldn't have survived in the long run.

"Well, I'm not going to pretend that I really have the best sense of what exactly is going on in this Terra place or how important you really are there or how much Rae is giving up, but I can tell you this. If the man you're referring to is the same one who gave you this letter"—she pulls a small envelope from her purse—"then you need to do everything and anything possible to get back to him, because let me tell you"—she fans herself with the piece of paper—"this guy is *not* someone you never want to see again."

With a gasp, I grab the slip from her hand. "Where did you get this?"

"Rae gave it to me to give to you."

I scowl as I bring it protectively to my chest. "Did you read it?"

"Of course."

"Becca! These are meant to be private."

She grins slyly. "I can see why. Who knew my Molly was such a harlot of a pen pal?"

I turn red. "Oh my God. I am not a harlot."

"From the sample of this man's writing, I certainly would be."

I can't help it. I tip my head back and laugh. And oh, does it feel good. So many of my recent days have been filled with somber realities and hard choices. It feels wonderful to let it all go, if only for a moment.

"So you really love this guy?" Becca asks once I've regained my composure, a look of inquisitive amusement alight in her gaze.

"Dev?"

"Dev." She nods.

I glance to the envelope in my hands. "Yes. More than anything. He's…he's…" I shake my head. "He's my everything."

"Then it's settled." Becca places a hand on my shoulder. "We're getting you back to him."

Chapter 13

Time must be laughing at us,
with its fickle nature to move slowly when we need
it to go fast.
Move fast when we need it to crawl.
If you ask me, I think it's in need of a good hug.

—*Part of a letter from Molly to Dev*

THE RESTAURANT WAS filled to the brim, a mostly private affair with the Vigil, who were celebrating their most loyal and dedicated brethren. The few Nocturna in attendance represented the small numbers who were aware of the Dreamer and what was happening tomorrow.

In the corner, Dev sipped his drink, giving off an air of relaxation and enjoyment, even though what he felt was anything but. He was a ball of anxiety, excitement, and dread. All the things that could go wrong swam before him, not to mention what would happen if everything went right. He would be gaining and losing two great people in his life. He could barely contain his impatience to finally see Molly again, touch her, breathe in her scent of honeysuckle and sunshine. But these emotions were sobered by the thought of what was needed to get her here.

Taking in the guests, Dev's eyes stopped when he found the man of the hour. Rae talked with the establishment's owner, Elario, in the back of the room. Behind them a replica scene of a Tuscan landscape rolled for miles on the other side of the glass partition. It was in there that most of the ingredients for Elario's restaurant were harvested. The dining establishment was located in Anima, a controlled biodome of all Earth's ecosystems and which took up a large section in the south part of the city. A deep laugh brought Dev's attention to the rotund man standing with Rae, his shortness exaggerated by his friend's height. Elario had been a great companion to him and Rae over the years, his restaurant the base of many fond memories. It often served as a getaway from the madness their lives usually brought, and whenever either of them had something they needed to discuss, or *didn't* want to discuss, they met here, Rae usually emptying Elario's pantry while Dev overindulged on the plethora of desserts the old man never seemed to run out of.

As if sensing an audience, the two companions turned to meet Dev's gaze, and with a smile Elario waved him over. Maneuvering through the crowd and around tables, Dev made his way toward them.

"We were just talking about you," Elario said, a twinkle of mischief in his brown eyes.

"Oh?"

"Rae was telling me about the time the two of you took a trip to Port City—and the bridge fiasco."

Dev leveled a chastening gaze on his blond friend, all too easily recalling the memory of their time in one of the smaller cities to the south of Terra. "I thought we were taking that to our deaths."

Rae shrugged, and the side of his mouth quirked up. "It's not like I'll be around to suffer the consequences of it now, only you."

Dev's smile dropped at the same time Elario cleared his throat.

"Oh, come on, guys," Rae said with an eye roll. "I was making a joke."

"Well, it was a bad one," Dev muttered.

"Since when were you the expert of funny?"

"Since hearing your attempt at comedy."

Rae snorted. "Elario"—he turned to the small gray-haired Nocturna—"that was funny, right? Or is the mood of the party ruined now? Should I tell everyone to go home?"

"I know better than to get in the middle of a lovers' quarrel." Elario held up his hands. "I think it's time I ensure everyone has enough wine." And with that the restaurant owner scurried away.

"No backbone on that one," Rae said with a shake of his head before catching Dev still frowning. "Come now." Rae slapped him on the shoulder. "If we can't joke about this, than what can we? You of all people should understand that. Or do I need to remind you of all the times you used levity during inopportune situations? Hint, the biennial Security Council gathering during Alex's speech."

Despite himself, a small grin forced its way onto Dev's lips.

"Exactly." Rae chuckled.

"Alex got his revenge though," Dev said with a smirk. "Which was only softened by Aveline also being forced to clean up the Metus droppings with me."

Both men laughed at that, the memories of their past circling Dev in a warm embrace. How much they had been through together, learned from one another. He trusted the Vigil with his life, and on this last thought his smile softened to a stern line again, reality setting in.

"I feel guilty," Dev said after a moment. "How can it be right for me to be happy when you're doing what you are?"

"You would do the same thing in my position."

Dev studied the amber liquid in his drink. "Perhaps."

"Don't kid yourself. You would. We all have our purposes, Dev, our duties. And honestly, if you want to know the truth, I'm not sacrificing as much as everyone thinks. Sure, I'm losing this." Rae looked around the room, to all the friends who had come to say their farewells. "But I'm gaining a life with a woman I love, and now so are you. I might even have the better end of the stick." He grinned slightly. "At least I'll have a better survival rate on Earth. I might even grow into old hair now."

"I think the saying is, 'grow into old age,'" Dev said.

"Whichever." Rae waved a dismissive hand. "The important thing is, Terra is getting their Dreamer back. *You're* getting her back. And the love of my life knows the truth about me and accepts it. We can all live happily ever after! It's a win-win."

Dev shook his head. "You're disgustingly positive sometimes."

"Why, thank you." Rae bowed.

"You're probably also enjoying the fact that I now have to work with Hector."

Rae's lips twitched. "You're forgetting that he and I will *also* have to work together."

"Not the same."

"It's not my fault that I'm more amiable, forgiving, lovable—"

"Does she know that he's replacing you?" Dev cut off his friend, knowing he would have gone on ad nauseam in listing his many virtues.

Rae's grin fell slightly. "No, I didn't want to overload her with any more things, but she'll find out tomorrow. He's going to be there at the transfer and guide her in portaling here."

Dev felt like a bird was trapped in his chest at the thought of his midnight being back here, with him, so soon. It almost felt unreal. Visions of her dark eyes, soft skin, and full lips swam before him. He shifted on his feet as his fingers drummed against his glass impatiently. How ironic it was that these small hours of waiting felt more torturous than the three months she'd been away.

"I wonder how she'll take the news," he said, referring to Hector.

"She doesn't really know him." Rae flagged down a waiter carrying a small plate of food. "But I'm sure once she finds out about his connection with Aaron, she won't be the biggest fan, not to mention whatever happened between him and her grandfather. He's also done a fine job keeping himself from ever returning to Earth. I'm curious, now with him being forced back, if he'll consider visiting Robert. That is, if Molly lets him." He grabbed almost the complete array of crab cakes from the offered tray, ignoring the waiter's astonished expression. "I'd accompany them of course, but I do wonder how Robert would react to seeing his old Vigil guard."

"Well, let's hope it doesn't kill him if he did. Molly wrote to me about his recent health issues."

"Yes, but that man is a tough nut. I think he's got some time on his side yet."

"Let's hope."

Rae used his beverage to wash down the lot of appetizers before peering out at the gathering. Aveline was off to the side talking with Tim and a few Vigil guards, Tim pretty close to being back to his full self. Aurora was there too, looking thinner than what was healthy as she stood away from the crowd, her partner, Ezekial, beside her, stealing a worried glance at her every so often. Dev would say hi soon, knowing he should try to maintain their friendship despite their conflicting feelings toward a certain man. He owed that much to the woman who helped lessen his grief all those years ago. If he was being honest with himself, she probably was the main reason he still stood there today.

Seeming to follow Dev's gaze, Rae said, "I heard you went to see Aaron together."

"I observed their visit."

"The elders weren't very pleased to learn you were granted access."

"Are the elders ever pleased about anything?"

Rae grunted agreement but stayed silent.

"He's still got his hooks in her." Dev observed Aurora a moment longer before turning back to his friend.

"Does that surprise you? He's her brother. They say such a bond is greater than anything we can understand."

"Perhaps, but it doesn't make me feel any better about it. You should see the way he tries to control her. I fear he's going to take advantage of her if their meetings continue to go unsupervised."

"There are Vigil guards always present," Rae said. "She's never alone with him."

"They don't know what to look for." Dev shook his head. "Aaron acts like he's crazy, but there's lucidness in his eyes. I've seen it. He knows exactly what he's doing. I just hope his trial comes soon and that his sentencing is termination. None of us will truly be safe until he's gone." Dev's hand tightened around his glass. "And I can't even think what he'll do if Molly returns safely and he finds out..."

"First, she *will* return safely." Rae gave his friend a steadying look. "And second, her security is going to be so thick it will practically be suffocating when she gets here. You might even have trouble getting to her."

Dev shot the Vigil a disapproving glare, and Rae smiled.

"It was a joke, my friend. Only a joke. By the stars, I'm really bombing tonight, aren't I?"

"Sorry." Dev rolled his shoulders, trying to relax. "I'm a little on edge."

"You don't say?" Rae teased. "But think of it this way—at least it's not *you* who's about to have his DNA reorganized."

Dev held back a weary sigh as he tried to maintain some levity. It was becoming apparent that Rae was using humor to mask his own fears. "Yes, I guess there's that," he said and then after finishing off his drink added, "Elena said everything looks good for tomorrow."

"Yeah, it's been gone over more times than I can count. Everyone is confident in the transfer's success. Sonja and Raymond said it should be quick. Some discomfort is inevitable, of course, but shouldn't be any worse than anything I've already lived through."

Dev's jaw set as a contemplative silence fell around the pair. Regarding the man beside him, Dev took in his strong features and the small scars visible on his dark skin, knowing exactly how each one was acquired. While siblings were almost nonexistent in Terra, Dev undoubtedly thought of Rae as a brother. He loved and would do anything for him, just as Rae was doing for Dev.

"Thank you," Dev found himself saying, his voice thick with an emotion he had hoped wouldn't surface until he was alone. "What you're doing…" He cleared his throat. "I'm honored to be your friend."

Rae studied Dev for a long while, his golden eyes shining with his own intense feelings. "Nihil familiā carius," he said and extended his hand.

"Nihil familiā carius," Dev returned, and the two stood there, letting the words flow through each other. They would have the rest of the evening to reminisce and joke and laugh among friends, but here, now, as they looked into one another's eyes, they knew this was their parting words of honor. For no matter the distance that was about to be forced between them, they would always remain bonded, friends and brothers.

"Nihil familiā carius," Dev found himself repeating.

Before my family comes nothing.

Chapter 14

This will be my last note to you
delivered by another.

—*A letter from Dev to Molly*

IT'S RAINING AS we pull up to the storefront in Brooklyn. Becca says it's a sign of luck, like at weddings, but I always thought that was a lie told to keep brides from turning into bridezillas. Nothing about the overcast gray sky and pellets of cold rain screams good omens. Nevertheless, I try to keep the paranoia to a minimum, as my nerves are already cranked to high. I barely slept a wink last night, despite Rae chastening that I'd need to be in my best mental shape for today. Even after the reassuring call with my grandfather, and Becca staying over to watch movies into the night, I wasn't able to calm my mind enough to slip into a restful sleep. But can anyone really blame me? I'm about to have my body Frankensteined, for Terra's sake. Plus, the thought of finally seeing Dev, of looking into his mesmerizing blue eyes and feeling his strong arms around me is enough to make me sick with anticipation.

Will this really work?

Will we survive it?

Swallowing back the constant rise of nervous bile, I walk with Becca and Rae through the empty storefront. Chunks of drywall hang down in corners, and the floor is covered with a chalky dust, the space's renovations apparently paused after the Vigil procured the building.

"Charming," Becca says as she peers around the debris. "The bookstore didn't exactly scream cleanliness, but at least I wasn't nervous about contracting tetanus."

Rae chuckles as he guides us through a few sets of moveable walls, all barriers to what hides in secret beyond, and I catch the look he gives Becca as she walks beside him. To say that he seems like a renewed man would be putting it mildly. His positive attitude came back with abundance since Becca's reappearance, and the way he regards her now, all gooey and doe eyed, under regular circumstance would have me gagging, but currently I'm too busy being happy for them. Having Becca's acceptance is enough to make *me* want to kiss her, let alone what her boyfriend must be feeling. For everything Rae's willing to sacrifice for my sake, I'm glad there still seems to be a silver lining in it for him. Now for the transfer to only go smoothly.

"How many more of these secret passages are there?" Becca huffs as we walk down a set of dark stairs leading to the basement. "Just put a sign that says *Bed Bug Infestation*, and I can *guarantee* no one will set foot inside this place."

Rae wasn't entirely convinced Becca accompanying us was a good idea, since she wasn't even technically allowed to know about any of this, but after a great deal of pleading from both our ends, he conceded. It wasn't just me that needed my best friend more than my next cup of coffee though. I'm pretty certain Rae wanted her there as well. Besides, good luck to anyone who tried keeping Becca from doing something once it was cemented in her mind.

As we stop at the back of a dark storage room, the only light source two bare bulbs dangling overhead, I wring my hands as Rae places his palm against a metal plate on the wall. A bright light outlines around his hand right before there's a rapid succession of metallic clicks, and with a slight shudder, the brick wall shifts to the left, revealing the pristine lab beyond. The whiteness against the black we stand in is like two squares on a checkered board, and I hear Becca's intake of breath.

We all step inside, and the partition behind us moves back into place, closing us in with a barely audible sigh.

"Now this is impressive," Becca says as she takes in the sterile setting of chrome tabletops and lab equipment spread out in various stages of experimentation. Her eyes linger on the smaller glass room in the far corner, where the two Molecular Chambers sit, their innocuous pill shape camouflaging the immense power they hold. After a moment I realize she's asking me questions, but my heart's hammering so loudly I barely hear her.

"Hey." She touches my shoulder. "You're going to be fine, little fish," she says, her green gaze soothing. "Nothing will go wrong. I'm your good-luck charm, remember?" She gives me a small smile. "Plus, look at this place." She gestures to the gadgets and monitors. "It would appear these people know a thing or two about science."

I grin at that.

"Come on," she says, reassured. "It's time to introduce me to your alien friends."

Sonja and Raymond walk over to greet us, each holding curious expressions as they regard Becca. I would have expected them to be a bit shocked or at least ill at ease, but it seems Rae prewarned them about our new guest, which is huge relief. I can only deal with so much going wrong today—meaning zero.

"Oh," Raymond says, his already wide eyes made wider from his lenses, "I can see why you're not so upset about becoming human, Rae."

Becca chuckles. "Well, you're certainly my favorite. I'm Becca."

"Raymond." The small Vigil enthusiastically takes her hand in his. "Rae has informed us about your recent...access into our world."

"He's also ensured your trust in staying quiet about it," Sonja adds with an assessing gaze. Her gray hair is swept up into her normal tight bun, her angular features made sharper, while a lab coat fits to her slim figure of black slacks and sweater. She definitely looks like the intelligent, otherworldly creature she is.

"And I have no intentions of breaking that trust," Becca says, looking Sonja straight in the eye. Whatever the Vigil scientist sees must convince her, for she gives Becca a respectful nod.

"I'm Sonja," she says.

"Pleasure." Becca shakes her hand.

A shadow in the corner has me stepping back to find an additional member of our group. His tall and thin black-clad frame stands rigid as I take him in, and from the pale hair tied in a low bun, to his razor-sharp green gaze, one eye made slightly disfigured by a ragged scar sliced over it, he looks every bit the villain from a nineties movie.

"Hector?" I ask, shocked. "What are you doing here?"

He frowns while glancing to Rae. "You haven't told her?"

"I thought it would be best to do it together," Rae says.

"Do what?" I ask. "What's going on? And Rae, why do you have the habit of telling me things at the last minute?" I huff.

"Molly, who is this guy?" Becca chimes in, studying our new companion with unease.

"Remember how I said you'd be having a new Vigil guard when you get to Terra…" Rae starts to explain.

"Please"—I close my eyes briefly—"don't say what I think you're about to—"

"Hector is your new guard."

I let out a deep sigh. "Of course he is."

"Is this a bad guy?" Becca asks in a failed whisper. "'Cause he looks like a bad guy."

"Hector was my grandfather's Vigil guard," I explain, her now knowing my ancestral secret too. "Like how Rae is to me, Hector was to him."

"Okay." Becca blinks. "So what's the problem?"

"It's a long story." I turn to Rae. "Why was he chosen and not the handful of others you said were being trained for this?"

"I have an idea," Hector chimes in. "Why don't you ask your new guard, who's standing right in front of you?"

"Oh." Becca nods. "I get it now."

"By all means." I gesture for Hector to explain.

He tips his chin up. "None were deemed ready for this mission, and no other living Vigil has the years of experience that I do with guarding a chosen Dreamer."

"Fine," I say. "But I have to ask—didn't you end up abandoning my grandfather? How can I trust you to protect me in Terra?"

"He did what now?" Becca whips a glare at Hector.

His jaw tightens. "Not that it's any of your business, but I was much younger then, and my actions that day...what I did to Robert, well, mistakes won't be repeated," he says with conviction that I'm unsure is for my benefit or for his.

I narrow my gaze. "What exactly *did* you do to him?"

"We'll have plenty of time to learn all each other's secrets soon enough," he says tightly, "but for now, I think it's time we begin." He nods at Sonja and Raymond. "Shall we? Elena wouldn't want us to get off schedule."

"Yes, please let's all make sure to remain punctual when we're about to completely alter two people's lives," I say with a wave of my hand. "Wouldn't want to keep Elena waiting."

Rae places a gentle touch to my shoulder, a silent gesture to say *breathe*, which I do.

But come on—is it really my fault I'm a bit testy today?

Guiding us toward the back of the room, Sonja pairs off with me, while Rae and Raymond group together, each giving us an extremely detailed examination. Urine samples, blood work, weight, height—all things they've taken before but need again. And lastly, making sure I haven't eaten in the last twelve hours, which I assure her, even if I was allowed, I wouldn't have had the stomach to ingest anything, my nerves being what they are. After what feels like forever and at the same time like a blink, we're ready to be led into the Molecular Chambers.

Food or not, I think I'm going to be sick.

The two white pods rest on the floor, their glass tops open, waiting for us to get in, and the multitude of clear wires run from one machine to the other, looking like a tapestry in the midst of being woven. Other than one monitor beside the Molecular Chambers, the rest of the room is empty. Sonja and Raymond will conduct the transfer from outside the room.

"We'll need you to take your clothes off," Sonja says while typing something into the computer near the two pods.

"Um, what now?" I ask.

"Your clothes," she repeats, gesturing to my body. "We can't have any foreign cells interfering with the transfer."

Rae starts to strip beside me, and as I catch a peek of his ridiculously defined abs, I swivel away at the same time Becca jumps in front of him. "Whoa there, big guy! I'm all for showing you off, but there are *some* things I'd like to keep for my eyes only."

"And I'd rather not be the star of a peep show," I add.

"Once you're in your Molecular Chamber, you'll be covered with the amniotic fluid we discussed," Sonja explains. "It's opaque in color, so no one will be able to see anything."

"We'll leave the room in the meantime." Raymond nods for everyone to exit.

Swallowing, I turn to Rae, his honey gaze still on Becca's retreating form before it collides with mine.

We both stand in a trance, the reality of what's about to go down almost paralyzing me to the spot now. "Before we do this," I say, "I want to let you know, what you're giving up...for me...I—"

Rae taking quick strides toward me, bringing me in for a hug, cuts me off, and I cling to him, breathing in his unique fragrance of summer and mint.

"I know, Mols," he says into my hair. "We've had some crazy adventures, you and I. This is just another."

I step back and peer into his handsome face, take in his full lips that always seem on the edge of a grin and the way his golden curls fall in contrast to his dark skin. "I love you," I say. "We might not share blood, but you will always be my family."

His eyes shimmer. "I love you too," he says gruffly. "Little sis."

With my heart full, I hug him one last time. Then, with him turned around and eyes closed, I get into my birthday suit and slide into the plush material of my pod. It feels very similar to my white coffin in the Village Portal Bookstore, the texture's temperature slightly warmer than my body, and it molds to every curve, keeping me from feeling as exposed as I am. Still, none of it is enough to keep me from shaking with nerves. I have absolutely no idea what I'm about to experience or how I'll feel after.

If we make it through, how much of us will still be us?

No one, not even the Vigil scientists, know exactly what to expect. All of which is *super* reassuring.

Sonja's voice comes through the room's intercom, meaning Rae must be in his pod as well. "We're going to activate the amniotic simulation now, so try to relax. All of this is what we've already gone over," she says as a foggy gel seeps into my pod. My muscles completely relax as I float up and then become stationary as the liquid stops filling right as it outlines my face. Besides my eyes, nose, and mouth, everything else is completely submerged in the gray fluid. The sensation is strange. I can barely feel any part of my body, as if I only have my face that's exposed to the air and nothing else.

"Rae?" I call out, my voice sounding small.

"Yes?" Comes his deep reply, which is slightly muffled from the liquid filling my ears.

I swallow, hating what I'm about to admit, but needing to. "I'm scared."

There's a beat of silence.

"Wherever we're about to go, we're going there together," he says, and it's like a phantom sensation of his hand grasping mine.

"Together," I whisper right before the buzz of people enters the room.

I hear Becca's muffled voice close by, saying soothing words to Rae before her freckled face is hovering above me. "You look ridiculous," she says, and I attempt a chuckle, but the fluid surrounding me makes it difficult.

"Famous last words," I say.

"Oh, don't be so dramatic. You're just altering your DNA. It's an in-and-out procedure these days."

"Evidently."

She grins before her green gaze becomes serious. "I'll be right outside," she says. "This is going to work."

I stare up at her, a tightness forming in my throat. "Thank you."

"For what?"

"For believing me."

Her eyes hold mine before she slips a silver chain forward from around her neck, showcasing the scripted word *Dove*. It's the necklace I gave her for her birthday. "You're my turtle," she says, referencing my own piece of jewelry that goes with hers. "Turtledoves stick together."

My stomach flutters with adrenaline and emotion. "I love you, Bec."

"I love you too," she says and then bops me on the nose, breaking the intimate moment. "I'll see you soon."

As Becca ducks away, Sonja replaces her image, her Vigil features pinched in concentration. "I'm hooking in your oxygen now before we finish filling the pod. You'll also feel a pinch at the base of your neck. Raymond is going to give you a light sedative. We can't have you fully out, but we can help to dull any potential discomfort. The amniotic simulation is to aid with the electric current, but hopefully not make it as acute."

I swallow. "Do you think...will there will be much... discomfort?"

"I won't sugarcoat it. This won't be pleasant, but it shouldn't be as bad as getting hit by lightning."

"How reassuring," I say, having the urge to shift my body, but it's like I'm a toy stuck in a Jell-O mold.

"Are you ready, Molly?" Sonja asks, her gray eyes searching, and it's like the world stops spinning, waiting for my answer.

"Yes," I eventually say. "I'm ready."

She nods once and then inserts a breathing tube into my nose and over my mouth. It's only a little uncomfortable. "Take deep breaths in," she says. "Yes, just like that. You're doing great." Glancing forward, she gives a thumbs-up to someone before returning her attention to me. "You're going to feel that pinch now."

I scrunch my face as two small needles hook into the back of my neck, and then, like a veil, any worry I had slips away as everything falls out of focus, a blurred image beyond a rain-covered glass.

"Good, Molly. Good," comes Sonja's silky voice through the haze. "Close your eyes now. We're filling the rest of the pod."

Her smooth features are the last things I see before the room blinks to blackness, and I'm barely aware of a cool gel flowing over me until I become nothing. I'm just a brain floating in liquid, my body detached. A strange hum fills my ears, the pod lifting off the ground, and then everything returns to quiet, my breathing the only thing in existence.

In. Out. In. Out.

A part of me knows I should be worried, freaking out, screaming that this is all wrong, but I can't seem to do any of that. I'm merely a vessel experiencing my existence pass by. And the longer I lie docile, uncaring, the longer the concept of time dissolves along with everything else. My thoughts drift, wander, float until those break apart as well, transferring my state of existence back into particles, into atoms of barely there consciousness.

But then, just as my mind expands further into thoughtlessness, it's violently jolted back together, a kettle's whistle going off, and like a boiling pot of water, my skin begins to tingle until it starts to burn, and I want to thrash and move away. But I can do nothing except be still and let the thousands of needles prick me in waves.

Again.

And again.

And again.

No part of me safe from the onslaught.

My body is fire, smoke, and my cells are suffocating, screaming for it to stop. But it doesn't. My skin keeps twisting and tearing as though it's being raked inside out, and a metallic tang grasps to every one of my taste buds. Yet I still lie motionless, a prisoner within my own body, no sense of escape.

And so it goes on, for days, weeks, millennia, my mind stretching out infinitely as whatever is changing me, becoming me, snapping me apart, only to put me back together, overtakes everything.

I am no longer Molly.

No longer human.

I. Just. Am.

Colors flash behind my eyelids, galaxies spinning, and I fly through them, racing toward an unknown destination. And at the moment the conscious part of me accepts this new existence of pain as my forever—my normal—the world explodes in a kaleidoscope of sensations until it gets vacuumed into white, into nothing. This is where I stay, floating in some In Between, a disembodied energy. But then a light materializes in the distance, and I push my mind toward it, gradually become aware of a coolness flowing over me. Whatever held me trapped, paralyzed, begins to recede, and suddenly, like a punch to my gut, my chest jerks forward, and I blink my eyes open on a gasp.

Reborn.

Chapter 15

Soon I'll be standing in front of you,
where I always should have been.

—A letter from Molly to Dev

THE ROOM WAS a buzz of barely contained nerves, Dev not the only one waiting in anticipation. His skin felt like it was on fire, his heart threatening to kick through his chest as he stood in the back of the room. The wait was like nothing he had ever experienced. He felt frozen in time, screaming on deaf ears for the universe to start spinning again, to do *something*. But it all remained still, a held breath unable to sigh.

Cracking his knuckles, he took in the two layers of guards separating him from the portal that lay dormant in the center of the space, their presence more amusing than annoying. *Try to keep me from her,* he thought. The elders stood off to one side, their six white-robed figures statues of feigned boredom. Elena was the only one making conversation with a Vigil next to her, a stout woman with copper hair. She was one of the lead scientists in the Dreamer Containment Center, and Dev tried to recall her name, only being introduced moments ago, but it proved useless, his mind too preoccupied to retain much of anything.

His roommates stood beside him, having been granted access to the facility after Dev's relentless and rather threatening insistence. He knew they would be a comforting sight to her, something familiar after all the unknown. Tim was to his left, hands clasped in front of him, perfectly at ease, while Aveline was to his right, leaning against the wall. She blew a lock of blonde hair from her face as she played with the transmitter wrapping her wrist, no doubt sending a message to one of her many friends. The thought of Dev's own recent loss of a companion hit him low in the gut, and he rolled his shoulders back, keeping them from hunching forward from the pain. What was done was done, and he knew Rae wouldn't want any of them to wallow. His choice was made as much for himself as for everyone else. Even so, the sting of never being able to see him again would take a lot longer than a few days to fade.

A high-pitched whir sounding throughout the room interrupted Dev's melancholy thoughts, and he looked up. The portal in the center was turning on, and in an instant everyone fell silent, their attention turning toward the slowly brightening light. Dev watched, mesmerized, a swallow stuck in his throat as he took a step forward, his heart a race of beats. He tried to peer over the Vigil guards' shoulders, take in what was happening, but they were pinched too closely together, blocking any visibility. Grinding his teeth, he was about to start knocking them back when a burst of white shot out from the portal, followed by a gust of wind.

Dev shielded his eyes before glancing around frantically.

Was she here? Was that it?

Elena made her way forward, a small gap opening in the circle, and Dev stepped behind her. *Breathe*, he told himself. *Remember to breathe*. Beyond all the bodies, he thought he glimpsed a shoulder and a bit of dark hair, which sent his mind tumbling, desperate, before guards stood in his way again, blocking and keeping him back. Dev barely contained a growl as his muscles coiled, hands balled into fists, and he pinned each Vigil with a stare that spoke of quick deaths if they didn't move. With meek expressions, they hesitantly stepped aside, allowing him to march forward, ready to end any threat that tried to get in his way again. But even in his haste, as he walked past the last row of soldiers, he stopped, his body seizing on a vision, one made of familiar curves and deep-brown eyes set in midnight.

He drank in Molly just as she drank in him, and that's when everything disappeared

as

Dev

fell,

swimming in starlight.

Each will come to us,
the brightest among the stars.

It will be for us to guide
and for them to lead.

—Tome of the Elders, Vol. II;
The Dreamers, Article 328

Chapter 16

IT'S TOO BRIGHT and loud. Black-clad bodies encircle me, a line of austere expressions trapping me into the center of some room. I blink, trying to focus my new vision that seems to want to pick up every detail—an errant lock of hair on the shoulder of one of the guards, a faded scar on the neck of another. Retaining Vigil DNA ended up giving me more than just access to Terra's portals, but also new senses, or more accurately— heightened ones. How Rae functioned like this, I have no idea. Everything is so acute, sharpened to the point that it almost hurts to open my eyes. Sonja and Rae seemed to think I'd soon get used to it, but even with spending a few hours after the transfer with them, things have remained extra sensitive. Rae said I shouldn't complain, considering he feels like he's now deaf and blind with how dull humans experience things. This of course elicited Becca to punch him in the arm and ask if that felt dull.

My lips twitch at the memory before quickly remembering where I am and everything that happened to get here—waking up safe after the transfer; the relief mixing in with the sadness now that Rae was human, and me…something else; Hector prepping me to walk through the portal; and the unimaginable pressure as

I passed through, like I was some cartoon being stuffed down a bottle's neck only to pop out the other side unharmed. Whatever happened between Earth's dimension and Terra's was not a memory that could be retained. It merely fell away like water through a mesh bag.

Returning my attention to the room, I study the person who now stands in front of me, taking in her immaculate chin-cropped blonde hair and intense blue eyes—Elena. She looks every bit the same and as put together as the last time I saw her, and I watch as her mouth moves, saying things like how happy she is that I returned safely, that the Dreamer is now home. But I can't concentrate on any of it, and it's not because of my discombobulating new abilities.

With my stomach in knots and my heart a hummingbird's wing, I look past her, searching for someone else, someone I need more than abiding by manners and sharing pleasantries, more than even realizing I'm finally back in Terra. I search for the one person I risked my life to see again, and just as my chest grows heavy, only finding strangers among the crowd, there's a commotion to my right, and I turn, the Vigil guards parting, letting a tall man walk through. My breath catches as the black-clothed form now takes up my everything, dissolving the room, the people, the noise to nonexistent as I become lost in his aqua gaze that drinks me in. His angular features, which a second ago were tight and hard, soften as he stands before me, and his muscles strain against his T-shirt, as if he's trying to control something wild from escaping. I forgot how large he is, how consuming, his presence eclipsing that of anyone he stands near, and I'm desperate to be absorbed.

"Dev," I whisper, and watch as something in his features flash, his eyes roaming my body like a lick of heat before they connect with mine again. I sway forward, an invisible finger curling, inviting me to come closer, but before I can will myself to move, he's the one taking a step toward me, slowly, carefully. Blood swooshes between my ears, and my breathing grows ragged, hungry, desperate as he stops mere inches away. My heightened senses take in the fluttering pulse against his skin right below his jawline, the same jawline that's covered in day-old scruff and yearning for my fingers to run across it.

"You're here," he says, the sound of his deep voice soaking into me like melted butter. How could I have lived so many months without hearing it?

"I'm here," I return, and then I'm being pulled into his arms, pressed against his hard chest, and finally, thankfully, his soft lips come crashing down onto mine.

The world is on fire—flashes of lightning in my veins, behind my eyes, and from the faded hum that's reaching my ears, I have a feeling they are physically manifesting throughout the room as well. But I can't bring myself to feel embarrassed or even care, because I'm home. That's the only way I can describe what it's like to be surrounded by this man again, to be kissing him, tasting him, breathing in his scent of night and spice. Dev's hands are in my hair and pushing against my back. My arms wrap around his neck, and I have a selfish desire to imagine ourselves somewhere else, somewhere alone, but before I can turn my wish into a reality, Dev is slowly moving away, leaning his forehead against mine.

"Please tell me this is real," he says.

My grip tightens on his arms. "It's very real."

"Molly," he moans and kisses me again, chastely.

It's not enough.

I clamber to get closer, and Dev chuckles as he brings me into a hug. I've never felt so panicked and at ease all at once, like my mind doesn't fully believe what's happening, but my body is *very* aware of it.

As I tilt my head into the crook of his arm, I see two familiar forms walk into the circle. "Tim! Aveline!" I immediately reach out, bringing all of us into a group hug. I hear Tim laugh, while Aveline grunts her annoyance.

After a moment more, the four of us step back, Dev and I still connected with my hand in his, neither of us ready to let go of the other, not after everything.

"Tim, you look great." I glance at the smooth skin of his arms, no longer blackened and deformed. His whole body seems stronger, in fact, renewed.

"Thanks to you."

"No." I shake my head. "Your doctors did more than I could—"

"Molly." Tim places a hand on my shoulder. "It's time you learned to take a compliment."

I fight a grin while simultaneously trying to hold back tears. Is this really happening? Am I really back? Turning to Aveline, I watch as she backs up a step.

"Oh no," she says. "I can tell you're about to get real emotional on me, and let's skip that, okay? I'm happy you're back, but more so because this guy"—she gestures to Dev—"can finally stop acting crazy."

Dev gives Aveline a steely glare.

"What does she mean?"

"Nothing," he says, bringing me under his arm. "Ignore her."

I open my mouth to press the issue, but before I can, a high-pitched whine followed by a bright flash of a light bursts from the portal behind us, and Hector steps out.

"Ah, good. You didn't disintegrate," he says as his green gaze finds mine, and Dev stiffens beside me. I forgot these two don't get along, and I wonder how Dev took the news about Hector now being my Vigil guard in Terra.

"Nope," I say. "Made it in one piece. You were right about holding your breath. I don't feel nauseous at all."

"Good." He smooths back his white hair that doesn't need fixing. "After a couple more times through, you won't need to."

"Thank you, Hector." Elena steps forward. "For guiding Molly through the process. From her presence here, can we assume Rae is doing well?"

"Yes." He nods. "The transfer was successful on both ends. Each just needs a little time to get used to their new skin."

"Wonderful." Elena smiles. "Well, there will be plenty of time for that later, but unfortunately, not at this moment. There is much to fill you in on, Molly." She turns to me. "We'll need to save the official reunion for after. There's a packed room of Council members awaiting our arrival."

"There is?" My eyes dance between her and Dev's.

"Yes," she says, a slight glint of a smile. "And I think it's time for an introduction."

Chapter 17

THERE'S A FEELING I get when I'm receiving other Dreamers' memories. Even though I'm in their body, looking out through their eyes and taking in everything they do, I still have a sense of detachment. Their skin doesn't quite stick to mine, and I float, a spectator in their worlds.

That's how it's like for me now as I sit in the Council meeting, listening to the members' collective outrage grow more deafening. Scrunching my face, I resist the urge to plug my ears from the overwhelming sound. This certainly isn't helping me acclimate to my new Vigil senses.

Elena sits beside me, casually looking out at the sea of bodies, having just finished sharing everything I am and the history that comes with me. As the evidence in front of us shows, the Council didn't take it well. The room has been in an uproar for a good twenty minutes, no one willing to go past stage two of the grieving process—anger.

I know I should be worried, nervous, feel something, *anything* about how I'm being received, but for some reason I can't. I'm still wrapping my brain around the fact that I'm indeed here, in Terra, sitting next to the man I never thought I'd see again. Nothing seems as big of a problem now that I'm back beside him, our fingers threaded together under the table we sit behind.

Catching my gaze, his hand squeezes mine, and it takes all my effort to turn away from his angular profile, the slip of his grin. *Seriously, is it possible he got even hotter since I've been gone?* Shaking my head, I attempt to finally concentrate on what's going on. Sitting at the front of a large circular room on a slightly raised platform, I share a table with the elders, a few Vigil from the DCC, Alex—the Nocturna's head of Security—and Dev. Tim, Aveline, and Hector are filed away among the three-tiered stadium seating that wraps in a semicircle in front of us. Every chair is filled for this meeting, each body a representative from the various government sections of Terra, and though they started off sitting, mostly now stand, faces pinched with anger or confusion as they look in our direction—my direction. Well, all accept the Vigil members. They sit calmly among the irate crowd.

A giant ball of Navitas rests high in the domed ceiling, the only light source in the room, and I can't help tugging on the energy every so often, not having been able to tap into my power for so long, and it feels glorious, a gulp of water in a parched mouth. Now wearing the Dreamer vest, the same one I wore during the fight against the Metus and that helped me save Tim, my connection with the Navitas is even more fluid.

Before walking into the meeting, Elena insisted that I put it on, announcing the safety mandate for it to be part of my public uniform from now on.

Elena raises her hand beside me, requesting silence, and a hush slowly falls over the crowd. "We understand this comes as a shock," she says, her voice booming with authority even in its softness, "but it's news you all must see as a gift. We have a Dreamer amongst us. She sits right here, our salvation to this war, and unlike any that have come before her, she is not with us through a dream, but a living, breathing embodiment of the race we live to protect. She is here to help, as you will soon see and as some of you have already heard." She pauses, making sure she has the full attention of the room. Not even a cough breaks the silence. "The girl who could fly?" She goes on. "Who could hold Navitas in her hands? They were not rumors. That was a Dreamer, this Dreamer." She gestures to me. "And that was just the beginning of what she's capable of."

A wave of gasps and astonished chatter fills the space, a multitude of eyes glancing my way, and I swallow, trying not to be unnerved by being on the receiving end of so much negative attention.

"But I still don't understand," says a blond man in black robes, speaking above the noise. He sits in, what Dev explained, is the education section. "Why were these Dreamers kept a secret from the Council? If they've been our key to winning all the wars in the past, why hide them from us?"

Council members murmur their agreement.

"As Elena mentioned previously, it was for the Dreamers' protection," answers another Vigil elder, surprising me. I've never heard this one speak before. Actually, I've never heard any but Elena speak. Even during the one time I had an exclusive audience with the elders, Elena had led the meeting, acting as the group's ambassador. Curious, I study the man, taking in his weathered face full of folds and wrinkles, which seems out of place when the rest show no real signs of aging. But this man, now that I'm paying attention, stands out among his pack. With his short-cropped white hair and papery skin, he is much deserving of the title *elder*. Still, despite the appearance of age, he exudes a strength, a hidden fire that warns that looks can be very much deceiving. His posture is straight against his high-backed chair, his frame thin but sturdy, and he seems almost bored as he uses his thumb to spin a thick silver band that adorns his pinky finger.

"Protection?" The Nocturna who asked the question sputters. "From what?"

"Don't be naïve, Victor," the elder says in a tired tone. "Greed is not an emotion Terra lacks. Nor, evidently, is stupidity. There are always those who selfishly seek more than they have, who hate what they don't understand. Until Molly, the Dreamers have come exclusively to the Vigil for centuries, our world giving us a sign on how to proceed, and we've dutifully abided by it."

"But you said this one came to Dev, a Nocturna," chimed in another Council member.

"Yes," Elena says. "Which has put us on our current course. The Dreamers will no longer be a secret—this war's magnitude calls for a new way forward. We have decided that along with the Council, we will tell the citizens of Terra. All will know the key to ending our wars, and it is up to us to show our support for the Dreamer and to reassure our people of her good intentions. A power such as Molly's will undoubtedly create a backlash from certain groups. We all know there are those who are dedicated in their beliefs that the Navitas we collect from humans is meant to be regulated and shared, not contained for a sole person to control."

"Yes," says a smaller, rounder woman from the crowd. "Because we've all learned from watching humans what can happen when one person has ultimate control." Her narrowed gaze lands on me. "How do we know this human isn't susceptible to the same temptation?"

"We don't," Elena says, which causes a quiet stir from the group. "But I can tell you what makes her different from those of whom you speak of. Molly never sought greatness or power, never thirsted for it like they did. She was thrust into this role unwillingly, just like her predecessors. She has been forced to learn all that she is and her capabilities to lead. She comes from humility, a pure heart, and I, along with a few others in this room, have seen how far she will go to save another."

I shift uncomfortably in my seat, not used to hearing such praise, and glance to Tim. He sits in the middle of one of the tiered sections and, catching my gaze, flashes a supportive grin.

"The road before us isn't easy," Elena goes on. "But none worth taking ever is. We have achieved many things in our great nation and overcome even darker ones. The addition of the Dreamer among us is a positive one, and your elders are convinced this marks a great new path for Terra. But we need all of your cooperation to ensure this. The Council is the backbone of our society. To be split on this subject would be detrimental. That is why"—Elena tilts her chin up, her posture becoming even more authoritative—"we will be requiring a binding oath where every member must pledge their loyalty to the cause." The room erupts again, but Elena continues over them, undeterred. "*If* there are any who feel, after given the proper time to process, that they cannot willingly agree to their consent and support, we will be revoking their access to any future Council meetings that pertain to the Dreamer, for Molly's safety is our topmost priority."

This elicits another rush of comments and questions, one barely answered before another is flung forward, and I want to slouch lower in my seat, to hide under the table. But even I know with so many watching eyes, I can't give them any more reason to doubt what Elena has said about me. So I take in a deep breath and remain still.

But to be forced to take an oath of support? For a person they hadn't known existed a mere hour ago... *By the stars*, couldn't the elders have come up with something a little less...shackling? Talk about too much too soon.

Sweeping a gaze over the raucous mass, I grow nauseous with my overwhelming nerves. How will I do this? Fulfilling my duty in secret was enough to choke me into panic, but now, shoved into the spotlight and forced to be...this person, this savior, while this world watches, well, I hope the elders are prepared to hand out a lot of refunds to the show.

As if sensing my unease, Dev tightens his grip and leans in. "You're doing great."

I scoff. "Considering I've done nothing but sit here, I would hope so."

Dev muffles a laugh as he sits back, his thumb stroking my palm, which normally calms me but currently makes me more anxious and a little frustrated. Being so close to him, after so many months, without—per Elena's words—"a proper reunion" is tortuous.

As the Council talks over one another, none of the elders doing much about it, Elena presses her hand to my wrist, causing the familiar jump of my power in my gut.

"Molly," she says softly. "I was wondering if you could calm them."

"Me?" I arch my brows.

She nods. "Yes. I think a demonstration might set some things straight and hurry this along."

"Um…" I think I might be sick.

"Make something that would ease you." She tugs at my energy again, sending a comforting heat across my skin. "Create a place that can take away your doubts and fears."

I bite my lip and stare out at the crowd. "My doubts and fears?"

"Yes," she murmurs. "Where do you find peace?"

Glancing to the ceiling, to the source that has been reaching out to me since I entered the room, I search for the answer to Elena's question, and like a gentle gust of wind it comes to me. Taking a deep breath and glancing to Dev to find his reassuring nod, I stand.

Almost immediately the room silences, and before I lose my nerve, I block out everything, everyone, and concentrate on the one thing that has always calmed me in my moments of panic. With my belly warming, I awaken the Navitas inside me, connecting it with the swirling blue-white mass above, and instantly I feel whole, perfect, and euphoric, finally able to work with my magic. On a sigh I push out my desires, imagining the ceiling crumbling away, disintegrating into particles of dust that sparkle and shine as they fall to the floor. With a prick of cold to my head, each section recedes to reveal Terra's sky, the spinning black mass of endless shooting stars now rolling out to blanket us, the roof of the Council's chambers now gone.

I hear gasps, a cry of surprise, but I don't let it knock my concentration. I keep pushing forward, willing the stars—the

Dreamers—closer, imagining the bright orbs to shrink and spin around the room, illuminating the space in a dazzle of warm fairy light. I pull out feelings of love and safety from the thick tendrils that wrap the sleeping souls, cocooning them in a warm hug of peaceful sleep and, for the first time, let the audience experience what it is to slumber. I cover everyone in the illusion, lulling their minds into calm, that sweet moment right before you slip into unconscious and travel to the other side, where magic is real and memories come out to play. I have it go on and on, my own heart humming with pleasure as the stars graze along my skin, my soul soaring as it's finally connected with the source that has been trapped inside me on Earth. I feel happy, bright, and expansive— the color yellow, and only after an endless moment of weaving these sensations, these realities into the citizens, do I slowly bring it to end.

Softly I lift the illusion, sending the millions of tiny stars to pop, showering the space with a glittering dust, and like a rug being rolled out, the sky above gets covered back in white, the ceiling once again settling in place.

Even though I felt no wane to my strength, I can't help but let out a deep breath, a breath that gets caught in my throat, however, as I glance out to a quiet audience. Every eye is trained on me. Not one sound breaks the silence, as if they are hypnotized, waiting for the snap of my fingers to awaken them.

But I can do nothing but stare back, barely hearing the voice of the male elder speaking nearby.

"Yes," he says. "She'll do."

Leaning against Dev in one of the rooms that's connected to the Council's chambers, I close my eyes as his fingers rhythmically draw patterns of comfort along my back. I only hope this means we are done for the day and the two of us can finally have some time alone.

After my demonstration, where the crowd either quieted from shock or realizing I could actually help, Elena said a few more words before adjourning the meeting. Our dais was immediately flooded with members, all scrambling to get a word with me, but before any could get within an arm's length, I was surrounded by a dozen or more Vigil and shuffled out a side door. Though I haven't done much since coming here, I'm completely drained.

Dev's body tensing has me opening my eyes to find Elena and the male elder who spoke before.

"Well done, Molly," Elena says with a smile. "You handled that perfectly."

"I'm glad you think so. I wasn't really sure what I was supposed to do."

"Which merely proves my point that you're a natural. It will be impossible for the citizens of Terra not to follow you."

I frown. "But I don't want followers. I just want to help."

She shares a speaking glance with her elder companion, as if to say *see*, and he nods ever so slightly.

Who is this guy?

"Molly, I have the great honor of introducing Cato," Elena says as if reading my mind. "He specializes in overseeing the political temperature of Terra and ensuring the populace, as a whole, is happy."

I glance to the man, whose green eyes regard me with a shrewd sharpness despite being housed in the folds of soft, wrinkled skin. Now that he's standing, I see he's no taller than me.

"It's nice to meet you." I extend my hand, which he merely glances at quizzically before lifting his own, knuckles up. Though a little confused, I grab his fingers. To say it's the most awkwardly limp handshake I've ever had would be putting it mildly.

He pulls back with a disgusted purse to his lips, and hearing Dev's stifled chuckle leads me to believe I might have just committed a faux pas.

"Yes, well, there's obviously a lot to work on," Cato says, glancing at me from head to toe, "but there's promise."

"Uh…"

"And after your earlier show, there's definitely a lot we can do publicly with demonstrations. I've already pulled together some ideas that would be crowd-pleasers."

"Crowd-pleasers?"

"For your tour," Cato explains.

"Tour?"

"Am I not speaking the same language as her?" Cato raises an impatient brow at our group.

I ignore the jab. "So wait…I'm really to go on some junket thing?"

"Yes, after we make your public announcement." Elena gestures to her companion. "Cato will be accompanying you through the city and to our various ports and smaller villages. He will be in charge of your PR campaign."

"PR—" My mouth drops. "Are you serious? I mean, I get that we need to introduce me to Terra carefully, but don't you think I'll be busy enough with the war going on? Shouldn't I be concentrating on that?"

"One is equally as important as the other," Cato says. "If we don't have the citizens on our side, we'll not only be dealing with a war with the Metus, but possibly a civil one as well. Now that you're with us as a whole and don't have Earth as a distraction, you can use the time you spent there for this."

Earth as a distraction... My face grows hot, and I'm about to reply with something equally as pointed, when Aveline jogs up to us, her features worried.

"Did you get that message?" she asks Dev, who just finishes pressing his finger to his ear, his jaw set tight.

"Yes." He turns to the elders. "They're attacking the damaged wall again. We're needed for backup."

"Go." Elena nods.

"But not Molly," Cato adds.

"What?" Dev and I ask in unison.

"Your team is more than capable of handling this," the elder explains. "The Dreamer should not be risked for every Metus attack that comes forth."

Dev's eyes narrow, about to respond, when I rest my hand to his chest. *I've got this*, I silently say before turning to Cato. "While I appreciate your concern and understand your logic, I must disagree. I just spent the last three months concentrating all my thoughts, energy, and efforts into finding a way to get back here and help with this war. I got fired from my job, almost lost my best friend, had to sacrifice a life of one of your own, and underwent a risky and life-altering genetically modifying experiment. I made it through all those obstacles to stand before you today, a loyal Dreamer, willing to do practically anything to ensure the safety of my two worlds. But you must understand something." I hold on to his green gaze. "After all that, the last thing I will allow for is someone else to dictate when they think my 'talents'"—I air quote—"are necessary and when they are not. Every Dreamer has been brought here to protect, and I will continue that legacy."

Cato's chin tilts up, and I can tell he's dancing between being completely aghast or impressed, but before I can learn which, I glance to Elena, who wears a look of hidden amusement and... yes, I think that's pride.

Chapter 18

THE WIND RUSHES against my skin, a cold washing of reality as I fly forward on the zipline. Dancing between Terra's glittering skyline, the buildings whip by in a blur of lights and steel shadows. Despite what we're about to encounter, I briefly close my eyes, allowing myself the feeling of exhilaration this form of travel always brings me. I let it sooth and settle within my bones before I blink open, following Dev's darkened silhouette as it sways in front. His strong back muscles contract under his movements as he readies to land on the approaching platform. In preparation for my own descent, my hands grip my Arcus tighter as my path zooms toward the western wall. A line of Nocturna soldiers stand ready, their black-clad bodies pressed against a small fortified lip. In quick patterned bursts, they shoot flaming arrow after arrow at something directly on the other side. The only things currently in my line of sight are an angry glow of red and the endless grassy landscape that stretches to the distant horizon.

As my feet touch down, I unlock my Arcus and step beside Dev. He's already talking to a dark-skinned woman with an austere expression and buzzed head. I half listen to their conversation as I peer down into the chaos, my eyes widening as I cover my nose. Even from our high vantage point, the sounds and stench overwhelm my new senses, and I wonder if it's as distracting for the rest of my companions. The entire field is ablaze with orange and crimson and liquid mucus as the two packs of Metus attack from every angle. I hadn't laid eyes on these nightmares in weeks, and yet my memory of them didn't so much as dim in my absence. They're every bit as ugly, terrifying, and hungry to destroy as I remembered. Their seven-foot-tall bodies slosh forward as razor-tipped claws dig into their own chests to pull out fiery chunks of flesh, launching blobs at all who get in their way. Giant sections of singed metal scaffolding, which the engineers must have erected to aid in their fixing of the damaged wall, lay collapsed and useless in the grass. The Metus concentrate on hitting the weaker joints in the structure while the soldiers above and below fight back with their various Navitas-charged weapons. This is the closest I've ever seen the nightmares get to breaching the city. With the buzz of adrenaline, I absently touch the vest around my chest, my power stirring to enter the fight.

"There were three packs when we got here," the woman says to Dev, "but we've been able to reduce it to two." From her authoritative tone and stance, it's pretty obvious she's one of Terra's generals. "The wall guards saw them coming and set off a Navitas shield, but a handful were willing to sacrifice themselves to overwhelm our equipment. They created an opening there"—she points to a break in a blue-white fiery wall in the distance—"and the rest were able to approach."

"And the engineers?" Dev asks as he transforms his Arcus into a working bow.

"All were removed in time."

"Good," he grunts. "If your archers can watch our backs from here, we'll engage below."

The Nocturna glances to me, a questioning crease marking her brows before she nods to Dev.

With Aveline and Hector joining, we climb down part of the scaffolding that's still sturdy enough to take our weight and regroup at a center platform. Crouching down, we're shielded behind a thin metal wall, and as my companions talk, I try steadying the onslaught of sensations forcing their way toward me from below. Everything wants to be heard, smelled, and seen at once, and only taking in large breaths seems to calm me. How will I fight like this?

Beside me, Hector rhythmically clips together a sleek-looking gun, only stopping to push back a white lock of hair that fell from his tight bun. I'm still not used to his presence. Seeing him only brings up memories of whom he replaced, and I try not to let that mar my judgment. After all, he did guard my grandfather, and despite whatever ended their partnership, my grandfather had trusted him with his life. Plus, Aveline enjoys his company. If nothing else, keeping her happy and distracted from her usual sarcastically barbed self is worth having him around.

"I want you two"—Dev points to Hector and Aveline as he peers over the lip of our wall—"to stay here and take out the Metus that are the closest below, while Molly and I propel down. We'll hold the off rest until you're with us. Then I want to group attack. There are too many to have our backs open, despite the guards on the wall."

We all nod, and I take in another deep breath, about to stand, when a voice calls Dev's name from above, and I watch as Aurora and her partner, Ezekial, jump to our landing.

I almost stumble back in shock as I take her in. She's so thin, her once voluminous strawberry-blonde hair now limp and oily, her usually lively green eyes hollow. She looks sick, and I'm about to ask if she's okay, when her gaze meets mine, and I swallow my words. As quickly as her eyes show surprise, they narrow into icy coldness.

"Molly," she whispers.

Dev is instantly in front of me, his shoulders tense. "What are you doing here?" he asks Aurora, his tone clipped.

"We got the com about the attack," she says slowly, her gaze unable to leave mine as I peek around Dev. "We were told to meet up with your group."

"Hi, Aurora." I smile and try to push Dev aside. He holds me back, an intense uneasiness radiating off him. I frown. "Dev, what's wrong with you?"

He presses his lips together as he glances between Aurora and me, Ezekial watching the exchange with a strained expression. "There's time for reunions later," he says. "Aveline, fill them in. Molly and I are going to make our way down." With no further instructions, Dev ushers me to the opening of our little hideaway and, attaching a grapple to a beam, grabs around my waist and jumps from the ledge. I squeak in surprise, my stomach flying up with the rush, but then we hit the soft soil and are instantly thrown into action.

As Dev lets go, two Metus charge our way, one swiftly put down by an arrow from above. Dev spins to dodge the other's giant swiping claws, lodging his glowing Arcus straight into the monster's back. It howls as its dripping red form fills with a blue-white light and then, on a gurgle, bursts apart. I sidestep out of the way, the mucus splatter singeing the dirt by my feet. I pant, trying to catch my bearings. Though I continued my training with Rae, it still takes a second to remember this dance, which I'll have to recall quickly because another wave has advanced. Now that we're on the ground, the sheer number of Metus—at least twenty—overwhelms me.

Dev steps to my back. "Get ready," he calls, his Arcus aimed at the few in his line of sight. Straightening my shoulders, I turn to watch the approach of the ones in mine—three. With my acquired Vigil senses, I can make out the details of their churning lava skin, the way it pusses and bubbles, the steam coming out of open orifices and letting out poison-laden air. My lip curls. *Gross.*

Staring them down, I call forth the power that has been bouncing ready in my chest since I landed here, and like a lit match, two balls of Navitas spring to life in my palms. "Let's go, fellas," I say. "I know you've missed me."

On a bone-chilling cry, they attack, and I don't hesitate as I let fly my orbs of energy. They soar fast and true, colliding with the oncoming mass and sending the group to the ground, where they howl in pain. The Navitas coats them from head to toe.

Just as they devour us, I devour them.

They struggle to push back the consuming energy, but it's useless, and as soon as it seeps into their liquid skin, lighting them blue-white from within, the energy that's still linked to me senses a sigh of relief, a gentle peace, right before they explode into nothing. I rock back on my feet, forgetting about that part, the connection I feel when putting these creatures down. I swallow back my unease. My empathy for these monsters has always been the hardest part. But I'm left little time to settle my emotions before I have to continue to defend as Metus after Metus swarm us.

Eventually Aveline, Hector, Aurora, and Ezekial make it to us, and the six of us form a circle, backs to each other, as we move through the battle. Other Nocturna form into a similar fashion, none giving the chance for the enemy to sneak up from behind. A few Nocturna regard me in surprise as I bring forth Navitas from thin air, but their years of training keep them from being distracted for long, and soon they settle on the task at hand. All questions for later.

The grass grows sticky under my feet as more and more Metus are reduced to thick puddles. And as one of my boots gets lodged in a small pile, I hold back a gag as I try dislodging it. The remnants of the monster are now tar black, which means it's no longer a threat, something I learned after Tim's accident. If it's red and burning, it has the capability to consume anyone who touches it. But deadly or not, as I try to remove one shoe, the other merely gets lodged even deeper, and with a panic I realize I'm stuck, suctioned in.

Oncoming nightmares howl in front of me, and on a gasp I raise the ground by their feet, tripping them. But that bides me little time, for they soon rise again and charge my way. With a bone-chilling scream, one launches a fireball straight at me, and I hit the ground, my butt and hands in grass, my feet still in tar.

Shit, that was close.

Making sure no one in my squad got the brunt of it, I turn back. "Okay, guys." I glare at the Metus, who now regard my trapped state with drooling orifices. "You want to play dirty? Let's play dirty." Gathering a large amount of energy in my mind, until the cold is almost unbearable, I push out a wall of Navitas directly from my chest. The layer of white light rushes forward, slapping into the awaiting Metus, and like a child's finger to a bubble, they burst apart. My whole body sags from the effort, even from the aid of my vest. I need a moment to recharge.

But as if sensing my sudden vulnerability, two more Metus appear, and like a nightmare-induced magic trick, they step into one another, creating a mammoth-sized monster. What was once seven feet tall must now be nine, its width growing along with its height.

"Oh shit." I peer up into the burning sludge of overwhelming hate as the evil flowing off this mega beast is now so potent that my body shakes in fear, my confidence swiftly dwindling into defeat.

"Oh God oh God oh God." I grunt with the effort to use my powers to free me, but I'm tapped out, can barely produce a flame of Navitas without my mind screaming in protest. Desperately I glance around. I need help, an energy boost, and the first person I see is Aurora. She looks from me to the colossal monster.

"Aurora!" I call. "My feet, they're stuck!"

She glances away for a moment—as if to check that she's in the clear?—before her head whips back to me, hesitation in her gaze.

"Aurora!" I cry out again, trying to clamber away from the approaching giant, but my legs are rooted to the spot, the black goo holding strong as my struggles only seem to make it worse. *Shit.* "What are you doing?!" I scream to her. "Shoot it!"

But again, she does nothing. *Why isn't she helping?!*

The monster is only feet away now, its eyes burning red with hunger, and in desperation I try erecting a wall between us, but as I feared, my mind is hit with icy shards. I gasp in pain. *God damn it!* Glancing around, I frantically search for someone else, but Ezekial is holding back a barrage of his own enemies, and Dev is heavily involved in fighting three Metus with Aveline. If I call to any of them now, I could get them killed. I lock eyes with the useless form that is Aurora one last time before I growl in frustration and turn back to the monster, whipping forward my Arcus while still on my butt. I'm not the best with this weapon, but it's better than nothing.

But before my tar-laden fingers can reach for an arrow, a dark form flashes in front of me, and the sound of a knife slicing through wetness rings through my ears right before I'm flattened and covered by a heavy body. There's an explosion of heat and stink, pushing us deeper into the wet grass, and we lie there until the last mucus pop is heard. Slowly the person rolls off, removing his jacket that has chunks of red lava on it, the material sizzling as he throws it to the ground. Blinking, I look up into Hector's scared gaze, bright from the action. Locks of his white hair are plastered to his porcelain skin, which is marred by a few brown smudges of dirt.

"Need some help?" he asks, extending a hand, and now that he's only in his black T-shirt, I'm surprised to find his arms painted with graceful muscles. I've always assumed him to be scrawny under his conservative clothing, given his lean body, but he has definite strength, reminiscent of a ballet dancer.

"Thank you," I say and grab on to him. He gives me a good tug, freeing my legs, and I wobble for a moment, letting him hold on to me until I find my bearings.

"That was an unpleasantly large beast," he says in a tone that's way too casual for the moment.

"Two Metus gooed themselves together to make it."

One of his brows rises, impressed. "They are coming up with all sorts of new tricks these days."

"Yeah, all kinds," I agree distractedly as my gaze searches out Aurora in the distance. Her forehead is pinched, a multitude of emotions playing on her face, but before I can make them out, she notices Hector's attention on her as well and turns away, reentering the battle.

He glances to me, curiosity in his eyes, but the last person I want to confide in is someone I barely know. So I push away the questions swirling in my mind, and gesture to the glowing weapon at his hip. "My vest seems empty. I need you to shoot me with your gun."

"Excuse me?"

"The Navitas in your gun, I need you to hit me here." I tap on my chest. "It will rejuvenate me, at least a little."

"And then what will you do?"

"*Then* I hope this will all be over."

"Hmm." He glances to our surroundings, the storm of chaos, thank Terra, seeming to be quickly passing.

After a moment more of his silence, I let out a huff. "Never mind. I'll ask Dev—"

"By the stars." Hector cuts me off with a laugh. "You're an impatient little one, aren't you? I'll do it. No need to call the boyfriend."

With reflexes that are much faster than I would have assumed, he flips out his gun and shoots two crackling blue rounds into my chest. I tumble back from the impact and then straighten as the energy bursts through every nerve ending, and my eyes widen. It's all at once overpowering and at the same time exhilarating. I sigh and wet my dry lips, feeling extra alive, a little jittery, and slightly euphoric.

"Interesting," he murmurs.

Not liking his examining gaze, I look away, finding Dev across the tall grass. As he notes me standing with Hector, his features grow tight, and he waves me over.

I turn back to my new Vigil guard. "Um, thanks again for—"

"No need." Hector holds up a hand. "There's much more to atone for before I deserve your gratitude."

"What do you—"

"Another time," he interrupts again. "You should go to your boyfriend before he decides I need to be taken out with the rest of these monsters."

Glancing behind me, I watch Dev cut down a Metus as he makes his way toward us, and with a resigned sigh, I nod to Hector before turning to leave. I'll deal with all the weird that just went down later. For now, I want to finish this and then take the longest bath of my life.

The fighting goes on for much longer than anyone was prepared for, our side suffering more losses than I have ever experienced while battling the Metus. But even with the disheartening number of fallen soldiers, the Nocturna don't back down until the area is cleared, the field falling into a grim visual of singed grass, black and red puddles of our enemy, and the putrid stench of burning flesh.

Rubbing my temples, I try to ease the dull ache that has blossomed there, all the while breathing through my mouth. Men and women run around me, collecting the injured and preparing them for the medic vehicles making their way from the city.

With the nonstop action, I hadn't had the proper opportunity to take in our surroundings, but now as I glance up to the wall, I gasp. *Holy Metus fire*, it's much worse than I thought. Even though the sleek silver scaffolding of the engineers covers half the damaged area, I can still make out a large section of the titanium structure that is melted and singed black, as if a giant asteroid smacked right into it. How close had the Metus come to tearing a hole straight to the other side? Dev never mentioned anything about them attacking the fortification in his letters, and I begin to wonder what else he left out, my mind unable to stop from flipping back to the two beasts joining into one, and Aurora...what has happened to Aurora?

Turning to Dev, who's talking nearby with Aveline, I take in her dirt-soiled, but otherwise uninjured, form and watch as he brushes some mud from her shoulder, an almost paternal gesture. I step closer when the whispering and glancing of a few Nocturna catches my attention. Some I recognize as those I recently fought alongside, the ones who obviously saw me use my power. *Great.* This will definitely speed up the timing of my announcement, for no one will be able to stop the rumors and questions that will come from today's events.

"Molly, what is it?" Dev asks, tucking me under his arm.

"I think it's time for us to leave," I say, watching as some soldiers walk toward us.

Dev, noticing them too, stands taller and slowly moves me behind him, but before our two parties connect, a sleek black hover car stops in front of us, blocking the oncoming Nocturna. With a whirl, the glass top falls away, revealing Hector and a team of Vigil guards, who step out and encircle me.

"Your chariot awaits," Hector says as he gestures to the vehicle.

I blink, surprised. "How did y—"

"Cato instructed I call your entourage as soon as this was over, so I did."

I let out a frustrated huff. "Can you please stop inter—"

"It's hard not to when what you say is so predictable."

I grind my teeth.

"Is this for all of us?" Aveline asks.

"My pet, there's *always* room for you." Hector smiles, which merely earns him an eye roll from her.

Too tired to stand here deliberating any longer and not wanting to stick around for when the Nocturna make their way around the car, I crawl in. The interior is cool and clean, the seats soft and inviting. It's almost unsettling, given the dismal scene outside.

Aveline and Dev follow, Dev sharing the seat next to me. "You did good out there, midnight." He leans over to whisper against my temple before giving it a quick kiss. "I almost forgot how terrifying you can be." Blue eyes meet mine, a hidden smirk. "Almost."

I hesitantly smile. He obviously didn't see what happened with Aurora, and I debate telling him, but as he leans back, letting out a sigh as the tension in his shoulders eases, I decide to save it for another time. This was enough for today, enough for a lifetime. So I stare out the window, watching as we slowly maneuver through the tangle of soldiers, thinking about how this battle was merely the first of many I'm about to fight. What will change once the city knows of my existence, what I'm meant to represent? As these questions tumble through me, my gaze falls on a group of guards who've stopped in their task of cleaning the charred landscape to watch us pass. A few murmur to one another, frowns marring their foreheads, and even though I know they can't see me through the tinted glass, I still find myself slouching down. What must they be thinking? Will these men and women eventually grow to support me? Will they see past the centuries of the Vigil keeping me a secret to allow me to continue to fight with them? Dev wrote of the hidden whispers shared among his people, of many who hoped what they'd heard was true, that a Dreamer had indeed come to Terra. But what about the ones who aren't happy?

Biting my lip, I'm about to turn from the exhausted scene outside, when a pair of green eyes in the crowd catches my attention, and finding who's attached to them, my heart stutters. Aurora stands in the tall grass, the illumination from the nearby city painting half her face in a cool blue, the other in dark shadow as she follows our moving vehicle. With the assumption that no one is watching, the emotion she hid earlier now shines clear as day, and my chest explodes in a panic. Gone is the teasing light of the friend I once knew. Now only a stranger with a shivering passion of hate regards the place where I sit.

Chapter 19

THE WATER FALLS in a constant stream down my face, my eyes closed as I lean into the warmth, letting it seep into every one of my cells. Now with my strength returned, I could have easily imagined myself clean after the battle, but washing away the grime is not merely a physical act but a spiritual one. I need this small moment of solitude, away from all the demands and expectations, to finally collect myself. It's the first time since coming here that I actually let the reality of being in Terra settle in.

I did it.

We did it.

The memory of Rae back on Earth after the transfer swims forward. His look of astonishment as we both climbed out of our pods had revealed the small amount of doubt he'd had about surviving it. He had kept this emotion so carefully hidden, but I saw it then, and it made me love him even more fiercely—to sacrifice even with such doubt. I know friendship such as his and Becca's is rare, hardly ever found in one's lifetime, and I'm well aware of how lucky I am.

Pushing back my wet hair, I allow the water to continue pouring over me. I'll need to get out soon, step back into reality, but

I resist it for a second longer. I know who will be waiting for me when I do, and my chest flutters. I can still feel the heat of his blue gaze when I announced I was going to take a shower after returning to his apartment, and if I was honest with myself, I'm nervous. It's been so long. So much has happened, and after being shut out, the emotions I went through…well, I'm terrified to realize how much I need this man. Could I live through losing him twice?

Abruptly I turn off the shower, forcing away that thought as I warp myself in a towel and step into the steam-filled bathroom. It's all white tiles, chrome fixtures, and hushed cream lighting. Using my hand to wipe the fog from the mirror, I stare into my large brown eyes. I look tired, which is probably because I am. After attending a short debriefing right after the battle, Aveline, Hector, Dev, and I made our way back to the apartment, where, thankfully, I'm still given access to stay. I have no doubt Dev had a lot to do with this and only under the strict terms that my Vigil entourage remain close. As I stand here now, a dozen or so guards stay on watch in the hall and hidden in the shadows of the streets below.

Even though I'm used to being continually surrounded by people in New York, having these dedicated men and women constantly around me feels different, unsettling. But I understand their purpose, their importance, and can only imagine their numbers growing once my announcement takes place. Which Elena and I are to discuss in more detail tomorrow, but for now I just want to push all that to the back of my mind and have a moment to actually appreciate the here and now, of being back.

Using my powers, I imagine myself in the soft gray shorts and white tee I usually wear to sleep in New York, and in a burst of energy, my limp wet hair dries to hold a soft brown curl. This is one talent I definitely missed on Earth.

Regarding myself in the mirror one last time, I step into my bedroom, where my heart immediately kicks into overdrive. For as expected, Dev is there, freshly showered himself, sitting on my bed. He wears his signature black pants and T-shirt, the sleeves clinging to his biceps, and in the dim lighting, his features are cut in severe angles, his day-old scruff shadowed. His gaze comes up from staring at something in his hands, and his cobalt eyes sweep over me in a quick heated pass. I remind myself to breathe.

"How are you feeling?" he asks, his voice deep and soothing.

"Okay," I say, leaning against the doorframe to my bathroom.

He regards me a moment, his astuteness knowing there's more of an answer than that, but he doesn't press. "Come here." He raises his hand, and I walk forward, letting him pull me to sit beside him on the white comforter. "I have something for you," he says and lifts an open palm.

"My shell." I gasp in surprise.

"You said to give this to you the next time I saw you." His features hold a deep fire as he watches me take it, and I trace the spiral design, swallowing back a ball of my own emotions.

"I did, didn't I?"

There's a moment of tense silence as each of us take in what's in my hand.

"You know," he says. "I came here a lot when you were gone."

"To my room?"

Dev nods. "You forgot to make your bed that day," he says gently.

I study my room, everything how I remembered it. A modern dresser and circular mirror rest against the far wall, while sheer white drapes frame the floor-to-ceiling windows behind us, giving us a breathtaking view of the dark, twinkling city outside.

"But I always make my bed."

"Yes." He smiles. "But for some reason, you didn't that day, and after…" He pauses as his voice wavers. "After, I was glad you didn't, because even if it left you a ghost in this room, at least I could feel your presence."

The depth of emotion swimming in his crystal-blue gaze is too much to bear, and I turn away. How much we both have suffered.

"Molly." He says my name in such a way that it causes me to look back at him. "I love you."

My eyes burn. "I love you too." His lips descend on mine, and in that instant I break apart. As tears slip down my cheek, my mind tumbles to the stars and back. I'm everywhere in the room, my cells a collection of twirling, twisting desire as he gently lies me back on the bed. He tastes like mint, smells of his intoxicating fragrance of spice and night, and as the weight of him presses me into the sheets, I want nothing more than to be completely overcome by him. Too many hours had been spent trying to hold on to moments like these, grasping the memories that every day I spent away had threatened to slip from my mind. I loved him before, but here, as his hands slide over every inch of me, our energies twirling tightly together, I'm devastated for him. A dimension has separated us twice now, and yet we still have found our way home. This knowledge gives me a strange sense of confidence, of power the two of us have together. No matter what is laid across our path, we will always find one another.

Always.

With a kick of desperation, I pull Dev more firmly to me, wanting to fuse the two of us together, but despite my greedy insistence, he forces us to start slow. His kisses are torturously languid, agonizingly exploratory, and I'm embarrassed to say I actually whimper, wanting so much more.

The rumble of Dev's chuckle does nothing to help my desperation, for it goes straight through me, lower, heating my skin to burn. "This is going to last awhile, my midnight." He grazes along my neck. "So you might as well get comfortable."

I tilt my head back on a sigh as he kisses and licks my throat, slowly, painfully inching down my body. *By the stars*, how I missed him. Without realizing it, my mind must have imagined Dev shirtless, for suddenly my hands are smoothing against warm, taught skin.

"Molly." He leans back with a laugh. "You're cheating."

I bite my lip as I greedily take in his defined chest and abs. "I'd say sorry, but then I'd be lying."

"Oh, how I wish I had your power right now," he says, a devilish glint in his eyes. "But because I don't, it's a good thing I brought this." Pulling something from his back pocket, he snaps a band around his wrist. I frown at the glowing white lightning bolt in the center.

"No fair," I whine.

It's a Dreamer repellent band, something that when worn by the Nocturna protects them from my powers, but when on me renders me powerless.

He pulls my hands over my head, holding me in place. "Now, where was I? Oh yes." Pressing his hips into me, eliciting a gasp, he dives back into tasting every inch of my skin, and my mind shuts off as I merely become a ball of twisted, highly attuned senses and feelings. His touches become flashes of colors under my lids, his groans notes of ecstasy across my nerve endings, and we both sigh as eventually, thankfully, he rips my clothes from my body and skin touches skin. He mutters my name over and over as he praises my beauty, and I'd return the compliments if my mind wasn't a putty of lust. Spreading my legs apart, he allows my hand to be freed so I can dig them into his strong back as he slowly enters me. That's when the room falls away, along with the city and this world. It's just the two of us learning the other again, remembering, floating in a timeless dimension of pleasure. And for the first time in a long time, every responsibility that has been a constant weight on my shoulders, a reminder of what's to come, disappears, and I fly. Fly, wrapped in the arms of the man I love.

Chapter 20

AFTER A TIME that can't be quantified, my bedroom walls softly fall back into place, our surroundings coming into focus as Dev and I lay tangled in the sheets, sedated. Dev plays with strands of my hair as I snuggle closer, wanting to drink in his scent. Literally. Give me a glass of it, and I'd gladly gulp it down, because my God, it should be illegal to smell this good.

"This is new." Dev tugs on a lock of my hair, bringing me out of my stalker-like thoughts. I don't have to look at what he holds to know what he's referring to.

"Yeah, it happened after the transfer. Rae has a black one."

The only visible side effect that happened after completing the DNA transfer was that Rae and I now each have an inch-wide stripe of the other's hair color. Becca thought it was cool and "punkish," while Rae and I were just relieved it was the only physical mutation, at least so far. Visions of doubled limbs or his face morphing with mine had definitely flashed in front of me when Sonja mentioned that our appearances might alter slightly.

"I like it," Dev says, tucking the blonde piece behind my ear. "It makes you seem edgy."

I laugh. "And here I thought I already had that on lockdown."

"Oh, you do, but now you can tell by looking at you."

"What? You couldn't before?"

Dev holds back a grin. "Before you seemed as sweet as a sip of Traub."

"Well, that sounds gross."

Dev chuckles. "Traub is a sugary drink made from Terra grapes. I'll give you some later."

"Oh." I frown. "Wait. If that's true, how did anyone take me seriously before?"

Dev props his head on his hand, amusement shining in his gaze. "You think you have to look scary to be taken seriously?"

"It certainly helps."

Bringing his thumb up, he traces the line of my jaw to my bottom lip. "Often the best weapon is camouflage." He draws his finger closer to the opening of my mouth, and I bite it. He grins. "Precisely."

"I like this form of teaching," I say, wiggling my brows. "Give me another lesson."

He laughs. "Gladly." Leaning down, he kisses me. "Did you know Cato's an original," he says. "One of the first elders in Terra."

My eyes pop open. "What?"

Dev nods. "Which makes him also one of the most powerful."

"Oh God." I cover my mouth. "But back in City Hall I ..."

"Told him to shut it?" Dev offers with a wry grin.

"Oh God," I repeat. "No wonder he looked sick when I grabbed his hand. I totally messed up, didn't I?"

"Cato has seen many things in his lifetime. A little sparring from a Dreamer certainly can't be the most shocking. I'm sure it was even a welcome change for the old man."

I swallow. "I certainly hope so."

"I loved it," Dev says as he combs his fingers through my hair. "It was a turn on."

I roll my eyes. "Of course it was."

"A big one," he clarifies as he brings his lips back to mine.

I let him nip and massage them open, savoring every one of his touches, the way his tongue moves against mine. I could do this forever, and just when I'm about to suggest such an idea, Dev moves away, resting his head back against his pillow.

I hold back a groan of displeasure.

"I meant to ask earlier," he says, weaving his fingers into mine, "but how's Rae?"

"He seemed...okay before I left. Having Becca there helped, and I think...I think he's going to be happy."

Dev's features run through a gamut of emotions before ending on resigned acceptance. "I'm glad."

"He's a good friend."

"The best."

"You know," I say. "I did overhear Raymond say something about them working on a dimensional video connection thingy." Dev's eyes lock with mine. "At the very least, having the portal boxes able to carry electronics without jumbling the feed." I smile slightly, but Dev merely frowns.

"Let's not play that game," he says.

"But—"

"I appreciate what you're trying to do, but I can't...Rae and I said our good-byes. If something becomes possible with time, we'll address it then."

I study his furrowed brow, the way his eyes dart from mine, trying to hide what I can clearly see, and that's when I realize how much of a hit Rae's sacrifice really was to him. I always knew it would be hard, but I guess I never thought about *how* hard, considering I will still be able to see our Vigil friend. I feel disappointed with myself. Of course losing Rae weighs heavy on Dev. They don't have siblings here, but it didn't take long with being around the two to know they were like brothers, closer even. Memories of what I went through when I thought I had to give up Becca, my family, like I almost did, falls on me hard, and I suddenly want to give Dev a bone-crushing hug. But I don't, because I know he'd interpret it as pity. So instead I murmur that I understand and I won't mention such things again.

"Thank you," he says before we settle into a silence, each of us wrapped in separate thoughts.

"Can I ask you something?" I eventually ask.

Dev turns to me.

"What's going to happen to Aaron?"

His blue gaze immediately darkens, the lightness of our moment gone, but I had to ask. The Vigil has been a constant thought since getting here, and Dev talked very little about him in our letters. Besides snippets that Rae would pass along, I hardly know the state of things. I knew both men must have done it to ease my mind, considering the white-hot anger that goes through me whenever I think about Aaron, but it's time I face reality.

"He will have a trial," Dev says after a moment, rolling to study the ceiling.

"To be banished?" I ask.

He shakes his head. "Terminated."

I sit up straighter. "What, like *killed*?"

He nods.

I lean back, taking this in. Aaron...sentenced to death. I didn't know Terra even did that sort of thing. "Does...does Aurora know about this?"

Dev's jaw clenches. "Yes."

"Oh God." My hand goes to my mouth. "That's why..."

"Why what?"

I swallow. "Just...she didn't seem too happy to see me." I don't know why, but I can't tell Dev what happened during the battle tonight, not yet anyway. I mean, of course she'd be mad at me, blame me, but she'd never intentionally hurt me. She'd been kind, despite my jealousy toward her and Dev. No, she's not the sort of person who would do that...

"Her brother has a way of manipulating her," Dev says. "I've told her to stop visiting, but she's blind when it comes to Aaron. She always has been." His lips press into a tight line. "I don't want you around her without me present."

I gawk. "You can't be serious."

"I've never been more serious."

"But that's ridiculous. And anyway, I'm *never* alone now." I glance to the window, reminding him of the Vigil guards outside.

"Even so," he says, pulling me closer. "She's not been herself. Her eyes...there's something unstable there."

"We should help her."

"I've tried." He shakes his head. "But it does little good when the person you're trying to help believes there's nothing wrong."

"But after everything the two of you've been through, you can't just give up trying to—"

"Mols." Dev cuts me off. "Let's not talk about this anymore. We only have a few hours left before one of us will be called for something. I don't want to waste it by talking about this."

I chew on my bottom lip, sensing that what Dev's asking is more of a plea. "Okay," I say, knowing he's right. Time, something I once took for granted, now seems like the most precious commodity.

But even as Dev tucks me under him, his soft lips finding mine again, my mind isn't completely free from worry. Because if I've learned anything since the night I got hit by lightning, it's that no matter how hard you try to ignore something, say it isn't true, it has a way of crawling out of the shadows when you least expect it, showing you how very real it is.

Chapter 21

THE CORRIDOR APPEARS endlessly long, the white walls stretching out before me like taffy pulled straight. The only things breaking up the monotony are the few doors evenly patterned along our path. As I take in a deep breath, I taste the sterile tang of air that's mixed with a sweetness, something I've only recently become aware is the smell of Navitas—my new senses allowing me to pick up the fragrance. My entourage of Vigil guards trail behind me as we travel at an even pace down the hall, various engineers and scientist bowing their heads as we pass. If my feet weren't already moving forward, they'd be shifting uncomfortably. Even though I've walked this corridor of the Dreamer Containment Center many times before, something has evidently changed since I've been gone, and I really don't think it's me. The employees here have always treated me with respect, but now…well, now it's borderline reverent.

And I hate it.

I might have picked up some new traits upon my return, but I'm no different than I was before. The change in their behavior seems unfounded, and I press my lips together to keep from yelling at them to stop it already and act normal.

Hector, who accompanies me, seems to pick up on my discomfort, and smirks. "I've never seen someone so displeased from gaining attention. You look like you're having a difficult time squeezing something out your butt."

I shoot him a narrowed glare. "Thanks. Are you always this charming?"

"Only every other day of the week."

"How lucky for me then, to get you on one of the every other."

"Indeed," he agrees with raised brows.

While I'm still not used to Rae's replacement, and can definitely see how Hector can be one trying SOB, there's something about his mocking undertone and flippant demeanor that I find rather amusing. I can certainly see how Dev and he wouldn't get along though. While their appearances are as different as night and day, they seem to share a similar sarcasm when it comes to authority, or anything for that matter. Such a trait, when put tête-à-tête, wouldn't mix well.

"I just don't get why they're acting like this," I mutter after I share another nod with a group of soldiers, who've all bowed low. It'll take all day to get to Elena at this rate.

"I suspect they've realized how much of a necessity you actually are now, given the war's escalation since you've been gone."

"Wouldn't they have known this from the Dreamers before me?"

"Not everyone here was present for them, plus memories fade, Molly."

I hear a trace of sadness in his voice, but his features show no signs of such an emotion.

Turning a corner, we follow another long colorless hall that will eventually lead me to my session with Elena, and my heart sinks seeing another round of various DCC employees whom we'll have to pass. "There isn't, like, a hidden passageway that will get us there faster, is there?"

Hector fixes his already neatly-pulled-back bun, his gray hair camouflaging into our surroundings. "None that I know of."

"Really? You never found any all the times you were here with my grandfather?"

Hector stiffens beside me, his green gaze finding mine in a quick, narrowed sweep. "No," he says tightly.

"Sorry, I didn't mean to—"

"There's nothing to apologize for."

"I know, but—"

"We're here," he says, stopping in front of a closed door that houses a glowing blue lightning bolt.

I frown, watching Hector gesture to one of my guards to unlock the room, and wonder what in all of Terra could have happened for him to act so strangely on this subject? The few times I've brought up Hector to my grandfather, he had nothing but fond memories to share, and while my grandfather did seem hurt by Hector's sudden disappearance during the war, he never mentioned anything that might have caused the abandonment. He seemed just as confused as the rest of us. What was Hector hiding?

"I'll be back once you're done." He nods for me to enter the room.

I open my mouth to say something, but decide better of it. He seems far from an open book. So I turn and walk inside, the door closing with an audible huff.

The giant domed space is just as I remember it. The walls are covered in panels of white, the area lit from some unknown source, and the petite blonde who waits in the middle, one hand on an ivory padded chair, all gives me a sense of déjà vu. I'm back in the Dreamer Memory Room.

"Welcome," Elena says as I approach. "I hope you were able to get some rest since yesterday's events."

"Yes," I say, glancing to the dentist-like seat between us. My stomach flips in anticipation. It's been so long since I've been connected to my predecessors, and it might be a strange thing to say, but I missed the feel of their presence. Even though it's never as strong as when I'm in the energy plane of sight, I can still sense an undercurrent of their experiences as I stand here now. They course through my central nervous system, ready to be called forth at a moment's notice to my mind. Riki, the strongest of them all, whispers my welcome home.

"Good." Elena smiles and indicates that I should take a seat. "We're going to start today's session a bit differently. Before I give you a past Dreamer, I would like to record part of your memories. We'll need to do a few sessions of this."

"We can't collect them all now?"

She shakes her head. "We've found this can affect your short-term memory if too much is pulled at once."

"Oh, then yes, let's space them out."

She smiles an amused lilt as she readies the equipment. A white podium rises from the ground, where a small glass container rests on top. It looks no bigger than a pint. "You really must not be taking very much."

"This can hold up to fifty years of memories." She types away on a tablet beside her, causing apparatuses to move and shift around the chair. "Now please lay back," she instructs as she presses tiny round sensors to my forehead, the material cool against my skin. "These tap into the Hippocampus section of your brain, which is responsible for your various memory functions. The retrieval process won't hurt. If anything, you'll feel a little tingle and some heat where the sensors are."

"And they will pull my memories into that?" I point to the empty container.

She nods. "Yes."

"But how? Are you going to connect a wire?"

"How do you think your Internet works? When you press Send on a text on your cell phone, how does it get to the recipient?"

"Uh...magic?" Is it pathetic that I don't actually understand the science behind something I use daily?

"Sure, let's call it that," she says as she hands me a small cup of liquid. "Drink this. It's a light sedative and will make your thoughts slow. We need your mind relaxed."

"What memories are you going to take?" I ask, realizing how extremely invasive this actually is.

"We aren't *taking* any," she says. "We're duplicating."

Is there really a difference?

"And we're going to start from the beginning, a few days prior to the lightning strike and go from there. Now sip." She pushes the glass closer to my lips.

I chug it down and wince. "Ug, that's disgustin—"

My mind goes blank.

The air is uncharacteristically warm for April as I walk down a small street in the West Village. It's my birthday, and a man waits for me, his tall, broad form leaning against a lamppost on the corner. Jared's hazel gaze lands on me, and my stomach jumps as he steals a kiss. Dinner is filled with conversation and laughs, comfort and a silver charm bracelet. My life is simple, calm, everyday. I'm happy, if not somewhat bored.

It's dark and raining now, and I'm soaked to the bone. The buildings I run past become illuminated with the flashing of lightning, and I jump as the reverberating crack of thunder follows. I'm almost home. *Let me just make it home.* Another loud splinter sounds through the air, and then there's nothing but pain and my silent screams as my body is ripped inside out. It lasts forever as I disappear into an abyss.

The scene shoots forward at a nonstop pace—my time in the hospital, my parents beside my bed, Dr. Marshall's smile, my subconscious screaming that it's not who I think it is, but it's useless. All of this has already happened, already been set in motion.

My thoughts move on.

I take in Terra for the first time, the wonderment of the spinning sky with its shooting stars and the mysterious illuminated city. I meet Dev, his blue gaze piercing as my soul fuses together on a sigh. There's Aveline, Tim, Rae, and Elena. I fly through skyscrapers, nightmares, and manifest my desires into existence.

This recalling goes on until it stops at the moment I learn who I am, my purpose, and I'm devastated and excited and confused. I stand under the canopy of a single tree at night as an endless field stretches out before me, only ending when it hits a glowing metropolis in the distance. The only sounds are the sway-ing of the grasses as they dance in the breeze, and the rhythmic chirping of insects. My life is no longer simple, calm, or everyday. But yet I'm still happy and most certainly not bored.

My eyes blink open on a giant intake of air, and I glance around, discombobulated. I'm back in Terra, in the Dreamer Memory Chair, in the present. There's a gentle tug to my core, and I glance to my right to see Elena touching my arm.

"You did wonderfully," she says, her voice muffled.

I blink again, and a blue glow catches my attention. The once empty container on the podium is now filled a quarter of the way to the top, the liquid inside shining with an array of blue rainbow hues. Turquoise, azure, cobalt, a wink of silver. It's the most beau-tiful thing I've ever seen—my memories.

"Elena?" I say her name, mainly to root myself in the now.

"Yes?" She begins to remove the round sensors from my forehead.

"I—" I don't know how to talk for a second. Reliving all that...I feel exposed, raw, and I have an urge to burst into tears.

Elena's blue eyes meet mine. "Are you okay?"

I swallow, eventually finding the strength to nod, to speak. "Yes, I think so."

She watches me a moment longer. "Good, because we must go on."

"On?"

"Yes, while your mind is still penetrable. I'm going to give you a Dreamer."

My muscles tense. "I think I need to rest for a second."

"Unfortunately we don't have time for that, and all your vitals are reading normal. This Dreamer will be quick. His experiences are necessary to prepare you for what Cato has planned for your announcement tomorrow."

My announcement.

Tomorrow...

I swallow. "Who's this Dreamer?"

"He was a son of a politician."

I frown. "How will that—"

"Lay back." She tilts my forehead to rest once more on the chair's headrest. "Now, take a deep breath and relax. We've done this before. You know there is nothing to fear."

Even so, it had never been in conjunction with my memory retrieval before. Surely there's some protocol to follow? I watch Elena's practiced movements. She hooks up the new Dreamer memory, swirling colors that lap inside a large, clear box. The Navitas within pulses and calls to me as it snakes through a clear tube—its destination the memory grid she snaps over my face, holding my head in place. I bite the side of my cheek in protest. I'm not ready. My mind is sluggish, sore, and tired. But none of that seems to matter as the glass over me pools with the reflective liquid, blocking my vision. And all too quickly two spots directly above my eyes drip down and force them open. It's a frostbite grip as my mind suddenly fills with white and then bursts open, painting a new world of color.

Chapter 22

I HURRY THROUGH the streets of Rome, the yellow dust from the cobble-paved road kicking up at my sandaled feet as I try to keep pace with my father. The air is uncharacteristically cold for summer, and I pull my wool wrap closer to my body. I am a young boy named Vibius, in my twelfth year, but I am also Molly looking out through Vibius's eyes at what I assume is ancient Rome. I—Molly—want to gaze at the bright painted frescos covering the buildings, but my head is dutifully facing forward, following the broad-shouldered man guiding our way. His cloak gleams the color of the purest milk under the early morning sun, the purple stripe down his right side vibrant in contrast. *One must always display his position proudly*, he would often say to me—to us—as our servants dressed him for the day. This of course made sense, him being part of the Senate, which in these times was made up by an elite group of the wealthiest men in Rome. It was a time for powerful growth from within these seats. After the assassination of Emperor Severus Alexander two years prior, Vibius didn't need his father to tell him how our great city would change. You could hear it being whispered in the kitchen, along the shops, and among the men who visited our home, not paying attention to the child who played in our atrium's far corner.

Vibius and I can't help shivering—the details of how our emperor's brutal end came by the hands of his own troops is not something a young boy would easily forget.

But now we are no longer a boy, at least not in our father's eyes. We are to be groomed to be like him. When born into noble blood, into a family with two decades of Senate lineage, your path has already been paved. We would do everything and anything to make our father proud.

Turning a corner onto one of the main market avenues, we pass tented stalls, the array of products showcasing Rome's far-reaching trade. Fine silks from the East, mosaics from the South, and painted pots are willingly made ours for a bartered price. But we are not here to shop, and civilians respectfully move out of the way to accommodate our father's confident strides. They know who he is—he's made sure of that—and as we pass, he smiles at each and every one of them.

Even the smallest ants, when grouped together, can move impossible things, he is fond of reminding us. *You never know where your strength will come from.*

So we study the way he nods and shakes a few merchants' hands, addressing them by name as we make our way to the Senate assembly. The citizens stand tall at his acknowledgment, and our father steals a glance our way. *Yes, I'm watching.* Always watching, learning, for we're to be him someday.

Time jumps forward, and we now know of two worlds, of Terra and Rome. The vision of our father by our bed, eyes rimmed red, swollen, and filled with relief once we finally awoke after the storm that left us asleep for days, asleep but living in another place, one filled with shooting stars and people who say we must protect them. Vibius and I resent this new world though. We don't want to accept this other duty when we have a more important one here. Our heart contracts, recalling the love our father showed in that moment, the emotion he usually kept locked away.

We will make him proud.

We will support him in every way.

We will be like him.

The room shifts and changes. Vibius and I now stand by our father as he gives a speech to part of the Senate. He booms about how we must support our agriculture, pay attention to what we have to trade, nurture it, for the prosperity of these commodities will make us more powerful than any army. We stand tall, mesmerized by his words, and narrow our gaze at those in the room who dare challenge him. His belief is not popular. It is considered weak in the eyes of many, but they are all fools.

A movement by the back door of the hall catches our gaze, and our stomach flips, finding the tall blond man who is supposed to remain in our dreams. I—Molly—can feel Vibius's heart pound faster, a mix of anxiety, resentment, and excitement to see him now here.

The Vigil's green eyes, set against tan skin, latch on to ours, a small smile barely touching his lips, and we stare at those lips for a beat too long.

"Julius," we whisper.

Years pass, and Terra is taking up too much of our strength and time, time we wished we had here, at home. Vibius's desire to call forth the power found only in our sleep grows daily as more and more members of the Senate are heard muttering against our father. We want to end them the same way we do the Metus, for surely the same nightmares must be festering in the hearts of these corrupt men. Julius is there beside us, a staying hand to our shoulder, a silent word telling us to ignore them, to be calm. We listen even as our pulse jumps at the contact. He is our Vigil guard, but we—Vibius—wish he could be so much more. With the warm looks we catch Julius giving us, we know it could be possible, if we were brave enough.

Vibius's memories keep coming, days turning into weeks and then months, but unlike the other Dreamers I've acquired, I stay with Vibius mainly on Earth. The nights of Terra are few and far between, and I can only assume Elena, or whatever engineers are responsible for gathering past Dreamers for me, have clipped these out so I pay attention to what Elena deems more important.

The time without a proper emperor has now gone on for a decade, and Rome is suffering two wars, agricultural failure, and political chaos. The taxes are high, too high, and the people are angry. But our father, always so careful to take care of the ants, has finally found himself in a popular seat in the Senate. They know of the persuasion he has among the working backbone of our great nation.

Remember, Vibius, when victory is closest, so are our enemies.

We are more alert now, for our father is running to be one of the two elected consul—those who will now rule our empire. And after the years of following and watching, we have cultivated the tongue of the serpent and the wit of the owl. Easily we flirt in this game of social graces and seamlessly walk the lines of the sticky web, eluding the spider. But still, we fear for our father. Already the few consuls before him have not sat long on their seats. Lies, deceit, and murder fill our everyday, death now a constant, both asleep and awake.

In an uncharacteristic moment, we find ourselves alone, sitting on a bench hidden away in our peristylium, the back garden of our house, while our father holds a social gathering for his cause. Wine, music, fine foods, and ornate clothing adorn our guests, Tonight we are too tired to smile and nod and engage in the usual conversations. For once the politics of it all is draining rather than providing us the usual rush of accomplishment. We feel lonely and overwhelmed, this life leaving little in the way of true friendship. Is this to go on forever? Our thoughts are interrupted by the sight of a tall man, beautifully dressed in purple silks and gold trimming, walking out into the garden. An entourage of people follow him, and our heart quickens as we take him in. Julius's blond hair is pale under the moonlight, his angular cheeks and strong jaw clean and smooth. We watch as the crowd of men and women are equally as charmed by whatever he is saying. One woman touches his arm with a laugh, and a spike of jealousy goes through us. We turn away.

Time jumps forward. It's late. Low candlelight flickers on the table before us, the only illumination in the political chamber of our father. We sit back with a sigh and rub our forehead, staring at the crisscrossed mosaic floor that stretches out into the darkness. We stayed up to organize the notes from our father's latest meeting, for he is now one of the two elected consul.

Even the smallest ants can move the most impossible things.

While those ants didn't have a vote, they surely had a role in our victory. We've dismissed the scribes early, wanting to be close to the parchments that have our father's words scratched across. Our fingers linger over the etched-in symbols, the wisdom collected for all those in the future. A sound beyond where our light reaches brings our head up and our body to stand, but as we watch who steps out of the inky darkness, our mind calms while our skin grows warm.

Julius stands silently regarding us, his green eyes, made honey-wheat under the candle's glow, never waver from ours. His white toga is simple tonight, easily displaying the strength of his arms, and it's not only Vibius who is under the spell of this man. I too take in this Adonis of a creature and understand his appeal.

Slowly, Julius winds around the table until his sandaled feet hit up against ours. He removes the scroll that was tightly grasped in our fingers and, without looking away, places it on the desk. Vibius swallows, his heart wanting to jump from his chest, while I—Molly—feel guilty to be witnessing such an intimate moment. We glance to the lips in front of us, the way the bottom looks heavy, weighted in its fullness, and I can sense Vibius's desire— strong, consuming, desperate. How long we've yearned for this moment, waited for our bravery to surpass our duty. And I, Molly, understand Vibius's fear for the possibility of happiness in a world that is so often wrought with peril. But life is short, often unfairly so, and in this moment with this man, Vibius suddenly cares very little for any of those things, and finally, with a new strength, leans forward and claims Julius's mouth with ours. It's soft yet urgent, and as he responds to our kiss, pulling our body closer until we are no longer two souls, but one whole.

The weeks that follow are filled with maneuvering political spiderwebs, exchanging secret Senate deals, and collecting intel on the quiet murmurs of a possible revolt among the Roman people. Famine has hit hard, the crops not responding well to the uncharacteristically cool summer, and two wars are being fought—on Earth and in Terra. It has been the toughest time we have ever had to endure, but it has also been the happiest. Taking Julius's hand, we give it a quick squeeze, a smile shared between us, before turning the corner to the back entrance of our family home. The usual sounds of life, of servants and guards, are absent as we walk through the doorway, the atrium strangely deserted. The cool night air stirs the drapes that hang as separators to our garden, the few burning candles in the corners setting the space in a golden haze. The only noise comes from the trickling of rain water as it falls into the pool that rests in the center of our atrium, where the statue of Janus, our household god, juts proudly from its shallow depths.

Something is wrong.

We sense it even before Julius steps in front of us, attempting to shield our gaze that has already noticed something on the floor beyond the statue. We push past him, knocking away his arm as he tries to hold us back. *No no no*! Our heartbeat thumps in our head, and time slows as we lock on to what we refused to believe would happen. Instantly Vibius's world, my world, collapses to dust.

Abruptly I'm torn away from the scene, and I—Molly—gasp as my eyes blink open, released from the liquid that held them. I squint into the brightness, back in Terra, back as me, strapped into the Dreamer Memory Chair. It takes a moment for my body to fall into itself again, but once it does, it still holds the chill of the last image I was given, the last memory, and my stomach turns over in anguish. Glancing around, I find Elena's puckered brows by my side, her lips pinched tight in silent frustration. I have a feeling I wasn't supposed to see that last part. I swallow, the metallic taste filling my mouth like it always does after receiving a predecessor's memories, but this time it mixes with the bile that has climbed its way up my throat.

"Why did you show me that?" I ask, my voice hoarse and sounding odd after living through such a different person, in very a different time.

"It was the closest experience we could find amongst our Dreamers that could prepare you for what you might experience after your announcement. What you and Cato might deal with."

Memories of the public gatherings with my father, Vibius's father, speaking to the people, winning their favor, float before me. But so does the betrayals within our own Senate, the lies, violence, and never knowing whom to trust.

"When was that?"

"It was around 240 CE, as humans have deemed it." Elena returns the memory to the library of many along the wall, the glowing blue box enveloped as it fits snugly back into its place. "What is also known as the Crisis of the Third Century," she explains. "Where the Roman Empire nearly collapsed."

"Well, they certainly named it accurately." I rub a sweaty palm over my pants. What had happened to Vibius? To Julius after that day? My heart grows heavy at the thought of the likely outcome.

"Was that to warn me?" I ask. "That last part?"

Despite Elena's next words, her features stay their usual blankness. "The engineers messed up in their splicing. That wasn't something you were supposed to see."

"But I did."

"Yes." Her blue eyes hold mine. "You did."

"So what now?"

She takes in a slow breath. "Do what is intended after these sessions. Learn from it."

Learn from it.

I frown.

My mind easily brings forth the last vision with Vibius, starting with the square stitched mosaics pattered across the floor, the pristine stone shining under the low light of the candles. Our eyes travel the length of it, stopping when it met a pale hand. Following the arm, we slowly walked around the statue that blocked the rest of what was hidden, our skin numb, disbelieving. The man's robe lay in violet waves around his body, his other hand draped across his chest, where a chalice seemed to have dropped from his fingers, rolling a few inches away. Red wine marked its path, a stained pool that flowed under his body, dampening his toga and drawing attention to the bit of crimson snaking down the side of his mouth, mixing with white foam and purple lips. His eye stared up at nothing, and we fell to our knees, wishing we could share the same blindness. As tears streamed down our cheeks, we silently yelled for him to blink, but he never did and never would, for the fate of all those before him had found its way to us. No matter how well we played the game, despite our honorable intentions or our belief that goodness conquers all, we still found ourselves there, staring at our father—poisoned.

Gone.

Chapter 23

Sitting on the zipline platform of Dev, Aveline, and Tim's building, I study the stars shooting overhead in their constant stream, trying to count how many souls must be sleeping. Tucking my knees to my chest, I lower my gaze to the lit-up metropolis that expands before me. The skyline glows blue and white and is cut by the crisscrossing hairs of zipline wires woven between buildings, the stillness of the city interrupted every so often by quick dark spots of citizens flying by. No one was home when I got back from my session with Elena, leaving only Hector and me. While I sit up here, he's sprawled on the couches downstairs, book in hand. I was happy to get a moment alone. Despite the meditation after Vibius's memory, my mind still twirls with too many thoughts and worries.

Strands of my hair, which is pulled into a ponytail, brush across my face as a breeze passes by, and I push them back. The air is warmer than normal, reminding me of summers at my parents' house, of my backyard and the fireflies that flash between the grass. I used to think they were fairies dancing. Despite my melancholy mood, the memory has me grinning, and I decide to manifest them here. With my energy growing warm to cool in my mind, I imagine their yellow glowing bodies twinkling around me. In an instant the space I sit is lit by dozens of winking lights. They hover around me, the beginnings of an impressionist painting, and as one comes to float in front of me, I lift my finger, and it lands on the tip. Its black wings flutter as its backside pulses with light, sending a soft sheen to my skin.

"Hello," I whisper, and as if it understands, it winks in response. I smile.

"Am I interrupting?" A deep voice comes from behind me, and I sit up with a start, glancing over my shoulder. Despite my sensitive hearing, I hadn't noticed anyone approaching, a testament to Nocturna stealth. Dev slowly walks forward, his Arcus strap barely moving across his broad chest, and my heart kicks into a new beat seeing him.

His eyes sweep over my tiny blinking friends as he sits beside me. "What are these?"

"Fireflies."

His head jerks back as one comes close to his nose, and I bite back a laugh.

"Fireflies." He studies them suspiciously. "You have them on Earth?"

I nod.

"That's a bit dangerous, don't you think? How is that one not burning you?" He frowns to the one on my finger.

I wiggle it, and the bug jumps into the air, mixing with all the others. "They don't actually have fire inside," I say, amused. "That's just what we call them."

"Hunh," he says dubiously, watching as I slowly bring the bugs to shimmer out of existence. With the last one's disappearance,

Dev looks to me, his blue gaze holding a bit of wonderment. "You know"—he pulls one of my hands into his—"you're not supposed to be out here alone."

I barely hold in an eye roll as I glance to the four corners of the roof, indicating my Vigil guards dutifully standing watch in the shadows. "Don't worry. I'm not."

"Still, I don't like you out in the open like this without anyone close."

"You're close," I say with a teasing grin, one he can't help but return.

"Don't try to charm your way out of this."

"Says the pot to the kettle."

His brows pinch in. "What?"

I shake my head. "Never mind. I just mean, look who's talking."

"Mols, I'm being serious."

I sigh. "I know, but can you really blame me for wanting a little alone time before my announcement? This might be the last chance I get to just..." I glance around. "Be."

Dev's gaze softens. "When are you meeting with Cato?"

"Soon." *Too soon.* My stomach bunches with nerves at the thought. Cato is to give me a quick debriefing before I'm announced to Terra tomorrow.

"I'll be with you," Dev says. "Through all of it."

I chew my bottom lip, turning back to the city. "I wanted to talk to you about that."

He waits.

"I was thinking... Maybe you should wait to see how the crowd takes the news first before you connect yourself with me.

I don't want to put you in a position where you'll be standing against your people."

Dev's silence has me glancing his way, finding stone features.

"Do you really think I care two Metus turds about that?" he says, and I open my mouth to respond, but he continues. "To even think such a thing..." He shakes his head. "When I would get your letters that talked about everything that was happening with Becca and Rae, the violence that was getting worse on Earth, I felt sick that I couldn't be there by your side. Do not rob me of being able to stand with you now."

"Dev," I say, touching his arm. "I'm sorry. That's not what I—" I pause, searching for the right words. "Of course I want you beside me, *need* you there. I just didn't want to hurt you in the process."

His blue gaze is severe, focused, as it stays locked to mine. "You and me, we're a pair—do you understand? Anchors in this storm that's about to hit. The only way you'd hurt me is by leaving me again."

My throat constricts at the thought. "Never," I whisper.

A gentle smile tugs at the corner of his lips. "Good."

And then he's pulling me to him, kissing me so softly that it nearly breaks my heart.

With a moan I bring him closer, my hands wrapping around his neck, and he responds instantly. His muscles coil around my form, a wall of strength, of support, and I wish we could stay like this—in such a simple moment where all I want is him and all he wants is me.

But I'm no longer so naïve to believe such a life exists, at least not at the present, and as if to prove my point, the sound of someone clearing his throat breaks through our locked embrace.

Pushing apart, we see Hector standing at the top of the stairs that lead to the landing platform where we sit, his upper lip curled in disgust.

"Now that I've properly lost my appetite for a few Earth cycles, I'm here to tell you it's time."

Blushing hard, I detangle myself from Dev and stand, my heart racing for a very different reason than what it was a moment ago. But before I can follow Hector, who's already made it off the platform, Dev tugs me to a stop, his gaze capturing mine again.

"Anchors," he says quietly.

I watch him closely, drinking in his confidence and determination. "Anchors," I repeat, and then with his hand in mine, we make our way forward.

-->|=◉ ◉=|<--

The room Dev, Hector, and I walk into is on the top floor of the City Hall building and is, for a change, not all white mixed with more white. It's ornate in design and grand in height and length. Actually, it's less like a room and more like a long library. One that has a complicated tiled floor of black and white, and Corinthian columns that stretch up to a curved glass ceiling, reminiscent of the top of a greenhouse—patterned with crisscrossing framework that gives way to the view of the shooting stars. This is where the main illumination of the room comes, and despite the stars' distance, they cast a startling brightness against walls lined with thick leather-bound books. Hector leads the way, and I have trouble keeping step with his gliding strides as I find my pace slowing, taking in the multitude of small marble statues placed on pediments in front of each texted alcove that expands the hallway's length. The statues are displayed like art objects in a museum, and as my eyes go from one to another, I realize that's exactly what they are. Toward the middle I spot a familiar form and come to a complete stop. While no colors but pure white marble shape the figure, it's all too easy to see who it represents, for the leanness of her limbs and strength in her shoulders give her away. Not to mention the drape of straight hair that frames her petite face, one that's frozen in a severe stare. A statue of Riki gazes out from her perch, one hand planting a Bō staff securely by her side. Even in her two feet of height, she's still fierce to behold.

"Who is she?" Dev asks.

"She was a Dreamer," I say. "Her name was Riki." Glancing down the line, I recognize a few more of my predecessors. *What is this place?*

"You received her memories?" Dev asks, connecting the dots.

I nod. "She was the first I was given."

I know it sounds strange, but as I gaze upon Riki's likeness, it's as if the weight of her energy is pulled from her sculpted form to mix with my own, and in a strange wave, my nerves to settle with comfort, if only for a moment. *I am here*, she seems to say. *We all are.*

"Have you seen this place before?"

Dev shakes his head.

"This floor is the elders' domain. I've only been granted access into Elena's office up here."

"Are you coming?" Hector calls to us, his voice echoing through the cavernous space. Reluctantly I tear my gaze from Riki's.

"Where are we?" I ask Hector as we return to his side.

"The elders call it the Gallery of Stars," he explains. "It houses information on all the Dreamers that have come to Terra and is a connecting passageway to each of the elder's chambers." He nods to the six doors evenly patterned along the wall. "It also leads to the main balcony that overlooks City Hall Square."

At the end of the long room stands a giant wooden door that, even from a few yards away, I can make out the intricacies of. In layered sections are scenes of the spinning Terra sky mixed with lines after lines of some sort of ancient Latin. At least, I think it's Latin, given what I've seen used in this city.

At the base of the door stands a cluster of people all watching our approach. Elena is there with Cato, her white wrap dress at opposites with his black uniform. He wears an outfit similar in appearance to the Nocturna guards, yet his is structured to the *T* with long sleeves and a high collar that barely sits below his sagging chin. The rest of the elders are there as well, gray robed and standing off to the side as if they want to blend into the walls. I hardly give them a second glance as my eyes skim over Alex, a few other Council members, and search out two individuals who seem to be missing.

"Where are Tim and Aveline?" I ask Dev before we reach the awaiting group.

"They are in the crowd. We thought it best to have some of our people below." He touches his ear. "They'll be communicating what's going on."

I frown. As nervous as I was for Dev to be at my side, I can't help feeling even more on edge with Tim and Aveline below. Surely some have seen us all together, know that they support me. What would happen to them if this goes badly?

"Welcome, Molly," Elena says as we come to the end of the hall. The Vigil guards who accompanied us spread out to semicircle our group. "I see that you've recognized some of our Dreamers here." She gestures to the library behind us.

"Yes." I turn back to the opulent space. "Are they all here?"

"We have another wing where more are located and"—she gives me a gentle smile—"where there's a space waiting for you."

It's an attempt to raise my spirits, but it actually has the inverse effect. The idea of being immortalized in stone leaves me feeling unsettled. All the figures that we passed seemed like such warriors, stoic figures to be respected. I don't belong among them...I mean, what would I even be holding, a cell phone to my ear?

"We hear your last Dreamer onboarding was a success," Cato says beside Elena, his white head tilting to the side as his calculating green gaze falls on me.

"If you mean I didn't lose my mind after, then yes, I would say it was a success." Acquiring the memory of Vibius's father's death, however, was not.

"Yes, well, it will be beneficial for you to now bring forth what you learned," Cato says. "Remember to not let your emotions show, despite how strong they might be in the moment. Everyone will be watching you. They will be looking for how they should react based on your reaction. Confidence is the only thing acceptable in this moment."

Funny how his speech does very little to incite that.

"Alex will go up first," he continues, gesturing to the general, "and discuss the temperature of the war and how big of a threat it has become. He will play up this desperate time we are in."

"Does it really need to be exaggerated?" I ask. "Isn't it *actually* desperate?"

Cato looks at me coolly. "He will paint a picture that we are in need of an offensive advantage," he clarifies, and I glance to Alex, whose shoulders are set straight with confidence, his hands clasped behind his back. He looks every bit the lead general of an army and at ease in this moment of planning.

"Elena will go next," Cato continues, nodding to his elder companion, "and will prepare our people for the reveal of the Dreamer."

"That's you," Hector whispers in my ear.

"Thanks," I mutter without removing my gaze from Cato. "I won't have to say anything, right?"

He and Elena share a glance.

Oh no.

"*Right?*" I ask again.

"Depending on the crowd's reaction, you might," Elena explains.

My stomach has officially dropped out my butt.

"No." I shake my head.

"Moll—"

"No," I say again, as if that might change things. "You don't understand. Any confidence you want me to exude with my mouth closed, I can do, but as soon as I'm forced into public speaking, *especially* with a whole world watching...well, forget about it."

"You did wonderfully during the Council meeting," Elena points out.

"Because I didn't *say* anything."

"Then do the same," Cato suggests.

I blink. "What?"

"Talk with your power, not your words," he says. "If anything will sway them, it is what you hold inside. Show them the beauty you can create, the things you can promise, and the elements you can demand. Terra already honors those who dream. We now must show them that it is okay for one to walk among us. Your powers, while dangerous, are always routed in good. Show them, Molly. Remind them."

The hall falls silent as I take in Cato's words. Glancing to the ornate carved door, the only thing that separates me from what I'm about to do, I truly try to prepare myself. "Remind them," I repeat softly, shifting around the energy that is held within my chest, wanting to be freed. Always wanting that.

Cato watches me and waits. The whole group does, even Dev, and something in me, in this moment, decides to play the person these people want, need.

Because, really, what other choice do I have?

So with the memory of Vibius standing stoic beside his father and the sure gaze of Riki, my spine straightens and my chin tips up.

I am the Dreamer, I tell myself. One among a long line of many, and I will do my best to make their sacrifices worth it.

"Okay," I say to Cato and Elena. "I can do that."

It's all that's needed for everyone to move into position. Like a choreographed dance, the elders stand in front, followed by the few Council members, and then Hector, Dev, and I, with me in the middle and our Vigil guards circling us from behind.

There's a pregnant pause, the elders and guards preparing themselves, and despite my efforts to stay in control, my breathing quickens.

Fingers weave between my own, and I glance up to Dev.

Though he stays silent, his blue gaze says it all—no matter what, he is with me. I manage a small smile right as the doors open with a strained creak and the roar of the crowd below floods through.

Chapter 24

I'VE BEEN ONE in thousands at stadium concerts and maneuvered through the masses in Times Square, but neither comes close to what it's like to stand on this balcony, gazing down upon Terra's sea of people. The bodies stretch out, a wave of black, going farther than my eyesight can follow. The only thing breaking up the churning force is the cluster of trees that line City Hall Square.

Six large screens hover in front of the Roman columned buildings that circle the perimeter, projecting our image for all of to see. The noise grows louder as we come into view, the elders in front, the rest of us behind, and the reverberating beat hits against my skin like an ocean's wave. I want to plug my ears and shrink away. It's too much, the definition of overwhelming. But I can do none of these things. I can only force myself to stand, hands by my side, shoulders back, mimicking the stance Vibius took beside his father.

Even the smallest ants, when grouped together, can move impossible things.

Never have I believed that statement more than I do now. Somewhere, among so many, Tim and Aveline watch, and my stomach tightens into a crumpled ball of unease. *Please, by the elders, let this go well.*

I steal a glance at Dev beside me. His gaze is forward, scanning the people with empirical confidence while his hands clasp the Arcus strap across his broad chest. He looks every bit the fearless warrior in this moment, regarding the large populous below as if it's nothing out of the ordinary, his everyday. How I hope I look the same.

Elena walks to the center, where a thin silver microphone is placed, and with her approach, the screens focus in on her as the entire crowd grows silent. Not even a cough can be heard, and I'm unsure which was more unsettling—the overbearing noise or the fact that such a large mass can all be commanded so quickly.

"Salvete." Elena's voice booms over the city.

"Salvete." The people below respond in thunderous unison.

Dev leans closer to me. "Our traditional Terra greeting."

I nod, not taking my eyes off the back of Elena's blonde head, her white dress seeming to glow under an invisible spotlight.

"Welcome, people of Terra," she says while raising her arms. "Your elders thank you for attending today's gathering. We have not all been brought together for many Earth cycles, and as most of you know, it is usually under distressing circumstances. So first, let me put your minds at ease. While what you are about to hear will touch upon such matters, you will also witness something that is to be celebrated, something that will change our future forever and mark this evening as a historical event."

Elena pauses as a murmur slithers through the crowd, and I'm reminded of her expertise in theatrics. The way she gives information has you always on edge, hanging, waiting, and wanting her next words. And just when you can't take the silence any longer—

"We have much to share," she booms. "So please, let us begin." Turning, she gestures to Alex behind her. "General Alexander, our head representative of Security, will explain the current temperature with our oldest foes, the Metus."

Another stirring of the crowd as Elena steps back to allow Alex his time at the mic.

Though a stout man, what the general lacks in height he more than makes up with in his confident posture and demanding presence. I only manage to listen to the beginning half of his speech, his words on the war and the Metus, how their numbers have risen beyond what has ever been seen before. He speaks of the things that are being done to ensure Terra's victory, but how we will need something more—a strength not of this world, and that's when I begin to tune out. It would seem the least proper time to do so, but my mind can't help it. It must be subconsciously trying to stave off a panic attack. I catch words like weapon, ambush, powerful, and then I find myself studying the way the grays in Alex's close-cropped hair seem to wink as he turns his head this way and that. It's strangely soothing, like a glimmer of diamonds under a light.

Then there's a commotion—the citizens' collective voices slowly growing, and that's when I realize Alex has ended his speech, leaving them on a note of anticipation, of nerves, and I watch Elena return to the center of the balcony. My breathing grows heavy, my heart a *thump, thump, thump* of a racehorse's hooves. What did he last say? Something about finding a key to the war... Damn my stress-induced ADD.

Elena raises one hand, her sign for all to settle, and they do, but there's a buzz now, an energy to the center of this city that hangs on a precipice.

"I know what General Alexander has shared is filled with fearful prospects, but it is our belief that you all deserve to know the truth of what is happening in our world," Elena says in a tone bordering on motherly, "so you can prepare just as you have done so many times before. We have lived through many of these wars, risen to meet the crest of the approaching dark wave, and we will do so again. But this time it will be with the full transparency of the advantage we now hold."

I squeeze my hands into fists, my vision tunneling.

"For we have an individual among us that our very race has been created to protect, who holds the energy we harness in our everyday. Their kind has come before, just as they have now, during times of war, of need. They are brought to regain the balance of our two worlds, Terra's and Earth's." This is where she pauses, just for a moment, allowing the information to seep into the thick silence—and in my mind, drown in it—before she goes on. "In the past they have exclusively come to the Vigil, in secret, for our protection, but today is a new chapter in our history books, for the one whom we speak of has entered our world outside our usual protection, and we believe it is so all of us, Vigil and Nocturna, can finally work as one to beat our enemy. My people of Terra"—her voice raises an octave—"you've heard the rumors of the girl who could fly, who held Navitas in her hands and brought a man back from the brink of death. Well, I say to you, stop your whispers and open your eyes, for it is all true. The girl exists, and she is among us. Gaze upon the key to end this madness." Elena turns to the side, throwing an arm to me. "I give you a Dreamer."

The hidden cameras now swing to my face, plastering it across every screen, my too-large eyes staring straight ahead, and I can barely register my relief that my mouth isn't gaping open like a helpless moron.

I can't move. I'm frozen just as the rest of Terra, until someone behind me—I'm pretty sure it's Hector—actually, I *know* it's Hector—pushes me forward, right as the crowd falls into chaos.

There's yelling, shouts, collective outrage, and confusion. The thunderous noise of the crowd flipping out below pushes against me, causing me to want to run, to turn away and find Dev's reassuring embrace. But I know I cannot. This moment is my responsibility, and mine alone.

Elena's blue eyes hold mine, her presence the only thing enabling me to put one foot in front of the other and go to her, a fish on a hook being reeled in. Her hand gently rests on my shoulder, a burst of her comforting energy seeping into me, and the two of us peer across the ocean of citizens, our faces plastered across the screens. Elena appears sure, confident, and regal in her billowing alabaster dress, while I...I look like no one I recognize. My hair is pulled tightly back, the white strip in it bright against my dark locks, and my cheekbones jut out in a severity I never knew I had, the invisible spotlight above creating a hardness to my features that is unfamiliar to me. The boning of my protective vest forces my posture straight, my shoulders back, and though I feel like a chicken without its head, I resemble anything but. I look tough, a soldier, someone who can indeed make a difference. In this moment I am so reminded of Riki's statue in the Dreamer Gallery that my breath hitches. Have I truly changed so much and not known?

Something strange happens then, taking this in—something inside me clicks into place, something that feels a lot like acceptance, or maybe it's finally understanding. I truly *am* a Dreamer, just like those who came before me. I might have told myself that before, but here now, standing above all of Terra, I am overcome with a strange sense of what I'm meant to do.

With the roar of the angry crowd below seeming unending, I step out of Elena's embrace, now truly alone, dangling above a world, knowing this will be the most important test of my life, the start of my legacy. With the collective centuries of Dreamer memories at my disposal, I pull forth what I need, and with a deep breath, tip my chin up and force my eyes forward as I blink into the plane of energy. Everything bursts into blue light, the thousands of souls below illuminated with their life energy that twists inside them. Riki is here, Vibius, my grandfather, and all the other Dreamers I've acquired. We stand together and we wait, wait for the crowd to understand our desires as we push it out to cover them. It's a blanket of our thoughts, our will. *Quiet*, we tell them. *Ease yourselves*, and after a few gasps of shock, of sighs, the noise dies down. It's just me and the gentle wind passing through as every pair of eyes in the square gaze up.

And this is when I speak. "What your elder has shared is true," I say, my voice booming through the energy-laden air. "I am your Dreamer, *a* Dreamer. My people fly above us"—I gesture to the sky—"the souls you've gazed upon endlessly, and while their energy brings life to this world, while I carry it with me here, I assure you I am no different from each one of you. I still need to breathe to live, eat to survive. I have the same desires of peace for both Terra and Earth and know the importance of their survival. I'm not sure why I was chosen to come here, to help in this war, but I have seen the lives of the ones who have come before me, of their sacrifices, and I will do everything in my power to continue their legacy as well as move a new step forward with my own." I momentarily pause, the crowd murmuring as I ready myself for what I know must come next. "Elena has spoken of rumors, of things I can do, and I'm sure some of you recognize me as the one who has fought alongside you. I want you to know that I will keep fighting, keep helping until the very end. But I also want to show you that I am not merely here to be a weapon, to destroy. You must remember the origin of my powers, what I'm made of." I glance out to the awaiting mass. "And that is dreams." With the echoing of my last words filtering through the speakers, I let the energy I hold within me zip down my arms to my hands. It sizzles and tingles along my nerve endings, and I just have to think it once—*fly*—to find myself floating up, my feet leaving the ground, until I'm hovering in midair for all to see. There are gasps, a few cries of alarm, but I block it all out as I close my eyes and switch my mind to automatic, to what calls out for me to create, and when the coldness in my head collects to near freezing, my eyes blink open, and with a burst, I paint the night in light.

Chapter 25

I⟋ RISES AT the far end of the square, the yellow glow of the sun seeping between the cracks and alleys set by the close cluster of skyscrapers. Lines of warm light filter over the crowd, wrapping around buildings that have only ever been touched by dark. Like golden threads weaving into a blanket, it covers everything, and I watch as heads turn, a wave of movement, to glance behind them. The sound of astonishment, of confusion and shock are a dull hum in my ears as the energy within me soars, mimicking the rising ball of fire, and my mind prickles with the cold collection of Navitas. With muscles tense and my hands palms up, I roll out a blue sky to mask out the black one, the shooting stars replaced by white clouds and a fluttering of birds as they make their way south. The sun now sits high over City Hall Square, nestled between two fluffs of cotton and bringing everything below to life with new colors. The leaves of the trees shine green and fresh, the whitewash of the surrounding marble lit in a warm yellow hue. I pop flowers from the ground, imagining their petals a rainbow of shades, their stalks tall.

The citizens move back as they spring up by their feet and gaze mesmerized as butterflies flap their delicate wings to dance around them. I pull ivy from the base of the columns that surround us, and I let it climb and crawl and sprout emerald-green leaves as it overtakes the buildings. I construct a jungle of life, a world that I know these people have only seen under a glass dome and others not at all. I allow the most beautiful animals in. Peacocks roam free, a buck with a crown of mossy antlers stands atop City Hall's stairs, while leopards and cheetahs prowl docile. I let it all remain there for a moment, to thrive and fill the air with fragrance. I let Terra take it in, see it, believe it, believe *me*, and then slowly, delicately, I pull it all back until the sun sets and the world is once again in its constant night. The only dash of color is the reappearing orbs in the sky as they fly to their dreams, to a place I was able to pull my energy from.

With my creation's end, so is my flight, and I rest my feet once again on the balcony. I now stand, regarding the silence as I take in two breaths and then three, a nagging fear that this might have been a horrible mistake, but right on the precipice of my fourth breath is when it begins.

The square erupts in cheers, and my legacy is born.

→━◉ ◉━←

In the days that follow, Dreamer information booths are erected throughout the city, Vigil representatives who, in my opinion, are given a rigid script of appropriate answers, are set to man them and pass out pamphlets. For even though my announcement went as smoothly as it could, it wasn't enough to keep out the suspicion and doubt.

Who's to say she won't use her powers against us? How could they have kept this from us for so long? Isn't it dangerous to have something so uncontrollable here? But shouldn't we worry about her carrying those diseases humans so often get? I hear she can read minds!

I mean, for Terra's sake.

Hearing the nervous whispers of the citizens is enough to make me happy that I've been momentarily stuck indoors.

Well, almost.

While my physical training with Hector and sessions with Elena continue, my days are mostly filled with meetings with Cato. And nothing about these hours improves my opinion of him, or more accurately, changes it. I can't quite put my finger on my discomfort, but something about him seems...well, robotic.

I get glimmers of similar apathetic behavior from Elena, but she at least appears to have a soul warming her body. I'm not sure if it's from living for more centuries than I care to count or something that happens with the elders after a time—or both—but Cato is the epitome of dull. He's all rules and musts and pinched brows followed by condescending pursed lips. How he's supposed to be the go-to man for the temperature of Terra's happiness is beyond me. I haven't seen him smile once. Well, maybe once, but I'm pretty sure that was from gas.

The worst though is that the elder seems more than okay with usurping every hour of my free time. Despite my earlier argument against it, he's still managed to stop me on more than one occasion as I made my way to help fight a Metus attack. The only thing keeping me from stomping my foot like a petulant child is Dev's reassuring gaze telling me they'll be able to manage without me—for now.

Even as we travel to the first stop on Cato's rather ambitious Dreamer PR tour, he still insists I sit with him to go over the schedule. Who cares that I've already heard it a dozen times? Might as well make it thirteen. So here I sit, in a very swanky decorated airship across from Cato and Elena, listening to the elder of the elders go through the itinerary.

"When we get to Port City, we will meet with the elected delegates first before doing a boat and walking tour," Cato says as he reclines, legs crossed in a puffy leather chair, his age-spotted finger scrolling through his tablet. "After that you will attend a dinner in your honor." His green gaze flickers my way. "While this outpost has our highest Vigil population, we have invited enough influential Nocturna to have this visit be beneficial. And all of us are in agreement that having Dev as your evening's companion will help persuade any Nocturna skeptics."

I bite the inside of my cheek, more than a little uncomfortable to have Dev act as some pawn. Sure, use and move me around, but I'd rather keep the rest of the people I care about out of it. Dev of course has no problem being included in this political game. In fact, he seems to gain a weird pleasure from it. Glancing beyond Cato, I look down the long belly of the beige-carpeted ship to where Dev sits with Hector in a corner booth. Dev looks a little tense, given his present company, but lately the two men have been able to put aside their differences and work together somewhat amicably.

"We will have a small demonstration the following day," Cato continues, and I catch Elena's gaze, a sympathetic tug at her mouth. Even she seems sorry for my predicament, and I'm not sure if that's reassuring or not. With a quiet sigh I peer out the large window.

We've been in flight for about an hour, and the dark landscape has gone from the grassy field closer to the city of Terra to the sandy desert I remember visiting with Dev when he showed me the Sea of Dreams. I can just make out its blue glow on the horizon, the racing stars above curving in the sky to reach their desired resting place—the Sea where they can finally dream. The tragic event that occurred the last time I was there, with Alec, settles like a weight in my stomach, and I push my mind to other things.

Studying the barren landscape, I wonder how much longer we have in flight. Dev told me Port City is the closer of the three smaller outposts of Terra, and I know these aircrafts can travel at an almost lightning speed, yet we're moving at a leisurely pace. Something about this causes me to shift in discomfort, for taking one's time has never been something I've been able to afford.

"Molly." Cato brings my attention aback to him, his wrinkled face set in another signature pucker. "Have you been listening?"

"Yes," I say quickly. "I'm not to speak about my DNA transfer or mention Rae becoming human."

Cato taps his ringed pinky on his crossed knee, seeming a little put out that I was, in fact, listening. "You understand the importance of this, yes?"

"No, actually." I turn completely toward him. "Isn't Rae's sacrifice an important one? Shouldn't he be honored in some way?"

"His close Vigil friends know what he did," Elena says. "And his name will be added to our wall."

My fingers dig into my armrest. "But he's not *dead*."

Cato raises one delicate brow, as if to say, *And?*

I resist a growl. "All of Terra deserves to know what he did. *Rae* deserves it."

This elicits an amused snort as Cato flicks a speaking glance to Elena. "Molly, really, use your head. What do you think would happen if the citizens of Terra—if the *Nocturna*," he clarifies, "knew they had a chance to see Earth, of having a potential life there?" My silence seems to be his desired response, for he nestles more smugly in his chair. "Exactly," he says. "This was an experiment done under extreme desperation and will *not* be repeated. It cannot be. Life here is already too delicate for such a technology to exist, let alone the fact that it would most definitely be used in the black market, thus making it unmanageable. Our anonymity from Earth would be sabotaged, and I hardly care to imagine what humans would do if they knew of us. I mean, by the stars, races from your own neighboring countries are hardly allowed to pass your American borders. It would be chaos."

I chew my bottom lip. I know when Riki was alive, her village seemed to know of Terra, but the world was much smaller then. Differences in faith was something universally understood and accepted, not fought over. What would happen if Earth knew of this place? I hate to admit that Cato's prediction is correct, but the more I think about it, the more I find myself begrudgingly agreeing.

"Am I correct in thinking we've covered everything?" Elena asks Cato, her composed form not moving an inch since we took off. Her hands are still politely folded in her white lap, her chin-length hair coiffed just right.

Cato answers by waving a tired hand.

"If you'd like"—Elena turns to me with a knowing grin—"you may sit with your friends now."

With a grateful nod, I make my way to Dev. Upon seeing my approach, his scruff-filled face showcases a welcoming smile, and he makes room for me beside him in the booth, where I slide into the crook of his arm.

"How was it?" he asks.

"*Riveting*," I say with as much sarcasm as I can muster.

"And that's where I don't envy you." Hector drapes one arm across the back of the beige leather couch across form us, his longs legs set in an impressive sprawl into the aisle.

"You mean you'd gladly be responsible for the life of two worlds otherwise?" I ask with mocking raised brows.

"No," he muses. "I suppose not. But I would be *more* than happy to conjure anything at will. I'm rather surprised you don't more often."

I'm distracted by a passing steward asking if I need anything. Declining any refreshments, I turn back to Hector, taking in the way his usually severe scar appears softer under the warm lighting of the ship. "It takes more focus than you'd think," I say. "And...I don't know. I forget sometimes."

Hector laughs. "*You forget?* By the stars, Molly, you really are the chosen one, aren't you?"

"Stop it." Dev cuts a glare at the Vigil.

"I'm not trying to be insulting." Hector settles more comfortably in his seat. "I honestly find that incredible."

"Find what incredible?" I ask.

"You." He waves a graceful hand toward me. "Such humility. Do you know what others would be doing right about now if they had your powers? Everything but what you are now, probably."

"And that's why they don't have her powers," Dev says dryly.

"Perhaps." Hector drums his fingers on the back of the couch while looking back to me.

"Why, what do *you* think I should be 'conjuring up'"—I air quote—"right about now?"

"A gluttony of food or music," Hector suggests. "I mean, at the very least some beautiful women to help us pass the time."

"I'll be sure to share that last part with Aveline." Dev cocks an unamused brow.

Hector merely gives him a slick smile.

"So you'd want me to use my powers on frivolity?" I cross my arms over my chest.

"One man's frivolity is another man's treasure."

"That's not how the saying goes," I clarify.

"No?" he says in faux confusion. "Well, it should be."

I regard him for a moment, the way he carries himself with such indifference and yet such grace—a bored royal. "And you and my grandfather really got along?"

Hector immediately stiffens, his mocking grin changing into a tight line. "Like brothers."

"Hmm" is my only response, watching my Vigil guard sit up straighter, his attention moving to other parts of the ship. I still haven't learned what exactly happened between him and my grandfather, why Hector grows so uncomfortable any time I mention him. I never seem to get the right opportunity to approach the subject, but I realize now could be just that.

"We're here." Dev peers out the window to our right, and I move closer.

"Whoa." I breathe, taking in the scene below. In the middle of the dry terrain rests a large lake, the waves twinkling from boats soaring across the water. Right in the center is a blue glowing city settled on ringed strips of land. They start small in the middle and then grow larger, like a ripple with water canals dividing each from the other. As we fly nearer, I notice the variant of bridges that connect them and sleek-looking boats that fill the channels. Our ship tilts, turning in the direction of one of the central buildings on the middle island. Its metal sides jut high into the night, pulsing with the familiar blue-white often found in Terra. I make out a crowd gathered on the roof where we're to land, and my hand finds Dev's as my heart picks up pace.

He turns to me, his azure gaze steady. "You'll be perfect," he says softly.

My attention slides back to what draws near. "I hope so, since it's my only option these days."

"Not with me." The seriousness in his tone has me glancing at him. "Not with me." And with a quick, gentle kiss that does a rather good job at calming my nerves, we turn back to the window and enjoy the last few moments of quiet before the noise of responsibility floods in.

Chapter 26

THE MOMENT WE step out of the ship, only one thought consumes me, and I hate to admit that it's a shallow one—I have absolutely no idea how celebrities do it. How on earth do they function, let alone not become blinded and deaf by the flashing of so many cameras and the yelling of so many people wanting their attention? While I wasn't completely oblivious to some of the press coverage the elders were allowing, I still had no idea it would feel quite like this. Screw Cato's rules of etiquette and proper topics of conversation. He should have stuck me in a booth with millions of sparking lights and taught me to keep my eyes open while smiling like I wasn't in pain.

I'm terrified of the video footage that the hovering cameras are capturing of me exiting the ship. I can already see the headlines: "Dreamer Appears to Have a Nightmare upon Landing in Port City." Or something of the like. But as much as I want to shield my face and possibly fall into a fetal position, I manage to force my head up and allow my Vigil guards to move me through the crowd. Elena's white dress walks in front, acting as my focal point, and I can feel Dev and Hector at my back, the inner circle to my inner circle. I'm desperately thankful I have them with me. Yes, even Hector.

The next moments are a flurry of meeting the awaiting Port City delegates, eight in total, and whose names leave my mind just as soon as they are uttered. I smile and shake hands and then turn for more smiling as Cato whispers for me to face the press before entering the next transport, the next destination the start of our walking tour. I barely keep from diving into the smaller airship, the interior's quiet a gift from the gods, and take a seat in a far corner. The rest of the entourage filters in, and I notice one of the delegates, a particularly smart-looking redhead, smiling familiarly at Dev as he talks to the group. He says something that has them laughing before he turns, seeking me out. As embarrassing as it is to admit, I find myself momentarily distracted by his graceful strides and the way his long-sleeved black shirt hints at his impressive build as he removes the quiver across his back. Clearing my throat, I sit up straighter and tear my gaze away before he catches me in my ogling act. Terra knows I don't need his smug teasing right about now. But as I move my attention elsewhere, I notice the redhead from earlier just as transfixed on the back of Dev as I am on his front, and I purse my lips as her eyes settle on a much-lower part of his anatomy. I mean, *really*, doesn't she know staring is rude? There's a wink of light on her arm—a Dreamer repellent band. I know all the delegates have them on as a precaution, but for some reason seeing it on this woman is like a child facing a button that says *Do Not Push*. I want nothing more than to test just how well it works.

"You okay?" Dev's asks as he takes a seat next to me.

His face is close, close enough to kiss, and I can't help thinking, *Wouldn't that be shocking?* Dev and my relationship isn't meant to be a secret, but I also know showing my need for him in such a public way could easily put each of us at a disadvantage. Weaknesses, especially of the heart, are the best fodder for an enemy—a horrible lesson I learned from Vibius and especially Aaron. So despite my immature need to publically claim him in front of a certain someone, I resist.

Realizing Dev's been waiting for me to answer, I say "Yeah" and half smile.

But his shrewd gaze misses nothing, and I know he doesn't believe me, yet he lets the matter drop. "I haven't been back here in a long time," he says, kicking one ankle to rest on his knee and facing the open haul of the ship. "It's nice to visit again."

I follow the direction of his gaze, taking in the mostly oc-cupied padded seats that line either side of the transport's dark interior. Where our larger ship was lit with warm hues of yellow and beige and comfortable seating areas, this is painted with the usual Terra grays and black of their military vehicles.

"Did you know Port City is the oldest outpost to Terra?" Dev asks. "Our other two are fairly new."

"Which means they're still probably older than America."

"Probably." He smiles.

"How come the Nursery doesn't count as a city?" I ask.

"It's more of a facility, a compound of sorts. It relies on Terra for most of its day-to-day needs. I think if it was more self-sus-taining it could be considered one, but as it is now, it's too small. And even though it has the most concentrated storage of Navitas, it's rather fragile and serves mainly one purpose."

Ever since learning about the Nursery, I've been so curious about the place where Terra's population is delicately managed. No memories of it are available for me from past Dreamers, and I didn't see it on Cato's list of tour stops. I wonder if I could suggest a possible visit.

"You'll love it here," Dev says. "The Vigil claim it has similarities to Venice. Have you been there?" I shake my head. "I've always wanted to go though."

"Have you traveled much of Earth?"

"I did a road trip across the States and have visited some countries in South America, but I haven't had the chance to go beyond that." I pause, realizing something. "Well, actually…if I can count my Dreamer memories, then I've been almost all over the globe."

A charming grin lights up Dev's face. "I think you can more than count them."

With a shared smile I turn back to the ship's interior and soberly realize what I thought was a private conversation between two people was actually a very public tête-à-tête. For all the eyes of our new Port City companions are curiously pinned to us. With a swallow, I remember. Here I am no longer Molly. Here I can only be the Dreamer.

→━● ●━←

Dev's prediction on how I would feel about Port City is more than accurate. In fact, it might have been an understatement. As we set out on our walking tour, I'm exposed to beautifully paved streets that line the edges of breathtaking canals. The winding water shimmers with silver as the sleek boats ride the waves, their sails billowing in the constant breeze, white puffs speeding forward. This metropolis is very much a city that embraces its surroundings, for every detail has some sort of reference to the lake, to water, and to what must swim within it. Fish are a largely used emblem, gracing windows in blue-stained glass or placed into the names of passing establishments, all with the facades of large gray stones. The crest of waves curls along metal railings of bridges, and even the uniforms of the people have a more navy hue than black.

And speaking of people, they fill both sides of the streets to capacity. Everyone has come to see the Dreamer. And while I see a few regarding me with hesitant stares, with mistrust, the majority cheer my arrival and even reach out in a desperate weeping gesture. Yes, actually friggin' *weeping*. As if I were some savior whose touch could create miracles. They call my name, and when I go to them—my Vigil guards sticking close beside me—to shake their hands, they grip me tight and sputter their thanks, their praise. The Metus attack on this port right before I was cut off is clearly still in their minds. But despite the discomforting adoration, nothing is as unnerving as seeing the men and women who have streaked a part of their hair white.

Unconsciously I touch my bleached strands that are pulled back into my ponytail, and the few who wear the fashion yell louder, as if my movement was a purposeful acknowledgment of their visual dedication. I drop my hand. This is too much. Don't they know I'm just as much flesh and blood as they? But despite my discomfort, I keep smiling, understanding the thing I represent is more important than any truth I might feel about myself. Terra needs this, needs a Dreamer, and I will give them that for as long as I can. So I continue to nod and murmur my words of comfort, of appreciation, and when the requests become unbearable, concede to demonstrate my powers, Cato's schedule of me reserving that for tomorrow be damned. As we walk along the river's edge, I pull creatures I suspect a town like this would appreciate into existence. With the coolness collecting in my mind, I envision manta ray to float and flap their large gray wings beside me, their tales swooshing as they glide forward. I call streams of water from the nearby canal to arch overtop of us, imagining multicolored fish to swim within, a ceiling of aquatic life. Pink jellyfish puff through the air, their tentacles harmless as they string out behind them, occasionally passing over an outreached hand. The crowd gasps, applauds, and squeals. Even the doubters are unable to hold back their smiles as they stare up at the wonder. Each and every one of the citizens' happy souls reaches out to me, and despite not being in the plane of energy, I can sense the brightness, the good intentions, and positivity. Their simple desire to merely live a life of peace and beauty. All of it feeds my energy, sending my creations to spark with new vigor. I can feel myself growing stronger, a similar euphoria I experienced when I stood on the balcony in City Hall Square after my demonstration. Taking in the collective pureness of those present is so overwhelming that it threatens to bring me to tears, and it's in this moment when I realize what I'm truly fighting for, what we *all* are. The blessing of existence, the miracle that is creating and imagining, and I take in a stuttering breath as this settles deep within my heart. Gazing across the people, their hope palpable among the lapping water and the shooting stars overhead, I pray for one thing—

That I won't let them down.

Chapter 27

To say that I'd rather be curling up in the giant fluffy bed that greets me as I walk into my private suite than attending my honorary dinner would be 100 percent accurate. Despite the energy the crowd momentary afforded me, I feel drained, empty, exhausted. So after my guards sweep my room, I let out a giant sigh as they shut the door behind them to stand in the hall outside, finally, blissfully, leaving me alone.

Removing my quiver—more of a prop these days—I sag into a nearby chair, its cushions embracing me with softness. "Thank you, beautiful silence," I murmur and kick my booted feet onto the marble coffee table. Glancing around I take in the Grecian-style architecture of my quarters. Despite the more modest homes that lined the various canals in the city, the hotel I'm staying at is grand to the extreme. My suite features a large open foyer that connects to the living room where I sit, which then opens to a balcony, a bedroom off in one direction, and a bathroom that's the size of my studio back in New York. As my gaze swings back to the table in front of me, I spy a plate of cookies resting next to a large bouquet of flowers and a tray with a pot of coffee.

Coffee!

I nearly fall out of my chair as I sit up.

They have coffee!

I want to cry. I am crying.

I have no idea how they've acquired it, since Terra has no need for the caffeinated beverage, but even if they went to extreme and unnecessary lengths, I can't bring myself to feel bad. I mean, it's coffee! Pouring myself a large cup, I ignore the burn of drinking it too soon and gulp it down.

"Ah." I audibly sigh. "I love you, sweet beans from the gods."

I wish Rae were here. He'd have a thing or two to say about the ridiculous grin now plastered on my face. Becca would defend my enthusiasm without question, of course, sharing my obsession for the holy liquid. As the thought of them has me softly laughing, it just as quickly fills me with a sudden pang of homesickness. Which is rather odd, considering I've never missed home when I've been in Terra before... In fact, I hardly ever thought about it. But this time, with everything that's going on, all the pressure and needs for my attention, I'm actually missing my simple life back on Earth. Don't get me wrong—I *certainly* don't miss being cut off or only being able to travel here while I sleep. I just miss... well, the slight reprieve it offers. The ability to take a deep breath between all this. I wonder when I'll have the chance to go back, how everyone is doing. Is Becca handling pretending to be me and texting my parents to keep their calls at bay? I cringe. Please let her not be as bad as Rae.

The sound of approaching footsteps in the outside hall brings my attention back to the present, and a smile edges my lips. Dev must be coming to see me before the event. Nerves flutter in my stomach. We practically ignored each other on the walking tour, him keeping an official distance away while playing the part of another one of my guards. Running a hand down my T-shirt that doesn't need fixing, I head for the door, ready to give him a proper hello. But when the large wooden frame opens, I come up short, seeing someone who's very much *not* Dev. A tall, striking women walks in, her spaghetti-strapped seafoam-green dress swaying like liquid by her heeled feet, the silk cascading down her pale skin, while her gray hair is tied into a neat, high bun on top her head, bringing attention to her startling almond-shaped silver eyes.

"Sonja?" I say in shock.

The Vigil scientist that I last saw before I stepped through the portal in the Brooklyn lab gives me a friendly smile. "Hello, Molly."

"What are you doing here?"

"I was asked to attend," she says, stepping farther into my suite and glancing around. "Elena thought it might be beneficial to have as many people you've been connected with at tonight's event. Your friends Tim and Aveline were supposed to accompany me, but a small matter with the Metus unfortunately kept them back in Terra. But don't worry. I can more than vouch for you and your good intentions." She winks.

I slowly realize this gala dinner is going to be more of an interrogation.

"How have you been?" I ask, walking with her to the sofas, and as we sit, I take in her light fruity fragrance.

"Great." She leans forward to grab a cookie. "More than great actually. The success of our experiment with you and Rae has really opened up a lot. Dr. Mackenzie and I have been able to make huge headway on a few projects we previously were hitting a dead end on." She wipes a crumb from her lip after taking a bite of the dessert. "Of course, it's nothing quite as severe as what we did with you, but it will definitely help the medical community."

"Oh, well, that's good," I say, remembering the name of the human scientist Sonja was working with at Vita Corp. I wonder if Dr. Mackenzie has any curiosity about *why* they've made such sudden progress. "How's Rae?" I ask, pouring another cup of coffee, and when she declines any for herself, I'm secretly relieved. Yes, I'm a coffee hoarder.

"He's doing well," Sonja says. "Still getting used to some things, like being able to sleep, but doing well nonetheless."

My brows raise. "I never thought about that—that this would be his first time sleeping. Does he like it? Oh!" I lean forward. "Has he had any dreams?"

"No, he hasn't reported dreaming yet." She shakes her head. "But he definitely finds sleeping strange. And I can certainly understand why. I would *hate* to be so mentally vulnerable and shut off."

Hunh. I never thought about sleeping in that way, being vulnerable, but I guess if I were someone like Sonja, who is constantly using her brain, it would make sense. "Wait…" I nearly drop my cup. "Does that mean…could he potentially come back to Terra if he does? Dream, that is."

Sonja regards me with a sympathetic smile. "No, Molly, I don't think that, even with him dreaming, he'd be given access to be in Terra like you were. He's not a chosen Dreamer, after all. He'd merely be one of the many passing stars."

"Oh." My shoulders droop in disappointment.

"But I do have something that might make you feel better."
She lifts her small golden clutch and snaps it open. "These are
from Becca and Rae." She hands me two sealed envelopes, and
my heart jumps. I want to rip them open, but I miraculously hold
off, preferring to be alone when I read.

Sonja seems to understand this, for she nods ever so slightly
and stands. "Well," she says, "it seems our Cinderella has a ball
to attend, and lucky for you, your fairy godmother happens to be
standing right here." Walking to a side table, she presses a button
beside the com, and after a short beat, the doors to my suite swing
open and in enter a man and a woman pulling a rack with more
designer dresses than I'd ever be comfortable trying on in New
York. They give me radiant grins as they begin to set up.

"What's this?" I ask.

Sonja does a quick sweep of my body. "Did you think you'd
be attending the dinner dressed as you are now?"

I look down at my black uniform. "Um…"

"Precisely." She pulls out dress after dress. "Now you can
either go take a quick shower or Dreamer yourself fresh and
clean. Either way, when you get back here, we're going to have
a bit of fun," she says before turning to the two stylists. "We'll
need something gold if she wears this one, and her lips will
have to be a cherry pink and—*by the star*, definitely *not* this one.
Remove it from the rack altogether and hand me that teal number, will you?"

My eyes widen in silent respect. Who knew lab-rat Sonja was
a closet fashionista?

⊶⊷

The opulent hotel lobby is filled with the echo of our steps along the smooth stone floor as I follow my entourage of guards into tonight's event. Large Ionic columns of silver and white stretch up to an arched ceiling, where a depiction of the sea is painted in swirls and crashes of indigo blue waves, while hanging chandeliers of Navitas cause the water to appear in motion with its spinning light. Taking it all in, I try not to trip in my heels.

After spending a majority of my time in my flat, sturdy boots, I forgot the skill it takes to manage stilettos. Why I decided to go with such strappy ones is beyond me, but it seemed I couldn't help going all out with Sonja by my side, especially after she pulled out a deep-blue scoop-neck, floor-length dress that shimmered with bits of violet as she turned it under the lights. It felt like baby wings as I draped the thick silk over my body, feeling it hug all the right curves in a flattering silhouette. As I caught my reflection in the mirror, I actually became a little breathless. With a team of people helping, I certainly cleaned up nicely.

Yet despite feeling like a princess, I also feel incredibly vulnerable. Without the protective layer of my black clothes and weapon-ready uniform, I can't help the sensation of being extremely exposed, almost naked. My arms are uncovered, my back bare to where the soft material rests right above the dip in my lower spine, and my hair is down, resting in waves around my shoulders. I've never showed this much skin…well, ever.

I knew tonight's dinner was going to be a big deal, but I hadn't realized what a black-tie affair it was, and my fingers flutter nervously by my side as I walk. I was hoping to enter with Dev, but Sonja said he had something to attend to and would be running a bit late. Even though disappointment settled in my chest,

I pushed it away, needing as much composure as I could muster. So as I make my way through the hotel, I keep my shoulders back and my chin held high, ignoring the curious stares and whispers of the few hotel guests who have been cleared to remain in occupancy. They fill the main floor of the lobby as my horde of soldiers and I walk through. The entire establishment, in fact, is peppered with guards, and if they ever wanted my presence to be inconspicuous, they certainly chose the wrong tactic.

"We're almost there, ma'am. It's just through these doors." One of my Vigil chaperones, who I've learned is called Odi, says to my right. He seems to sense my unease, and I give him a grateful smile, catching the way his inky-black hair tints red under the lights. With the addition of his big brown eyes and beautifully tanned skin, if he were from Earth, I'd guess his heritage lay in India.

After passing another security checkpoint, I enter a lavish room, where another large decorative chandelier of Navitas is set in the center, pulsing blue-white above the small gathering. The sound of my heels clicking against the black-and-white checkered tile floor seems to lift a few nearby heads, and then it's like a wave of realization goes through the room, and everyone stops their conversations to take in my appearance.

I hold back a nervous swallow.

"Molly." Elena materializes next to me. "You look exquisite."

"Thank you," I say. "So do you."

And she really does. Wearing a silver-gray wrap dress that ties around her neck, her milky skin is exposed, bringing her blue eyes to startling vibrancy. Her hair is pulled back in a simple twist.

"Thank you." She smiles. "Let me introduce you to some of the delegates. They've been very anxious for your arrival."

I merely nod, not trusting my voice to not waver.

As Elena guides me to one corner where a few Nocturna delegates stand, the room slowly resumes its buzz of conversation. Immediately I notice the redhead from earlier within this group. While her hair color might be the same as my best friend's, it's the only visual trait they share. Where Becca is a summer breeze of friendliness, this woman is sleek, painted in gloss, her burgundy mane pencil straight and draped to her moss-green waist. A waist, I might add, that's close to the same circumference of a quarter. I mean, dear God, how is she able to remain standing? She talks with two men of similar age—well, they at least *look* to be in their forties. One is short with a jovially round belly that stretches the material of his gray suit, while the other is stockier with wide shoulders and a thick head of white hair.

"Coretta, Elek, and Ormond." Elena gestures to the three. "I'd like to once again present to you our Dreamer, Molly."

We nod our hellos.

"That was a marvelous show you put on today," the small, rounder delegate, Elek, says to me with a slight bounce. "We were just discussing how remarkable it was, weren't we, Ormond."

"Quite," Ormond agrees.

"Thank you," I murmur.

"So how does it work exactly?" Elek goes on, his brown eyes bright with curiosity.

"Using my powers?" I ask.

"Mmm."

"Um...I'm not really sure how best to describe it." I catch Coretta's unwavering stare. She seems to be measuring my every move and word. "But I guess it's a bit like when you get thirsty or hungry."

The two men's brows scrunch.

"How so?" Ormond asks.

"Well, when you're hungry, do you start to think about what you'd like to eat? Start to visualize a particular food?"

They both nod.

"If you were to concentrate harder on that, really hold it in your mind, if you were a Dreamer, you could eventually imagine it into existence."

"Incredible," Elek breathes.

"That's a bit too easy, don't you think?" Coretta says dubiously.

"Well, I was trying to explain it simply." I give her a sweet smile, which she does not return. "While what I explained might sound easy, it's my own energy. It still takes a great amount of concentration and is not a limitless ability. I can and do get drained from using it too much."

"Then let's hope you have a high amount of stamina." Elek chuckles.

"Yes, we'd hate to lose a fight against the Metus because our Dreamer has gotten tired," Coretta mutters, and takes a sip of her wine.

Elek shoots her a reproachful glance, while Ormond merely seems amused.

"You have nothing to fear," Elena chimes in, a confident smile lighting her face. "Our Vigil engineers have been busy creating things to aid Molly with her power and make sure she's more than equipped in battle."

"Excellent." Elek claps his hands together.

"Will we see some of this equipment?" Ormond asks.

"Most certainly." Elena nods. "Now if you will excuse us, I would like Molly to chat with the other delegates before we sit for dinner."

"Thank you," I whisper to Elena as she guides me away from the group. I still feel Coretta's narrowed gaze on the back of my neck.

"Don't thank me yet," the elder says. "That was merely the warm-up."

I groan. Stick me in a room full of Metus, and I'd be more comfortable than I am now.

"You'll make it through," Elena says, sensing my distress, and with a knowing look adds, "You have with worse."

The predinner conversations carry on in a similar fashion, Cato eventually taking over Elena's position, much to my dismay, and making sure I say at least one word to everyone in attendance. Throughout all of it though, my gaze can't stop moving through the room, wondering when I'll see a certain Nocturna male. But just when I turn to tell Cato I'm going to search Dev out, I catch a tall, dark figure making his way through the main doors.

And as he comes into view from a break in the crowd, I lose all sense of thought.

Dev stands in an impeccably tailored black suit, the lines simple and straight, the top two buttons of his charcoal-colored dress shirt unbuttoned, allowing his smooth, taught skin underneath to peek through. His face showcases his signature day-old scruff, now slightly manicured, but only just, his strong jaw appearing even more defined and enticing. His blue eyes spark bright, a churning, seductive energy surrounding him as he takes in the room. I have to remind myself that he's not only a warrior on the battlefield but in the political arena as well. He *would* find tonight a pleasing game to maneuver and win. I'm rendered paralyzed watching him. He's so beautiful, so consuming, and I have a jolt of satisfaction that he's all mine.

As if he can sift through all the stares pinned to him, he finds mine. His gaze lingers from my eyes, down my body, then back up again, my cheeks growing flush, my skin too warm, and I pray to all of Terra that I'm not also raising the temperature in the room. Dev's features grow dark as he steps toward me, his lips parting slightly, the bottom one weighted and wanting to be bitten. I force myself to look away in case I cause the whole room to burst into flames. Dear God, this man is too good looking.

But before Dev can reach me, someone announces dinner, and Cato pulls me toward the dining room. I glance over my shoulder, finding Dev regarding my retreating form in silent frustration. *The feeling's mutual*, I want to yell. Instead, I'm hoping we're seated next to each other.

We are *not* seated next to each other.

Elek and Sonja sit on either side of me, my two dinner companions, and then Hector beside Sonja. The table stretches out to accommodate up to fifty guests, delicate plating and ornate cutlery resting in front of each diner, our wineglasses never lowering below two sips before a server swoops in to refill it. Rich foods steaming with exotic fragrances are set in an unending stream in front of us, and by the fourth course, I feel like I'm going to pass out from overindulgence.

The only solace I have is that Dev is sitting across from me. But even as I'm grateful for this small mercy, it's offset by who's beside him. I have a feeling she planned it this way. Coretta laughs at something Dev says, placing a hand on his arm. A hot bubble of annoyance crawls up my throat. *Breathe*, I tell myself for the fifth time since sitting down. It wouldn't do well for me to imagine her wineglass pouring all over that green dress of hers. I smile. Or maybe...

"So, Molly," Elek says beside me. "What do you think of our city?"

I turn to my cherub-cheeked companion, who, to be fair, has been rather enjoyable. He's seems nice enough, with his easy laugh and gift for finding the humor in all things. He just has this *tiny* habit of chewing with his mouth open, like a cow with hay. But thankfully, he's sans food right now.

"I find it beautiful." I give him a genuine smile. "I love how the visual of water is incorporated into a lot of the architecture."

Elek puffs up with pleasure. "I'm glad you noticed. Port City may be smaller than Terra, but we pride ourselves in the arts." He leans in conspiratorially. "Did you know we are considered the capital of culture in Terra?"

"I didn't know that." I tilt my head with interest. "But it doesn't come as a surprise. I can tell everyone here has impeccable taste. Oh, and before I forget, I wanted to thank you."

He blinks. "For what?"

"Given your obvious knowledge in fashion"—I wave to his suit—"I can only assume you had some influence with the dresses I was to choose from tonight. They were all stunning."

Elek practically squeals under my praise. "Oh, yes, well, they *do* say I have a bit of an eye for such things."

"I have no doubt they do." I nod.

Turning back to my plate, I catch Dev watching me. His mouth is curled in a half-amused grin, his eyes twinkling in a strange intensity that flips my stomach over.

What? I mouth silently to him.

You, he mouths back.

I bite back a smile.

"I see you have your eyes set higher these days, Dev." Coretta's voice cuts through our moment, and he turns to her. She pierces a glance my way. "But from what I remember of *our time* together, you were always ready to take on a challenge."

The emphasis she put on *our time* was really unnecessary, but she clearly wants to drive the point home.

"We seem to be in agreement there," Dev says, and Coretta frowns.

"We are?"

"Yes." He looks at me again. "Molly is certainly worth fighting for."

I choke on a laugh and then meet Coretta's annoyed gaze head on. "And so is he," I say.

If that wasn't a clear enough statement to back the Metus up, I don't know what is.

The dinner finishes with an absurdly delicious chocolate dessert, one that might have moved me to steal a forkful off of Sonja's plate when she wasn't looking, much to Elek's delight, before we're ushered into a parlor room.

Needing a bit of air before I'm launched once more into the dance of political conversation, I seek out Odi and ask if there's somewhere I can pop out for a moment. "It will just be quick," I assure him when he regards me hesitantly, and then to seal the deal, say, "Cato told me to step out if I was feeling a meltdown about to happen, and it's definitely about to happen." I cross my eyes for a moment while feigning a drunk's expression.

He sighs, his broad shoulders losing their stiffness. "Follow me." Grabbing a few more guards, he walks me down a side hall. "Ten minutes," he says as he opens two tall bay doors that lead to a courtyard.

I nod, an obedient child. "Could you…maybe also wait in here?" I ask and then seeing him about to say no, add, "The entire hotel has been swept, and this is a contained courtyard. I just need a *little* sense of privacy. A second. Please, I've been surrounded by people nonstop."

He frowns.

"*Please.*" I say again, hitting him full force with what, I hope, are my biggest puppy-dog eyes.

"Fine," he grumbles. "But we'll be *right* in here."

"Yes, of course!" And without giving him an opportunity to change his mind, I skip into the open night.

It's only a little chilly on my bare skin, but the salty freshness of the sea air is a welcome relief.

I duck under a small hedged doorway to enter the center of the courtyard, my pace slowing. For in the middle is the most beautiful fountain I've ever seen. Bursting through a multitude of twisting marble waves is a large coiling serpent, its scales a variety of silvers that sparkle and shine under the quickly passing stars.

A variety of fish, their colors changing in rainbow shades, lap in the pool below, a few jumping out to slurp up the streams of water that pour out of the snake's mouth. Its head is tilted up to the night sky, and I listen to the soothing rhythm of the cascading liquid.

Elek was more than correct in saying this place excelled in the arts. Everything I've seen so far has such attention to detail and obvious love in being created, this fountain a prime example. The water trickles peacefully in front of me, calming the small throb in my head from tonight's activities.

I'm so lost in the moment that I don't sense him approaching until his intoxicating scent of night and spice wraps around me. My heart skips a beat.

"Did you know the serpent is one of the oldest mythological symbols in both our worlds?" Dev's deep voice slides over me just as the shadow of his nearness does, his large form eclipsing the light, and I briefly close my eyes. He doesn't touch me, not yet, but I feel his heat against every inch of my exposed skin.

"It represents the duality of good and evil," he continues softly. "In Port City, it is particularly important because of its connection to water."

He lets his words hang in the air and weave into the ripples expanding at the base of the fountain, right before I feel a light, secretive trace of his finger draw a line down the center of my back. My shiver is instant. He slips my hair to one shoulder as his lips graze the back of my ear.

"You've been magnificent," he says, his breath hot on my skin, soaking into me like a quick fog on a mirror. I barely hold back a moan. Slowly, with hands that retain so much strength, he smooths them over my hips, turning me around so I find his blue gaze burning hotter than the stars that fly overhead. "*You're* magnificent," he clarifies, tugging me forward for a kiss.

If there was ever a moment to swoon, this would be it. With legs already made weak by my ridiculous choice of footwear, I slump, putty in his hands. His strong grip holds me up against his broad chest, and my hands wrap around his neck. His mouth is soft but demanding, and I run my fingers through his short-cropped hair, bringing his mouth closer. He groans, and I can sense him trying to control himself.

"I can imagine us back in my room," I say breathlessly between kisses. "*Very* easily," I add, my own inside joke to Coretta's earlier remark.

With a small chuckle, Dev pulls back. "We can't," he says as his hands roam down to my backside, where he gives a gentle squeeze. "But by the stars do I wish we could."

"We can do anything," I say and kiss him again, but he moves back—again, his gaze suddenly serious. "What?"

"We can, can't we?"

"Can what?"

"Do anything. You and I."

I smile, my heart filling. "Yes," I say. "We can."

"I love you." He brings his lips to mine, his arms remaining securely around me.

"I love you too."

"When I saw you in this dress tonight..." A low growl escapes him. "All I thought was, thank Terra you're mine."

I laugh.

"I wouldn't think that would be considered funny," he says.

"It's not. It's just that I thought the same exact thing when I saw you in this suit." I run my hand over the finely woven material. "It's the first time I've seen you in anything but your uniform."

"That's not true. You've seen me naked."

"Dev." I snort. "That doesn't count."

"If you're trying to decide what I look better in, I think it does."

"*Dev.*"

He merely gives me a coy grin. "Well, doesn't it?"

I roll my eyes and flicker a glance behind him, finding the far doorway empty. "Where's Odi and the rest of my guards?"

"I told them to leave."

I lift my brows, astonished. "And they listened?"

"They know you're more than safe with me."

I scoff. "But yet the one who's supposed to have limitless powers and the ability to save two worlds can't take care of herself."

He shrugs. "Their rules, not mine. Though I tend to agree with anything that will keep you out of harm's way."

"You do realize what I'm meant to do here, right?"

"Yes, but it's not Metus I'm worried about."

I regard him a moment, take in the way his brows pinch in slightly, his gaze sliding away from me. "You're worried about your own people." It's not a question.

"People can be a very different kind of beast."

"Yes," I agree softly, the terrorism and violence happening on Earth enough of a testament to this. Feeling the need to change the subject, I ask, "Where were you earlier? That made you late?"

My question pops us out of our moment, and Dev drops his arms from around my waist to run a hand through his hair. "I had to take a call with the Council."

"Oh?" I wait for him to elaborate, which he seems less than pleased to do.

He takes a deep breath. "It's Aaron. His trial date has been set."

I feel my face paling. I actually managed a few days without thinking about the man. "When is it?"

Dev's eyes dance to mine. "Tomorrow."

"Tomorrow?" My chin juts back.

He nods.

"But...I have to be there."

His eyes cut to mine. "No, you don't."

"Yes, I do."

"Molly—"

"No, Dev. This is the man who tried to kill me, remember? I should be there for his sentencing. I'm surprised they don't need me to testify."

"We decided against it."

My mouth hangs open at the knowledge that he had a say in it.

"Your testimony wasn't going to be necessary," he adds quickly. "Aaron's fate is already firmly sealed regardless of you getting on the stand."

This I, of course, knew. Termination. A sentencing that is very, *very*, uncommon in Terra, life being as precious as it is. But even so, I don't know for sure whether this is what Aaron will get.

"Dev," I try again, more calmly this time. "I have to be there. If not for me, then for Aurora."

This only seems to unnerve him more, some hidden emotion flickering through his teal-tipped eyes, but after he clenches and then unclenches his fists he says, "Okay."

I stand, shocked. "Okay?"

"Yes," he sighs. "I'm coming to learn what I can and can't fight you on."

I deflate a little, relieved. "Thank you."

"Don't thank me yet," he says, his words strangely echoing Elena's from earlier, and without either of us saying it, we feel the whispers of our next thoughts.

No matter tomorrow's outcome, either way won't be good.

Chapter 28

A HORRIBLE THING happens when returning to work after a vacation. Somehow all my memories of the blissful hours lying in the sun, drinking margaritas, and rising late are sucked from my brain and devoured by the mere act of walking back into the lobby of my job. I'm not saying my trip to Port City was like a beach vacation *or* that returning to Terra is anything like my old marketing job, but the few days away in another place, experiencing new things, did carry the illusion of a mini getaway. Maybe being near water helped weave this. Whatever it was, as I now sit in the intimidatingly cavernous courtroom back in Terra, it's like Port City never happened. Any confidence I gleaned there from the citizens accepting me or success I felt from properly maneuvering political conversations with the city delegates, it's all gone the moment I watch Aaron being led to the circular podium in the center of the large marble-domed chamber.

It's the first time I've seen him since the night he stuck a knife in my gut, and as if it's still lodged there, my hand unconsciously goes to cover the spot. Only soberness and anxious dread fill my veins as I take in his appearance. His frame is shockingly thin—now so much like his sister's—as his prison scrubs hang loosely on his shoulders. His once thick dirty-blond hair is now long, limp, and disheveled. But despite all this, his hazel eyes still hold a lucidness, a calculating air as he's shackled to his dais and glances around. The threat he poses still manages to exude from his weakened body, and as a tiny smile dances upon on his lips, I'm terrified of whatever sick thoughts swirl in his mind. How this was the jovial doctor who treated me at the hospital is mind boggling.

A mass of Navitas rests high in the ceiling and shines a blue-white spotlight directly onto him, bleaching his pallor further, and a packed house watches on in the shadowed bleachers that circle the space. Above them are three more balconies of onlookers. The sound of their collective whispers echoes in the chamber, the gray marbled space feeling cold despite so many bodies to warm it. My seat is in a heavily guarded private tier, receding enough into the wall that my presence is hopefully indiscernible. Yet I still shift restlessly, nervously, for I'm directly in front of Aaron, and my breath is in a constant state of being held, waiting for him to look up. But his attention is directly below me, on the elders and Council representatives who sit in the inner ring on the ground floor. Dev is among them, only the back of his head visible to me, and I look around wondering where Aurora is.

Tim, Aveline, and Hector sit in my box, Tim resting a hand on mine, a supportive nod, before facing forward once more. I chew my bottom lip, wondering which sentencing the old guardian is hoping for and strangely find my own desire just as illusive. Despite the amount of agony and fear I experienced when ripped from Terra, from Dev, I can't find it in me to hate Aaron, not enough to wish for his death. I mean, I came back in the end, right? There were repercussions to that of course, but none that actually took a life, in the literal sense. Plus, there's Aurora to consider. What would happen to her if her brother truly died? They say twins here have a bond greater than any other connection. Would she perish along with him? Or could she survive it?

The immediate hushing of the courtroom brings my attention to Elena standing below. "We are here to bear witness and judge the crimes of the accused—Vigil made Nocturna guard, Aaron." Her voice booms through the space, traveling all the way up to the farthest balcony. "Prisoner G543," she says to Aaron, "you have been accused of an unsanctioned abandonment of post, unauthorized dimension travel, wrongful impersonation, theft, and first-degree murder. How do you plea?"

Aaron gives no answer.

"Accused, how do you plead?" Elena repeats louder.

To that Aaron gives an inaudible mumbled response, his head now dipped down, his long curls hiding his face.

A small impatient sigh passes from Elena before I feel a ripple of energy shoot through the room and watch, in amazement, as Aaron's head gets thrown back, his back forced straight.

"*How do you plead?*" Elena forces a lightness to her tone. I hold in my surprise, while the rest of the onlookers shift uncomfortably. I've never seen Elena exhibit her powers like this before. Had no idea she even could. I glance to the other elders. How much Navitas are they capable of tapping into, using externally? I hate that I can find no instances of it in my memory Dreamer bank.

Aaron chokes, whatever power Elena has wrapped around him apparently not comfortable. "Guilty to all but one," he finally spits out.

A murmur goes through the crowd.

"And to which do you plead innocent?"

"Murder," he croaks.

Instantly, he slumps back into his chair, Elena releasing her grip.

"I see," she says. "What evidence do you have to fight against this accusation?"

A slow, twisted grin slides along his face. "Because she's not dead," he says, and then, just as I feared, his eyes travel up to find me in the shadows. "In fact, she's right here."

My skin erupts with a cold sweat, my stomach curling in on itself as the threat of bile climbs up my throat. My guards instantly step closer, all but blocking my view of the man who appears extremely pleased with himself.

People twist around to gaze where Aaron does, to see the Dreamer, me. Below, the Council and elders mutter among themselves, Dev the only one not part of their conversation. Instead he's turned, looking up at me, his brows drawn together in a severe frown. This is precisely what he feared, Aaron aware of my presence. But there's no way he can get to me from where I sit. Absolutely *no way*...

But as I glance down into Aaron's glistening, mad hazel eyes, I know that's not true. He's able to touch me just by holding my gaze, acknowledging that he sees me, *sees me*, and knows of my return. Phantom sensations of his hands wrapped around my neck, his hot breath on my skin as he whispered his words of hate surround me—the violation of it all. And like a switch, I'm suddenly angry, livid that he holds such power over me, even when he stands so far below, restrained. Despite my early convictions that he should be spared, a rage I've only felt at my darkest moments edges along my vision. *He should be punished*, it whispers. *He showed you no mercy. He took everything from you, everyone. Do the same.* The words echo in my mind, and I can't help the lick of dark-oil energy that pulls from my stomach, a fire directed straight at him, and before I know what I'm doing, Aaron is screaming in pain as I ignite his stand. The flames don't touch him, but I insert the illusion into his mind that his skin is burning, melting brutally to the bone.

The crowd shrieks in horror.

"Molly." Hector's calm but insistent voice breaks me out of my manifested revenge, and instantly I blink back to reality. Aaron's wails reduce to groans as the fire snaps out, leaving small wisps of smoke in its place. But just as the room is enveloped in a shocked silence, someone cries from the crowd, and I watch Aurora tumble down the bleachers on the first level, desperate to go to her brother, but snatched back by Ezekial.

"*What did she do to him*?!" she yells, struggling against Ezekial. "She can't do that!"

My nails dig into my chair's armrests as disgust, shame, and guilt slam into me. *What have I done?*

A laugh brings my attention back to the center of the room to find Aaron peering up at me. His skin is flushed red from my recent demonstration, sweat slipping down his cheek, dampening his already slick hair, and his lips are white rimmed and dry. But his eyes…his eyes are excited and wild as he continues to chortle in pleasure.

"You all should be thanking me," he spits out. "Look how dangerous she is! It could be anyone of you that our dear Dreamer decides to play with. Who's to stop her?"

"Quiet," Elena bellows. "If you cannot control your outbursts, we will see to it that you will not be allowed to speak."

"*Me* control my outbursts?" He laughs again. "Was it *me* who just set a man ablaze? Was it *me* who just lashed out when I have done nothing but answer your questions? Am I to be punished for *her* abuse of power?" He looks to the crowd. "Let what is happening to me be a warning to you all. Do not trust—"

His words are suddenly cut off as Elena uses her powers to silence him. Nodding to the nearby Nocturna guards, they approach Aaron and place a bind to his mouth. But his damage has been done, for the citizens appear uneasy, flickers of resentment zeroed in on me as a few shout "go home," "freak!" I want to scream back, to tell them how easily they have just been manipulated, how easily *I* have been.

God damn it. He's gotten us all where he wants us, even as he stands chained and now gagged. It's in this moment I realize what his sentencing needs to be, and it chills me to the bone to accept it, to want such a thing, but I see no other solution. It makes me want to scream all the more, destroy something, but I don't because I know I can't, and when one of my Vigil guards whispers to me that the elders request my immediate removal, I sag in acceptance and slight relief. Without a word I stand, giving one last distasteful glance at Aaron, taking in the malicious, triumphant grin edged on his lips before turning away, somehow feeling guiltier than if I were the one on trial.

--->==◉ ◎==<---

While I await the news of Aaron's sentencing, I'm shown into the Nocturna recovery wing. Hector accompanied me out of the courtroom and surprised me with the smart idea to see to the wounded soldiers.

"Might as well prove Aaron's words wrong by helping where you're most needed," he said, and after taking a moment to calm myself to think clearly, I nodded sullenly.

Seeing such a packed room of injured men and women is only more proof that the war is slowly worsening day by day, but despite the dismal scene that tightens a vice around my heart, my earlier dejected spirit of failure lifts ever so slightly as I find myself doing something useful. At least here the Nocturna appear happy to see me. So I go bed to bed and talk with each one of them, listen to how they got hurt, and offer help where I can.

After lifting my hands from a particularly brutally burned leg connected to a brave-faced soldier—giving her some relief by channeling some of her pain to me—I wipe my brow. She's the tenth person I've felt the need to do that for, the nurses and doctors overwhelmed and backed up in handing out nerve sedatives. I know I can't keep this up much longer, my own skin growing sickly pale, and my tongue now covered in a metallic taste, but I feel the desperation to continue, the importance. Knowing it's my own self-inflicted penance for my earlier outburst and, no doubt, possibly ruining Cato's carefully laid-out plans to win over the people of Terra. I can't even imagine the lecture I'll soon be subjected to.

"Perhaps that's enough," Hector says beside me as we walk to the next bed.

"I can do a few more." I smile to a young man whose arm is in a sling, the side of his head being worked on by a hovering bot that's weaving stitches into a gash.

Before I can say hello, Hector pulls me up short, his green gaze finding mine. "I understand what you're doing, and I even admire you for it, but when I suggested we come here, I didn't do it for you to faint from exhaustion."

"I'm not going to faint," I say, holding back an eye roll, because I'm pretty sure the gesture would cause me to faint.

"Right," he says, unconvinced while crossing his delicately sinewed arms.

"What do you want me to say?" I huff. "These people need help."

He watches me a moment, the cut of his scar pinching with his narrowing eyes. "You don't have to punish yourself for what happened."

I turn away. "Don't I?"

"Molly." He says my name so softly that I glance back, surprised to find a drape of sympathy in his features. For some reason seeing such an expression on his otherwise arrogantly puckered face annoys me more.

"I understand how you're feeling, trust me, better than most." He shakes his head slightly. "But what you did back there was hardly a blunder. In fact, I'm pretty sure half the Council, not to mention the elders, were desiring the same thing."

"Don't say that."

"Why? Because you think it makes us bad people? Well, let me tell you something—it doesn't. It merely makes us mortal, or as you say on Earth, human. We're complicated creatures, Molly, with thoughts and feelings independent of what we might actually act upon—"

"But that's just it," I cut in. "*I* acted upon it!"

"Barely."

I let out a humorless laugh. "Right. Setting his podium on fire is *barely* acting."

"You could have done a lot more," Hector says with an edge. "We both know fire is the least deadly of your possible sins."

I jerk my head back. Wondering how much he knows about my ability to travel into the other plane of sight, to see the life's energy coursing through the room, through him. How I can stop it all with one concentrated thought.

"I'm not judging what you possess," he continues. "I'm just trying to prove a point. Not everyone could handle the things you've been given access to. Most would abuse it, *immediately*. I certainly would," he admits, and I'm not sure if that's true or if he's still painting himself the heathen. "But in all the days you've been coming here, have had the Navitas at your beck and call, what's the worst you've done with it?"

I give no answer.

"Exactly," he says. "So you let your emotions get the better of you *one time* to a person that tried to *kill you*. I mean, come on. I'd say that is well within your rights."

"I dropped a ceiling on Aurora."

Hector blinks. "What?"

"She was flirting with Dev."

Hector stares at me and then stares some more before his lips waver and his head is thrown back with laughter.

I glance around, embarrassed by the joyous noise in such sad surroundings.

"By the elders." Hector rests a hand to my shoulder. "I think I officially have a crush on you."

"Eww." I shrug him off.

"You wound me." He covers his heart. "Am I really so revolting?"

Luckily, I'm saved of needing to reply by Dev walking into the far door of the recovery wing. His mouth is set into a stern line, his black-clad body tense as he makes his way toward us. Without saying a word, he brings me into his arms and kisses me. I stiffen at first, shocked at his public display of affection, but then relax as the feel of him does what it always can—melts away my resolve.

Hector clears his throat, rather loud, beside us, while a few nearby soldiers let out a whistle. Eventually Dev pulls back, cupping my face with his palm. "I'm so sorry," he says.

"You're sorry?" I crease my forehead as I step back. "I'm the one who let Aaron manipulate me into making a scene."

"That was hardly a scene," Hector grumbles, while Dev says, "We should never have let the trial be public."

"Like you could really have changed that."

"We could've tried."

I let out a tired sigh. "Whatever, it's done now." And then wait a beat before asking, "What was decided?"

"Termination," Dev says quietly. "In seven Earth cycles."

I exhale slowly, letting the reality of his words seep in. Termination. I'd thought I'd feel a wave of relief or guilt, anything, but I only feel hollow and tired.

"Aurora?" I ask, because that's really all that matters now.

"She—" Dev swallows. "She didn't take it well. She'll be monitored by a physician until she can calm down."

It's like I've been punched. "We should see her."

"No," Dev says sternly. "I'm sorry, but you're probably the last person she wants to see right now."

"But she's my friend. *Our* friend."

"I don't think she shares the same sentiment at the moment."

I open my mouth to respond, but then shut it. He's right. As horrible and misguided as it is, of course she blames me for Aaron's sentencing. The look I saw in her eyes out on the battle-field floats in front of me, the hate... *In all of Terra*, how has so much gone wrong?

"This might be horrible of me to admit," Dev says, bringing me into his arms. "But I'm relieved. Having Aaron here... Now what happened can't be repeated."

Despite our public surroundings, I seek his comfort, wishing I could feel the same relief, the same assurance for a new future, but there's still so much to be done to accept it just yet.

"I'm sorry to interrupt," an out-of-breath female voice breaks into our moment, and we move apart to find a messenger. Her face is flushed as she pulls a letter from her satchel. "But I was told to personally hand deliver this message to you immediately."

"Thank you," I say, curious. Tearing the envelope open, I smile seeing Becca's familiar handwriting, but it slides off my face into a puddle at my feet as I take in the two simple lines.

"Oh my God." I cover my mouth as the world around me blurs.

"What's happened?" Dev asks.

"I have to go," I say, glancing up to find his worried blue eyes. "I have to go right now."

"What, where? Molly, what's going on?" Dev peers over my shoulder to read, but just then Hector pulls the letter from my fingers, his face growing even whiter as he reads. I know in this moment he and I are sharing the same cold dread and, as we lock eyes, are still seeing the inked words scrolled across the paper.

Come back now. Your grandfather, he's had a heart attack.

Chapter 29

IT'S STRANGE HOW much one person can endure. You'd think a species that depended so heavily on shelter, clothes, food, and regular sleep would crumble under the slightest pressure, the smallest challenge. But while our bodies tend to be weak and needy, our minds can surprisingly withstand an unwavering amount of onslaught. Even as the long list of high-priority responsibilities weighs down on me, all my swirling doubts and fears threatening to be the final drowning weight, I still manage to somehow hold myself together as I sit beside my grandfather's hospital bed. Not even a tear has so far crept from the corner of my eye, and I don't know if I should be proud of that or terrified.

This is my first time back on Earth after weeks away, the first time I'm naturally blanketed in the sun's warmth and am able to reconnect with Becca, Rae, and my parents. I remain beside my grandfather, who has just come back from surgery. Silently I watch his slow intakes of breath and count each beep of his heart monitor, waiting for the moment he wakes up.

Because he *has* to wake up.

My parents are outside talking to a nurse about the recent procedure and to find out how long he'll be comatose. I curl a hand into his cool wrinkled one and squeeze.

"Stop being so lazy," I whisper. "You always said oversleeping was for the addlebrained, and we all know you are *not* that."

I'm greeted with the rhythmic whooshing of his breathing machine.

"I got you a few sodas and bags of chips." Rae walks into the room, carrying a bounty of vending-machine snacks.

"I told him you didn't need so many carbonated drinks, but he wouldn't stop until he had one of every kind," Becca says, glancing to her boyfriend with endearing annoyance. Rae gives her a lopsided grin, looking every inch human in his unzipped gray hoodie, which is thrown over a white tee and dark jeans.

He deposits the snacks on a nearby table, while Becca plops into the chair beside me, her green summer dress pooling around her legs. Even with our current circumstance, they look happy together, and I can't help noticing a lightness in Rae that wasn't there before. Which is saying something, since he was already the most positive person I had ever met—well, besides Becca.

Turning back to my grandfather, I take a deep breath.

"Where's Hector?" Rae asks, handing me a soda.

"He said he was going to check on something." My attention goes to the open door, where my parents stand a few feet away.

After more than sixty years of not seeing my grandfather, Hector had astonished us all by saying he would accompany me home. We hadn't talked much in the moments that took us from the recovery wing to the hospital in Pennsylvania, but as I had watched him gaze upon Robert's prostrate form with tubes

connected to every inch of him, Hector's mouth had opened on a silent gasp before a swallow bobbed down his throat. His green eyes grew large and then narrowed to angry slits as his hands curled into fists by his side.

That's when he announced he would be right back, mumbling something about hunting down at least one intelligent human who called themselves a doctor before fleeing the room. I let him go, knowing despite whatever excuse he gave, he needed a moment alone.

"How's your new job?" I ask Rae, catching him in the middle of pouring the last remnants of a bag of chips into his mouth. He smiles sheepishly while dusting the crumbs from his chin.

"We don't need to talk about that, Mols," he says.

"I *need* to talk about it actually."

He and Becca share an understanding glance. "It's good." He settles against the wall, running a hand through his hair, the brown strip mixing into the blond strands. "They seem open to me messing around with the material of the boards. Even gave me a space in the back to work."

"That's great," I say, happy for him. In their earlier letters that Sonja delivered to me, Rae wrote that he found a job at a surfboard startup company who just opened a shop in Brooklyn. It's a perfect first human job for my old Vigil guard. With his honey-brown skin and sun-bleached locks, he already has the surfer appearance down. The fact that he actually has a passion for the sport and, to Becca's delight, was quite good at it was a bonus. They managed to make a few trips out to California since my leave, Rae wanting to show her a favorite spot of his that he'd often visit when Terra allowed him the time.

"He might have found a way for the boards to be quicker in the water." Becca beams proudly.

"*Might* being the key word," he says. "I can't take direct technologies from Terra, but I am allowed to figure out how to organically bring some here."

"Loopholes," I say.

"Precisely." Rae winks.

I'm startled by the small chuckle I let out, feeling like I haven't laughed in a very long time. "God, I've missed you guys."

Becca's hand covers mine. "Turtle, you have *no* idea. I mean, Rae *hates coffee*," she says with a disgusted shudder. "It was very nearly our deal breaker."

"I thought my refusal to watch rom coms was the deal breaker."

"Yes, well, you made up for that in other ways." A blush momentarily blossoms on her freckled cheeks. Thankfully, my parents walking back into the room closes that particular conversation.

"What did the nurse say?" I take in the tired appearance of my mom and dad. They stand in their matching lounge clothes, dark circles under their eyes, while their usual primped and tucked-in appearances are nowhere in sight. My dad hasn't shaved since the incident, and my mom's brown bob needs a good washing.

"Your boyfriend has been very…beneficial," Mom says after a moment of searching for the right word. "Especially for never meeting your grandfather before."

"He's not my boyfriend," I clarify. "Just a friend."

"Well, whatever he is," she says, "he's been extremely helpful. He's managed to get us the official surgery's test results much quicker than we would have otherwise."

"Oh, well, that's good." I shift in my seat, not used to feeling gratitude toward my Vigil guard. "What were they?"

"His heart attack was due to severe plaque buildup," Dad answers wearily as he goes to the other side of my grandfather's bed. "They thought they might be able to put in a stent but realized quickly they needed to do a coronary artery bypass grafting."

"A what?" I ask.

"It's removing a healthy artery or vein." Hector's voice brings our attention to his tall form now blocking the doorway. "And replacing it with the blocked section. It creates a new route for the blood to travel to the heart."

"Are you a doctor?" Mom asks, clearly impressed.

"No" is Hector's short answer as he steps farther into the room and hugs the wall, his eyes never leaving Robert's body.

"Hector likes reading about this sort of stuff," I say in a way of an explanation.

"Oh" is Mom's simple reply.

"So how long do they think it will take for him to wake up?" I ask.

"Could be in the next twenty minutes or the next day." My dad moves a few displaced gray strands across my grandfather's forehead back into place. "They said at his age he's lucky to even have survived the attack, let alone the surgery."

The room falls into a thick silence. Eventually my parents engage in some polite conversation, asking how my work is. I haven't told them about getting fired yet—I'll need to figure out an alibi at some point, a way to live what little time I spend on Earth without drawing suspicion. Another problem for another day. For now, I say it's fine, explain that Hector is a friend of Rae's from his new job. Rae and Becca go along with my lie, and then I convince my parents to go back home, which is, luckily, only a few minutes away. If not to get some rest, than to at least freshen up and eat something that didn't come from the hospital cafeteria. I said I'd call if anything changed.

Becca and Rae remain with me, nothing I say moving them from their seats, and Hector stands frozen against the wall. I want to ask him how he is, what exactly is going through his mind, but we haven't yet formed such a relationship. While I'm used to his presence and have grown to like him, there's still a distance between us, a gap of intimacy that comes more from him than from me, as if he's holding things back.

A low moan emanates beside me, and I turn to see my grandfather shifting ever so slightly.

"Grandpa!" I go to his side, Becca and Rae standing with me. "Grandpa, can you hear me? It's Molly." His wrinkled eyes blink open a few times, his mouth moving in an attempt to speak. "Shh, it's okay. You just got out of surgery. You had a heart attack, but you're okay." I stroke back his hair, this time finally feeling the tears come.

"Molly," he eventually rasps.

"Yes, it's me. I'm here. Charles, your son, he just left, but he'll be back. And my mom, Kathy, you remember her?"

He suddenly tries to sit up but then gasps from the impossible effort.

"No, don't move, Grandpa. You've got wires covering you. You have to stay put." I glance to the others. "Get a nurse," I say, and Rae immediately leaves. Hector just stands there, his breathing uneven, the pulse against his neck fluttering rapidly.

I turn back to my grandfather. "Just try to relax," I say softly. "You had a major surgery. You need to relax."

Soon a male nurse walks in, followed by Rae. The nurse mutters calming words to Robert, checks his liquids and charts, scribbles some things down, and then says a few more words, which my grandfather tries to respond to. The fact that he's showing signs of lucidness brings a sigh of relief, and the nurse explains that all looks fine, that he just needs to rest.

As the nurse leaves, we circle his bed, well, except Hector. He's still planted on the far wall, and part of me wonders if he should leave—discreetly. Maybe it wasn't such a good idea that he came. Robert *did* just suffer a massive heart attack. I can't see how the sudden appearance of Hector wouldn't induce another.

"I feel like I've been hit by a truck," my grandfather grunts.

"Well, you sort of were." I gently sit on the side of his bed.

"It's all those cakes your mother makes," he moans out. "She put me here."

"Grandpa," I admonish, unable to hide a small smile, knowing *he's* the reason she makes them, his addiction to the sugary treat. "That is *not* true and not a very nice thing to say. You better keep that to yourself when they come back."

He merely *harrumphs* and then, seeing Becca on the other side of him, a twinkle forms in his eyes. "Have you been assigned to nurse me back to health?"

My mouth pops open at his cheekiness, and right after nearly dying, no less!

But Becca merely laughs and says, "That depends. Can my boyfriend here be the one to do your sponge baths?"

"Becca!" Rae and I both say in shock—well, Rae actually says it more in disgust.

My grandfather merely chortles from his bed before choking on a wince of pain.

"Don't make him laugh." I glare at Becca, who says sorry.

"Don't yell at her," my grandfather wheezes, clearly not as strong as he was trying to let on. "I'd *rather* go out laughing."

"Well, I'd rather you not go out at all, especially from a gross innuendo."

"That wasn't really an innuendo," Becca clarifies and then pinches her mouth closed as I pin her with a glare.

Throughout this entire exchange, I forget the other person in the room, but as I catch my grandfather's eyes narrow at something at the end of his bed, I turn to find Hector now standing there.

My heart pounds, my skin prickling with nervous energy as I scan from my Vigil guard back to my grandfather. Each man stares at the other, and I watch as my grandpa's eyes slowly fill with recognition and then shock, his head pressing farther into his pillow.

"Hector?" he whispers, the words as softly spoken as the ghost he surely thinks he's seeing.

"Hello, Robert." A hesitant, almost shy smile inches across Hector's lips. "Been a long time."

And then the machines monitoring my grandfather's vitals begin to blare.

Chapter 30

A WEARY SIGH escapes my grandfather's lips as whatever sedative the nurses recently attached to his IV drips into his veins. It took two of them and a doctor to bring Robert back to a stable state after his shock, and I shove Hector, hard, as soon as they leave the room.

"What the hell! Was that *really* the right moment to reveal yourself? Jesus. He *just* woke up after suffering a heart attack."

"Mols, maybe lower your voice a bit?" Becca nods to the few people peering in through the small glass window to our room.

I pace away from the Vigil, unable to look at him anymore.

"Hector?" my grandfather croaks, his eyes darting around to locate the Vigil, and I bite the inside of my cheek to stave off another wave of anger.

"Grandpa," I say softly, going to his side. "I think we should let you get some rest now."

"Was that really Hector?" He looks at me imploringly. "Was it?"

I close my eyes briefly, letting out a breath of defeat. "This better not kill him," I say over my shoulder to Hector, who's hovering just beyond my grandfather's view.

"Yes, it's me," Hector says in a gentle tone, kneeling on the other side of Robert's bed. His hands flutter awkwardly, like he wants to take Robert's hand but is unsure if he should, or can.

"Hector," my grandfather sobs. "Where did you go?"

Hector swallows.

"You never came to see me."

As if that simple statement breaks whatever wall Hector was desperately trying to keep in place, he slips his hand between Robert's, the smoothness of the Vigil's skin in contrast with the age-spotted wrinkles of the other. "I'm seeing you now," he says in a hush. "I'm seeing you now."

My grandfather grip tightens. "I tried to find you after, but they wouldn't let me leave the Center, and you never came back."

"I'm…I'm sorry." Hector's brows pinch in before he lets out a small gasp of surprise as my grandfather lifts his finger to trace the scar across his left eye.

"This. This is why." It's not a question.

And then Hector does something that stops my heart. He leans over and sobs.

Becca, Rae, and I wait outside my grandfather's closed room, my attention unable to move away from the scene of him and Hector talking quietly. Even with my new sensitive hearing, they mutter too softly for me to make out anything, and I huff in annoyance.

"What do you think happened?" Becca asks beside me.

"That's what I'm trying to hear."

"Let them be," Rae says.

"Do *you* know what happened?" I look up to him.

"No." He shakes his head. "I know it has to do with the war, but the specifics are lost to me."

"Hector cried," I say for the fifth time.

"There's nothing wrong with that," Becca replies. "He obviously cares about him."

"I didn't say he didn't."

"Then why are you so surprised by it?"

"I don't know." I tap my finger on my leg, gazing into the room. Neither one has moved from the closed-in conversation. "It's just that it's *Hector.*"

"I get it," Rae says, pulling out a granola bar from his pocket. "He's never been one to show many emotions besides blithe indifference or sarcasm."

"Well, I like him," Becca quips, flipping her red curls over one shoulder.

"You just met him," I accuse.

"And does that mean I can't form an opinion?" She raises a brow. "Plus, I met him once before at the lab, remember?"

"Oh yes, your friendship goes way back."

She punches me in the arm.

"Ow!"

"Please." She rolls her eyes. "You fight nightmare monsters. That hardly could have hurt."

"It did in spirit."

She snorts and then swallows it back as Hector walks out of the hospital room.

"He wants to see you," he says, his eyes fluttering to me before returning to the ground, apparently deep in thought.

Without answering, I brush past my guard and shut the door.

Taking the seat Hector previously occupied, I scoot closer to my grandfather. "Hi." I curl my fingers into his cold hand.

"It's getting bad," he says.

"What is?"

"The war in Terra. It's getting worse, isn't it?"

"Um…" I lean away slightly, thinking this topic isn't the best idea. "Maybe we should talk about something less…stressful."

"Listen to me, Molly." He pulls me back in. "I don't know how much longer I'll be here—"

"Don't say that."

"I'm in my nineties, dear," he says tiredly. "I might be strong willed, but I'm hardly imperishable. And I've lived a good life, more than one, I like to think."

"Yes, but—"

"There are no buts about it. It's a reality for all of us. But life's mysteries are not what I wanted to discuss right now." He huffs another labored breath, talking obviously taking more strength than he has. I swallow and hold on to his hand more tightly.

"Then what?"

"I want you to know that I'm extremely proud of you."

My chest tightens. "I know, Grandpa. You've told me many times."

"Yes, but it's important that you never forget. You're about to face a very large challenge. One that rivals all previously. Trust me," he adds, seeing me wanting to respond. "You need to remember to remain strong. Never forget the power of good that's in you. You will find yourself doubting it. Fear will do that. It blocks out the light. You'll wonder what the point of your efforts are when hate seems to always be a constant. When every life you save merely is met with ten deaths. I almost lost my way a few times, brought to the brink of my ending more than once." His forehead crinkles. "But the people I knew who loved me, that were waiting for me, got me through it. I made myself survive for *them*." His wise eyes, circled in soft, puffy skin, hold mine. "Do you see?" he whispers forcefully. "I will keep trying to survive for you and Charles and Kathy, but, like any lucky soul, I will hopefully slip from this world naturally. You, or anyone else, cannot fight this. And when the time comes, I want you to remember my words to you now. I believe you can stop this evil like those before you. Like me," he adds with a secret grin. "You have always been a force meant for greatness. Show them."

"Grandpa," I choke out, tears forming in my eyes.

"I love you," he says and then loosens his grip. "Now I must rest for a bit. I know once your parents come back, I won't have another chance."

"Okay," I say. "I love you too." Then I kiss him on the cheek, leave his room, and do the only thing I can after that.

I look for Hector.

⋆⟶▆◉ ◉▆⟵⋆

The night air is crisp as I exit the hospital, the summer fragrance of newly cut grass its perfume as I find Hector sitting on a nearby bench. Joining him, we watch the quiet, dark parking lot in front of us. A nurse strolls to her car, the white teddies on her scrubs shining under the moonlight. A little girl helps her father carry a bouquet of flowers as they make their way inside, her skipping feet a gentle rhythm of hope.

After a moment more of silence, I speak. "I used to think hospitals were a sad place. So much sickness and death contained in one building." I lean back, crossing my legs at the ankles. "But then a week before my fourteenth birthday, I got hit with strep and bronchitis. If you don't understand how bad that combo is, imagine shoving two spiked golf balls down your throat. It was horrible." I wince at the memory. "But what sucked more was when I found out I needed to get my tonsils removed. I was miserable and terrified. I mean, it was the week of my *birthday*. But it couldn't be helped, and two days before I turned fourteen, I went in for surgery. I ended up spending half of my birthday in a hospital bed." I take in Hector's frown as his gaze remains forward. "But the most amazing thing happened. My room was filled with flowers and balloons and presents from the friends that were originally invited to my party that got canceled. They visited with their parents, and we ate so much ice cream, *too* much." I laugh, remembering the cartons the nurses brought in. "It turned out to be one of the best birthdays I ever had, and I realized something. Hospitals aren't just a place for the sick and dying, but also for survivors. It can be a place to celebrate life." I pause for a moment, watching a new car pull in, its headlights flashing across where we sit. "Profound things happen here," I go on. "True friends are realized, love is renewed, and probably one of the most important things of all, forgiveness is given."

There's a beat of quiet, the gentle buzz of insects and whooshing of cars on the far-off highway filling the void. I'm not sure why I felt moved to share that story, but something about what I saw in Hector's gaze as he left my grandfather's room made me understand something about him, something he has probably tried to hide for forty years.

With a shaky breath, Hector leans forward, dipping his head into his hands. "I don't deserve forgiveness."

"I think that's for the ones you've wronged to decide," I say. "And it seems like he has."

Hector's pale face turns to mine, surprise in his green gaze. "Robert told you what happened?"

"No."

"Then how do you know…"

"Give me a little more credit than that." I incline my head and allow a moment of pensive silence before asking, "Will you tell me?"

I'm not sure if it's because of what I just shared or the exhaustion of the day or both, but with a sigh he begins his story.

"Robert and I…we were inseparable. I hardly had to speak for him to know what I was thinking or feeling, and oftentimes we would go days without saying a word. We didn't need to. I could predict what he wanted just as easily as I knew I needed to take a next breath. Robert…his friendship was like nothing I'd ever known." Hector twists his hands in his lap. "I had been Robert's Vigil guard for nearly ten years before he was called into the war. I, of course, enlisted with him, making sure we were in the same troop, and eventually we were placed into the Thirty-Fourth Division, sent off to Italy to fight the Germans southward to Monastery Hill. The terrain was filled with mountains covered with boulders and cut by ravines and gullies. The ground was so rocky we couldn't even dig foxholes for safety. We had no shelter, and the weather was freezing cold and wet. Plus, there were no nearby portals for me to meet with Robert back in Terra when he did eventually give in to sleep. It was torture watching over him those nights, not knowing what was going on back at home. After weeks of this, my control started to slip. I became anxious and jittery, every small noise..." Hector stops for a moment, swallowing back the hoarseness. "The Germans had three months to scout and prepare defenses before we arrived, and everywhere seemed to be planted with mines and booby traps. It was on a night trek that it happened. We got ambushed. There was firefight everywhere, explosions that caused the wet dirt to cake the fallen bodies." Hector's coloring is ashen. "I don't know what happened, but I...I snapped. I ran. *Away*." He forces the word out with torment. "Robert, he...he went after me, was yelling at me to stop, but I couldn't hear or see anything but the massacre around us. It seemed so much worse than the Metus back at home, so pointless. But then I heard it, a mine going off behind me, one of our brothers setting it off, and I was thrown to the side. When I came to, I knew my face had gotten hit with shrapnel, but I also knew, *knew*, Robert was closer to the blast range."

I take in a sharp breath.

"I eventually found him unconscious in the mud. He had so much blood covering his uniform that it was hard to tell where the largest wound was." Hector lets out a snort. "And they said he was one of the lucky ones...lucky," he repeats in disgust. "His leg got the brunt of it, but the doctors thought they could save it, save him. I stayed by his bed as long as I could. Until I knew he was in the clear, and then...then I left."

"You resigned," I say.

"I failed him," he corrects, scrubbing a frustrated hand down his face. "Failed in my one and only duty."

"And you didn't let them treat your scar."

"A reminder."

I press my lips together to hold in the *oh, Hector* I was about to breathe, pretty sure that's the last thing he wants to hear. So instead I sit with him, quietly, and let the space around us hold his words, his memories, before the wind carries them away.

It all makes sense now. His years of torment, of reducing himself to the lowest rank and appearing heartless—all fueled from thinking that's what he was, what he deserved.

"No matter what you think," I eventually say, "my grandfather would never have blamed you for what happened. He lived, Hector. If anything, he seems upset that you left."

"That made it worse." Hector stands with a jerk. "I knew he would forgive me. He would never have held me responsible. He was always so understanding, *is* so understanding. But I *ran*," he says with a curled lip. "When I was supposed to be the protector, I ran, and my cowardice almost got us both killed. I couldn't look at him without feeling all my shame and failure. I couldn't..." Hector trails off, seeming to no longer have the energy for words.

"But now?" I ask.

"Now...now I had to. I had to see him, for his sake. I needed to tell him why I left. And even if he forgives me, I still don't forgive myself."

I watch him, the way his tall form stands still against the night. "Accepting forgiveness or not, it doesn't stop the fact that it was brave of you to come."

"By the stars," Hector snorts, incredulous. "Can you Speros get any more selfless?"

"You can certainly try me." I give him a light smile.

As if my words draw another thought from Hector, his gaze turns inward.

"What?" I ask.

"I have to tell you something."

"Okay..."

He regards me cautiously. "It's about Aaron."

Instantly my stomach tightens.

"It's because of me that he was able to find you."

My head jerks back. "What?"

"We traded," he explains. "But I didn't know who he was besides a defected Vigil. We swapped information, news on Robert for things happening in Terra. It's my fault, Molly." He balls his hands into fists. "It's because of my stupid fear of returning to Earth that led Aaron to you."

The ground grows unsteady under my feat.

"But if I knew who he was, what he was planning." Hector sits beside me again, his expression desperate and imploring. It looks completely awkward on his usually smug face. "I would *never* have done business with him. I swear."

So much pain, so much torment that he's brought onto himself. It's enough, I think. All of it. I just want to start anew, fresh.

"No," I say. "I don't think you would have."

He blinks, shocked. "You believe me?"

"What good would it do for you to lie about this?"

"But...you're not mad?"

I let out a large breath. "Yes, your interest in my grandfather might have led him to me faster, but Hector, Aaron was *already* looking for the next Dreamer. He would have found me eventually."

"He…how do you know that?"

"Because he told me."

"He did?"

"Yeah, right before he stabbed me with a knife," I add dryly.

"Oh" is Hector's only reply, and then after a moment, "Well, you took this a lot better than Dev."

My brows climb up my forehead. "You told *Dev*?"

"I was rather forced to." Hector straightens, his temperament of superiority slipping back in place. "It was one of Elena's conditions for the two of us to work together. Something about clearing the air."

I let out an astonished breath. "I'm surprised you survived."

"I'm sure Dev wished I hadn't."

I don't contradict him.

But by the stars… Dev knew this and didn't tell me. I normally would get annoyed by something like this, but for some reason, after everything, I find myself too tired for such an emotion. Dev telling me earlier versus Hector telling me now would have made little difference. We're still standing where we are, knowing the truth.

"We good?" I ask. "Or do you have a few more confessions you need to get off your chest?"

Hector surprises me by chuckling, and right then I see the young man that my grandfather would have been such good friends with. "Yes," he says, "I think we are."

As we reenter the hospital, a slight grin on both our lips, I think how strange this visit home has turned out. I came here thinking it would be filled with heartache, but it's proving to be a huge leap in not only Hector and my grandfather's relationship, but between Hector and my own as well.

Through the next few days, my grandfather's recovery appears stable, enough so that I feel lighter, and dare I say happy, as I return to Terra.

But as I walk through the portal to the DCC, I find Dev waiting for me along with my entire entourage of Vigil guards, now double in size.

I glance at them curiously, barely able to say a hello, before I register Dev's panicked gaze and coiled muscles. In quick long strides he comes to me, grasping my hands and forcing out words that poison the very air I breathe.

I feel the blood drain from my face. The lights in the room spark and flutter as my energy spirals in havoc.

This can't be real.

This has to be a sick joke. For how can fate really be so cruel as to not allow me a moment to hope? To rest?

"Molly." Dev shakes me slightly. "Did you hear what I said?"

I look at him, look into his ruggedly handsome face, and want to scream, *YES! Yes! I heard you.* But I remain motionless, silent, catatonic as his words tumble over and over and over in my mind.

Aaron has escaped.

Aaron has escaped.

Aaron has escaped.

Chapter 31

"I STILL THINK this is a bad idea," Dev says as he and Hector follow me down the white corridor, my oppressively large entourage of Vigil guards circling us.

"And I still don't care," I say as we turn a corner in the Prisoner Barracks, a building located on the eastern side of the city. The majority of the facility lies underground, and I try not to draw parallels it has with the DCC. "Elena didn't forbid me."

"And Cato?" Dev asks.

"What Cato doesn't know won't hurt him."

"I'm sure he would beg to differ," Hector muses.

"And anyway," I say, "he's an elder. He probably already knows, and I don't see him trying to block our path, do you?"

"She's got a point." Hector glances to Dev.

"Shut up," Dev mutters before tugging my arm, bringing me to a stop. Odi steps forward with pursed lips, zeroing in on Dev's grip.

"It's fine." I wave him back.

"Think about this for a second." Dev pins me with his blue gaze. "She's the one who helped him escape."

"Wait, *what*?" I ask in shock before rolling my eyes. "Yes, Dev, I *know*."

He merely glowers. "You should be on lockdown, not strolling in to visit the enemy."

"And that's what you think Aurora is now? Our enemy?"

"No. I'm just saying..." Dev groans, scrubbing his hand down his face. "She obviously can't be trusted!"

"I know," I say hotly and then, after a calming breath, say more softly, "I know."

"Then what are you looking to gain from this?"

"I—" I'm not sure. I just need to see her. Ask her why. How could she betray us, me? Aaron's out there now, *she* helped him get out there, and if he was smart and I was lucky, he was now very, *very* far away. But something tells me he's not. Something tells me he's much closer than any of us would like, and waiting. For what? I'm not certain, except it can't be for anything pleasant. Holding back a shiver, I glance to my guards. I feel ridiculous with so many now orbiting me, but it was either this or, as Dev so eloquently put it, be placed on lockdown, stuck in some windowless room deep in the DCC for Terra knew how long, until they could locate the escaped prisoner. Well, I was *not* about to allow that to happen. I was the Dreamer, for Terra's sake, have taken down bigger and badder nightmares than Aaron. And still will.

"I want answers," I say to Dev, and before he can utter another word, I nod to Odi to continue our quick pace to where Aurora is being held.

Her gray uniform covers her hunched-over form that sits behind the chrome table, her arms locked together by blue rings of

Navitas in the center, and I take in her dead stare that's fixed onto the table's surface. Dev, Hector, and I stand on the opposite side of a one-way glass, Dev's anger palpable.

"I don't know how much you'll be able to get out of her," the ward, a rather large burly Nocturna, says from behind us. "She hasn't muttered a word since she got brought in."

"She looks horrible," I say.

The ward merely grunts.

"Are you sure about this?" Dev asks again.

I nod.

"You won't be given that much time with her," the large man says. "And you'll need at least…" I can sense him looking around to my guards. "Five of your Vigil to accompany you."

"Six," Dev says curtly.

"Seven," Hector adds.

"Guys." I turn to them. "She's literally in chains."

Their joint resolute glares let me know they aren't budging. With I resigned sigh, I nod for them to follow, and with the sound of multiple locks unlocking and a whoosh of air, we're shown into Aurora's cell.

She doesn't look up as we enter. In fact, the only movement she makes that tells me she's aware of our presence are her fingers tightening as they rest threaded together on the table.

I glance to Dev, watch as his jaw muscle ticks and his blue eyes swim with a multitude of emotions as he stares at her. What must it be like for him to see her like this? After everything they've been through, helped each other survive. Has that all been erased now? I know with Aaron on the loose, my life is now in danger, but really, when has it not been? And can anyone really blame her for not wanting her brother to die, blackhearted monster or no? I'm still pissed by her actions and feel betrayed, angry, and hurt, but I also understand. We do crazy things for the ones we love.

So with a steadying intake of air, I approach Aurora, only to be held back by Dev's hand coming down on my shoulder.

"No," he says quietly, not so much a demand as a plea. "This is close enough."

But I merely rest my fingers atop his and, with a small reassuring squeeze, step away.

"Aurora," I say lightly, taking a seat in front of her. "Can you look at me please?"

She doesn't move, her drape of tangled strawberry-blonde hair blocking her face.

I try a different way in. "I'm not mad," I say. "I even understand why you helped him."

Still silence.

"But what I don't understand is how you let him put you in such a position. He's out there"—I gesture to the general space around us—"while you're now locked in here, forced to deal with the repercussions of his actions. Again."

That gets her attention. Her head snaps up, her green gaze boring into me, the malice pouring from it like a slice from a razor blade. "You know *nothing* of our relationship," she bites out. "He would have done the same for me."

"Would he?"

"Yes!" She jams herself forward, her chest hitting the table, and I lean back, shocked at her feral demeanor. I sense my guards stepping closer, and I hold my hand up. *Stay*, I demand silently.

"Aurora," I continue. "Look at yourself. This isn't you."

"What do you know about who I am?"

"Well, I like to think we are friends, but it seems you no longer feel that way. And…I'm not sure why."

She barks out a laugh while sitting back in her chair, wincing as the Navitas cuffs sizzle part of her wrists that brushed against it. I feel sick seeing what's happened to her.

"You sentenced my brother to death," she says through clenched teeth. "How could I be friends with you?"

"From what I remember, it was *Aaron's* actions that led the Council to decide his fate. I didn't cast one vote into the decision."

"But it's because of *you* that he acted like that in the first place. Because of both of you." She cuts a narrowed look behind me to where Dev stands.

"Aurora, are you listening to yourself? You sound just as delusional as he is."

"He is *not* delusional."

"Crazy then."

"No!"

"Mad?"

"Shut up!" she yells. "Shut up! Shut up!"

And I do, knowing I should never have antagonized her in the first place, but I'm finding my patience growing thin. I don't know how to reason with this woman. How could someone so sane, so lucid, and levelheaded be reduced to such a creature? Her logic is scattered like marbles from a fallen bag.

"Aurora," I say again with forced calm. "Your brother is suffering from heartbreak, one that happened long before I arrived here. Every action he has taken since that day has nothing to do with me. Can't you see that? He's trying to look for someone to blame, because I can only assume he blames himself for what happened to…Anebel." I force her name from my lips and watch Aurora's breathing grow heavy, her nostrils flaring with each puff of breath. "He's lost his way. His hate and self-torment has twisted him into someone that I believe is not the brother you knew so many years ago."

"That's not *true*!" she bellows, and tries to throw herself at me again, but the Navitas cuffs instantly shock her to sit back down, while two Vigil guards push her shoulders back. "He's my Aaron, and I'm his *mia gemella*," she pants on a wail. "I will always be his *mia gemella*! You did this." She can't seem to stop. "You and *Devlin*. You were going to *let him die*! My brother. You were going to kill him!"

She's lost it, gone mad. How could Aaron have reduced her to this so quickly? How could he so easily abuse the endless love she has for him?

I feel sick, cold, as if the mere act of sitting so close to someone so full of hate and torment can seep into me… I gasp, a realization forming.

"Molly?" Dev questions.

"Just wait," I whisper, and in the next moment, I change to the sight of energy. What I find nearly knocks me out of my seat.

Aurora's blood flows blue-white with the interwoven strands of Navitas locked to her cells—her life's energy. But now a dark sludge wraps around those threads, a black tar I've seen many times before, but only in one creature—the Metus.

How did this get here? Inside her and so fused? Is this what manifests after so much hate stays in one's mind? *By the stars*!

Aaron. Could he really have transferred his negativity like an airborne virus, like the Metus?

Even though I never looked into his soul, saw what truly lurked within those vein, I knew I didn't have to. The sick cloud that perpetually hovered over him, how his mere presence mutated the nearest space to something ugly, was answer enough.

With these thoughts swirling, I hesitantly let my power reach out to the darkness floating in Aurora's veins. But as soon as it touches, a flash of nightmares shoots to my brain, and I recoil, returning my vision to normal and placing a steadying hand on the table.

"Dear God," I whisper.

"Molly." Dev pulls me up and away. "Are you okay? What happened?"

I don't find the strength to answer him until much later, for all I can do now is watch the snarling girl in front of me, knowing of the monsters that lurk unseen inside and that I'm completely helpless to fix it. I realize my grandfather was right—I am about to face a very large challenge, and the doubt, well, it's most definitely creeping in.

Chapter 32

Our hover car flies over the darkened field at a breakneck speed, the scenery outside the glass an angry wipe of an artist's brush. Immediately upon leaving the Prisoner Barracks, I made sure we went to help at the Navitas generator, where we were alerted of a Metus attack. I need something to put my concentration into, something I can immediately fix.

When I touched the darkness flowing in Aurora, I not only snapped back from the horrors that flashed in my mind, but also the surprise of what I felt. While the black energy was similar to Metus', there was also something new, something foreign that leaves me lost on a solution. When helping Tim, and even trying to with Alec, the intruding tendrils were so different from their own life force that I was able to separate it like liquid from a solid. But with what I felt in Aurora...it was so interwoven and complicatedly sewn it would be like trying to compartmentalize different colors of mixed sand—painstaking and nearly impossible.

I gnaw on my bottom lip as I glance out the window, my Arcus strap across my chest feeling too tight. I haven't yet told Dev what I saw. I will of course, but I need more time to process it, figure out what can be done. Mainly, I need to talk with Elena and, ugh, yes, probably Cato.

Dev's hand rests on my knee, bringing my attention to the fact that I was bouncing it restlessly.

"Sorry," I say.

"Nothing to apologize for." He looks at me softly. "Can't your boyfriend put his hand on your leg?"

I give him a distracted grin, my thoughts still barreling forward along with our movements, all the things I need to do. A thick hush fills the interior of the car, our companions busy with their mental preparations for the upcoming fight. A few of my Vigil guards are in attendance, while Dev's Nocturna team packs the majority of the seats.

"You're going to chew that off," Dev says, nodding to my lip.

I immediately set it free from between my teeth, and after a moment quietly ask, "What will happen to her?"

His features grow tight. "It will be up to the elders to decide."

"The elders? But what about the Council?"

"Things like this go through them before it comes to the Council."

"Oh…well, that could be a good thing, right?"

The dark look he gives me is answer enough.

As we approach the threatened Navitas generator, the orange glow of the attacking Metus filling the sky, we ready ourselves. Assault weapons are double-checked for ammo, Arcus straps are tightened, and glowing blades are pulled from sheaths that sit across a few Nocturna backs. Each of Dev's team members has been specifically selected to fight in a unit, each lending his or her own diverse talent to the mix. And lucky for me, they are extremely professional when it comes to my presence. I suffer no side glances or hidden whispers like I often do with the other Nocturna, and I couldn't be more grateful. Catching eyes with a short-haired blonde woman, who I've learned is called Minka, she gives me a respectful nod before going back to placing small bombs into a holster around her waist.

"Disengaging top cover," the driver announces just before we stand, the audible whirl and click of weapons hoisting into place. I shift slightly in my Dreamer vest, the palms of my hands beginning to tingle with the Navitas that I pull to them. I hold the energy just below the surface, waiting.

"Ready?" Dev says to me.

"Ready." I nod and take in one last breath of fresh air before the putrid wind of our enemies hits us as the glass top falls away. The battle sounds are deafening, but having finally grown accustomed to my new senses, I am no longer overwhelmed. The field is covered with Metus, their red dripping forms attacking the smaller dark bodies of the Nocturna. The generator stands tall and proud a good distance away, the blue-white top crackling with Navitas as it reaches for the sky, for the souls that pass overhead, lending down their dreams.

The beginning of these fights usually start out the same. For as long as they can, Dev's team attacks as a group from the vehicle, using its sides as a shield from the fireballs thrown our way, before we are all forced to engage from the ground.

Once we hit the soft soil, Hector and I follow Dev to where we see Aveline fighting a few yards away, the tall grass thwacking our shins as we run. Tim is with her, having been cleared for battle a few days ago, and I watch as he lets loose a flaming arrow into a charging Metus. The monster dodges just in time, but Tim already has a new one nocked, and this time his aim is true. With its head thrown back, the beast gurgles a scream before bursting apart. From Tim's quick abilities one would never guess he suffered such life-threatening wounds a few months ago.

With silent acknowledgment of one another, we stand in a circle, back to back as we attempt to hold the nightmares at bay. My mind tingles with my use of power, warm to cold as I shoot out blazing ball after ball from my palms, any monster that gets in the way quickly removed. But with each pop of their bodies, the air is filled with fouler odors, and I have to hold back, more than once, retching all over myself.

"The tower!" someone yells, and I glance over my shoulder to see a band of five tightly packed Metus storming through a set of Nocturna. The soldiers don't stand a chance and are soon covered in burning lava as the grouped enemy merely plows through them to get to what they truly desire.

"No!" I yell and run forward, feeling my Vigil guards and team following.

"Careful, Molly!" Dev calls just as I skitter to a stop, watching the forms of the once-living man and woman now rise as our enemy. Their bodies are bent at odd angles, their new skin a mix of flesh and burning red mucus, and they walk awkwardly forward, no solid joints to hold them up, only a sick thickness of evil.

"No!" I say again, knowing it's too late to save them, at least in the way I want to. The other way I'll leave to Dev, still unable to bring myself to put down the turned.

The sound of Hector cursing beside me tugs my attention to the group of Metus that have now reached the tower's base. They slap their sludgy palms onto the black metal siding, slugs inching up hungrily to reach the top.

"We need help!" A nearby soldier yells as his small team throws everything they've got at the monsters. Aveline rushes ahead, her pale hair whipping in the night wind, and I'm quick on her heels. With a flick of her wrist, the Arcus she holds flips around to become a double-barreled shotgun, and without losing a beat, she rests it into the crook of her shoulder. She lets out two loud *thwak thwak* of Navitas-charged ammo. One hits a climbing Metus square on the back, its torso filling with the blue-white light before spreading to the rest of it, and on a howl of pain it falls the two stories to the ground to splatter and explode. The Nocturna jump back as chucks of burning liquid splash across the grass, and one woman does the due diligence of stabbing what remains with her glowing sword, killing any lingering energy and turning the mounds to black.

As if sensing the new layer of foes, the four Metus left clinging to the side of the building suddenly join together as one, the power of such a combination sending out black waves of malice and hopelessness.

"*Shit,*" I whisper as visions of this happening once before pass by. But while they were two, these are four, and they create a beast so monstrous the soldiers below are rendered momentarily still by the sight. It's like King Kong hanging on the Empire State Building, except this creature's howl sends shards of devastation through my core.

Screw this.

Jumping into flight, the added concentration pulling a good chunk from my vest, I hover in front of the mutation. One large clawed hand swipes toward me, but I move back and draw my Arcus. Using my Navitas would only drain me quicker, so I dip into the talents of the past Dreamers, letting their muscle memory flow through me as I fling arrow after arrow at the erupting blob. But besides it hissing in discomfort as the poison-laden energy lodges into it, its skin seems to swallow the energy whole, merely creating a black spot of dried lava on the area it touched.

It shrugs me off like I'm merely a gnat flying by its food, and continues to climb.

By the stars, why didn't that work?

"Molly!" my name is called from below, but my mind is racing too fast to divert my attention. I need something stronger to take this thing down, and quick. If it reaches the top, we are more than fucked.

Staying in midair, I briefly close my eyes and internally channel every last ounce of energy I have. This will do a number on me afterward, but I don't have time to question it. Calling strength from my predecessors, I switch to the sight of energy, looking at a world now dancing in flames. My mind sings with icy heat, my limbs vibrate with contained power, and I glance to the Nocturna and Vigil below. They are nothing but white spots, the continuous ammo shot from their weapons trails of bright light. Looking forward again, the dark mass in front of me is so void of life it takes on the appearance of a black hole as it slowly slimes its way up the tower, its hunger palpable to reach the top. And this is where I make a slight mistake. I check out the Navitas swirling above, and seeing it in this plane almost knocks me sideways.

It's so...everything. It's life and death, hopes and fears, dreams and nightmares. It's so pure and honest and full of love that it makes me want to weep. It's more potent than any other Navitas I've been connected to, and in my distracted haze, I wonder if this is what it would be like to look at the Sea of Dreams in this sight.

I'm not sure what does it—if someone yells or my flight falters—but suddenly my hypnosis breaks, and I'm hit hard with an answer. An answer that will either save us all or be the stupidest thing in the world. Clenching my jaw, I throw out a lasso string of Navitas to connect with the blinding energy cracking at the tower's tip. Like a punch to my back, I gasp as my chest arcs forward. The heavily concentrated power pools into me, a water dam set free, and I nearly drown in sensation. My veins are doused in euphoria, in perfection as my soul sighs in relief while at the same time greedy for more. In this moment, I understand why the Metus thirst for this, can think of nothing else, for there isn't anything beyond this feeling…nothing that could possibly compare, and I want it to go on forever.

But it can't, a woman's voice whispers in my ear. *It is not yours to keep.*

Riki.

As if she's gripping my cheeks, telling me to come back, to concentrate, I dash away the hunger slipping into my bones, just in time to see the dark soul of the Metus a hair's breadth away from wrapping itself around the top. With the crackling of lightning channeling into one of my arms, I throw out the other, shooting sparks from my fingers to stab my victim. It throws its large head back in a scream of shock and elation as it becomes locked in, the three of us—the generator, the Metus, and myself—held together in a circle of blue-white fire. I watch the blackness of the monster's soul ooze toward me, wanting to consume me in the hopes to get at the source just beyond, but I grind my teeth and hold still, forcing myself to keep flight, keep my concentration. My face drips with sweat, my body dangerously overheating as my mind is sliced with thousands of cold-tipped blades. With a growl, I suck in every drop of strength, as much of the pure light as I can before I slam it into the beast.

With a continuous scream I don't stop, I channel wave after wave of the generator's energy straight into the monster. It flows through me, my body merely a vessel as it guzzles into the Metus. I can sense the creature's instant sigh of relief. It grows stronger, larger as I feed it, overindulge it. I give it everything until it's too much, until the flames fill the monster to the brim, and I watch with blazing eyes as the once-black hole fills with light, the skin of the nightmare ballooning under the pressure, under the pureness. Its pleasured mewls change to moans of discomfort, then to howls of pain as I overdose it with all the hope and love and dreams I can. I poison it with the very thing it craves. And right when I can no longer hold any of this, can no longer be used as a connecter, a vibration racks through the land, and the bloated Metus bursts into dust of twinkling diamonds, no lava sludge to be seen.

With its disappearance, my arms droop, every connection severed, and my body does what it only can when I'm no longer able to hold it in flight.

It falls.

Chapter 33

THE OFFICE OF the oldest elder is lit in a warm glow, the ornate candelabras patterned around the room flickering and sending dancing shadows across the high-ceilinged space. Elaborate woven tapestries cover the walls, scenes depicting an array of human activity from stories of ancient battles to more leisurely pastimes, such as families picnicking in a park, are woven in gilded threads. The chamber's decorations give an air of high-maintenance regality, something that its master exudes in abundance.

With fingers steepled, Cato thrums the tips together while his elbows rest on the ornately carved armrests of his high-backed upholstered chair, his dark-green gaze unwaveringly pinned to me.

I shift slightly in my seat, which—like everything here—is designed for looks rather than comfort. My body winces from the meek movement, still sore from my fall three days ago. Cato's already permanent scowl deepens, catching what I am trying to hide, and I turn my gaze away, to the other elder in the room.

Elena stands a step beyond Cato, beside a large roaring fireplace, her hands clasped behind her back as she stares into the blue-white flames. Her alabaster skin is bathed in the mixture of the contrasting warm-to-cold lighting, and her hair shifts from blonde to ash with the crackling fire.

"I'm told your injuries have healed well." Cato's steel-tipped voice finally fills the thick silence.

"Yes." I instinctively roll my right ankle, amazed that it shows no signs of having been broken.

After falling the two stories at the Navitas generator, I suffered more than a fair share of injuries, the least of which was Dev's and, as it appears now, the elders' wrath. I'm more than lucky to be in a place with such advanced medicine and, given who I am, receiving the best treatment from the finest Terra doctors. In the end, I only suffered from pain for no more than an hour before my ankle was mended, two splintered ribs restored, and the severe bruising along one entire side of my body reduced to a fading yellow stain. The durability of my vest kept me from suffering any spinal injury, and the thick layers of my clothes took the majority of the impact when I hit the ground, saving my neck from snapping. Terra only knows how I didn't crack my head open.

"I hope you remember that your body is *completely* here now and, despite what we were able to do for you this time, *some* injuries are rather permanent." Watching Cato twist around the ring on his pinky, I'm more than aware that he means death. "That was a very risky thing you did."

"We had no other options," I say.

Cato watches me, his weathered face a valley of deep ravines under the candlelight. "How did you know it would work?" Despite the vagueness of his question, I understand exactly what he's asking.

Gnawing on my lower lip, I give a small shrug. "I didn't exactly, but since I've always been able to connect directly with the Navitas, as well as with an individual's life energy, I thought it could work to do both at once. And when I was in it, I knew I could use myself as a pathway to focus the energy and overwhelm the Metus."

"Hmm" is Cato's only reply as he reaches for a glass of Traub resting on his side table. He takes a slow sip, his eyes studying the purple liquid before they rest back on me. "Well, despite the success of your efforts, it seems Terra is keen on disliking you at the moment."

I remain still, having already heard such news from Hector. Dev would never want me to know such things.

"This, of course, is of no real surprise," he goes on. "People always need something to blame when things go badly. Before they knew of you, it was the Council's fault. Before that, humans and their weak minds."

"But never the elders?"

"They know better than to go *that* far," he says with a superior tilt to his chin.

A snort escapes me, and behind Cato I catch Elena fighting a grin.

"There are still those who support you, thank Terra," he continues, ignoring my reaction. "And believe in what you are meant to do here, but there's a greater number who have been swayed by the scene that occurred during Aaron's trial."

See, Hector, I think. *It* was *a scene.*

"With the Metus attacking more frequently, spirits are growing lower, and the last thing we need is a revolt on our hands. We need our world united on who the enemy is."

"Well, they can't possibly think I'm their *enemy*?"

"They see you as representing the start of this madness, despite the fact that you were brought here unwillingly. They also don't completely understand what you are. The humans they have watched over the years appear very different. They don't have powers to wield such as you. And besides, anger is often the result of people not understanding something."

I let out an exhausted breath. Thoughts of my grandfather's health, the threat constantly at Terra's wall, and one psychotic man on the loose should be my main concerns—correction—*are* my main concerns. Yet it seems that's not enough to shove onto my plate. I now need to somehow fix this *too*?

"So what should we do?"

Cato glances to Elena, as if to say *your turn*.

"We are going to stage a demonstration," Elena says, walking over to gracefully lower herself onto a settee next to Cato. Her white dress wraps her calves as she crosses her ankles.

"But I've already done those," I say. "And they apparently have done squat."

"This will be different from the others," Cato clarifies.

"How?"

"Leave that up to us." He waves a dismissive hand. "For now we need you to rest and conserve as much of your energy as possible."

"Why?"

"Because you'll need all of it in two days' time." He casually takes a sip of his drink again.

"Two days—" I take in Elena's impassive face. "Don't you think I should know what you're planning so I can prepare?"

"We're still working out the specifics," Cato says.

"Still—"

"Molly," Cato cuts in. "When there's more to tell you, we will."

Well, I don't believe that at all.

"Elena." I address the elder specifically. She's been way too quiet this entire meeting. "What about Aurora? What I saw."

I was quick to fill her in on Aurora as soon as Elena visited me at the hospital after I was treated. She seemed shocked and appalled as I described the black threads woven along the Aurora's life energy. After I finished, she left to, I assume, visit Aurora and see it for herself. Well, *feel* it at the very least, since her ability allows her to tap into an individual's energy. Maybe that's why she's been so out of it since I walked in here. What she felt must have terrified her as much as it did me.

"We've discussed it." Her blue eyes meet mine. "And we think we've found a way to treat it, or try to at least. Before we can though, she must stand trial for her actions with Aaron."

My heartbeat quickens. "But if what I saw in her is like a disease? Then she can't possibly be completely to blame for her actions. Her mind's obviously not all there."

Elena nods. "Yes, all things to consider."

"What can I do to help?"

The two elders share a glance.

"What?" I sit up straighter. "If there's something I can do, I want to know."

"Two days, Molly," Cato repeats while pressing a call button beside him. "Prepare yourself for the demonstration in two days. That's what you can do."

And with that, my Vigil guards enter the room. With a frustrated breath, I allow them to escort me out, but before I step through the door, I catch Elena watching Cato with a frown. Though I don't know the reason behind it, a shiver dances through me. For I've only seen that expression on Elena a few times, and always when something wasn't right.

⭤ ⭤

Dev takes the order for me to get some mandatory R & R with extreme seriousness. In the following days he makes it his life's mission to pamper me into exhaustion. Which, as I've recently found out, *can* happen. He gives back rubs, foot rubs, baths, and forces me to consume so much decadent food that I'm surprised I'm not a puddle of limp muscles and glazed-over eyes on the ground. I'm still not sure how he manages to get the cooks in the DCC to whip up these treats, but I'm not complaining. Especially not now when he and I lay tangled in the sheets in my apartment that's located on one of the lower levels in the compound.

It was hardly a shock that I was moved here after Aaron's escape, especially now with so much negative attention from the citizens. Although it's been slightly maddening and a little weird to not be allowed outside for the past few days, it has been more than convenient to keep residency here. My training sessions are easier to slip in and out of, and having Dev stay with me has actually given us a good deal of privacy that we've otherwise lacked when living with him.

"Do you think, when all this is done, we'd be able to get our own place?" I ask, tracing patterns in the light dusting of hair on

AAAAAAAAAAAA

his taught chest. One of his arms is securely wrapped around my waist, holding me to him.

"Are you asking me to move in with you?" The smile in his voice causes me to look up at him. His black short-cropped hair—that he's let grow a little longer these days—is beautifully mussed, and his blue eyes twinkle as they take me in.

"What if I am?"

"Then I'd say that's the best idea you've had in a long time."

"Um, wasn't it *me* that suggested our recent game of strip I Spy?"

"Ah yes, your poorly hidden attempt to get me in bed."

"A.k.a one of my best ideas."

He laughs deep and throaty, and the sound is beautiful and long overdue. As if we've both had the same thought, he pulls me closer, bringing my wrist to his lips. "I'll need to thank Cato the next time I see him."

I raise my brows questioningly.

"I can't remember the last time we've had so much of this." He glances to where we lay in my dimly lit bedroom, the main light source the blue glowing sconces on the walls. "Life almost feels…normal."

"I know I should feel guilty not having been out there helping with the Metus these past few days, but…if I were being honest, I don't. Does that make me horrible?"

"No." Dev nudges my cheek so I look at him, his gaze intent. "That makes you normal. You've had nothing but demands, things to fix, and fight since you've assumed your role. No one can keep that up without a few reprieves."

"I wish we had one more day of this," I say with a gentle sigh. My upcoming demonstration—that I still don't know the specifics of—is taking place later tonight.

"We still have a few more hours," Dev points out. "And lucky for you"—his mouth curls into a wicked grin—"I know just how to fill them."

Taking my face in his hands, he kisses me and doesn't stop until I all too easily slip into another puddle of euphoria, where I stay, swimming and forgetting about everything but the two of us until eventually there's a heavy knock on my door, forcing us back to a place where reality is all that's left.

⊷⊶⊙ ⊙⊶⊷

The crowd is deafening as I peer out of our private balcony into the arena. The stadium must be filled with close to forty thousand people, their raucous roars rumbling through the bleacher.

When Cato said this demonstration would be more like a show, he wasn't kidding. As we made our way to tonight's location, a giant sports-like dome that sits on the west side of the city, Dev explained its main purpose was for gladiatorial-type contests and a popular Terra game called Pila, which sounds very close to American soccer, or football as most of Earth's citizens refer to it.

Standing on the outer ledge of our balcony, I gaze out at the structure that stretches twenty floors high and is open to the night air. The stars streak the dark sky overhead in a layer of urgency. *Rush, rush, rush,* they zoom by as if to escape the wave of commotion directly below. While the materials of the building are sleekly modern, all steel and glass, the center of the pit is covered in tightly packed dirt and sand.

Taking a steadying breath, I turn back to the group that's with me in the private tier. Tim, Aveline, Hector, Dev, half the Council representatives—including Alex—and the elders fill the space, while the wall behind them is lined with guards. Half of them (mainly the elder half) look more than relaxed standing in front of so many people, while the others look like they ate something that doesn't agree with them. These are the people that I'm on the same page with. Despite being continuously shoved into the limelight, I have yet to feel at ease there. My stomach is a mess of nerves, and I never quite shake the feeling that I'll need a bucket at any moment.

Glancing to Cato, the ringleader for all this, I ask, "And what exactly am I to do here?"

The elder has donned one of his better uniforms for tonight, its black material cutting and hugging in all the right places, giving him the appearance that he's much taller and more built than he actually is.

"It will demonstrate a different use of your power," he says. "One the citizens haven't seen yet. We needed something bigger, something that properly demonstrates your invaluableness."

"Okay…" I catch eyes with Dev. His brows have been in a permanent scowl since we got here. "And what's that exactly?"

"Your ability to heal."

My turn to frown. "What do you mean?"

"You have an incredible gift, Molly," Cato explains. "One that no other Dreamer has been given before. It's our game changer. People have only heard of what you did for Tim. But what if we *showed* them?"

All the hairs on the back of my neck stand on end as alarm bells go off in my mind. "Cato," I say slowly. "What exactly are you asking me to do?"

"I'll show you" is his less-than-satisfying response before he nods to a nearby technician in the corner. The young Vigil, who stands in front of a hovering control board, presses a few buttons, lighting up a center section of the arena, and I watch as a hole opens in the middle, bits of loose sand falling into a black abyss right before an underground elevator brings forth a small form. The individual looks scared and weak standing alone in the giant space, her gray prison uniform bright and offensive under the harsh lighting, and her head whips back and forth in havoc. Gripping the balcony railing, I keep myself from collapsing in shock as all the blood drains from my body.

"Aurora," I whisper and then turn to Cato. "What's she doing here?"

"She's going to help with tonight's demonstration."

"Help? How?" I glance between him and Elena. The female elder's hands are clasped tightly together, her lips pressed into a firm line. She looks as if she's fighting a multitude of emotions, and that alone is enough to send me into a panic.

"Tell me!" I demand.

But Cato merely gives another nod to the technician, and three more circles open up at the farthest sides of the arena, where angry orange-red glows begin to rise from their abyss. Seven-foot-tall Metus now stand in the pit, their churning lava skin spitting fire and dripping mucus onto the ground, the sand sizzling as it lands. Under the spotlights, their razor-sharp claws wink with their movements, and the crowd's cries of surprise and horror shudder the very foundation of the structure.

"Oh my God." I step closer, watching as Aurora, who's a field's length away, takes panicked steps back. Thankfully the three beasts have yet to realize she's there, their attention still on the loud roar of the onlookers.

"Get her out of there!" I shout, spinning back to the elders. Dev has already taken steps toward Cato but is being held back by the guards.

"This is insanity!" he growls.

The rest of our companions look shocked stupid. Alex's mouth opens and closes as if he's fighting between his deep-rooted sense of duty to obey or putting a stop to this craziness. Tim appears tired, exhausted, as if he's given up trying to understand the will of the elders. Aveline, well, she looks like a ghost, her lips rubbing together with worry as her eyes flicker from Dev to me to Cato and then finally back to Aurora's small form in the distance. Hector's expression is unreadable, and a terrified part of me wonders if he knew.

"Stop this!" I plead with the elders. "Please!"

"That is *your* task now," Cato says. "She wronged you. Her actions with her brother directly affect you and your safety more than anyone else's. The people of Terra know this."

"What the fuck are you talking about?!" I yell, my mind tumbling down a hill of horror and dread as a bone-chilling wail from the beasts below fill the air. The crowd momentarily grows quiet, hushed, seemingly lost as to what to make of this scene. And it's like I'm sitting right there with them, disbelieving, as I listen to the next thing uttered from Cato's lips.

"This is to be her trial," he explains. "And it is for you to decide her fate."

Chapter 34

THE WORLD IS only darkness, hope momentarily wiped away by Cato's words. They rattle around inside my brain like ice cubes in a glass, cooling everything they touch and rendering me frozen.

"You're a madman!" Dev leaps from the guard's grasp only to be held at bay again by another. He backward head-butts the Vigil and surges forward, but before his fingers can so much as graze Cato's black pressed uniform, he screams in anguish and drops to his knees.

"Dev!" I dive to his side. "What are you doing to him?!" I cry out, glaring at Cato, who merely arcs an icy brow as he stares at Dev. *My* Dev, who moans in pain, his eyes squeezed shut. Switching to the sight of energy, I catch the cord of Cato's power hooked into Dev's chest, controlling whatever illusion of torment he has pinned to him. Letting out a growl, I lash out with a strand of my own, severing the connection, and Dev droops in relief in my arms.

"Well done." Cato regards me with a look of approval, and it takes all my efforts not to throw my energy back at him. With an audible grunt, Dev allows me to help him stand.

"Enough of this." Elena steps forward. "We did not agree to this plan to make enemies of each other." Her razor-sharp eyes rest on Cato, who huffs and looks away.

"Molly." She gracefully comes to me, her blue gaze uncharacteristically gentle. "I know this seems unfair and a bit manipulative—"

"Because it *is.*"

"But," she continues, "we had no other choice but to present it to you this way. You wouldn't have agreed otherwise."

"And I still don't agree!" The Navitas in me jumps with my rage, growing dangerously restless to retaliate.

"Yes, but here we are nonetheless, and if you want to put a stop to it, I suggest you go help Aurora before it's too late. Unless"—she looks at me meaningfully—"you think she deserves to die for her actions."

"Of course I don't." I gasp in a shocked whisper, horrified she would even think such a thing. Despite Aurora's lashings of hate when I met her in the prison—blaming me for Aaron and wishing I had never come here, that I never came *back*—I know those words came from a dark and twisted place, one provoked by whatever sickness of negativity her brother transferred to her.

"Then I suggest you act now."

A girl's scream echoes around the stadium.

With a burst of energy, I fly down and land in front of the lunging Metus. Their laboring steps rumble like a stampede as they charge toward Aurora, her frightened form pressed against the far wall. A thick titanium barrier wraps the circumference of the field, its surface too flat to climb, its height too tall, leaving any who enter without a way out, an animal trapped. Upon reaching the pit, I realize two things. One, these beasts are much taller and wider than any I have come across before, their dripping acid skin more red than the usual orange, and I wonder if these are a new breed of nightmares. The thought momentarily terrifies me, for I have no idea what sort of deadly abilities to expect. The second thing is that the crowd is reacting to my presence as if they are watching some game, and either their favorite or most hated player has just entered the ring. Shouts of excitement and support mix with insults and boos. It makes me sick, but I have no time to react, for the three beasts quickly approach.

With a deep inhale, I reach into the Dreamer vest strapped across me, pulling at the energy stored within, and with my mind prickling, raise my palms and pump out a blaze of Navitas straight into them. The arm of the nightmare in the middle gets shot off, causing that Metus to stumble before pitching forward. The other two swerve, eluding the shot. I start to backpedal as I attack again, posting myself between Aurora and the monsters, but they realize my plan and split off. I curse and force myself to hover just off the ground to gain leverage on their new locations—the armless Metus in front, two on either side of me. Raising a wall of sand to the left, I attempt to hold off one while I take care of the others, but before I get too far, I sense a presence behind me, and I spin just as I hear Aurora's scream of rage and watch her body hurling my way. I quickly float back, but she snags my leg, collapsing us both to the ground. Sand and mud ooze between my fingers as I try pushing myself up, but Aurora jumps on top of me, forcing me back.

"What the hell!" I yell and wrestle her away. "I'm trying to save your ass!"

"I hate you!" she screams as I try pinning her down. I grunt as her fist knocks against my jaw.

Holding it with my hand, I gaze down at her in shock. She pants like a rabid animal as I straddle her waist, no lucidness in her green gaze. She tries to punch me again, but I grab her fist, slamming it into the ground.

"Stop! Aurora, I'm trying to help!"

"I don't want your help!" she screeches before she starts to buck like a creature possessed, because that's exactly what she is—possessed.

"God damn it," I ground out. Not only do I have to get rid of the Metus, but I also have to hold off this crazy bitch without hurting her. As if sensing my frustration, a storm of red enters my periphery.

Without thinking about it, I call upon my energy, using it to flick Aurora up and wrap her in a cocoon of blue-white, momentarily holding her suspended high in the air and out of the way. She wails and spits out curses, as her arms are jammed tightly by her side. I care little about her screams though, as I find myself flattening onto the ground and rolling away as three fireballs slam into the spot I just stood.

"All right, guys," I say as the four of us circle each other. "It's just us now, so let's get this over with quick."

As if understanding, the armless one runs at me, but I instantly stomp one foot, sending a ripple through the ground. The impact flips it onto its back, and taking advantage of its shocked state, I jump to hover directly above it, launching a burst of Navitas straight into its chest. With little more than a cut-off scream of pain, its entirety is enveloped with light and bursts apart. Calling up a quick wall of energy, I shield myself from the backsplash. With my mind edging on a migraine, manipulating and using my power so fast, I take a deep breath to calm the adrenaline swooshing through my veins.

The crowd hasn't stopped their roars and cheers, and I wish they would shut up. Don't they understand what's at stake here? A life! And one of their own! But they don't get any of that, gorging themselves on the show. It's infuriating. Almost as infuriating as the two monsters running at me. As I prepare to send forth more globs of deadly energy, I realize too late that they aren't actually charging—they're using the momentum to hoist one on top of the other in order to reach Aurora's floating form.

"NO!" I shout just as I sprint forward, snaking out a whip of Navitas to cut off the bottom monster's legs. They both fall, but not before the beast on top reaches out with talon-laden fingers to grasp one of Aurora's ankles.

Her head snaps back with a blood-curdling scream, the audience's collective shrieks of horror a distant layer as I watch the lava of the Metus slowly working up Aurora's leg.

"NO!" I shout again. NO! NO! NO!

Switching to the sight of energy, I lash out with everything I've got, sending blue-white waves of my power toward the creatures. But as my knife-tipped bands burst straight through their chests, their wails of anguish on the wind, I feel no relief. Instead, I'm hit with a wall of confusion. No dark sludge fills their bodies like it normally would. Instead, I merely find a shadow of it. As if the blackness swimming in them is a ghost of what it really should be.

What are these things?

I have little room to think further on it, before their skin cracks and fissures with the overpowering Navitas filling them, and in the next second they explode, bits of red goop smacking into the dirt with a hiss.

Without losing a beat, I pull the still-screaming Aurora from her hovering state and lay her on a clean patch of ground. Keeping her arms securely at her sides with tendrils of my energy, I lift the cocoon and, while still in the sight, survey the damage. Her veins remain filled with the black and blue-white strand mixture, her life essence contaminated, while the lava from the Metus slowly crawls up her leg, just as it did with Tim. But this...this feels and looks much different. Like the smoke of evil I saw in the other Metus tonight, and after a moment more of watching it, the way it curls and inches forward but not actually connecting with the energy under Aurora's skin, not turning it the inky blackness of the monster it came from... *By the stars*, they aren't real. These Metus were simulations, like in the engineers' lab. The world bends with my disbelief, and I place a steadying hand on the ground as I peer up into the tiny box set into the stadium's wall, where I know Cato is watching, where all the elders are.

They tricked me.

They used my emotions, the fact that I care for Aurora, to win whatever game they're playing with the citizens of Terra. A clap of lightning flashes overhead, illuminating the stadium as my anger explodes. The onlookers gasp in terror and shock. But I don't care. I can't see past my own frustration and exhaustion, and the only thing that pulls me from it is the small whimper by my knees, and I look down to find Aurora staring up at me. In a rare gap in time, her green gaze is clear, lucid, a hint of the girl still somewhere inside. And in this moment I decide that if anything is to come out of this, it will be what *I* control. What *I* know is a real attempt to save a friend, not merely a spectacle to win over a people who have lost their way along with the humans of Earth.

So on bended knee, I block out the world around me, dim it to shadows, as I call upon all the Dreamers of my past. *Help me*, I whisper. *Help me heal her.* And like winks in space, I sense each one pop into this plane, the plane where energy and memory collide, where essence is power and the rest of life moves slow. Riki is beside me, always the closest of them, the most real to me, and I briefly close my eyes in a sense of relief as I feel her hand upon my shoulder, and I know what I must do.

Unstrapping my vest, I throw it to the ground. For this I will need the purest of pure, what lives in me, what rests in my heart.

Watching Aurora's gaze slowly slipping back into her feral state, her mouth curving into a snarl as she regards me above her, I act quick, and with a thump to my back, as if someone slapped me, a cloud of myself bursts forward, of smoke. It's not me, but it is…a specter of my power… And this Molly drapes herself over Aurora and seeps in. I feel myself dive into her bloodstream, coursing along every one of her cells, running the length of the complicated woven black thread that hooks into the white, and like medicine attacking a virus, I coat every inch. I'm no longer human, but trillions of cells split apart, created for only one thing—to erase the darkness. I have no idea how long we search and connect to the sickness, how long it takes to find every last centimeter of hate that's nuzzled deep within Aurora's heart, but when we do, it's like there's a click in our souls, and we know. I ask my past Dreamers to lend me their power, pour it into me. And they do. We join until we are as bright as a burning star, orbiting wisps of hope and love and forgiveness. And then we eradicate it in one fell swoop, a flash of white that burns through the dark.

Slowly everything recedes back into place. My predecessors leave me, my sight returning to normal, along with the arena and row upon row of spectators.

I sag, out of breath, out of everything. With both my hands on the ground, my head pounds with a ringing. A ringing of the world gone quiet, finally, the only sound the labored pants of the person by my side. I turn my head to Aurora holding her chest, her eyes wide as they stare up into the sky, her skin slowly gaining its usual honey color that had been sucked from it for so long. Her brother had stolen her, but he's no longer here to contaminate her, no longer haunting her thoughts.

"Molly," Aurora croaks out.

"Yes." I scoot to her side. "It's me."

She blinks, and as her gaze finds mine, her lip trembles.

"Shh," I say, reaching for her hand. "You're okay. You're okay now."

"I'm so sorry," she whispers. "Aaron...I did it. It was me."

"Shh, I know." I stroke back the damp hair plastered across her forehead. "I know, and it's okay."

But she just shakes her head and keeps mumbling. "It was me. I did it. Molly, I'm so sorry. I did it."

Her words go on and on, her confession seeping out of her. So I wait until she empties, left only with her sobs as I pull her into my arms.

Chapter 35

Nothing matters.

Nothing but my rage.

With the last ounce of my strength, I fly Aurora back to the private box where the elders and Dev wait for me, the applause of the citizens below a backdrop to whatever it was they saw when I healed one of their own.

Depositing Aurora in Dev's arms, the only person I truly trust to handle her in this moment, I turn away from his imploring gaze. He wants me to go to him as well, *needs* me to, but in my current mental state, I have no use for soft words and gentle touches. I don't want consolation. I want to yell and scream and set this whole place on fire. But even more than that, I want to be alone. I feel dirty and used and manipulated. And I know until I can rid these feelings, I don't trust myself around anyone I care for. I don't want to have to regret the things I'd end up saying, doing, or not doing.

The Vigil guards close in around the elders as I approach, and they are right to. I'm not sure I even trust myself in this moment. Elena half smiles as Cato opens his mouth to speak, but I cut them off.

"I know they were simulations," I say, my voice rumbling with rage. "The Metus—they weren't real."

"Of course not," Cato says.

I take a step back at his easy admission. "What?"

"We wouldn't *actually* put you at such a risk," he explains with a near eye roll. "What you do on the battlefield is one thing, but here..." He shakes his head with a scoff. "No, you're our most valuable asset."

The low lighting of our box flickers with my fury, and I catch the few Council members shifting uncomfortably in my periphery.

"I want you to listen carefully," I say with icy slowness. "For I'm only going to say this once, and only once." My hands curl into fists. "You will *never* do that to me again. Do you understand? You will *never* manipulate, lie, or use someone I care for against me. *Those* are actions of an enemy, and I wouldn't think you'd want an enemy out of the Dreamer." I purposefully glance to all the Dreamer re-pellent bands adorning some of the people in the room, a mocking sneer on my lips. "Especially now that I've won the favor of the people." To prove my point, I step back, bathing myself in the arena lights that creep onto the balcony. The noise grows deafening as I stand in view, and I throw my hand out in a wave as the stadium shakes with the chanting of *Dreamer. Dreamer. Dreamer.*

Slipping back under the canopy, I level the Council with my most severe glare. "Do we have an understanding?" I make a point to hold Cato's gaze.

His face is frozen in stone, but a gleam in his green eyes wavers on a challenge and sense of respect. I care little for either.

"Yes," he says after a moment more of the two of us glaring at one another. "We have an understanding."

"Good." My attention bounces from Hector, to Elena, to Odi, past Alex, hesitating on Dev, before returning to Cato. "Now, I'm going to leave, and *for the love of Terra*, I want to leave *alone*. I think I've earned that much." And without another word, I pivot and storm out the door. Dev calls my name, but I don't stop, even as guilt hits me in the gut. I merely break into a half run, desperate for the outside.

"Slow down!" It's Hectors voice this time, the sound of his feet slapping against the tiled floor to catch up to me. "Mol—"

Me throwing up a wall between us cuts off his next words.

For Terra's sake, I said *alone*.

Turning down the last hall in the building, I shove open the doors. The cool night air slaps across my skin, the peace of a quiet night, and I finally take my first real breath. Looking down the darkened side alley, I find the government hover that brought me here idling nearby. Two Vigil guards, who were casually leaning against the building, stand straight when they see me. With barely a glance at them, I activate the sliding door and crawl inside, another soldier already siting in the driver's seat, protective helmet on.

"Take me to…" *Oh God*, I have nowhere to go. No, that's not true. Home. That's what I really want—need. I want to go back to Earth. "Take me to the nearest portal," I tell the driver just as the other two Vigil guards climb in. With a barely audible whirl, the car turns on and zips through the streets. With my leave, true exhaustion sets in, my body slinking low in my seat, my muscles sore, my throat in desperate need of a glass of water. But I'm even too tired to ask or conjure one up. So I gaze quietly out the window as the scenery passes by, my mind turned off. The occasional pedestrian or bicyclist is seen as we move along the darkened street, but other than that the city is the emptiest I've ever seen it. All must have turned out for the big event, and I scoff. I hope they got their money's worth, because that show won't have an encore.

Running a hand over my face, I let out a weary sigh, feeling the curious glances of the two guards who sit facing me. I inch closer to the window. I know it's unfair to run away like this, if that's even what I'm doing, but I need at least a second to stand under the sun, to share a smile with Becca, a laugh with Rae. If I can get a few moments of that, it will be worth it. I need a few hours—days—of normal, of joy. Even with the violence on Earth, it's nothing compared to what's happening here. My chest already feels lighter at the thought. Yes, this is what I need. Then I can come back and fight the next big battle, the next challenge the elders throw at me. I'll do it all after I can refuel. I only wish Dev could come with me, and I regret not saying good-bye to him.

Catching sight of a long, domed warehouse, its metal siding glimmering under the star-streaked night, I realize we're in the outer part of the city, heading toward the wall. "Um, guys?" I sit up straighter, bumping knees with the Vigil in front of me. "Where are we going?"

The Vigil looks out the glass and frowns. Tapping the tinted partition that separates us from the driver, he asks, "Hey, Kyle, where are we going?"

The driver doesn't answer.

"Kyle?" the Vigil asks again. "Stop the car, man. We definitely skipped a few portals."

Slowly the hover pulls to the side. The guard who tapped on the glass turns back to me with a smile. "Sorry, ma'am," he says as

the partition behind him falls away. "You'll be there soo—gwah."
A line of crimson bursts from the Vigil's neck, a quick flash of
a silver knife as the helmeted driver cuts deep into his skin. A
gurgle of pain and blood spit from the guard's mouth and wound
as his eyes go wide before they all too quickly fade to nothing. His
life, just like that, gone. I scream and jump back right as the other
guard dives in front of me, but with a bright burst of blue set off
by a gun, he collapses into a heap by my feet, the Navitas hitting
him in the one vulnerable gap between his gear.

I don't know if it's because I'm in shock, too worn out from
my recent efforts at the stadium, or I just can't find it in me to
fight anymore (or all of the above), but as the driver opens a canister that springs forth a long blue-white glowing rope, I don't
even use my powers as the cord—with lightning speed—slithers
completely around my body, pinning my arms to my sides and
clamping across my mouth. Instantly I know my powers are stuck
inside me, unable to be freed no matter how hard I try forcing
them out, and with a cold trickle of dread, I realize why. I'm being
held by Dreamer repellent. I saw a similar roped weapon back in
the engineers' lab with Raymond and Elena.

Lying on my side, the seat cushioning my fall, I watch help-
lessly, tangled in a boa constrictor's grip as the driver presses a
button on the side of his helmet, taking it off.

And though a part of me knew, sensed it, my heart still stops
beating as I take in the man before me.

"It's rather poetic, isn't it?" he coos, turning to face me, his
hazel eyes flashing yellow, catlike, under the dim light of the car.
"My sister saving me, and then you saving my sister…" Aaron's
words trail off, swimming in the glee of the situation. His long,

dirty-blond hair is tied back in a bun, but strings slip out to plaster against his oil-slick skin. His lips crack as they stretch into a grin, watching me, hardly looking any better than when he was on trial. With a sense of desperation, I wriggle under the bines, try to yell over the muzzle, but the rope only digs further into my skin, the pain bringing tears to my eyes.

His smile grows wider. "To be honest, I didn't know what to expect tonight, if you indeed were going to forgive her, but I should have known better. Of *course* the benevolent Dreamer would," he says with a sneer. "But no matter. My plans for you were going to be the same either way."

The way he says *plans* brings ice to my veins. He's not going to kill me then, which only means he's going to do something much, much worse. I jerk against the constraints again. Mistake. They tighten so much that one of my shoulders threatens to pop from its socket. I groan against the rubber across my mouth and flicker my gaze in havoc around the car. There has to be something, *anything*.

"Shhh, shhh, don't work yourself up," Aaron says sweetly as he twists on a new barrel to his gun. "We have quite the journey ahead of us, you and I. I'll need you with some of your strength."

My body threatens to betray me. I feel it wanting to shake with panic and fear, and an earlier Molly would have given in to it. An earlier Molly would cry in a puddle of tears from her quick surrender.

But I'm no longer that girl. For good or bad. So instead I grit my teeth, biting the side of my cheek to keep myself in check, and hold back the wave of hopelessness that wants to overtake me as I defiantly stare into Aaron's crazed eyes.

He laughs at me, as if he finds my determination endearing. "Sometimes you remind me of her," he says with a nostalgic shake of his head. "Sometimes I can see her looking straight at me through you. But then I remember"—his face grows hard, his gaze filling once more with venom—"she's dead." And with the tranquilizer needle sparking painfully from his newly constructed gun, Aaron pulls the trigger, and my world tips sideways as I'm swallowed whole.

Some will not survive.

Others will.

All will leave a legacy to follow.

—Tome of the Elders, Vol. IV;
The Dreamers, Article 12

Chapter 36

What if this doesn't work?
What if that night was our last together?

—Part of a letter from Molly to Dev

WHITE FLASHING LIGHTS of the security vehicles lit the dark night and whipped against the surrounding warehouses' titanium walls. A small crowd of onlookers were being held back by tape while a group of Vigil soldiers explained the scene. They were looking into an abandoned government vehicle that was possibly stolen. This was not a lie, of course. The car *was* stolen. They were just leaving out the horror that was found inside and the person who was now gone—their world's hope abducted.

Dev's chest heaved up and down, up and down as he took in the blood-splattered interior, the two dead Vigil slumped against the black leather seats. He felt a world away as he gazed in. Floating somewhere far off, out of reach of the emotions that awaited his return.

He couldn't do it.

He couldn't live through it again.

He couldn't... *In all of Terra.* Bringing both hands to his skull, he gripped it as if that might keep it from exploding. His rage was like a slow swell of a tsunami. For that was exactly what he was about to do—level this whole nightmare, forsaken land to find her.

"Molly," he whispered, his voice cracking. "I'm so sorry."

Aveline stood next to him, a statue. But even in her stillness, he could feel her thoughts, her doubt. It froze his veins while simultaneously filling them with fire.

"She's alive," he said for them both to hear, but more for him. "She's alive," he repeated, his gaze moving across the stained upholstery.

How much is hers?

No! He rid his mind of it, for no other reason than he might add to the gore if he didn't, the next person to walk by an unfortunate victim of his fury.

By the elders, why did he let her leave without him?

"Dev." Hector's voice brought him out of his spiraling emotions. The Vigil guard walked around the front of the car. When they first got here, Hector nearly collapsed on the spot along with Dev, seeing what awaited them. His hand flew to his mouth, as if to keep from vomiting, and his face bleached of color. Hector genuinely cared for his charge. Dev saw it when he chased after her, and in his eyes, the way a bit of his soul broke, just like Dev's, to learn of Molly's abduction.

"They found this on the front dashboard." Hector's brows remained glued together as he hesitantly handed Dev a small piece of paper, the Vigil's gaze momentarily locking with Aveline's in warning.

Dev's fingers shook as he grasped the slip, but if his companions noticed, they said nothing as he read the words that were scrawled in a messy rush across the parchment.

He read it again.

And again.

His mind trying to retain their meaning, their truth, while violently rejecting them.

His thumb rubbed over the few droplets of crimson soaking its surface. A distant part of his brain wondered if Aaron purposefully added them for a dramatic flair, because if anyone doubted it before, this note was proof enough of who was responsible for this and who now had Molly. But whether or not the blood was hers, it didn't matter, for the message still did its duty in filling each of Dev's cells with a crazed panic, of all out insanity.

With the corners of his vision warping, blurring out of focus, he slowly closed his hand into a fist, crumpling the paper.

I promise you'll see her again, the note read, *all the pieces of her.*

With a roar that broke through the thick night air, quieting all who were present, Dev charged the abandoned car, slamming his fist into the glass.

Over and over.

Not even stopping when he felt his knuckles shatter under the pressure or when small cracks spider-webbed across the durable surface. He kept punching and hitting and yelling until his voice turned hoarse and blood painted the window, his blood mixing in with the others'. With *hers*. And on this last thought, he collapsed to his knees, his dripping and broken hand covering his face as he momentarily surrendered to something he hadn't in over four decades.

Dev cried.

Chapter 37

I often wonder what you're doing at this exact moment.
Do our lives ever mirror in an unseen reflection?
I'm holding my hand over my heart. Are you?

—Part of a letter from Dev to Molly

MY HEAD FEELS like it's filled with cement, weighted to the cold, damp surface where my body lies, every muscle laced with barbed wire as I hesitantly test moving.

Lightning heat slices across every cell.

With a groan I resist passing out again and keep still. Even taking a breath hurts. So I force my pants to remain shallow, yet that brings on a gagging cough, the air here so stale and rotten. If my eyes weren't already watering from my pain, they would be from the stench. The only silver lining is that I'm pretty sure I know where I am—the underground tunnels. Which, I guess, isn't *that* much of a silver lining, considering how sprawling and far reaching these go. Who knows how far away I am from the city. Plus, the odor most definitely means Metus are either close by or frequent travelers of this section.

Loose dirt starts to worm its way into my nose, my cheek pressed firmly against the ground, with my hands bound behind my back. I dare to turn ever so slightly away, but just as I feared, the same sharp pain splits down my spine.

"*Mmmf*," I groan, my mouth still bound by a rubber adhesive. The rope that was lassoing the length of me is now scrunched into a thick belt around my waist, the blue-white glow from the Navitas—that so beautifully works against me—the sole illumination in the cave. Luckily, it doesn't hurt to move my eyes, and I attempt to see past the small halo of light where I lie. Even with my slight night vision, I can barely make out anything more than a few small boulders peppering the ground, a rocky wall curving a good distance away, and the slimy mucus that covers it. If there's a ceiling, I cannot see it, my belt's glow only going so far. With a jolt of surprise, I realize my legs are free and not bound together. My breaths come quicker as I glance around again. It looks like I'm the only one here. I could run. Could try to—

As soon as the idea enters my mind, a bubble of laughter strains to escape my muffled mouth. Yeah, I can run *just* like I can do a simple task like turn over without wanting to vomit.

What did Aaron inject me with?

As if on cue, I hear footsteps stepping on the loose gravel floor, and I close my eyes, letting my muscles fall back into the appearance of unconsciousness.

"Your possum game won't work with me." A smooth voice speaks through the dark, a new warmth of a light on me. I remain still. "I heard you moaning," he continues. "So I thought you might like some water."

Water.

My mouth is instantly the driest thing in the world.

God, I hate how that works.

Aaron must sense my internal battle, for he jiggles whatever canteen he holds so I can hear the liquid sloshing inside.

With frustrated defeat, I slowly open one eye and then two.

"Good morning." Aaron smiles down at me, the gesture so much like the nice doctor I met at the hospital. His ability to slip to and from his different personas terrifies me.

He's still wearing the black uniform of the guard he impersonated, and I try not to think what he had to do to get it. A vision of red oozing from a man's neck flashes before me.

Stepping closer, Aaron kneels down and reaches for my gag. I flinch away and then flinch again from the agony of moving.

"Easy now," he says. "You can't drink with this over your mouth, now can you?"

He must have dropped me near a wall, for my back presses up against a rough surface as he goes for the strip over my lips again, removing it with a quick pull.

"*Aarrgg*," I gasp, feeling like he just ripped off a layer of skin.

"Sorry about that," he says in a tone that sounds anything but contrite. "Only way those suckers can come off."

I spit in his face.

He stills, his eyes closed as my saliva drips down his lids.

I draw as much satisfaction from this as I can, a terrified part of me knowing it won't last long.

"I suppose I deserved that," he says tightly, wiping himself with the back of his arm.

"You deserve a lot more than that." My voice sounds foreign to my ears, rough and dry.

"Hmm, I can see how you'd feel that way."

I merely glower at him right before he hoists me up to lean against the wall. A scream of pain rips out of me, the echo floating down a long tunnel hidden in the dark. We must be at the back of a cave. I'm surprised I can even take in this detail as I pant and try to keep from fainting, my skin flush and no doubt pale from the sensation of my bones splintering.

"Here." Aaron shoves a silver canister to my mouth, and I pinch my lips shut. My eyes blaze as I stare into his silver-flecked ones, the blue glow from his lamp and my belt painting his features in whites and grays and highlighting the hollowness of his cheekbones, deep grooves of shadows.

"Your stubbornness is admirable," he says with a sarcastic droll, "but I highly suggest you drink, because I'm not sure when I'll be so inclined to give you another."

I wish I spat at him again, turned away, told him to eat shit, anything than what I actually find myself doing. But because I know he's not a man to threaten lightly, I lean forward and let him pour the cool liquid down my throat, sending the smallest amount of relief to my discomfort. All too soon he's pulling it back and closing the lid.

I lick my dry lips, carefully watching him while testing the material of the binds at my wrist, cutting into the flesh. They feel like simple plastic zip ties, and it's maddening how easily I could break them if I could only use my powers. But I can't. It stays trapped, the belt hugging my stomach and slowly suffocating the ball of energy swimming inside.

"Now that we've got that out of the way," Aaron says, "let's begin." Taking a seat on a small rock in front of me, he places the plastic canteen and lantern by his feet. Once again I find myself longingly staring at the swirling Navitas inside the lamp.

"It rather surprised me when I heard you were back in Terra," he says conversationally. "Actually, shocked is the more apt word. Which, if you weren't aware, is a rare emotion for me." He weaves his fingers in front of him, assessing. "I don't like being surprised *or* shocked, Molly. I've worked quite hard to avoid it actually. So I ask you, how did you do it? How did you get back to Terra?"

I blink, momentarily stunned, and not by the lightness of his tone but from his question. Did Aurora not tell him? My mind flips through all the details of me and Rae's transfer, the secrecy of it. Was it possible she was kept in the dark?

"Is that why you did all this?" I ask dumfounded and almost amused in my disbelief. "Because you want to know how I got *back*?"

A flash of something plays across his eyes, annoyance perhaps. "I think it might be best to introduce the rules of how this will work before we go any further," he says while slipping on black gloves he pulls from his pocket. Removing a small box that was attached to his belt, he lifts the lid, releasing a red-orange glow. With careful precision he plucks a tiny round marble from within—at least it looks like a marble, except that it has an angry red flame that dances in the middle.

"Don't let the size of this fool you," he says, holding the ball between his gloved thumb and pointer finger. "They are quite the nasty buggers."

I swallow, unable to remove my gaze from the small fire.

"Now, I'll ask again. How did you get back to Terra?"

"Why?"

Without hesitating, he flicks the red marble in my direction, and as soon as it hits my shoulder, there's a bright-orange flare right before there's a sensation of thousands of knives carving into my body. "AAAAAAAH!" I scream and fall over, chest heaving, tears streaming along my dirt-speckled cheek.

"I told you. Nasty buggers." Aaron plucks out a new one. My body shakes. "So, do you think you can give me that answer?"

Even though I now understand how this will go, I can't bring myself to give him what he wants. Terra only knows what he'd do with the information. Gritting my teeth, I try my best to sit up and hold his gaze as I ask, "Where did you get those?"

"Oh, Molly." He shakes his head in disappointment and then throws another my way.

A flash of red followed by my familiar scream, my body convulsing under the splintering pain.

"This can all be averted," he says, leaning forward to rest his elbows on his bent knees, half his face painted in crimson, the other in blue. "Just answer my question. How. Did. You. Get. Back?"

I spit onto the ground, my mouth filling with the taste of iron from where I bit the inside of my cheek, and roll to my back. "Fuck you," I pant out, my skin dewing with a sick perspiration.

"What was that?" Aaron asks. He's giving me one more chance.

I close my eyes, my hands cramping as they dig into the rocks under me, and muster as much courage as I can. "Fuck you!" I say louder right before my world becomes nothing but fire and cries and chokes of terror.

Four more rounds, four more blinding lacerations of misery before my body does what I only wish it did sooner—it slips into unconsciousness, letting the sounds of my whimpers and the smell of my urine-soaked pants be washed away by the darkness.

Chapter 38

I'm so mad. I lost my favorite ring the other day.
But I'm not going to search for it.
Lost things never like to be found until they've been
forgotten.

—*Part of a letter from Molly to Dev*

HER HAIR SHINED healthy and new, its color returning to its attractive strawberry blonde as it rested on the pillow she was propped against. Her complexion was no longer bleached of life, but flushed pink, restored. Yet despite all this, the shadows remained under her green eyes. Dev watched as her hands clasped one another tightly in her lap, her fingers restless, too scared to leave the protection of her white gown. The private recovery room was located in a guarded section of Terra's hospital, only one guest visit allowed a day. Dev had filled the slot for the past two.

"And he never said anything about where he was hiding when he came to Terra? He had to have shared *something* about where he was staying for all those years," Dev said, trying hard not to let his maddening frustration come through. He sat on a chair beside

Aurora's bed, waiting for her to pull her lip from between her teeth and answer him.

"No, I'm sorry," she said. "He only ever mentioned that he never stayed in one place very long."

"But was he hiding in the city? In one of the outpost towns?"

"I…I don't know." She rubbed her forehead, looking defeated and shamefaced.

Dev took in a calming breath, which didn't calm him at all. He didn't think he was capable of being calm ever again. Not until he found her, and even then he might not find peace, for who knew what state she'd be in— his throat tightened. *By the elders*, how was he to survive another second of this?

"Dev." Aurora's small voice brought his attention away from his fisted hands. Her eyes seemed so tired, even after all the medicine and rejuvenate therapy. Whatever evil Aaron's nearness seeped into her, using the connection only twins possessed, it potently took its toll. "I wanted to tell you…I'm…how I acted before, with Molly—"

"Don't." Dev cut her off. "We don't need to relive it. She knows that wasn't you."

"But that's the thing. It *was* me." Aurora sat up straighter, her brows drawing together. "I *did* have those thoughts. They might have been buried, but I was so angry at everything, and I didn't know where to put it. But Aaron…it was like he showed me the truth. I believed it was her fault. I believed…" She choked on a sob and covered her face.

Dev watched her a moment, her body shaking with her tears, before he gathered the strength to sit on her bed and console her. He worked hard to muster any empathy in this moment. It wasn't just because a deep, dark part of him blamed Aurora for this—he knew Aaron, the puppet master, was behind the show—but more because any emotion besides rage and fear were currently lost to him. He couldn't find it in him to care about anyone but the woman he loved, the one who was at this very moment most likely scared out of her mind in the company of a lunatic. Dev refused to think about the alternative possibilities. A shiver rippled through him.

"Aaron manipulated you," he said softly, soothingly rubbing Aurora's shoulder. "He used your love for his gain. Don't give him any more power by putting this on you. It was him, Aurora." Dev pulled back slightly so she could see the sincerity in his face. "It was *him*. Do you understand? All of it."

She hesitantly nodded and then looked away. "Will we ever be able to go back?"

Dev knew what she was asking, understood it was about the two of them and their friendship. "No," he said and felt her flinch in his arms. "None of us can go back. But maybe, after time, we can go forward."

The room fell into a heavy silence, the small beeps of hospital machinery filling the void.

Aurora suddenly shifted and leaned away, her eyes glazing over.

"What?" Dev asked.

"The tunnels," she whispered, her forehead clearing of wrinkles, as if something dawned on her.

Dev's heart beat faster. "What about the tunnels?"

"He did mention something about them." Her face puckered again, and Dev resisted yelling at her to find whatever it was faster.

"My time with him was so foggy towards the end." She shook her head. "I can only remember certain pieces of conversation, and he spoke nonsense most of the time, but...but I recall him knowing a lot about the tunnels. Specifically the ones near the Nursery."

Dev stood. "But we collapsed the tunnels running from Terra to the Nursery."

"Oh." Aurora's shoulders slumped. "Even the ones that don't connect?"

Dev blinked, time slowing. "What do you mean, that don't connect?"

"Well, I thought there were some tunnels that were just little burrows, like pockets around Terra. At least Aaron mentioned something about ones near the Nursery."

"And you didn't remember this yesterday!"

Aurora flinched before her gaze narrowed. "I could hardly say my own name yesterday."

"I have to go." Dev threw his quiver across his chest.

"But Aaron could have been lying," Aurora added as he turned toward the exit. "And I could be remembering our conversation wrong. If the guards that monitored our meetings didn't mention anything and you guys didn't find them mapped in those old schematics you found—"

"It doesn't matter." He pressed a button so the glass door slid open. "If you told me she might be stuck in the middle of the Sea of Dreams, I'd build a ship to search it."

And with that, Dev left to find Aveline and Hector so they could hopefully, *please, by the elders,* find the other half of his soul.

⊷⊷⊷ ⊶⊶⊶

The next two days were filled with oscillating rounds of hope and utter disappointment. Using Terra's laser scanning and ground-penetrating radar machines, Dev and his squad searched the western lands that circled the Nursery. They were astonished to find so many unaccounted for pockets of tunnels. And even though they uncovered two Metus hives among the five they located, there were no signs of Molly or Aaron in the other three. They still had a good portion of land to scan, of course, but that was far from reassuring. Terra only knew how many ancient burrows were left to find around the Nursery, not to mention the miles and miles of land to the north, east, and south.

Dev was about ready to lose his mind, more than he already had. Looking back at his first separation from Molly, when she was stuck on Earth, was enough to make him scoff. That was a walk in the park compared to this, this where he had no way of knowing how she was doing. Was she terrified? Scared? Hurt? With Aaron's company, he had no doubt it was all of the above. Holding in a growl, Dev scrubbed down his face, the stench of decaying flesh clinging to his clothes as he stomped into the apartment. His black protective gear was covered in the slime that caked along the tunnels, the shedding skin of nightmares, but he could give two Metus droppings as he slumped into one of the beige couches in the depressed living room. The apartment was dark and quiet save for the crackling of the blue-white fireplace. Dev stared unseeing into the flames.

"We'll go back out in a few hours," Aveline said, her thin frame a silhouette of shadows as she came to block his view. "But you needed to eat something."

"Why?" Dev ground out. "She's probably starving right now. Why should I not be too?"

"Dev." It was Tim's calm voice. He had insisted on helping in the search as well, his body now completely restored since the accident. "She would want you to take care of yourself."

Dev merely pinched his lips together, his fingers digging into his thighs before he slumped forward and hung his head in his hands. "What am I going to do?" His voice was painfully raw.

Aveline placed a featherlight touch to this shoulder. "We'll find her," she said, sitting beside him. "We'll find her soon."

A shaky breath escaped him. His muscles ached—so did his head and everything else, for that matter. His whole body was a ball of tension and agony. He felt horrible, guilty, and useless anytime he wasn't out there searching, and even then he felt close to the same. The elders had deployed seven other Vigil squads to stealthily seek out the lost Dreamer, use whatever hi-tech equipment they had hidden away in their engineer labs. But so far, just like with Dev's group, nothing. Considering Aaron was able to hide from their world while still making frequent visits left little confidence of finding an easy trail to him now. He obviously knew what he was doing. He'd only be found when he wanted to be.

Molly had been gone close to a week now, and the elders were determined to keep her disappearance as quiet as possible, for as long as possible. Terra forbid this interrupt Cato's carefully laid-out Dreamer campaign.

Dev frowned as he glanced around the apartment. "Where's Hector?"

"He got a message to meet Elena," Aveline said, cleaning a bit of dirt that caked the side of her quiver.

"I have some leftovers from the other night." Tim walked to the kitchen that connected to the open floor plan of their apartment. "I'll heat something up."

"I'm not hungry," Dev grumbled, his gaze moving back to stare into the fire that danced in front of him. He felt nauseous actually and, maybe because they were talking about food, had the strongest desire to see Rae. He needed his friend right now. He needed to hear him say something reassuring, something that would make Dev stop feeling like his world was spinning out of control while at the same time standing still in the flames of hell.

He felt completely alone.

He stood.

"Where are you going?"

He sensed Aveline's concerned hazel gaze following him as he walked to the door.

"Dev, you need to rest," Tim chimed in, dropping what he was doing in the kitchen and coming closer.

"Don't you *get it*," Dev growled, spinning back around. "There is no rest! Not when she's out there!" He threw his arm out. "*By the stars*, how could I possibly *rest*?"

Tim frowned. "I didn't mean—"

"She could be dying." Dev's voice wavered at the end. "Right now. That monster, he could..." He couldn't finish the sentence.

The room hung in a tense silence. Though his flatmates were trying to be nothing but supportive and reassuring, none of it mattered. No amount of gentle words could stop this. Stop what Dev felt in his very marrow. The torture. The words of Aaron's note forever branding his heart, wrapping it with barbed wire until it oozed and bled.

"I have to keep looking," he said. "I'll go out with one of the Vigil squads. I just can't sit here and pretend like nothing's wrong."

"That's not what we're asking you to do." Tim's brown eyes were gentle, his gray hair winking silver in the low light. "We all need our strength if we're going to get through this Dev. Starving and working ourselves raw will not help bring Molly back faster."

Dev swallowed, his hands fisting at his side. "It might," he said gruffly before he turned and yanked open the door.

Hector filled the frame just outside. The Vigil looked up from where he was staring unseeing at the ground, as if he had been standing there for a long time. His face was ashen, the scar over his left eye red and swollen, obviously from crying. Dev took a hesitant step back. *NO, no, no, no. Please Terra, no.*

"Hector?" Aveline walked over. "By the stars, what's happened?"

Dev wanted to plug his ears, to run before the man would say the words he was so terrified would be spoken. *Please, don't let it be Molly.* Foggily, Dev wondered how his heart was racing when it most certainly had stopped beating.

"Come here," Aveline spoke softly to her friend, apparently still at a loss to speak. Gently wrapping her arm around his thin frame, she ushered him inside. The two were always a striking pair. Both willowy and moon pale, white hair mixed with a touch of her blonde, all set off by their black uniforms.

Tim set a tray of tea down on the coffee table as the three sat on the couches, Hector in a daze beside Aveline. Dev hadn't moved from his spot by the door.

"Hector," Dev heard himself saying, his voice rough like sandpaper and laced with a slight plea. What he wanted from the Vigil, he wasn't sure. Just...*something* besides this quiet dread of the next second.

"Is this about what Elena needed you for?" Aveline asked.

Hector nodded slowly and then finally opened his mouth to whisper, "He's gone."

Tim and Aveline glanced at one another. Dev merely stiffened while simultaneously deflating. "He?" he asked. "Who? Aaron? Have they found them?" Dev's voice rose, unhinging as his body prepared to jump into action.

Hector blinked up at them. "Robert," he said. "There were complications with his recovery. After he got home, he got sick... a fever, and he didn't...he didn't..." Hector couldn't finish his sentence as he leaned forward and put his face in his hands.

Dev had a strange sensation that he was looking at a mirror image of himself not too many minutes ago. Robert, Molly's grandfather, was dead. Dev lost feeling as he tried to compartmentalize this news with all the other horridness.

"I'm so sorry." Aveline frowned, clearly hating to see Hector in pain, his body shaking with his silent tears. "I'm so sorry."

Words, Dev thought, never did the job the speaker wanted them to.

"He lived a long life," Tim chimed in gently. "A full one, with two worlds that loved him. I know I never met him, but from what Molly had mentioned, I think it was good you reconnected in the end."

"*Molly*," Hector choked out, his gaze filled with agony and loss. "What are we going to tell Molly? She'll be devastated. She didn't get to be there…"

"Shhh." Aveline tried to calm him. "We'll deal with it when we need to."

Hector shook his head. "No, you don't understand. The funeral, it's on Monday."

The room collapsed into silence.

"Four days," Dev whispered, and Hector nodded.

They had four days to find Molly, or her family would realize she was missing. Three days to hope she wasn't already dead or dying. Dev grasped his chest, his hand unconsciously going over his heart, as if that could stave off the sensation of it bleeding. He didn't need an end date for him to already feel like they were running out of time, but now…now it was inevitable, urgency on top of urgency. They had a new ticking clock counting down the seconds of the already lit fuse that was racing its way to both their worlds exploding.

Chapter 39

When you look up at Earth's night sky,
don't remember me in the stars.
I am the blackness in between.
I am the dark that hugs the light,
keeping it safe.

—Part of a letter from Dev to Molly

TIME, A CONCEPT written about for millennia, weaved in song and scratched out from a poet's pen. It's a daunting thing, really. A formidable companion to any living creature, for it keeps going even after we don't. It will leave us behind as it progresses forever forward. I wonder if it ever gets lonely, knowing nothing but itself will last.

This is one of the things that fills my head on repeat as I lie in my sightless purgatory, for time has never made much sense to me in Terra. With no sun or moon orbiting the night's sky, I found myself relying on my guards or my patterned schedule to tell me the hour of the day. Rounds with Elena usually happened during the "mornings," while my training and classes with Cato occurred during the "evenings." Fighting the Metus just came when they did, punctuality not evil's strong suit. And here, lying in this dark, damp cave, the only sound the occasional drip of slime hitting the floor in the inky blackness or a mewl from a creature passing through a far-off tunnel, I'm completely lost to its passing. I can only count it from Aaron's visits. There have been five, each as nightmare filled as the last, each more creative in punishment with his rising need for me to give him answers to his questions. How did I get back? Who helped me? Where was the DCC, and how can he access it? I'd like to say I've kept quiet, that my earlier heroics to remain tight lipped lasted, but...I'm pretty certain it didn't. I have no real way of remembering. Lucidity in those moments of all-consuming pain is few and far between. There are black spots in my memory, or rather blinding explosions.

Did I tell him how I returned, or did I tell him to each shit again? Or both? From the nagging guilt that swims in my chest, I'm terrified I've let something slip, especially since Aaron seems to be gone longer than normal. I try consoling myself by saying one's convictions can only last so long after certain...experiments are done to one's body. There's only so much a person can take.

Right?

As if on cue, a splintering spasm goes through me, something that has been coming in waves since Aaron's last electro-shock ministrations. Gritting my teeth, I wait for it to pass and concentrate on a patch of rocks near my feet. The blue-white halo of light from my Dreamer repellant belt slides over their gray surfaces. The belt has rubbed my stomach raw, and if I could lift my shirt, I'm certain there would be a multitude of blisters. But even though I can't, my arms still pinned behind my back and connected to a long chain imbedded in the cave wall, it's of little concern to me. I've lost the desire to assess my wounds. What do I gain from that? More reasons to cry, to feel disgusted with myself? No, I no longer have the energy to care about my current state. If the smell from the corner of the cave is anything to go by, I've hit a low point, and I'd rather not dwell on it for too long.

A sound in the distance causes my head to whip up, my nerves to vibrate in fear, but they are momentarily dashed away by a dizzy spell. I've been given very little water and even less food. If the unrelenting torture wasn't already enough to weaken my mind and body, my hunger and thirst certainly have done the trick.

Though my thoughts remain loopy and skittish, I strain to see into the inky blackness beyond my small orb of illumination, listening for any sound of the devil's return. But so far I hear only the occasional howl of wind and the muffled, eerie clicks from Metus talking to one another. They must share the same cavern we hide in. Why they don't make their way toward me, attacking, I have no idea. Maybe the belt I wear not only suppresses my power but also hides my energy, camouflaging me. Which, if I were in the right state of mind, would fascinate me. But I'm not, so it doesn't.

After another indistinguishable amount of time, I finally hear what I've feared and strangely anticipated—the familiar footsteps of Aaron treading along the ground. I keep from visibly flinching when his tall form seeps out of the dark, his dirty-blond hair hanging in stringy waves around his gaunt face, a black mask pushed down around his neck and blending into the standard Nocturna uniform he wears. His strides are purposeful as he walks to the opposite corner, dropping a small duffel on the floor. I curl into a ball, trying to make myself as small as possible, unnoticeable, as my teeth chatter, my muscles tensing in panic despite their soreness.

A hot flash of loathing rushes through me, directed at the Vigil and myself. I'm so cowered by him, puny when he's near.

I hate it.

I hate myself and what I've become, what he's made me.

The Navitas in me cries out to be used, the thought of revenge never tasting so sweet. It hits up against my internal walls to be freed, but it can't. It's stuck firmly inside.

I want to sob.

Suddenly Aaron stops in the arranging of objects from his bag, and crinkles his nose, glancing to the corner, which I've been forced to use as a toilet. "By the stars, you've created quite the stench in here," he says, turning my way with a curled lip. "And I've hardly fed you anything too."

My face grows hot with shame and anger.

"But I guess it's better than you having another accident in your pants. I still don't know why you won't let me change them for you. I brought you that perfectly good pair."

My body trembles more, but from a completely different reason than fear. Red tinges the side of my vision.

"I'm sure your current pair aren't very comfortable," he muses before adding with mocking sweetness, "and you know how much I care for your comfort, Molly."

My chest heaves with each one of my breaths, working hard not lash out with words, which has been my only weapon against him. He's goading me. I've learned this about him now. He likes to provoke me into saying something hateful, mean, so he has an excuse to start his sick games. So far he's won in doing so every time.

And he's about to win again.

"I wonder," I say through gritted teeth, my voice hoarse from all my screaming, "what would a sick bastard like you ever do with your time if you didn't have me around to make suffer?"

He barks a laugh at that before approaching. *Shit.* I press back into the wall, my body searing in pain. "You call what you've experienced here suffering?" He leans over me, his hazel eyes narrowing in disgust. "You naïve girl. You've been coming here for a total of what? Nine months, almost a year now? You haven't seen half of the nightmares lurking in Terra."

"I'm staring at you, aren't I?"

The slap is so sudden that I don't feel the sting until my head is done twisting sideways. The iron taste of blood coats my tongue. Slowly I bring my face to him again, my hands pulling on the binds, the chain clanking behind me, with my desire to cradle my tender skin and most definitely wanting to hit back. Aaron's gaze is wild and sickly pleased as he regards me. My blood runs cold with a new terror. This is the first time he's personally harmed me, touched me with his bare hands. While my injuries are vast, none are from his actual physical contact. He prefers the use of a third party. If it wasn't the tiny fireballs, it was mechanical spiders that climbed in between my clothes, stinging me raw, or shocks of electricity from a sleek black rod. All weapons I can only assume he procured from the black market.

Aaron and I stare at one another. Somehow I find the strength to hold his gaze even when my throat bobs with a dread-filled swallow. Whatever this is, it isn't good, and with his smile sharpening, he knows I realize it.

But before he can strike again, a red-orange glow lights up the rounded doorway in the distance, the entrance to the cave. Aaron turns, resuming his full height, but doesn't grab a weapon. The telling sounds of a Metus approaching echoes forward, its liquid sludge moving closer as the air fills with an even more acute stench of rot.

My eyes widen. Instead of grabbing the Navitas-filled knife I know Aaron has stashed somewhere on his person, he turns off the lamp by our feet. Once again the cave is filled with the single glow of my belt. Glancing over his shoulder to me, he puts his finger to his lips, indicating that I should remain quiet, just as the beast comes into view. It fills the entrance, its lava skin churning and climbing along its globular body as it illuminates the space in crimson. Its eyes are two bright flames of white as it peers around the cave, which is now overflowing with its depressed energy, of the horror it holds within. While I barely breathe, fearing it will hear the sound, I notice Aaron's relaxed stance in front of me. He seems almost unconcerned by the monster's presence, and a part of me fights the idea of yelling out and giving away our location. Surely it would be better to end this all now. But before I can do much of anything, I watch in utter amazement as the beast sniffs the air, once, twice, before turning and slinking away, its orange glow growing softer and softer until it's no longer painting the cave walls. Everything is thrown back into the flap of a raven's wing, indicating the monster's presence is gone.

Aaron turns the lamp back on and faces me, seeing the astonishment in my features. "Interesting, yes?"

"How…why did it not know we were here?"

His mouth curls smugly. "That thing around you is a doll of a device. Not even an Energy Sensor would be able to detect you."

So what I surmised earlier was true. Still, I frown. "But what about you?"

His eyes glow from whatever secret he holds. "Yes, Molly, what about me?"

Despite hating looking at him for longer than a few seconds, I study him intently, the way his skin is almost translucent in its paleness, his dark veins snaking just under the surface easily traceable. And his pupils…his pupils seem larger than normal, blacker, almost covering his whole eye. Without meaning to, a vision of the black tar that snaked through Aurora whirls before me. *Oh God*, could it be possible? Could Aaron's soul have turned so dark, so full of his hate, that he now blends in with the enemy?

"What are you?" I whisper.

His cool gaze seeps into mine. "I would have thought that was obvious by now." He leans over, gripping my chin painfully. "I'm your nightmare." And then he steps back, returning to his bag and pulling out a small silver object that looks like a remote. "Now, where were we before we were so very rudely interrupted?"

I stay silent, not about to remind him that he was about to hit me again.

"Oh yes." He presses one of the buttons on the remote, and the belt around me instantly coils out to wrap around my whole body, just like it did when he first trapped me in the hover car. I fall to my side with a grunt, my legs now secured together, the long rope traveling up to pinch my arms to my sides and wrap around my neck.

My panic explodes.

"There's been a change in plans," he says as he stands over me. "I've realized your knowledge is of little use to me. What I wanted from you, well, besides the pleasure of your company, of course"—he smiles syrupy—"would take much too long to acquire."

So there was a reason to this besides his mere thrill of torturing me? For some reason that fills me with the slightest sense of relief. Which is sick, I know, but is it so wrong to need my pain be for a purpose?

"Yes, it would have taken at least another month Earth cycle," Aaron continues, "and Terra only knows what this place would smell like if you were kept here for that long."

My curiosity gets the better of me. "What were you looking for?" I ask as I stare up at him from my awkward position on the ground.

He tilts his head to the side. "Normally I'd punish you for asking such a thing, but seeing as this day is a celebration of sorts, I'll give you a gift by answering." He crouches down, his finger gently rubbing along my cheek and pushing back a greasy lock of my hair. His touch brings bile to my throat, and I resist recoiling away as my heart pumps wildly. "I was going to become you," he says softly.

I blink. "What?"

"A Dreamer," he clarifies, removing his hand. "Or at least gain your powers."

I knew Aaron was crazy, but... "What are you talking about?"

His eyes search mine. "You don't remember, do you?" He shakes his head, an amused gesture. "You were under quite a bit of...stress at the time, so I guess you wouldn't. The transfer chamber," he says, and my skin turns to ice. "You and Rae's nice little swap. Who knew it was possible, but I guess I should have wondered more about this blonde piece of yours." He touches the strip in my hair that is the color of Rae's.

My mind spins in circles. I'd crumbled, just as I feared. How long did I last before I sang like a bird? I remember none of it—it's all just a muddle of pain and fire and nightmares. All darkness mixed with blazes of hate brought on by this man. *Oh God.* And I'm supposed to protect a world, *two* worlds, and yet I can barely protect myself. I'm weak, pathetic. Dev would never have broken. Dev would have rather died than give in to this man. It's this thought, of the man I purposefully kept buried deep in my heart, refusing to think about while stuck with this monster, that breaks me further. But oddly it's not tears that mark my unhinging. It's laughter. I laugh, big, racking guffaws that strain my chest against my binds, burning my lungs with each breath.

What's the purpose of any of this?

Of me?

Everyone thinks I'm someone special, someone unlike the other humans of Earth, someone who can make a difference. I laugh even harder at that, and Aaron watches, confusion bringing his brows together, but not without the slightest bit of mirth. He seems to enjoy my trip into his world of insanity.

"You…you thought you could be me," I pant out. "You want to be a *Dreamer.*" Laughter erupts from me again. "Do it! Take it! Please, take it all. Take my power!" I yell out. "You want it? It's yours." I roll to my back, giggling all the while. "It's all yours."

Aaron stands, his gaze no longer amused. "You find what I had planned to be funny?"

"Oh no, no. On the contrary. It's possibly the most brilliant idea you've ever had." I'm smiling. I'm actually fucking smiling. I've definitely lost it.

"I see." He pulls the remote from his pocket again. "Well, I'll enjoy seeing what you think of my new plan. If it will amuse you as much as now."

This sobers me a bit, my chuckles dying down to heavy breaths, and Aaron arcs a superior brow.

"But I think it will be more beautiful than funny," he says. "Yes, quite gorgeous actually, and maybe a bit poetic, like our interludes often are." He grins. "I'm going to end it, Molly. I'm going to end this sin-filled world right where it begins. And you're to be my guest of honor, and perhaps a certain blue-eyed man too. What do you think of that? Would you like to see him one last time? It would be rather gracious of me, I think," he muses as he twirls the remote between his two fingers. "Yes, let's bring you two together to watch it all burn. It's what I was given, after all, to look into her eyes as she died, as *I* died." He's quiet for a moment before he lets out a gentle sigh, bringing his hands to his hips. "And if I were to be honest, I've grown rather tired of all this. Aren't you tired?" he asks rhetorically, glancing down at me. "Of course you are. You look positively exhausted. Yes, I think you'll appreciate my new plan. After all, it will end the war. Ah, I see you like that," he says as my eyes widen slightly. "That's right, Molly. I'll be doing your job, for I've come to the decision that if she can't exist, none of us should."

And then with a flourish, he points the remote at me while pressing a button. Instantly the rope tightens like a vice, and I cry out in agony, the telling pop of one of my shoulders coming out of its socket filling the cave. If I had food in my stomach, it would be all over the ground.

"But you—" I pant against the searing pain. "But you haven't asked me anything!"

"Oh, I'm not doing this to get answers anymore."

My voice comes out small and fragile as I ask, "Then why?"

His smile is the very curve of evil. "Because I can."

As the lasso tightens and cuts off my air supply, my vision explodes with white dots. And the oddest thing enters my mind as I lie on the cold cave floor, slowly dying. I think how crazy it is that out of all the amazing things the human body does, the way we can think and feel and grow and learn and create—something as simple as blocking one's air supply for a mere moment, a few seconds, can stop all that. How something as complicated as a life can so easily be taken by another.

Because he can.

Chapter 40

I learned how I can get back today.
What needs to be done.
And while I hate to ask it, I must.
Is such a sacrifice worth being together again?

—Part of a letter from Molly to Dev

THE AIR WAS stale and humid, the darkness like spilled ink against the rocky walls, the only offset the low blue-white halo of their Glowers. A sheen of sweat ran across Dev's brow, and he blinked against the salty burn when droplets slipped into his eyes. It was the last tunnel his squad would search today, as another Metus attack had been reported along Terra's wall, which needed reinforcement. But as Dev waited for Aveline to scan one of the two tunnel openings they stood in front of, he wondered how it would look if he stayed behind. If they ended up empty handed after this, he was pretty certain he'd be useless on a battlefield. He felt useless a lot lately.

Minka shifted beside him, her cropped blonde head bent over as she checked the map readout. The hologram floated above the tablet, painting a twisted, circular web. They had found new pockets of caverns hidden a few clicks to the east of the Nursery and quickly set out to find an entrance. Minka glanced at Dev as the hologram flickered in and out, a sure sign they stood near an energy concentration, even though nothing was picked up on the scanner. Dev nodded once, his nerves instantly set to vibrate. *Please, by the elders, let her be down here.*

"We should split up," he said as he raised his Glower higher, illuminating the carved-out space where his team of eight stood in the bowels of a thin shaft. "Marcus, what's your sensor reading?"

A burly man with almond-shaped eyes and jet-black hair turned from the other opening, his radar machine gripped tight. "There's definitely something here."

"Yeah, I'm getting something too," Aveline agreed, not taking her eyes off the black hole in front of her. "I don't think it's a hive though. Maybe a pack. From the smell, I think we all can agree that there's a fair share."

"Can we tell which one they are down?" Dev asked.

Aveline glanced at Marcus. "My numbers are all around thirty."

"Same," Marcus said, frowning.

Collö, Dev silently cursed. "We'll split evenly then."

Divvying his team, Dev turned down the left bank, Aveline in tow, while the rest traveled the right.

"Minka, you hear me okay?" Dev asked, checking their communication.

"Loud and clear, Boss," came her raspy voice.

Careful to stay clear of the walls, despite wearing their protective gear, Dev and his squad kept an even pace as they maneuvered through the tunnel. Their way could only be lit a few yards ahead at a time, the black shadows fighting back against their illumination as they moved forward.

They might have traveled ten minutes or thirty. Dev wasn't sure, his mind too preoccupied with his racing thoughts to keep much hold on a detail like time. Which was funny, since that was all he'd been aware of lately. A pinprick of orange seeped out of the space in front of them, the stench growing richer. The Metus.

Dev turned off his light, his team following suit until they stood in utter darkness.

"Slowly now," he whispered as they crept forward, using the steady light of the enemy to guide them until they could hear the sounds of the monsters' movements, wet liquid steps flopping along a dirt floor, a slug sliding. Dev's stomach turned over.

He snapped out his Arcus, and there was a small echo of the rest of his men and women preparing their weapons as they came to stand just beyond the entrance of a giant cavern, the stalactite ceiling five floors high. Remaining in the shadows, he took in the five monsters that were almost lounging in their hovel, abnormally bloated in size. A sticky tar lined the entire space, a putrid energy of sorrows swimming in the air and burning the back of Dev's throat as he breathed in. He spotted piles of blue-white glowing balls spread around the floor. And he watched in horror as one Metus scooped one up with its talons, its mouth opening to a sickeningly wide degree, and threw it back. Smoke sizzled out as he chomped, the creature's mewl of pleasure echoing in the cavern as its size grew just barely plumper.

By the stars... How did they get energy orbs? Dev stole a glance at Aveline, who shared a similar look of dismay. Somehow the

Metus obtained an absurd amount of the Navitas used to power the vehicles in Terra. And then it dawned on him. Aaron. Aaron would do something like this. But why? What was he using them for? And did the monsters understand such a trade? His people still didn't exactly know how intelligent they were, but given their recent behavior, especially now, Dev was beginning to think Terra's soldiers grossly underestimated them. As these thoughts spun, a new one zipped to the forefront. *Molly.* She was here. She had to be. He felt it in the very marrow of his bones. Why else would he keep these creatures here, sedated, but here nonetheless, if not for a diversion? Guards against something he wanted to be kept hidden? Dev's gaze zeroed in on another opening on the far side of the cave. Two Metus slumped along the wall beside it. His heart beat so loudly in his chest he feared the monsters would hear it, but as he looked around at each of their docile and lazy forms, he realized that if this *was* Aaron's doing, he'd made a grave mistake. The creatures were so well fed on the Navitas that they seemed almost drunk, languid and apathetic to their surroundings.

Perfect for the picking.

With control he never knew he'd be able to possess, he resisted running straight toward the other tunnel and instead turned to his team.

Pointing to each of their various weapons, he indicated for them to pick a target. They would get as many beasts as they could from where they stood. The Metus outnumbered them by one, but it didn't matter. Dev was quick with his bow and would have one of his arrows flying at another before the first made contact.

Lining up next to each other, each soldier took aim, and with the loosening of Dev's first arrow, the rest followed suit. The creatures didn't know what hit them before they were all blown apart, coating the space with their slime, another layer against the black tar. A few of his team members bent over coughing from the overbearing smell, but Dev merely covered his nose and darted forward. He heard Aveline call his name, but he didn't stop, his only purpose to find Molly.

Please Terra, let me find Molly.

The entrance was smaller than the one they had previously traveled down, and sloped deeper into the ground. Dev had to dig his gloved hands into the wall to keep from slipping as he ran full out. But as he made it to the bottom, he hesitated when he heard the wail of a girl echo out of the darkness.

"Molly!" he choked out as he plunged forward, his light stick guiding his way as he rounded a bend, skidding into a smaller cave. He barely registered his leg hitting against a wire before he found himself ducking as a bright shot of Navitas flew straight at him. The rock wall broke apart beside his head. A booby trap.

Rolling into a crouch, he swept the area, landing on a tall male with hollowed-out cheeks and dirt-smudged blond hair, staring at him from across the cavern, a flash of surprise in his gaze before he pulled a gun from a holster at his back.

"*Aaron,*" Dev spat, every one of his muscles coiling to spring forward, but the Vigil's surprise switched to a smile as he pointed his weapon while simultaneously slapping a round contraption onto the wall where he stood.

"I wish I could stick around, but—" Aaron darted to the other side of the cave, where another opening was sliced thin into the wall.

Dev pounced, but Aaron held him off with a shot from his gun. Dev followed suit with one of his arrows, the two men sparring from their separate sides of the cave, lighting it up with sparks of blue and white.

"Uh-uh," the man tutted. "I'd choose wisely now," he said and glanced to where he previously stood, where Dev realized a timer was counting down. A bomb. "Which do you want more? Me or her? And I'll give you a helpful hint. If you don't decide soon, we'll all die, though that's rather an inevitable end eventually."

Dev's blood ran cold. *Her?* Swiveling around, he searched the shadowed cave, squinting as his eyes landed on a blue glow coming from the corner, a small huddled form wrapped in wire.

The world spun out from beneath him.

"Molly!" He ran, barely aware of the man at the edge of his vision slipping through the crack and disappearing. "Oh, Molly! Can you hear me?" As he crouched down, the girl flinched away while simultaneously curling into a smaller ball, a whimper escaping.

Dev's heart broke into a million pieces. "Midnight," he said more gently as his hands hovered unsurely above her. He didn't know exactly what was wrong with her, besides everything, and he didn't want to add to her pain. Glancing at the timer, seeing he only had a few minutes, he returned to take inventory of the woman by his knees. He scanned her bound hands behind her back, chained and connected to the wall. She had a thick, glowing belt around her waist that painted a grisly scene of the rest of her. Clothes, once a durable black uniform, were now a stained and tattered mess. Her skin was so covered with dirt and...other things, Dev could hardly make out if she had any cuts or bruises. Clumps of her hair were stuck together, worming over her cheek and across her chapped lips, and she looked half her weight. Red exploded in Dev's vision, his body quaking in unchecked rage. *He would kill him.* He would peel the skin off his body slowly, methodically, and enjoy every sound of terror that devil screamed out. Aaron would pay for this. He would pay dearly.

So consumed in his thoughts of revenge, Dev barely remembered cutting the binds from Molly's wrists and lifting her into his arms. She flailed in his grasp, seeming to confuse his help for another's torture, and Dev could hardly see past his own tears as he sprinted toward the exit.

He ran and ran and ran, even after the blast of the bomb shook the underground tunnels as he and his team burst through to the surface. Didn't stop when Aveline called his name, saying they were safe. Dev kept going, moving, getting as far away from that horror-filled cave, hoping with every step the distance would somehow remove all the seconds, hours, and days the woman in his arms had swum in nightmares.

--⊱⊰--

The next day and a half were...unbearable. Dev had her back, had her an arm's distance away, could look at her, smell her, yet she wasn't there. Molly was a shadow, a mirage of her once bright self. Even after Elena ordered the doctors to induce her into a coma so she could splice her memories, try and remove some of the sickness of what she'd experienced with Aaron, Molly only woke a hair's breadth better. She was given advanced medicine and high-carb-filled fluids to bring her gaunt body back to one that could stand without shaking. Her hair, so matted and stuck together, had to be cut. It now hit right at her shoulders, which helped in rounding out her face. But even after all of this, even when she returned to her correct body weight, the bruises, cuts, and broken bones mended, and her freckles returning to dust along the bridge of her nose and across the flush of her cheeks, her eyes said it all. They retained a slight glaze, a tendency to drift out of focus in the middle of a conversation. And though Molly had stopped flinching when Dev reached for her, even allowed him to hold her, which he so desperately needed, she seemed nervous, tight.

Dev was at a loss.

He knew the only thing that would truly mend things was time. And time, well, it wasn't something they ever had the luxury of having. Her grandfather's funeral was in two days, and he still hadn't told her the news of his passing. With a headache creeping along his temples, Dev scrubbed down his face as he watched Molly sleep, as he sat in the chair across from her.

She lay curled in a ball on the couch in her private chambers in the DCC. She preferred resting here to her bed, and Dev tried not to think about why. Even though he knew, saw along with Elena, the rest of the elders, and the engineers who took and spliced her memories. They watched what Molly couldn't relive in words, viewed what they needed for intel on a hovering screen in a sound-proof room. Though slightly muted, as if behind a veil, they heard Aaron's insistent questions, the screams, *her* screams, tears, pleas, and final confessions. They viewed it all until Dev had to leave the room in a burst of his own madness and blurred vision to puke in the hallway. His midnight had been broken and then broken again, and those sounds...scenes... *By the elders*, where would they go from here? Where would she? Dev had howled then, succumbing to the blinding rage to wrap his fingers around a certain Vigil's throat, watch as his eyes bulged in protest before they dimmed to the shade of death. The only solace he got was that Molly hopefully didn't have these memories anymore, even if Dev had them for eternity. It was the least he could give her, his third-person pain for her first.

Then there was Hector, who surprised Dev with his unwavering support and aid. He seemed almost as desperate as Dev to put Molly right again, even when dealing with his own grief. And while it sometimes annoyed Dev to have his place by her side so encroached, he was grateful to the Vigil. He knew he couldn't have done this alone. His small family of Aveline, Tim, and now Hector were the only things holding him together. If only Rae were here...

"Dev?" A soft voice came from the sofa, and he blinked out of his internal musings. Molly looked at him under half-closed lids, her head propped on a pillow, her soft ivory lounge clothes of sweatpants and tee twisting in the blanket Dev had placed on her. She had fallen asleep reading some human book about a beast and a beauty. Since moving in here, she had collected quite a few books.

"Do you need something?" He slid forward on his chair, ready to stand.

She didn't say anything for a moment, just watched him from her fetal position on the couch. "How did you do it?" she eventually asked.

"Do what, midnight?"

"Live after Anabel."

Dev sucked in a quiet breath. He wasn't prepared for that.

"How did you cope?" She remained lying on her side, the only movement her slow blinks and the gentle rise and fall of her chest.

"I just had to," he said with a frown. He would never tell her he had seen clips of her memories, would never give her reason to bring them to mind any more than they seemed to come on their own.

She held his gaze and then nodded softly. "I'll have to."

Dev was by her side in an instant, kneeling before her, his hand pausing in question. *Can I?* he silently asked.

Another nod.

Dev slipped his fingers into her curled ones. They were so cold.

"The difference is you won't have to alone," he said, brushing a bit of her hair from her face. She closed her eyes at his touch, and Dev didn't know if it was from pain or pleasure, her brows so stuck together it was hard to tell. The thought that his touch might cause her discomfort sliced another cut in his tattered heart.

Her lids fluttered open, her gaze going to their connected hands. "I…"

He waited.

"I'm sorry."

Dev pulled back slightly. "Molly, you have *nothing* to apologize for." He almost yelled the words. "Why would you say that?"

"I just wish...I wish I didn't feel like this. I wish I didn't let what he did...I want to be *me* again," she finished in a broken whisper.

And there it went, finally, his heart in pieces on the floor.

Not waiting for her permission, because he needed this like he needed to breathe, he shifted her around so he could hold her in his arms, cradled like a child. "And I wish I could tell you that you will be." He pressed his lips to her forehead. "But we both know that would be a lie. None of us can go back. By the stars, how many times I wished we could. But no, our world only turns one way." He leaned away so she could look him in the eyes. "I can tell you one thing though. While you might not be the exact same Molly and I not the same Dev, when we get through this, because we *will* get through it, we'll be something even better, closer and fiercer."

She scoffed, looking like she wanted to roll her eyes. Which was a good thing. The Molly he knew loved to roll her eyes.

"I'm serious," he said. "Being able to live past what life throws at us, live despite it, find our laughter again, well, that's what makes us a different breed of strength altogether."

She chewed her bottom lip, seeming to take in his words as her gaze dipped to his mouth, and something warm spread through him. And just when he thought he never would again, she said, "Kiss me."

His arms tightened ever so slightly around her. "Are you sure?"

"It's the only thing I'm sure about."

Without needing any more of an invitation, he leaned down, heart beating wildly in his chest, and gently brought his mouth to hers. It was like the first time all over again, out on the field, wrapped in the cool night air under the blanket of the shooting stars. His head went up in flames as he brought her closer, her lips so sweet, her small hands on his shoulders. He was desperate for her, devastated by her. He never felt so needy while getting exactly what he wanted. No, that wasn't true. He wanted so much more. He wanted skin to skin, wanted to taste more of her, to *feel* more of her, but he knew she wasn't ready. This alone was a huge step forward, and he had to remember to hold back, find a way to push down his overflowing desire to strip the clothes off both of them. With a low growl, he moved back and gazed down upon the woman in his arms. Her eyes, he was pleased to see, had a light in them that had remained out of sight until now, and her skin flushed a pretty pink.

"I love you," she said, bringing one of her fingers to graze along his stubble-filled chin. "I don't know what I would have done if—"

"And you'll never have to." He cut her off with another quick kiss before adding, "I love you too."

They fell into a comfortable silence, Molly drawing patterns along Dev's shoulder, and he wished they could stay like that forever and that the ghost of her cries would eventually stop evading his thoughts.

"I think I should go home for a bit," Molly said, and hurt bloomed in Dev's chest, hearing that she still thought of Earth as her home when his home was anywhere she was.

"Once I'm feeling a little better, that is," she added quietly. "I want to be here with you, but…but I think I need some time away from…this." She glanced to their surroundings. "I think it might help me…heal."

While his first reaction was to violently disagree and beg her to stay—*he just got her back*—he also knew what he wanted didn't much matter anymore, especially with what he still needed to tell her.

He took in a steadying breath. "There's something that you need to know."

She must have sensed the change in his tone, for she sat up. "What?"

Even though he dreaded saying the next words, the ones that would surely set them back, he had no choice.

He told her about Robert and watched her face go still, her eyes return to a glossy fog, a doll's unblinking gaze as she absorbed the words. But what happened next truly made Dev cold to the bone, for Molly didn't cry once, not a single tear. In fact, she hardly said a word. She just remained void—blank, an empty vessel. Like she decided right then, in his arms, that she was unplugging.

They were in big trouble.

For in a world that needed a hero, what were they to do when the one they had stopped caring?

Chapter 41

What must it be like to live with seasons,
by the sun and moon's rise and fall?
It must be nice to have warmth to eventually thaw the
cold,
light to even out the dark.

—*Part of a letter from Dev to Molly*

STREAMS OF SUNLIGHT filter through the funeral home's windows, golden dusted highlights caressing the rows of mourners and setting the bouquets of flowers decorating the room to an oversaturated glow.

Here, look! they seem to say, *there is still life to be found among the dead.*

I always thought it was an odd sort of condolence—flowers. Why give the aggrieved something else that will die? Or is that the point, to remind us that all life has beauty and that part of it is in dying? A ticking clock of sorts for our own grief. When the last petal falls, it's time to move on, to smile again. Whatever the reason, I'm currently glad they are there to draw my eye away from the black closed coffin that rests in the center of the room, a heavy brick of reality.

A shape moves outside the window, and I turn to watch a sparrow dart across the azure sky, its brown flap of wings quick against the slow-rolling puffs of clouds. I can't help but see the irony in it all. How long I had craved the sun and now find myself resenting it. Earth seems to be laughing at me, a jester to my bleak mood.

It should be raining, *hard*. Should be storming with sixty-mile-an-hour winds, cracks of thunder and lightning that shake the walls. A baby should be crying somewhere, alone. A cat left out soaked to the bone. *Some* dismal scene that can accompany my own, but instead it's a beautiful sunny day. One of the most gorgeous we've had all summer, in fact, according to the DJ on the radio as we drove here.

Gorgeous. Perfect. Happy.

I blink back to the aromatic beige room, watch my parents, with their puffy eyes and supportive arms around one another, murmur their thanks to the guests lined up to say their condolences. I still haven't cried. Not one wet drop squeezed out. And while I'm more than sad, heartbroken, it's almost like I can only feel it through a dense fog. The sick part is, I'm grateful for it, relieved even. After Aaron…if I could take in what was happening here, I don't think I'd be able to move again, not that I'm currently animated. But it's like my mind, having sensed this, placed me in survival mode. Now I'm just doing everything by memory: waking up, brushing my hair, teeth, chewing my food—even when it tastes like dust—nodding, and saying words when I'm meant to.

Rinse and repeat.

And no one questions it. No one sees my behavior as odd. I'm a girl who lost her grandfather, after all. Of course she'd look adrift and broken, have dark circles under her eyes, and appear like she was just tortured by a madman. At least fate gave me that, gave me something to hide my recent experience under.

How kind of it.

My fingers dig into my thigh as the memories of the painful hours left alone in a dark, wet cave mixes in with even more painful hours in the company of someone in a dark, wet cave. They flutter violently through me, phantoms that, despite Elena's attempt to cut them out, still drift by like a chill on the wind. I might not be able to see them, but my body knows they're there.

The only silver lining in any of this is that my grandfather's thoughts still live on inside me, the ones Elena has given. It's a small reprieve, but it feels like everything to be able to pull them forward and be with him, even if it's only in my mind. I try to do it now, try to think what my grandfather would say. What advice would he give to keep me going? His words about it getting worse, much worse, come back to me, and I almost laugh. Is this what he meant? Is this as bad as it's going to get? Is this when I shouldn't lose faith, when I need to keep going and be strong?

Strong.

I barely keep in a snort.

I've never felt weaker in all my life.

"Here, Turtle, I got you a water." Becca's gentle voice pops into my internal thoughts, and she takes a seat beside me on the front-row pew. Her wavy hair shimmers ruby red under the beams of sunlight that filter in, her short-sleeved black dress simple and to the knee.

"Thanks." I fiddle with the bottle's label as I hold it in my lap.

Becca has been with me since I stepped out of the portal in the bookstore. She held my hand the whole car ride to Pennsylvania and dressed me this morning when I found myself standing in front of the mirror in a blank stare. Out of all the horribleness going on, it is her unwavering support that has almost brought me to tears.

"I think Hector is scaring some of the visitors," she says, and I follow her gaze to where the tall, lanky Vigil stands cross armed by the foot of my grandfather's coffin. His white hair is pulled back in a severe bun, the scar over his left eye frighteningly red as he narrows his eyes at all who approach, as if he's watching for anyone who might defile the body inside.

While having his fair share of shadows pass across his features, pain in the pinching of his brows, he's accepted Robert's passing as gracefully as any could. Their reconnection at the hospital seemed to make some peace with whatever demons Hector had held on to for all those years. And I'm glad for it. I only hope my own serenity will come soon as well.

Though, I wonder if I'd even realize it if it did.

My parents have stopped questioning Hector's strange behavior toward a family member they believe he had never known. They now seem blind to it actually, too lost in their grief.

Rae steps over to sit on the other side of me, having just ended a short conversation with my father. Seeing him all in black again reminds me of our training days together under the dark sky of Terra, the laps we'd run around the city.

"We're going to leave soon to continue the smaller service back at your house," he says, draping an arm around me.

I nod.

"What can we do?" he asks softly, his golden eyes strained after another moment of us sitting in silence.

"This. Just more of this," I say.

And with that, Becca curls her fingers into mine, and Rae squeezes my shoulder, and we watch the rest of the wake pass by. A few distant cousins and friends of my parents come up to tell me how sorry they are for my loss. I thank them, murmur my agreement that yes, he was a good man. Yes, he lived a good life. Understanding they need to hear this more than I. After the things I've experienced, had to live through, people I've lost, I've come to realize that someone's presence oftentimes far outweighs one's words in comfort. So while I appreciate their need to pass on their regrets, it's that they showed up at all that means the most to me. And the fact that the two people on either side of me understand this is enough to slowly mend my broken heart. I only wish Dev were here. I could see the anguish in his eyes when I needed to leave, his anger with not being able to hold me through my sorrow, and the torture of letting me go only when he just got me back. When *I* just got *him* back.

I've never resented the difference in Nocturna and Vigil more than I do now. That he can't just as easily slip through a dimension like his brethren is maddening. For if anyone can thaw the cold that has iced over my heart, it's Dev. But even with my cells screaming out to be with him, yearning for his touch and reassuring gaze, I know I can't go back to Terra, not yet, not until I'm somewhat whole again. I'll be useless to anyone otherwise.

"Molly." My mother is standing in front of me, looking at the back of the room, her brown gaze questioning. "Do you know that woman?"

The three of us turn in our seats, and I nearly fall out of mine. A woman in an immaculately tailored long-sleeved black wrap dress stands against the far wall by the door. Her hair, which I know is pale blonde, is covered up by a charcoal scarf tied at the base of her chin. She slowly removes her large round sunglasses, showing off startling blue eyes. Two large men flank either side of her, looking every bit like the bodyguards they are.

Elena.

She's here.

On Earth.

Oh. My. God.

My mind spins. Is it possible? I guess she *is* a Vigil. But… *Oh my God.*

"Did you know she was coming?" Rae whispers to me.

I shake my head.

"Who is that?" Becca asks in awe, clearly impressed by the vogue being before us.

"Elena," I say.

"*The* Elena?" Her brows creep up to her hairline.

I cut her a look, telling her to not be so obvious.

"So, you know her?" My mother asks again.

"Um…yes." I'm slow to answer as I search around for how to explain. But just then Elena walks up the aisle, her pace slow and regal, and the entire room stops to watch her. Not only because she is such a rare rose among all us weeds, but something in her aura commands that we do. Even here she is ethereal, almost more so, and a shiver goes through me.

She stops in front of my grandfather's coffin and places a delicate hand on top. Not even a cough breaks the tense silence. It's like we're all waiting for something to happen. I'm not even sure what, but there's an anticipation in this moment that can't be explained. Her eyes are closed, her head bent, and I can barely make out the smallest bob to her throat, an emotional swallow. My chest tightens, all the memories of her and Robert flashing before me like a flip book. Their love. And then, ever so slightly, a weird heat expands in the room, starting from where she stands. Almost like a tickle of energy, and I sense my muscles relaxing, the throb of a headache at the back of my eyes lifting, a drop of relief, and I hear a sigh go through the guests when she lifts her hand away.

She approaches my parents, my father coming to step beside my mom, and they both regard her with dazed expressions. My mom looks as if she's staring into the eyes of some celebrity, and my father appears a bit like a gaping fish.

"Charles, Kathy." Elena's husky voice accompanies her grasping each of their hands. "I am so sorry to hear of your loss. I'm Elena. Your daughter and I work together, and I know how close the two of them were, how much he meant to all of you."

"Oh, yes, thank you," my father says, a bit delayed as he bounces a glance my way before returning it to Elena.

She smiles, and even in its subtleness, it's dazzling. "I've unfortunately experienced loss many times myself," she says. "And I've come to believe the pain that feels so suffocating at the time is merely your heart remembering everything beautiful about that person at once."

Even though she's looking at my parents, I know these words are for me.

"It's difficult to lose someone," she continues gently. "To understand why such things happen and to find your way back. But one of your great authors, Philip Pullman, once wrote something about death that I find extremely comforting. 'You'll drift apart,' he said, 'but you'll be out in the open, part of everything alive again.'" And then with another empathetic nod, she turns to me. "Molly," she says. "Rae." Her gaze holds his a beat longer, pride gleaming in their blue depths before she's walking away, her two guards following on her heels, as she pushes open the doors to the outside and steps through, letting the morning light swallow her whole.

"Whoa," Becca breathes.

I stand. "Um, I should go thank her for coming."

Just before I slip from the room, I hear my dad ask, "What did she mean, one of *our* authors?"

I squint at the accosting brightness that hits me as I exit into the parking lot and shield my eyes, finding Elena about to get into a black luxury town car parked under the shade of a tree.

"Elena," I call out, my heels clacking against the concrete as I approach. "What are you…I didn't know that…" I'm not even sure where to start.

"You look better," she says, ignoring my obvious sputtering and running an astute gaze over me. I blink as she takes in a deep breath and glances around. "I forgot what it smells like," she says and then seeing my confusion adds, "the sun."

"When's the last time you were here?"

She smooths a nonexistent wrinkle from her dress. "One hundred and sixty-eight years ago."

My mouth makes an O shape, but no sound comes out.

"It's much changed since then," she says nostalgically.

"I would think so."

She smiles.

"Thanks for coming. It really…it means a lot."

"I loved him too," she says softly.

I nod. "I know."

Her brows slightly pucker as she looks across the street to a young girl kicking a soccer ball with her father in a park. "Things are changing," she says. "Our world is becoming something new, and that means so will it here. I'm not sure in what way, but I'm hoping, with your help, it will be for the better."

I press my lips together and look at my hands, fiddling with my nails.

"Take the time you need," she says, placing a gentle yet strong hand on my shoulder. "Find the peace that this home can give you. But, Molly"—her blue eyes seep into mine—"you do need to come back."

Then she's slipping on her sunglasses and dipping into her town car, leaving me standing in the parking lot with the bright sun shining down and the jovial laughter of the young girl echoing around me as I watch her drive away.

The next week and a half goes by in a slow crawl of monotony.

And I love it.

No one has knocked on my door demanding my presence or commanded that I perform tricks in front of a crowd of people to win their favor. There's been no sounding of alarms to rush off and destroy monsters or sessions to infuse my memory with new thoughts and feelings of an old predecessor. I sleep in, eat home-cooked meals, watch horrible reality TV, and let my mind wander into caring about mundane things like, do I want to wear yoga or sweatpants today? It's funny how much I took such trivial matters for granted before, that I actually begrudged them. How naïve I was.

Becca, Rae, and Hector remain with me at my parents' house, and despite my quick and affirmative denial, my mother is convinced Hector is my new boyfriend. Even though we hardly speak to one another, let alone physically touch. Still, she has somehow gotten it into her head that there's a romance. Can we say, disgusting? And despite Hector's slight awkward stiffness around my mom's doting, obviously never experiencing something like a mother before, he actually infuses quite well with our little family. He's even sat back and watched a baseball game with Rae and my father. Something I was sure he'd turn his nose up at, he instead seemed to rather enjoy.

Becca has taken it upon herself to give me a makeover while she's got me trapped with nowhere to go, and I've let her. Knowing it's her way to make up for the guilt she feels for what happened to me, even though what Aaron did is in no way her fault. Still, I sense her anxiety, her silent frustration that she can't keep the threat of any more hurt coming my way. She doesn't agree with what I must do, what fate seems to have landed in my lap. I've even overheard her arguing in whispers with Rae about it, but I know she also accepts there's no way around it. So I let her paint my nails bright reds and purples, curl my new short hair into something of a 1950s pinup do because it gives her a sense of usefulness, of bonding with her best friend, who has recently been so unreachable. And the benefits of all this are paying off, for I actually am finding my laughter again. The first time was when I watched Hector's repulsive reaction to Rae and my father having an impromptu burger-eating contest. I've never seen a man actually turn green in the face before. It was hilarious.

So yes, my joy seems to be slowly returning, the part of myself that I thought was forever lost, stolen in the dark by a man and his vengeance, is showing itself again. And this is why, as I lounge on the couch reading a book, my parents and Hector preparing our dinner in the kitchen and Becca and Rae watching TV curled up on a smaller love seat next to me, I grow annoyed when the news turns on and a very dismal picture is painted of the state of the world. Gun violence reported in every state over the past month, terrorist attacks rampaging through Europe, nuclear threats in Asia, and all this mixed with natural disaster after natural disaster. The Earth is sick and only getting sicker, and my stomach curls in on itself, the weight of it all falling once again on my shoulders.

"Can we change the channel?" I motion to Rae, who holds the remote.

"I think it's important to watch this," he says pointedly, his gaze not reaching mine, but I'd have to be an idiot not to get what he's insinuating.

The news anchor chatters on about the latest mass shooting in Nebraska, the high body count. My breathing grows heavy, and I try plugging my ears from the inside.

"What's wrong with people?" My mom says in disgust from the doorframe that leads into the kitchen, one of her hands covered by an oven mitt. "Things have been such a mess." She unknowingly smears a bit of sauce onto her jeans.

E.J. Mellow

"Yeah," Rae agrees. "It makes you wish there was something you could do about it." He lets out an *oof* from what I assume is Becca jamming an elbow into his stomach. I grind my teeth together, reading the same sentence in my book over and over, before I close it with a thud and drop it on my chest. I know what Rae is trying to do, and I get his *need* to do it. I can't stay here forever. I can't ignore the inevitable. But god damn it, I really, really want to. And it's not just the droning of the news that is filling my stomach with acid. No, it's also the notes Hector has been passing between Dev and me, the ones from him that are filled with the growing onslaught in Terra. It's bad there. The pinnacle of the war has very much been reached, and yet here I sit, curled up on a couch, the sounds of a calm summer night coming through the open screened windows and the comforting chatter of my parents in the kitchen. But despite the serene scene, the TV obviously is telling a very different story. One that I'm forced to listen to for another hour, which, not surprisingly, puts me onto thoughts of death.

My life could have ended many times. It could have ended during any of the hours in that cave. But it didn't. So I wonder how many lives this cat has left and if I'd be willing to give the last one up for a greater good?

I'd like to think so. I'd like to think I'd sacrifice myself for the world, be that selfless person who understands the concept of one for many.

But here's the thing.

I'm not.

I don't want to die.

I want to grow old and see my friends and family grow old with me. I want to travel the world, both my worlds, and meet new people and eat exotic foods. I want to learn another language that *I* can speak, not through the memories of another, but from my own mouth.

This might make me the most selfish person across two dimensions, but I guess I'm her. I care about my own neck enough to search for all the other solutions before I reach the one that's my sacrifice. Because honestly, all those characters in books I've read and movies I've watched that think it's an act of heroism and nobility—I'm sorry, but it's simply an act of laziness.

If it's my ultimate demise that's written in the stars, fine, but I sure as hell am not going to walk out to the slaughterhouse willingly. No way. I'm going to fight tooth and friggin' nail until my last breath.

And that's when it hits me like a crack of lightning.

My grandfather was right. How can I enjoy any of this if there will be no one around to share it with? If there are no worlds left to explore?

I have to keep going for them. For us.

I bolt upright, ignoring the inquisitive stares of Becca and Rae as a new urgency fills me.

I need to go back.

I need to return to Terra.

I need to do everything I can to end this.

And this time, when a certain someone attempts to take my life again, I won't hesitate to do everything in my power to take them down with me.

Chapter 42

I'm coming home.

—A letter from Molly to Dev

THE WIND WAS a never-ending force against Dev's face, weaving between the gaps in his clothes and sending licks of icy caresses against his bare skin. His hands gripped the handles of his Arcus that straddled the zipline, giving in to the way his body swayed left and then right as he danced through the skyscrapers. The stars seemed brighter tonight as they zoomed overhead, accompanying him forward, both speeding toward a destination that only could be reached in flight. Dev's of course was a feeling rather than a physical place. He decided to take the longer route back to his apartment after the last security meeting with Alex, needing the sense of freedom and relief it brought him. Even though the information shared at the gathering was that of progress, it still left him in a foul mood. They found the leak in the energy orb manufacturing facility—an older Nocturna who was bringing the product onto the black market and who, though unknowingly, got them into the hands of Aaron and subsequently the Metus.

Terra only knew what other things Aaron used to manipulate the beasts, what else he had procured from the underground trade for his own gain. The thought of him using the bomb in the cave resurfaced as Dev's jaw clenched. *Did no one ask questions there?* As crazy as Aaron was, he was more than capable of covering his tracks. Not only had his whereabouts still eluded them, but there was no way, after the explosion, they could have taken inventory of what he had hidden in the place he took Molly. Dev's grip tightened, and he closed his eyes, forcing his mind to clear and erase the negative thoughts that had consumed him in the past weeks.

On top of the phantom memories of Molly's torture, he was sick of constantly being called to battle, sick of watching soldier after soldier give his or her life in the hopes that it would make a difference. How many of his men and woman had he seen die in the century and a half of him doing this? The answer was easy— too many.

His life in Terra had never been an easy one, his happiness such a fleeting experience that he almost feared the sensation. How long would it last this time? A week? An hour? A quick smile before she left again?

He let out a growl. So much for the zipline giving him some peace. He needed Molly. Needed to see her, touch and kiss her. She wrote that she was coming back, but when? Every second felt like an Earth's cycle, and he was getting more than restless to receive notice to go to the DCC for her return.

Catching sight of the quickly approaching platform on the top of his building, the glowing bull's-eye pulsing like a homing beacon, Dev prepared to land. His feet touched down, and he flipped his Arcus off the line, taking a hesitant step forward as he saw an obscene amount of Vigil guards covering the roof. A row lined the perimeter, with at least a dozen more manning the small door that led to the elevator bay. His heart kicked into overdrive. They'd only be here if...

Dev was sprinting, almost taking down the three guards who tried to get in his way. Thankfully for them, their supervisor called for their retreat, letting him pass, and he was off again. He charged down the stairs, too impatient to wait for the elevator, before he was bounding down the hall, squeezing past another layer of soldiers to swing open the door to his apartment. And there she was, sitting on the couch with Tim and Aveline, Hector standing by the fireplace. She looked up as he entered, her short brown hair with one strip of blonde twirling around her shoulders, her dark gaze connecting to his, and she smiled.

Dev took an unsteady step back. *In all of Terra...*

Molly smiled.

A reaching-the-eyes, toothy grin, and something dark and heavy disappeared from his chest. She was back.

"You're here," he said.

"I'm here," she repeated, her melodic voice curling around his skin.

Then they were both walking toward one another, the other people in the room forgotten, gone, before he took her in his arms, and because he knew he could, he kissed her.

Dev practically kicked open the door to his bedroom as he pulled Molly inside. Despite never needing to sleep, his bed was large and took up the center of the room, his gray sheets lit by a soft yellow light on his bedside table. This was one of his favorite places to read, and stacks and stacks of Terra and Earth novels lined the shelves that covered one side of his room.

"Dev." She laughed as he dragged her toward the sheets. "You didn't even say hi to anyone."

He hardly heard her words, his mind still playing the sound of her laughter over and over. *By the stars*, she was smiling *and* laughing. He kissed her again. "How are you?" he asked. "Before you left you were…and now you're just so…" He couldn't stop himself from touching her cheek, running his hands through her hair. Her eyes were bright, well, not as bright as they originally had been, but at least no longer the glossy voids from before.

"I'm better." She rested her hand atop his as he cradled her cheek. "It still hurts, thinking about my grandfather, but he left me his journals, and when I read them, I feel like he's with me again."

"That's good." Dev searched her face. "And…the other thing. How is that?" He hated to even ask, but he had to for what he wanted to do next. Despite his desperation for it, he wouldn't allow it unless she was ready. He watched as a quick phantom from her time with Aaron floated between them, her arms tensing ever so slightly.

"It's…still there, but not as all consuming," she said quietly, glancing to the side. "I'm able to work past it."

Would he?

He nudged her chin so she'd look at him again. "You can take more time."

Her smile was a touch sad. "No," she said. "I can't."

They both remained quiet, because she was right.

"I thought I'd be meeting you at the Center when you returned." He guided them to sit on his bed.

"I'm sick of being stuck indoors," she said, playing with their entwined fingers. "I needed to see the city again, the stars."

He nodded. They were alike in that way.

"Plus," she added with a secretive grin, "I wanted to surprise you."

His skin grew hot as he gazed into her deep-brown eyes, saw the desire and love shining out. "You can surprise me like that anytime." His returning smile was mischievous. "So long as we can do this after." Tugging her to his chest, he tilted her head back and tasted her lips. He explored languidly at first, both of them relearning the feel of the other. She sighed into him, her muscles relaxing in his arms as the temperature in the room spiked. It didn't take long for him to slip their clothes off and slide her under his sheets, worshipping every inch of her olive-tinted skin.

"Dev," she moaned, and he glanced up at her under heavy lids as he kissed her stomach. She was gazing down at him, her fingers combing through his hair. "I love you," she said. "I love you so much."

In a flash he was above her again, touching the new sunbaked dusting of freckles across her nose and cheeks, letting their bodies glide over each other. "Love doesn't do justice to what I feel for you," he said gruffly, kissing her again. "You are everywhere in me, taking up all the spaces in between. You consume me, Molly Spero." And then there was no more talking, only soft sighs and gasps, the lights vibrating with Molly's quickening heartbeat and climbing need.

They each took pieces of the other that night and gently fused them back together, so in the end there wasn't him and her, only them.

⇥━◉ ◉━⇤

Dev wished the next few days could be filled with similar pleasant endings, but as expected, Molly's return was consumed with security meetings and fighting the Metus. Day by day she fought them back as vehemently as she did her internal nightmares, not allowing either to win. The Metus were a constant wave upon the city though, the citizens now on lockdown, no one allowed outside the wall unless given special permission and accompanied by heavy artillery. All the outpost cities were operating under similar law, any trade currently at a standstill. Though this left the people moving in a tense energy, the mood wasn't as dismal as Dev had expected. Most were placing their hope in the Dreamer and what she could do to hold off the war from getting worse. After her demonstration with Aurora in the arena, any doubt of her capability, or intentions with her power, practically vanished. Cato was a smug elder, to be sure. His plan worked like a charm, despite who it hurt in the process.

This, of course, only left Molly more on edge. She knew the whispers about her, the reality of what was at stake more potent than ever before. And as Dev stood across from her at one of their daily security meetings, a hovering map of Terra between them, he wanted nothing more than to smooth the pinching of her brows as she listened to Alex talk.

"And we've just deployed two more units to the Nursery," the general said, his stocky arm pointing to the highlighted section that was a small replica of the outpost where all of Terra's life was created. "We'll most likely send a third once we've gathered enough intel."

As soon as the Council had seen what Aaron told Molly about ending it where it began, they immediately knew what the Vigil meant. The Nursery was where everything in Terra began, where everything with Dev, Aaron, and Anebel started. To threaten this place was to threaten the very existence of their world, and if Aaron's ultimate goal was to end it all, this was where one could do it. So with Molly still on Earth for her grandfather's funeral, a master plan was set in place to defend the Source at all costs.

"And what's this?" Molly asked, pointing to a bright spot in the center of the Nursery. The city was set up in a series of rings with six large tubes running perpendicular through them from the outer wall to the very center—highly concentrated Navitas pipes.

"This is the Source," Elena explained. "It's what feeds our young into creation and ultimately what extends to the rest of Terra. These"—Elena gestured to the six Navitas pipes—"run currents of energy to our city as well as to every other outpost in our lands."

"So it's important," Molly said dryly, and Dev bit back a smile.

"Very." Elena nodded.

"He'll attack there," Molly said.

Alex let out a disbelieving snort. "It's nearly impossible to penetrate. Not only because of the layers of guards, but the biometric locks, feet of titanium, solid walls, and airtight rooms all leading up to an even *more* secured vault that houses the incubators and Navitas."

Molly looked unimpressed. "He'll attack there," she repeated.

The room fell silent, the different Council members sharing nervous glances.

"This man has lived undetected under all your noses for over fifty years," Molly pointed out. "He's still eluded being found even with the use of Terra's endless hi-tech resources. He knows how to get protected weapons that you said only a handful of Vigil are even supposed to know about. He's cunning, slippery, determined, and"—Molly shared a glance with Dev—"has nothing to lose. That alone makes him the most dangerous. If I were him, this"—Molly nodded to the Source—"would be where I'd hit."

"She's right," Dev said. "Take this, and you take it all." As he watched Alex's forehead crinkle, he couldn't help thinking that his world really messed up in making such a precarious place— the center of all life. *At least install a backup generator or something.* But worlds, though seeming indestructible in size, were always made up of delicate ecosystems. If you tipped the scales one way, it all came crumbling down, a house of cards.

"Then we'll concentrate our efforts there," Alex said after another moment, and with a heavy sigh added, "There's not much else we can do."

Which was true. All that was left was to wait, wait and fight the Metus while looking for Aaron to make his move.

And on the third day he appeared.

But what he had waiting was much worse than any could have imagined.

Especially Dev.

Chapter 43

We have to believe going through darkness
will eventually bring us light.
Especially when night is our forever.

—Part of a letter from Dev to Molly

SIRENS PIERCE THE air as units of Nocturna soldiers run to their various ships, the giant hangar filling with flashing lights and the collective thumping of boots hitting the ground, the sounds of war. I watch it all from my own aircraft that rises out of the open top, changing the forms below to ants as we get swallowed up by the stars and zoom away. The city of Terra is now nothing more than a shrinking, glowing droplet in the dark land.

I turn my gaze from the window, adjusting the seat belt that crisscrosses my chest, to find Dev looking at me from across the cockpit. His blue eyes spark with determination in the shadows that slink between us, his mouth set in a grim line. His arm muscles tense up under their black protective layers as he grips his Arcus resting across his knees. Even though he looks every bit the warrior that he is, I know the worry that spins in his mind, the fear, for it's also my own. How many of us will be sitting here after today?

Dev's unit, along with Aveline, Hector, Tim, and Ezekial, fill the rest of seats in the airship, all either checking their weapons or sitting in pensive silence. The space almost chokes on it, the quiet loud with everyone's thoughts of what's ahead. There's a slight rocking of the cargo bay as the aircraft switches gear, bodies swaying.

My fingers flex in my lap, the energy that slips easily to and from my vest surging to their tips in anticipation. This is the moment we've all been preparing for, the one we've been dreading as well as anticipating, for one can only sit waiting for the devil for so long without growing impatient for the hell he will bring.

"Here," Hector says beside me, handing me a breathing mask. In its closed form it's nothing but a sleek black headband that's worn low behind the ears, but once engaged a glass partition will go over the entirety of the face, locking at the chin.

Putting it on, my already twisted gut curls even tighter, hoping it won't be necessary. We got the call exactly twenty-four minutes ago that the Nursery was under attack and that Aaron was definitely inside. Even with all the units standing guard, no one was prepared for what this one man had in store. And even though horrific, the choreography of how everything went down was just another testament to the power of the mind when determination and passion mixed.

By burying large crates of energy orbs belted with Dreamer repellent ropes, they were able to sit undetected, for Terra knew how long, in the ground on one side to the Nursery. Leaving

Aaron only to wait patiently, like a coiled snake in the grass, watching for the right moment to strike. And the right moment came when a large horde of Metus popped up to attack a nearby Navitas generator, a favorite of theirs, it seems. When the overwhelming numbers swarmed in and the Nocturna readied to hold them off, the hidden crates burst open, shooting out grappling hooks that fused to the wall and dangled the deliciously available energy orbs along the wire. The images projected to us looked like that of a town fair, lights strung from the ground to the wall's ledge, but instead of festive illuminations, these lights were filled with blue-white Navitas, which sang like beacons to the Metus. It was only a matter of seconds for them to change course and rush in to gobble them up, Pac-Men in a deadly game. And despite the guards along the Nursery wall working quickly to dislodge the grapples, enough beasts had ingested the energy to grow big, strong, and undeterred in climbing the wire up and over.

The Nursery was now compromised, and Aaron was headed toward its heart. While the majority of forces were sent to defend the north breached wall, the others were ordered to scour the south part of the compound, for this reeked of a diversion.

"Reaching destination in five." The female pilot's voice echoes through my earpiece, and Dev nods once. *I'm with you*, he seems to say, and I give him a small encouraging smile while rubbing my palm against my thigh. It's begun to bounce with my restlessness, and I catch his attention dropping to it.

"There in three," the voice announces. "Prepare for contact."

With synchronized clicks, our seat belts unlock, and we gather near the port end.

"Pair up." Dev's deep, commanding voice slithers through my earbud and down my body. His blue eyes find mine as I step beside him, and he hooks a new tether to each of our belts.

"Ready." A chorus of voices fills my head right before a hole in the ground opens, sending in a rush of wind and the light from the Nursery compound below.

In the next moment we each drop through, my stomach flying to my throat as Dev's arm wraps securely around my waist as we rappel to the ground. Our ascent slows right before our feet hit the pavement, and we unhook. Our unit surrounds me, positioning their weapons as they inventory our surroundings, and I can't help my jaw falling open. This breathtaking place is all beautiful cobblestone roads lined with tall marble buildings that have intricately decorative ironwork for doors and banisters. It's almost mythical the way the stonework shines and displays an unknown master's hand. If the streets weren't filled with terror-stricken adolescents and their instructors rushing them to armored cars to take them to safety, I'd have gawked for at least another hour.

Blinking back to the scene before us, my mouth presses into a hard line. Aaron's sickness knows no bounds, and it was no mistake that he positioned the Metus breach near the students' housing. Some of the older kids, who appear no older than thirteen, help in hauling the younger ones to the awaiting vehicles. Only a few shed tears. The rest appear stoic in their gray-outfitted uniforms, ready to take on the threat, to fight, most of their fates.

A high-pitched scream turns our heads to a giant orange beast lumbering toward an armored hover car, a group of young kids scampering into the truck as the Metus approaches. Its dripping lava form is bloated from the recent ingested energy, leaving it twice its normal size and more powerful. So when the guards attack, I'm not surprised when the blue electricity from their weapons only solidifies certain body parts rather than blowing it apart. I've seen this before, back at the Navitas generator when the Metus joined together to create one massive beast. Then, just like I'm guessing now, they could only be destroyed by a very high and pure concentration of energy.

But unlike last time, we're prepared for it.

"The hoses!" I shout to the distant guards as my mind pierces with a collection of cool energy right before I lift up the perfectly lined street right near the Metus. The stones smack into the monster, momentarily holding it off. But this is all the time we need for the Nocturna, understanding my command, to pull out a newly constructed weapon from the truck. It looks very much like a bazooka connected to a large vat of glowing blue liquid— water from the Sea of Dreams—and with a high-pitched whir, it turns on and, with two guards holding it up, shoots out rivulets to douse the beast. The Metus' howl of pain ricochets against the buildings, causing some kids to plug their ears right before its entirety is overdosed with the pureness and, on a kick, bursts into shimmering silver dust.

There's a moment of silent shock as the onlookers take in the new defense mechanism, and then, like a bad dream, a slow clap thumps from the speakers that line the city's streets.

We turn, seeking out the source.

"Well played," echoes out a familiar disembodied voice. "I see you've learned something about our lovely friends. And they say you can't teach old dogs new tricks."

Dev and I lock eyes as I hold my body very still. If I don't, I fear it will crumble. The sound of the man who tortured me, had me soak in my own filth and depravity, still has the power to fill my veins with icy fear.

But one thought pushes through all that, the knowledge that Aaron is here, watching us, which can only mean...

"The control room," Dev says, turning to Minka. With a nod, she gathers three members of their team and sets off on a run.

"Tsk, tsk," Aaron tuts out, "do you really think I'll be here when they arrive? You know better than to weaken your team like that, Dev."

Dev's knuckles turn white as they grip his Arcus, the distant sound of the fight continuing around us as we stand listening to this madman.

"Why don't you stop being a coward and show yourself," Dev calls out. "You've got us here, so let's get on with it."

"How impatient you are," Aaron muses. "If I were you, I'd want to prolong this moment with your love. But you were never good at appreciating what you have, were you?"

"Dev." I say his name gently. His nostrils flare, his breathing heavy, but his blue gaze meets mine.

"What buildings connect to the Nursery's control room?" I ask. "We should start there and work our way in. Cover any possible exit he might use."

Dev blinks a few times, lucidness returning, but right before he opens his mouth to answer, Aaron speaks again.

"Since you all seem to be in such a hurry, why don't I make this easier for you. You can find me at the Source," he says, and a chill goes through me. This might be the first time I wish I wasn't right about something.

"And to make this more fun," Aaron continues, "let's time it, shall we?"

Dozens of hovering monitors that line the streets switch on to display a red clock counting down from one hour. During our quick debrief of this outpost, I was told these were used for the students to get to and from classes on time.

"I'll also let you in on a little secret," Aaron announces. "You'll want to make sure you don't let the clock run out, for this world will get more than a tardy slip when it does."

"It's a trap," Aveline says as we stand outside the large octagonal building that houses the Source. It's a windowless beige structure with a flat roof, the center of which glows a bright blue-white. I could see it as we flew into the Nursery, nestled in the center of the compound, and the shape reminded me of the Pentagon, but without the hollowed-out center courtyard. Instead, a large condensed ball of Navitas, the sun to this world, occupies the middle under a glass roof. The streets here are quiet, the battle being fought against the Metus a far-off sound.

"Of course it's a trap," Hector says, waiting for a Nursery guard to open the security door. "We just need to figure out what kind."

"How did he even get in here?" I ask, watching the complicated code being punched in followed by a prick of a blood sample and eye scan. The heavy metal door gasps open, revealing a long white corridor.

"Unfortunately, you can obtain these methods of entry if you don't mind the gore of getting them." Dev glances at our guard again, specifically to his eye that was just pressed up against the scanner.

I swallow. *Gross.*

"I'll need you to help evacuate the building," Dev says to the young man. "Get everyone out, and quick."

"But what about—"

"Turn on the auto incubator for the life pods," Dev says to a woman in his unit, cutting off the young man. "The elders have given their consent." Pulling a chip from a small pocket on his arm, he hands it to the Nursery soldier. "Check this document if you need to, but we only have forty minutes left, so if you're going to do it, do it fast."

Dev ushers us inside, and the Nursery guard and the rest of his unit run in another direction to where I'm hoping they will start removing employees.

Our group is now reduced to Tim, Hector, Aveline, Dev, and I, and we pass empty offices, the workers here having taken the initiative to leave on their own, as we head to a shuttle car that will take us to the center of the building.

We're all breathing heavy as the door dings shut and the train zips away. The dimly lit interior has two rows of sleek seating and a middle aisle for standing. Our group hovers by the door as light from the darkened tunnel flashes inside, becoming one stream of illumination with our speed. I catch Aveline watching Tim carefully, her constant concern for his health since the accident still apparent. Hector is cleaning his nails, but from the slight pinching of his lips, I can tell he's thinking of far more serious things than a hangnail. I look at Dev. His scruff has grown a little longer over the past two Earth cycles, but his buzzed hair remains just as thick. His wide shoulders and height make the tram's interior feel miniature as he stands holding a center pole, his Arcus in the other hand. I want to cross the aisle and go to him, feel his strong arms around me, but if I did, I don't know if I could step away again. Sensing my attention on him, he glances up, and as we remain locked together, I'm nearly knocked backward from the intensity. He doesn't have to say a word for me to know what he is silently telling me. He's whispering endless words of reassurance, promising me a life away from all this, a life with him and the determination he has to get it. My throat tightens with my own desperation to believe it, to see it, and my grip on the handle I'm holding grows sweaty with my impatience to have it all now.

It's this look shared between us, this vow of our love, that I will recall many times later, a reminder that whatever ugly I come across, there is always that quick moment of quiet beauty that passes between two people.

And as we step out of the tram, entering into the locked corridor outside the Source, I find myself using the memory of that moment for the first time. For it's the only thing that can soften the sickening dread that runs across my skin as I glance down the hall to all the bloody bodies.

Chapter 44

The thing about our love
is we don't need to be near
to know its strength.

—Part of a letter from Dev to Molly

I'VE BEEN IN battle, watched as Nocturna and Vigil fall to the hands of monsters, covered in their mucus of hate until it burns their flesh to the bone and then resurrects them as the nightmares they feared. I've been in human wars, viewed through the eyes of my predecessors as men and women work like puppets to the same evil, fighting one another in a misguided cause for power and peace. But in all those instances, all that gore, I've never seen death for the pure pleasure of it, until now.

"By the stars," Tim whispers as we slowly make our way forward. Beside me Aveline gasps while holding her hand to her nose, trying to stave off the acute stench of iron in the air, all the blood.

A cold sweat breaks across my exposed flesh as we carefully step over body after body. Quick sprays of bullets put down most of the corpses, a thinning of the herd, but bile rises in my throat as I gaze at the few who have been purposefully mutilated. Empty eye sockets puss crimson while Nocturna and Vigil arms lie broken, mouths hanging open in a last scream as slashes of lightning bolts are carved on cheeks and exposed skin, a torture for answers, a sick calling card for the Dreamer, for me. There must be at least fifteen bodies that cover the white tiled floor, slick with ruby puddles.

"Why?" I hear myself asking, my body, in its shock, growing numb, desperate to detach.

"Because he can," Dev says, his voice tight as he moves closer to me.

Because I can.

Visions of Aaron's gaunt face hover in front of me, his manic smile and vengeful leer staring down right before his touch brings the only thing it can—pain.

In my daze I bump into a nearby desk and reach out to steady a mug, the tea inside still warm and steaming. My stomach knots even tighter. How recently this place was filled with life, the buzz of employees doing their jobs.

I shake my head to dislodge the illusion, a hand wiping through smoke, and force my gaze away from the slaughter. Little beeps from abandoned machines echo through the space, and even though I can't see the Source, I can feel the overwhelming concentration of Navitas close by, the blue-white power that sits nestled like a fallen star, feeding the souls of Terra's people who are still being created. From studying the map, I know this part of the building is made of up three rings, the Source at the core, which is wrapped with a special windowless titanium wall, another smaller hallway, and then where we stand, the monitoring circle. This area is wide with high ceilings and two rows of desks that line the walls and face a glass screen that travels the circumference. Energy readings fill some of the sections, red to blue heat sensory maps, while the majority now have the countdown clock.

Thirty minutes.

Thirty minutes left to figure out and fix this madman's plan.

It seems hopeless.

"He shot the majority," says Hector, breaking our mournful quiet. "And then must have tortured the rest until they gave him access inside."

The conclusion I came to as well and what explains the cut-out eyes and fingertips.

"What do we do?" I look at our small group.

"Ave, can you get us a feed to the inside?" Dev asks. "It would help if we can find his location. The Source may be one large room, but there are four ways to enter."

"He killed the cameras," Aveline says as she fiddles with a nearby computer. "We'll be going in blind."

Dev curses.

"Maybe we should wait for backup," Tim suggests.

"We don't have time for that." Dev runs a hand through his hair and, after a second more of thought, says, "We'll stick together and enter through the west entrance."

Falling in line, we leave behind the massacre and enter the smaller circular hallway, a smear of blood here or there marking Aaron's path. Our pace quickens until we are all running toward the door that peeks out of the curved wall, and right before we travel the last bend, a blaring alarm sounds and a glass partition slams down. I skid to a stop right before I smack into it.

"No!" Dev runs back and slams his fist against it, his voice muffled. I stand with Aveline and Tim, while Dev and Hector are on the other side.

I watch Dev frantically search for a way to open it, but there's nothing. We are separated, and whether this is Aaron's doing or not, it no longer matters.

I click on my earpiece. "Dev, look at me."

Worried blue eyes find mine. "We don't have time. We'll go to the south door and meet you inside."

His lips are pressed together, his brows bunching. "This doesn't feel right."

"I know," I say.

Dev lets out a growl and looks away before saying, "Tell me when you're at the door. We'll time it to enter together. Tim"—he looks to his mentor—"you still have the overriding codes?"

Tim nods, and then after one more beat, Dev takes in a deep breath looking my way. "Be careful."

"You too," I say.

"Don't worry, Mols," Hector chimes in to our moment, his smile oddly relaxed. "I'll make sure your man doesn't trip over his shoelaces on the way in."

"Shut it," Dev barks before we both turn and run in the opposite direction.

"Here!" Aveline says as we approach an identical metal door to the one we were heading to before. Bending down, Tim presses a button on the wall, and an eye, fingertip, and keypad, with the ancient Latin symbols, flip open.

"Dev?" I say.

Nothing.

"Dev, we're here. We're about to enter."

Still nothing.

I look to Aveline and Tim. Tim's gray-tinted hair twinkles under the bright lights as he turns to read the clock on his wrist. Twenty-five minutes.

Aveline gnaws on her lower lip. "Sometimes the high concentration of Navitas messes up our coms."

I nod, forcing myself to believe this rather than the hundreds of other possibilities, all of which aren't good.

"We have to go," Tim says.

"Yes." I pull out my Arcus as Tim enters his override code. With a huff, the large titanium door cracks open, sending out a stream of bright light along with waves of energy.

I take a step back. *Whoa.*

"You good?" Aveline's hazel eyes search mine, while the rest of her body is poised for battle, an arrow nocked, her moon-pale hair tied tightly back.

"Uh, yeah," I say, settling the new sensation within me. "This doesn't bother you guys?"

"Not like it would you," she whispers as we inch forward.

"I can't see Aaron on this landing," Tim says, peering around the door. "We'll enter quickly and hide behind a balcony wall until we can find his location."

On his nod, we burst through, crouching to a stop at the balcony at the far end of the long ramp. There are three others like the one we're on, connecting to the other entrances and stretching out to peer down at the Source in the middle. Even from my low position I can see the giant ball of Navitas below, the swirling light almost blinding as it fills the space. Its colors transition from blue to purple to gold, a myriad of shades that dance against one another, churning and turning around the core, an indistinguishable shade except for its hot brilliance, the center of a flame. I'm mesmerized as rivers of veins flow out to connect to thousands and thousands of small droplets, blue cocooned pods with children of various ages tucked into fetal positions—the people of Terra being created. They all circle the Source and go deeper than the eye can see, a bottomless well. And while this is all completely alien, it's also breathtaking, almost to the point that I want to cry. The energy in this room is womb-like, motherly, pure and protective. It's like a warm embrace, one that I never want to step back from. And just when I'm about to be overcome from the sensation of safety, of love, I see him, his dark figure bound and gagged, and the world around me explodes.

Dev dangles from a Dreamer repellent rope right over the Source. The blue-white glow twists around his body, wrapping his neck and sending a sickly pallor to his ghostly white face. His nose is bleeding, and one of his eyes is swollen and slowly beginning to close.

"DEV!" I stand, and just then a searing pain slices across my right bicep. Aveline tugs me to the ground.

"Aaron's armed," she hisses, but I barely hear her, barely feel the sharp pain from my wound as warm liquid seeps through my shirt—the protective material keeping it from going too deep—because all I see is Dev's hanging body, bruised face, and panicked gaze as it found mine.

"How did he get Dev?" I practically shout. It's impossible. Dev is strong, unbreakable. He can't have been captured, can't be dangling precariously over something that brought him life but now will surely kill him.

"I don't know." Aveline's voice cuts through my terror-stricken mind. "But we'll get him out of this." She grabs my hand, and I look at her. Sweat has crept across her brow, her jaw locked with determination.

"Do you understand, Molly? We'll get him out of this."

I nod numbly.

"I can't see Hector," Tim whispers as he falls back to his knees after inching around the top.

"Well, he's somewhere," Aveline says right before Aaron's voice fills the room.

"You all made it just in time," he says, and we each peer around to see him standing on the balcony directly across from us, a gun angled straight at Dev. His dark pants and shirt are stained darker from blood that's not his own, his dirty-blond hair greasy and stuck across part of his forehead, and with a flash of red-hot anger, I take in the protective band adorning his arm, my powers useless against it. Still, I can't help lashing out, practically growling when it does nothing more than hit a wall.

"And with fifteen minutes to spare." Aaron casually gestures with crimson-caked hands to two small silver balls stuck on either side of the arched room's walls.

"Collö," Aveline curses.

"What?" I ask. "What are those things?"

"We use them to wipe out the Metus hives," she says with a swallow. "They're bombs, big ones."

So he truly meant to end it all where it begins, but then why hold Dev? Flinging out my powers again, I try to manipulate the rope holding him, but it just bounces back. My mind screams as it races for a solution. *The controller,* that's the only thing that can manipulate this rope. My gaze runs over Aaron's form. *Where is it, you bastard?* My hand curls around the Arcus with a realization. After spending all those days stuck with him, I know how he likes games, and this stinks of one.

Standing, I ignore Aveline and Tim trying to tug me back down, ignore the dark figure that hangs between us and holds my heart. I ignore it all as I look straight at Aaron. He almost brought me down once. He won't do it again. "What do you want?" I ask.

"No hellos and pleasantries?" He chuckles. "And here I thought we had become such friends."

"What do you *want?*" I repeat.

His head cocks to the side. "I want what I've always wanted," he says. "For this world to stop pretending that their dead didn't exist, that *she* didn't exist. But maybe most importantly, I want *him* to pay," he spits out while glancing down to Dev. "Once these go off"—he points to the silver balls—"Terra won't be able to keep going like nothing happened. That is, if there's anyone left to pick up the pieces."

"So you would kill yourself to get your revenge?" I ask.

He laughs coldly. "Oh, I died a very long time ago. This will be my resurrection."

My heart pounds violently against my rib cage as I listen to each of his insane words, my adrenaline swirling my internal energy to near bursting as I search around for all the possible ways out of this.

"Twenty minutes," Tim whispers by my knees. "I can try and get a shot."

I hold my hand out, telling him no. I don't want to risk it just yet.

"But I've decided to give you a gift," Aaron goes on. "I'm giving you a way out of this."

I wait for his next game.

"I'm going to leave the fate of all of this with you, our dear Dreamer. For isn't that your destiny?" With a flourish he pulls out a remote, *the* remote, and holds down a button. Dev begins to slowly lower, drawing nearer and nearer to the Source. My heart stops.

"You can save your love, get out with enough time for you both to live, or stop this whole place from blowing."

My hands grip the balcony's railing for support as I watch Dev, the world teetering off kilter. "What do you mean?"

"I've placed a deactivator under one of the desks in the outer monitoring ring," he says. "If you leave now, you can find it and stop these from going off, but unfortunately you won't make it back in time to save him. But stay and save Dev, you'll only have time to get as far away as you can before the bombs go off. Just say the word, and I'll stop lowering him." Aaron's mouth curves to the side, the devil standing in checkmate. "The choice is yours, Molly. Dev or Terra, but you better choose quickly, for time is running out."

With a push, Aveline makes a run to the door behind us while shooting at Aaron, but Aaron merely ducks behind the balcony's wall, and suddenly Dev's ascent quickens.

"Aveline, stop!" I yell, and she skids to a halt. Dev's movement returns to its previous pace. Her eyes are wide, terror stricken, and panicked as she glances to her partner.

"No more of that," Aaron says while hesitantly standing. "This is Molly's choice, and hers alone. If any more of you move, you'll only force her to make her decision quicker."

I want to cry, scream, lay to waste every ounce of the man in front of me as my mind races for a solution, the energy inside me shooting like fireworks with my indecision, and I can almost see it coming off me in heat waves. If I don't leave now, I will destroy a world trying to save Dev, but if I go for the detonator... I hold back a scream of frustration. My soul can't take that option. I glance to Dev, watch as his gaze scans the Source below him as it gets forever closer, his body trying to pull against the binds, lift himself away. And then in a weird pausing of time, he looks up to me and stops struggling, his body going limp. With tears pooling in his eyes, he nods, understanding and forgiveness swimming in the blue depths. *Yes*, he says silently, *save our world*.

And I break apart.

I can't...I can't do it.

"This isn't a choice!" I yell at Aaron, and as I look up, I see a small movement near the far wall behind him, where Hector and Dev entered. A lanky white-haired man is inching forward on his stomach, gagged with his hands tied behind his back and a small trickle of blood dripping down his forehead.

Hector.

Oh God. Hector is here, alive. I try to control my breathing, to keep the madman's attentions on me.

"It's more of a choice than I ever had," Aaron sneers. "You should be thanking me!"

I swallow, chance a glance to my watch. Fourteen minutes.

Barely enough time for anything.

Only enough time for one.

Hector has wobbled his way to standing, and I barely hear the gasp from Aveline, which she quickly muffles.

"And how can I believe you'll stop lowering Dev?" I'm trying for a quick distraction so Hector can carry out whatever he *can* do bound and gagged.

"Your little faith wounds me," Aaron says with faux hurt, throwing a hand over his heart. "I'm a man of honor. When have I ever backed out of my promises?"

Hector is a few feet away now, and my palms are slick against the rail, knuckles white. *What are you going to do? What are you going to do?* Hector looks to the remote in Aaron's grip, over the balcony to Dev still lowering, then to the Source, the light channeling up and illuminating his face from below. Hector struggles to loosen his hands, but even I know it's impossible. His choices are few, just like mine are. With him also wearing a Dreamer repellent band I can't touch him with my powers, not even to free him.

Glancing up, he finds my gaze and holds it. What I see in his green depths raises goose bumps across my skin and shreds my heart. For I understand in that moment what he's going to do, and while I want to shout *No! There has to be another way*, I know there isn't.

Not without more time.

So I stand silently, unmoving, and soak in the love that Hector now, after so many months, allows me to see. Love for me, for my grandfather, for Terra, and, with his eyes staring behind me, to the girl who watches on.

It all happens quickly, and at the same time is the slowest thing in the world. Aaron begins to turn, curious to what my attention has gone to, and that's when Hector charges forward.

He lets out a muffled groan as Aaron gets out a shot, nicking Hector's shoulder, but it's not enough to stop him as he knocks into Aaron's side. They smack up against the balcony's ledge with a grunt, hanging suspended in what feels like eternity right before they go barreling over, straight into the Source below.

Aveline screams, Tim screams, yet I stand still in a moment of disbelief as their bodies hit the Navitas, disintegrating into the power in which they came. It's only when an energy surges into the room that I blink into action, feeling its intentions like a smack in the face.

"Run!" I yell to Aveline and Tim as I jump into flight, zipping to Dev, whose descent has thankfully paused. But still he screams against his gag, most likely telling me to get out too, but I don't move as the Navitas flames lick toward our feet, the heat unbearably close. Instead, I shut him out, block everything as I switch to the plane of sight, the room erupting with light, time creeping as I use the power in my vest to form a shield around Dev and myself. Though I can't touch him directly, I can still create a cocoon of safety, and I push away the acute pain from my mind cooling to an arctic degree, while the rest of my energy gathers in my gut.

Time has run out, but by the stars, this is *not* the end.

With my intention filling my thoughts, one that will either kill us or save us all, the Source thumps out in a barrage of power, a giant's foot crashing on waves, and my head tilts back on a silent scream as it all channels into me. My soul is ripped away, my body now emptied as it fills with all the lives of my collected predecessors, of all the Nocturna and Vigil yet to be created below, all their innocence, heartbeats, and incubated breaths as my arms fling out, shooting two thick cords of Navitas to suction

around the soon-to-detonate bombs along the wall. I'm nothing and everything as I soak in the self-sacrifice of Hector that
fills me from the Source. His selfless love drowning out Aaron's
sickness of hate, consuming it like the ocean to a sinking ship, it
more powerful than anything I've ever felt. It gives and gives and
gives, burning my skin from the inside out, thickening the shell
around me as I sense the timers ticking down and the cells cracking open with their explosion. And this is when I scream, we all
scream, the sound so piercing it would shatter glass as I force my
arms straight, keeping the shell wrapped around Dev while holding on to the two cords suctioning the bombs. The walls shake,
rumble in the threat to give way, but I only pull more of Hector's
purity into me. It wipes the darkness blind, turns it to light as it
feeds me its strength, making me strong enough to hold everything together as I crack apart. Wetness seeps out of my ears and
down my nose as my atoms turn to fire, sucking in the flames of
Navitas bursting from the bombs. I'm nothing but a vessel for all
of the energy, a gateway for it to travel through and turn gentle
as it links to the Source below. I hang there, a suspended bridge,
gritting my teeth against my muscles yelling that they can't take
it anymore, that I must let go, but I can't, not yet. I need longer,
we need longer, and this is when I feel a gentle touch to one of
my hands. I blink to see Riki with me in this space of in between,
Vibius, and slowly my grandfather. They float around me, link-
ing hand to hand to all our pasts, lending me their power, their
support. And right before the last two Dreamers connect, a burst
of lightning cracks out from below, and Hector steps through.
His eyes glow white, like the rest of theirs, his silver hair floating around his face in a gentle wind, and his scar is now gone,

his features peaceful. They no longer bear the heavy brow of the past that haunted him. He didn't run away. He faced the enemy, and in doing so saved a world, two worlds. My eyes water with his brilliance, tears unshed, and as his hands complete the circle, a jolt runs the length of me, and my mind switches to a timeless being, all of us now one.

In this moment our collected soul is everything, every living being born and yet to be made on Earth and in Terra. We're ideas, creation, and every emotion. We're the wind, a petal floating away from a flower, flame lashing out from a fire. We have no body, only energy, atoms of existence that break apart destruction to make solar systems and stars. Out of a death comes a life, and we empty it all back into where it came, back into the Source, the sun of this world. And after a time that can only be quantified as forever, the room that was about to erupt in chaos calms, and my soul reconnects with my body, my ancestors disappearing in the fading light, and my arms lower, move on their own accord to wrap around a glowing body floating in front of me. They stay there, tightly hanging on with no intention of ever letting go.

In this space is when I sigh, my first breath from my new self, and close my eyes, welcoming the darkness that no longer brings me fear.

Chapter 45

When this is over,
because surely such evil can't last forever,
what shall we do first?

—*Part of a letter from Molly to Dev*

THE WINDOWS WERE open, the drapes pulled to the side, letting in the glow of the passing stars and the fresh summer night's breeze, just as she preferred. Molly lay sleeping beside him, the gray sheets twisting in her legs and across her body. Her bare shoulder peeked out as alluringly as her midnight hair, with its one streak of white, fanned across his pillow. Her hands curled by her chin, and with lips parted, her steady breathing squeaked out in small mewls. Dev had yet to tell her she snored. He adored it, thought it was so human, so vulnerable, that he feared she would somehow stop if she knew. Her life was so public now, so part of everyone's in Terra that he liked to keep things like this for himself, bits of her that only he knew.

With one hand propping his head up, he used the other to brush a gentle finger across her cheek. It was soft and warm against his callouses. She stirred, but her eyes remained closed.

It had been a month since the Nursery incident, which is what the elders were calling it now. An *incident*, not attack or near catastrophe, just a blip in security that was tidily swept clean. It was better for the citizens to believe this, Elena had explained, than how close they actually had come to living in a dystopia. It allowed Terra to hope after such loss, for while the woman who slept so peacefully beside him held together the Source, the outer ring of the compound still suffered its fair share of blows. They lost half their guards that day to the Metus who broke through, and a sickening number of students before enough backup arrived to help fight back the beasts. Of course, they could have lost everything, a whole generation and more, if Molly hadn't retained the blast, if Hector hadn't sacrificed himself to aid her.

Dev frowned, his mind drifting back to right before it all collided. Looking up at Molly as he had dangled bound and gagged, had felt his soul screaming in desperation for her not to be harmed, his skin blistering against the tightly wound rope as gravity tried to pull him down, Aaron controlling him. He had believed in that moment that he would die, that Molly had no other choice but to find the device hidden so close in the other room and deactivate the bombs, save her along with everyone else. That was what all of it had been for, right? But yet she didn't move, and while Dev wanted to yell at her to snap out of it, to run and get far, far away, if he was to be honest, to be selfish, he was relieved that she didn't. He didn't want to die, not like that, not by the hands of Aaron. And especially not because of the death of a woman they both had loved. Anabel's life shouldn't be remembered in such a way.

So as he watched Molly's face lift from his, her gaze on something that changed the crinkle in her brow ever so slightly, he thought maybe, just maybe there was another way out.

Which he saw as the two men flew past him into the Source.

If anyone had asked Dev two months ago who in that room would have been the one to sacrifice himself to help them all, Hector would have been the last one named. The Hector he had known was selfish, vexing in his subtle cruelty, and would have rather slummed it with the abandoners in the black market than stand with anyone of honor.

Or so Dev had thought.

In the weeks leading up to his final moments, the Vigil had shown cracks of a different self, or rather, someone always there but hiding. Hector *was* honorable, brave, caring, and loyal—he just did a great job of covering it up. As soon as Dev saw past his own dislike for the man to what really floated below the surface, he felt like such a fool. For hadn't he hid under similar airs, maybe not as snobbish and cruel, but a facade of unfeeling? They were more alike than he wanted to admit. Both feared what they might relive if they followed the same paths as before. What tests would they have to relive to redeem their pasts, to change them? The only thing that probably saved Dev from becoming as bitter as Hector was Molly.

She was his heart, and she clung to him. And he to her.

After the Source settled below him, after Molly had shed her skin to shine brighter than any star or goddess he had ever seen, she wrapped her arms around him and wouldn't let go. And Dev was fine with that.

Even after Aveline and Tim had pulled them out from dangling over the potent energy, they'd had to wait until reinforcement showed up with the proper equipment to loosen the rope around him and then her. But still, when pried free she hadn't awoken, merely slipped into a deep sleep for three Earth cycles.

Three Earth cycles where he had sat beside her in the hospital, hugging Aveline to his side. He had seen Molly like this too often, and each time it took a piece of him to see her through it. He could only hope this would be the last for a very long while.

Elena and Tim visited frequently, and even Cato came to check on the Dreamer, but it was Aveline who stayed with him the whole time, mending her own wound that wasn't visible but just as devastating as a knife to the heart.

"I'm sorry, Ave," he had said as they watched over her, the gentle beeping of the monitoring equipment accompanying their silence.

Aveline just tightened her hold around him as she ignored the tears that slipped down her cheek. "You know," she eventually said, her voice breaking, "he always told me he wasn't a good person, that he didn't deserve my...friendship." She paused, letting the word settle. "Many times he tried to antagonize me to leave him. *See reason*, he would say." Aveline let out a small laugh. "He liked to talk like that, like those old Hollywood actors he was so fond of watching when he had lived on Earth. It always made us laugh when he would catch himself doing it."

Silence.

"But I knew what he was capable of, what he thought I couldn't see." She glanced up at Dev, her hazel eyes bright and wide. "Like you saw with me."

Dev swallowed against the tightness in his throat as his partner continued to share her heart.

"He left this world doing the one thing he thought he didn't possess. He died bravely, Dev. And I think...I think, wherever it is we go after, he's in peace now." She glanced back at Molly, to the gentle rise and fall of her breathing. "It hurts," she whispered. "It hurts, but...but I'm proud of him."

He looked down at her, waited for her eyes to come back to his, and took in how much she had changed since the young cadet he had chosen as his partner all those years ago. She was strong now, inside and out, passionate and every bit the Nocturna guard he believed she would become. They had been through countless battles, the deaths of many friends, heartbreak, and survival of a war. And though they had a bit more to go, to fight, this war was at an end. He could feel it in the air. Since Aaron's death, the sickness and hate that shadowed Terra was losing its potency, and it was only a matter of time before the world regained its balance.

Since that moment with Aveline in the hospital, as they had waited for Molly to wake up, Dev's prediction was right. In the weeks that followed, it was like the Metus knew they had lost. No longer made strong by the vengeful generosity of a man feeding them power, no longer able to hide out in the many twisted caverns below ground near Terra, all now found and destroyed, they slunk back to their tar pits of nightmares. And though it frightened him a little to think about it, when Molly eventually awoke, she awoke stronger than anything the elders had ever known possible. There was no way the Metus couldn't feel the shift in power then, in light from dark. It was like the sacrifice Hector gave that day had permanently settled in Molly's heart, lending a layer no Dreamer before her had worn or had access too. The whites of her eyes held a constant gentle glow now, like her connection to her energy, as well as all that surrounded her, no longer needed to be separate, something to switch in and out of. She was fluid, water over rocks, a breeze through the tall grass. And when she had entered the battlefield quickly thereafter, she eradicated the Metus in swift blows, barely tiring, her vest used more for protection than powering up.

She was exquisite.

And while Cato was both mesmerized and slightly disgruntled, for she barely listened to the elder now, Elena was a vision of excitement and pride. Though the blonde elder wasn't previously a favorite of Dev's, just like Hector, he now saw the way she cared for Molly, maybe in her own strange way, but cared nonetheless.

Molly was granted an invitation to sit as a figurehead among them, the Council and all of Terra accepting this like they tended to do with any change after a time. And while she accepted the role, she did so with humility and hesitant appreciation, never one to enjoy too much time in the spotlight. Even so, when in public she was gracious and giving, appeasing the citizens' wishes for her to create things whenever they asked, and most importantly she was just as curious of them as they were of her. This alone might have been enough to sway them to adore her, because for such a powerful being to ask about their friends, to show genuine interest in how they ran their food vending and constructed buildings, settled a loyalty in their hearts.

Not so long ago these same men and women had spat their disapproval of her, and now...well, now it was almost dizzying to watch how much they loved her. She and Dev could barely walk ten paces in public without a crowd following them. Her Vigil guards remained by her side, of course, but not the tense guards from before. It was obvious the people of Terra would no sooner hurt Molly as they would an elder. So while her notoriety left her and Dev little room for alone time while in public, it had at least given her permission to move out of the Dreamer Containment Center.

Molly now lived at the apartment, in Dev's room, until they could get their own quarters.

"You should take a picture. It'll last longer." Her sleepy voice brought Dev back to the woman he stared dazedly at. Molly's eyes were open, their brightness startling against her dark-brown irises. She smiled and stretched out, her gracefully toned arms reaching above her head. "Was I sleeping long?"

"Always," Dev said as his attention fell to a gentle sloping of skin that peeked tantalizing out of the sheets.

"Eyes up here, buddy," Molly chastened.

"I think my eyes are fine right where they are." Dev grinned as he tugged the covers away.

"Dev!" She threw her arms over her bare chest, but it was futile, for he quickly had them pinned to her pillow, her beautiful olive skin shining under the dim lights of his room.

"You're gorgeous," he said gruffly, sliding to rest above her, her skin cool against his hot. "You should never cover yourself."

"Hmm, I think you're right," she mused. "I'll walk through the streets of Terra butt naked from now on. Cato will love that."

Dev laughed. "I'm sure it would finally pump some blood into certain dead parts of him."

"Ugh, gross." Molly squirmed under him, and Dev's mind cleared of anything but this woman and his need for her. *In all of Terra*, what she did to him.

E.J. Mellow

She must have seen the change in his features, for she stopped moving, her breathing heavy. "Dev," she said. "We'll never get out of bed if we keep this up."

"Are you hungry?" he asked as he lowered his head to nip at her neck.

"No," she panted.

He licked his way down to her breast. "Need the bathroom?"

She gasped as he took the peak into his mouth. "N—no."

"Then there's no need to get out of bed."

And because she knew he was right, there wasn't anything pressing, she let him worship her body, for every inch of her was holy to him. He took his time on every dip and curve of her skin as the room grew hotter, each pounding of her heart sending it soaring, the lights flickering on and off. Only until she moaned his name a third time did he ease himself back up and into her.

On a husky groan he brought his lips to hers, savoring the way her nails dug into his back as he pushed them into their own dream state, one where they could go together. She sighed against his skin, and he cradled her closer, tasting her perfection, feeling it. Their long journey through hell and back had finally brought them to a place that was just for the two of them, a place where love lived freely, without the fear of loss in every passing hour. Dev was determined to keep it that way for as long as he could, specifically right then. So with forced control, he stretched them further in the sheets, feeling her tightening around him, and kept them there, deliciously long, torturously so. Until he could take it no longer, until she couldn't, and on her last beg, he swept them to the surface, where they both burst apart. But even then Dev merely kept them wrapped together, waiting for their breathing to steady before he kissed her heart open and did it all over again.

Chapter 46

When you come home, find me.
I'll be where I always found you.

—*A note from Dev to Molly, left on their kitchen table*

TODAY IS MY twenty-sixth birthday.

A whole two years older than the first night where my life was forever changed.

And I haven't even received one present yet.

Squinting into the sunlight, I flip my shades down from where they rested atop my head and let the ocean breeze float through my thin yellow chemise. The lapping blue waves rhythmically collide in an endless song in front of me, and I watch as a tall, dark, and shockingly blond-haired man throws a ball to a black Labrador on the beach below. It barks in excitement as it chases its projected flight, its chocolate coat glistening in the sun.

I sit nestled on a small cliffside patio of a cottage near El Matador beach in Malibu. The sun is high, a bright early afternoon, and I close my eyes, soaking in the peace.

"Okay!" Becca chirps, stepping out from the house. "I made us piña colada!" She flops into the lounge chair beside me and hands over one of the white frothy drinks. Her red hair is pulled up in a floral wrap, and her bright-green bikini peeks through the sheer fabric of her white dress.

"Isn't it a bit early?" I ask, poking at the overabundant mini umbrellas stuck in my beverage.

"I'm going to ignore that ridiculous question because it's your birthday," Becca says before taking a generous sip. She lets out an exaggerated *ah*!

I shake my head with a laugh and then dig into my own.

"Thatta girl." She smiles and then shields her eyes as she peers out to Rae playing with their dog, Caterpillar. When she told me the name, I hardly batted an eye. Becca and her pet names, pun intended, know no bounds of bizarre.

"How long do they usually stay out there?" I ask.

"Usually until one of them gets tired."

"So forever."

"Yup." She nestles back into her chair. "Which is perfect for me and my R and R time."

"I would think you'd have overdosed with R and R by now after moving here."

"Molly..." She laughs like I just said something cute, like a child trying to say asparagus. "You can *never* have too much relaxation."

"Some would beg to differ," I say while my nose bumps against four mini umbrellas as I try to take another sip. *I mean, really?*

"Well, *some* of us don't need to save worlds every other day. *Some* of us like to kick up our feet and smell the friggin' tanning oil every once in a while."

"I like to kick up my feet," I accuse. "What do you think I'm doing right now?" I gesture to said feet that are said *kicked up*.

Becca's lips purse. "I'll give you this one because you're the birthday girl."

I scoff. "You'll give me this one because I'm *right*."

She waves a dismissive hand and returns to watching Rae. He's in nothing but his surfer shorts, and his strong chest and arms glisten under the sunlight, flexing as he pulls back to throw the ball for Caterpillar. Even I can't help ogling him, and all too easily hear my best friend let out a contented sigh.

Rae and Becca moved to California a little over six months ago. The surf shop Rae worked for wanted him at their flagship store after some of his engineering changes to their boards landed them as one of *the* go-to suppliers for the world's champions. Becca easily found another producer job that allowed her to work from home most days instead of slugging the commute to Los Angeles. The culture on the West Coast is a lot more laid back than on the East Coast. It's easy to see that the move was a good decision for these two, especially from the glistening rock now resting on Becca's finger. Rae popped the question the very night they moved into this cottage, as they watched their first sunset. I know, puke-ishly romantic, but I couldn't be happier for them.

With the war in Terra ending, the violence that was slipping into this world subsided with it. Threats of terrorism still linger in certain parts of Earth, as do the Metus in certain parts of Terra, but the constant gun violence and seemingly random acts of hate between neighbors has all but disappeared. Life, it seems, has fallen into a nice, gentler pattern. One that I hope lasts a long, long time. The gift Hector gave our two worlds, not to mention me, is immeasurable, and I feel his soul swimming through me just as easily as I feel all my Dreamer predecessors. Which is why I've been working diligently with the Council to finally, *finally*, erect a memorial that all the public can see, of those now gone, those who gave their lives for their world. Not just some wall with their names tucked away deep within City Hall, but a space that can be viewed front and center. Because if I've learned anything from the experience with Aaron, it's that grief shouldn't be shunned and stifled. It should be let out, freed, and given a place to go. I'm just hoping the bill will pass soon so we can begin the designs and construction.

"So, have you checked under your seat yet?"

I blink at Becca's question.

"Under my seat?"

Her lips curl mischievously as I reach under me, my fingers hitting up against something.

"You got me a present!" I lift a polka-dot gift bag to my lap.

"Duh, monkey butt. It's not like I haven't mentioned your birthday like every other sentence."

Ripping away the tissue paper, I pull out a small black box and pop it open. "Oh," I gasp. "It's...it's..." I can't finish my sentence, for tears blur my vision.

"I'm hoping those are happy tears," she says.

I nod vigorously as I pick up the delicate gifts resting inside. Two small silver charms, a palm tree and the shape of the state of California, twinkle in the sunlight.

"I know you haven't worn your charm bracelet in a while," Becca says, "but I thought this would give you a reason to wear it again. It really is so lovely, and I think you should have something that will always remind you of here, of us."

Placing the gifts and my drink to the side, I turn and give her the biggest hug. "It's perfect."

"I love you, Mols."

"I love you too, Bec."

"Well, if I knew this is how your visit was going to turn out, I would have showered this morning. Care if I join?" Rae's deep voice comes from the stairs leading up from the beach.

"You wish." Becca throws a sandal at him.

He easily catches it and grins. "I meant the hug. But by all means, please tell me what *you* thought I meant?"

She throws her other shoe, and I laugh.

"I see Bec gave you our gift." He stretches out in one of the chairs, his muscular chest dusted with sand, and Caterpillar trots over to sit by his feet, her tongue hanging out. He absently pats her head.

"Yes, thank you."

"Of course." His white teeth beam against his dark skin. "Have you gotten Dev's gift yet?"

"Dev's gotten me a gift?"

"Babe! You ruined the surprise!" Becca chastens.

"Was it really a surprise he was going to get her something for her birthday?"

Becca harrumphs. "Still."

"Still nothing." Rae kicks out his long legs, crossing them at the ankles. "It's not like I told her that it was a—"

"Don't you *dare* utter another word!"

Rae chuckles while shooting me a wink. "She's adorable when she's frustrated with me, isn't she?"

"Adorable, perhaps," Becca quips, "but a lot less agreeable to engage in certain acts later, if you catch my meaning."

"I think Caterpillar even caught your meaning," I say dryly.

"*Molly*," Becca says tightly, "do I really need to remind you that as my best friend you need to be on my side in all things confrontational between Rae and myself?"

I merely hold up my hands appeasingly.

"Coward," Rae mutters.

"Hardly," I say. "I didn't actually answer her, now did I?"

Becca gasps, while Rae laughs. "Ah, how wise you've grown."

"I am twenty-six now."

"Yes, you're practically ancient," he snorts before standing. "Now, it's not a birthday without a cake, so who wants to help me bake it?"

Becca becomes engrossed in sipping her piña colada, while I rest my hands behind my head. "I was told that I needed to learn to kick up my feet more and smell the tanning oil."

Rae's brows furrow. "Why would you want to smell tanning oil?"

"Once you've made a delicious cake for Molly, we'll tell you," Becca answers.

"I'd be careful how you state your words next time, my love." Rae bends down to give her a quick kiss. "Because a cake for Molly and *only* Molly is what I'll now be making. Well, and me of course. You can sit in the corner and watch us eat it in bliss."

He barely dodges her punch to his shoulder before he disappears into the house, his laughter being chased by the pattering paws of Caterpillar.

"He's the worst," Becca mutters.

"You love him," I say.

"Too much," Becca returns, and with a contented sigh we both sit back, sipping our coconut flavored drinks and soaking in the sun of our new lives.

⟶▬◉ ◉▬⟵

My skin tingles as I step out of the portal back in Terra, quickly imagining my standard Nocturna uniform hugging my form. My designated reentry room rests close to my personal chambers in the DCC, and I'm not surprised to see Odi waiting for me, his back pressed against the far wall near the door. His dark-black hair sweeps across his forehead, while his brown eyes crinkle with his smile, taking in my appearance. After Hector's death, the role of my Vigil guard was left open, and it didn't take long for him to finish up the proper training and be promoted. I couldn't officially give my consent without warning that this position seemed a bit cursed, if my past Vigil guards were anything to go by. But Odi merely shrugged and informed me that all curses were eventually broken.

Only time will tell, but so far so good.

"Looks like you got some sun," Odi says, pushing off the wall.

"Yes, Becca certainly made sure of that."

"I have no doubt. That woman likes her lounging."

"To say the least." I smile as we step into the white hall, nodding to the various Vigil, and now Nocturna, engineers who pass us in the DCC. With the knowledge of the Dreamer going public, the two races now work beside one another when it comes to my future lineage and me. None of us, not even the elders, are sure what will happen with the next summoning of a human. Now that my twenty-fifth birthday has come and gone with absolutely no change to my connection here, the future isn't as predictable as it once was. The transfer with Rae obviously rid the barrier to only travel to Terra through my subconscious and, in effect, severed the countdown to my cutoff. Elena thinks I'll even live longer, aging as they do here, which will essentially keep me in my Dreamer position, as well as by Dev's side, for a long, long time. And honestly, I'm beyond psyched about this. Somehow I'm having my cake and eating it too. Well, I *did* have to go through some pretty deadly rings of fire and a psychopath to be able to do that, but still, I can have bits of both my lives, and I couldn't be more grateful.

The only thing we had to figure out was my "day job" on Earth, which was easily solved by giving me a position at one of the small Vigil-run financial firms in the city. And by position, I mean in name only. I never went in unless I needed to for appearance's sake if my parents visited.

With a smile on my lips, I pick up my pace as we head toward the exit, excited to see the man who's been my guiding light in all this. He was gone when I woke before heading to Earth for a quick visit with Rae and Becca, but I found his note and a beautiful bouquet of flowers on our kitchen table. Even though we no longer need to, we still write little letters for each other to find around our apartment. It might only be a floor above where Dev used to live, because how could we really move far from Aveline and Tim, but it's very much *ours*.

"Molly." Elena steps out from a doorway that we were about to pass. Her blonde hair impeccably cut straight to her shoulders, her white wrap dress spotless as her delicate hands rest, clasped in front of her. Her form shines brighter now that my connection with the plane of energy is more fluid, a halo of power, and I often wonder if this is how the elders see the world, in different forms of illumination.

"How was your visit?"

"Good," I say, Odi and I stopping. "Rae says hello."

She inclines her head gracefully, a small grin. "Have they set a date yet?"

"Not officially, but they don't want a large wedding, so they don't need to wait the usual year to be able to find a place. Becca was playing with the idea of a ceremony on the beach."

"I'm happy for them," she says, and I know she means it.

"You're invited, you know."

Her blue eyes widen slightly, and it might be the second time I've ever seen her surprised. "Oh, I don't think—"

"After what Rae did for Terra, it would mean a lot for you to be there."

She regards me a moment, her expression slowly softening. "Then I shall be there."

I smile. "Good." And with a parting gesture, we continue on our way, before Elena calls my name.

"The Council reached a vote on the monument today," she says once I turn back around.

My heart skips a beat.

"It passed."

My mouth opens to speak, but nothing comes out, my chest filling too quickly with warmth for the future, and I know she can feel the shift in my energy.

"Happy Birthday, Molly," Elena says gently, her gaze bright before stepping back into the room from which she came.

⊶⊷

The stars stream by endlessly, the billions of souls cocooned in sleep as they travel to their dreams, and I run my hands through the tall grass as I watch them zip in the opposite direction that I walk. Odi left me on the wall's platform, giving me this brief moment of solitary as a birthday gift, and I soak in the quiet night. There's no angry red glow peeking over the horizon or the smell of rot and death waiting to disturb me. The world is calm, the crickets chirping the song of tranquility as I make my way forward. A lone elm tree rests in the distance, and the closer I get, the more I have to keep myself from running toward it, for I know who will be waiting for me there.

As soon as I'm able to, I see his silhouette inking against the dark, his form tall, lean, and muscular as he leans against the trunk of the tree. His hands are tucked into his front pockets, and he watches as I approach, his blue flaming eyes never wavering from mine.

"Hi," I say.

"Hi." Dev's full lips inch into a grin.

"Have you been waiting long?"

"For you?" He gently pulls me to his chest. "My whole life."

Even after everything we've been through, Dev can still make me blush.

"How are the lovebirds?" he asks after a quick kiss.

"In love."

He smiles. "How monotonous of them."

"I know. They should take a note from our story or something."

"Or something," he says, lazily gazing down at me. His features over the past year have rid themselves of the haunted shadows, the furrow that had always seemed permanently etched between his brows is all but smoothed away, leaving a younger, brighter Dev.

With my heart lifting at the sight, I run my fingers through his hair, and his eyes flutter close. "I heard you had a present for me."

Dev's eyes immediately snap open, and he laughs. "Oh yeah?"

"Yeah." I smile.

Shaking his head in amusement, he reaches around to his back pocket. "I have a feeling blabbermouth Rae had something to do with this."

"Then your feelings are correct. Now, gimme gimme." I snatch the velvet pouch out of his hands.

"It's just a little something," he says, almost shyly, as I pull out a delicately carved silver charm in the shape of a shell, of my shell, *our* shell.

"Dev." I force down a swallow. I've already cried once today. It would be absolutely pathetic if I did it again. Yet, my eyes have different plans, and soon my cheeks are damp with my tears.

Dev brushes a thumb over their path to wipe them away.

"They told me what they were thinking of getting you, and while I might have hated that bracelet," Dev admits with chagrin, and I know it's because of the man who originally gave it to me rather than it actually being ugly, "I thought if it had a piece of me on there, of us, I might be able to grow to love it."

I peek up at him through my lashes. "Thank you. This means more than you know."

"Happy Birthday, Molly," he says and tugs me closer again, placing his lips to mine. We stay wrapped like this until our separate body heat mixes to one and my legs grow weak in the knees.

"Want to go?" Dev asks after we finally come up for air.

I nod.

Holding hands, we walk from under the tree's canopy, excitement pumping through my veins. While Dev and I might have our apartment to seek sanctuary from the constant crowds that circle me now, it would be maddening if that was the only place we could find our alone time. Luckily, we found a solution.

"Don't bounce around this time," I say. "It's harder for me."

"But how will you get better if I don't test you?" Dev fails at hiding his smirk.

"Always with the testing," I mutter. "Need I remind you whose birthday it is?"

Dev chuckles. "Okay, no bouncing, at least out here." He shoots me a wink.

"Oh God." I roll my eyes. "How you can go from a seducer to a cornball so quickly is beyond me."

"Don't be jealous of my overwhelming ability to be funny *and* debonair," he says. "Now are we going to do this or not?"

"*You're* the one who keeps distracting me!"

Dev's eyes dance with mirth. "Whatever you say, birthday girl."

My gaze narrows. "You know, I'm feeling rather weak today, like my power just might not be able to keep certain—"

"Okay, okay." Dev all out laughs now. "I get the point. I'll be good."

My turn to smile. "Good."

Settling my feet firmly on the ground, I pull and twist the energy that no longer lies purely in my gut but flows freely through every cell of my body, and even though I can't see it, I know my eyes are growing brighter, for Dev has told me they always do for this. Like a hot slice of fire, my power shoots out to hook into Dev's life source swirling in his chest.

On his gasp his emotions are instantly there for the picking, there to swim in and wrap within my own. Our love pulses strong, the surface like the soft petal of a flower, a butterfly's wing, and a pumping of trust enters my heart. Dev is giving himself to me, giving me every bit to do as I wish, and it feels like everything beautiful all at once. This connection is deep and rare in any universe, just like this man standing before me.

"Ready?" I ask a bit breathlessly while our gazes remain locked.

"Always," he says.

Barely having to think it, see it, I exhale, and our feet leave the ground. We lift up and up, higher and higher, suspended over the endless field where the walled city of Terra pulses in a blue-white glow in the distance. We hang there, sensing the freedom and the complete wholeness of the moment. For while Dev is my everything, he is also my equal, and I his. We are each our own shooting star that fills the sky, and when I feel his silent ask caress across my soul, I nod. And with a smile on both our lips, I tip our bodies forward and we fly.

Acknowledgments

I'M NOT GOING to lie—starting these acknowledgments was almost harder than writing this entire series. There has been *so* many amazing people associated with this trilogy being possible that it's almost dizzying. To start off, it would only be appropriate to thank you, the reader, for making this world so much bigger and fuller than I ever imagined possible. The love shown for these characters has fueled me to make it here, writing the acknowledgments to the final book in The Dreamland Series. What a ride we've been on! I can't be more appreciative or feel more blessed to have each and every one of you in my life.

To my family, who the first book was dedicated to, and to Dan, who has filled the spot for the last, you are my heart, my strength, and my ice tea on a hot day. I love you all.

To Corinna Barsan, I would cover your office with flowers every day if you would let me. Thank you for always being the first eyes to each one of my rough and filled-with-spelling-mistake drafts. You will always be my fairy godmother.

Dori Harrell, my editor superhero. I could get extremely gushy and emotional right now, but I'll keep it contained by saying this—you are irreplaceable. Raising a glass to all our future worlds we will explore together.

To my Mellow Misfits, you ladies are my rocks, my fireworks, and every joyous beat of my heart. Thank you a million times and more for being my biggest voices of support. I've said it to you before, but I could not be where I am today without each and every one of you. Biggest group hug!

To all the bloggers who took a chance on an indie author, specifically Cassandra (@thebookishcrypt), Farrah (@foksha_1996) and Demi (@Demeriahh), thank you for your tireless support. We authors are lucky to have you in our lives.

To all my friends, new and old, who have cheered me along the way, I bow down to you in gratitude. Every one of your emails, texts, calls, and conversations over a glass of wine has been an ember added to my fire to keep doing what I love. Thank you... thank you...thank you.

About The Author

E.J. Mellow is an Award Winning fantasy writer who resides in Brooklyn, NY. With a Bachelor's Degree in Fine Arts she splits her time between her two loves—visual design and writing. E.J. has no animals, but loves those that do.

The Destined is the third and final book in *The Dreamland Series*.

www.ingramcontent.com/pod-product-compliance
Lightning Source LLC
Chambersburg PA
CBHW020504020726
47493CB00001B/178